Timothy Kimball is the pseudonym for Kimball Bailey and Tim Garbett.

They met by accident in a sleazy rented house in north London in 1980 and have since shared interests in cricket, skiing, board and table games, food and wine and, of course, the 1920s.

Tim maintains that he is a Yorkshireman in exile. After university in Newcastle, he moved south to London where the streets were not paved with gold, and now lives in Twickenham, with Claire, daughter Elizabeth and labrador Toffee.

Kimball confesses to having been born in Essex, but moved quickly to London from Cambridge, where he read law at Magdalene after a brief diversion into Anglo-Saxon, Norse and Celtic. He now lives in Putney, just round the corner from Stockington's house.

Dark Designs is their first novel.

Dark Designs

Timothy Kimball

ALASTOR
PUBLISHING
LONDON

Alastor Publishing
44 Clarendon Drive
London SW15 1AE
www.alastorpublishing.co.uk

First published in the UK in 2012

A copy of the British Library Cataloguing in Publication Data is available from the British Library.

ISBN 978-0-9572015-0-7

Text designed by
Shore Books and Design, Blackborough End, Norfolk PE32 1SF

Cover design and illustration © by Ange Hart
www.hartanddesign.co.uk

Printed and bound in the UK by the
MPG Books Group, Bodmin and King's Lynn

Acknowledgements

Collaboration on such an enterprise is difficult to achieve, and it is a tribute to my friendship with Kimball that it survived this process largely intact. Without his drive and energy, the novel would never have been completed.

We have deliberately set this fictional work against a background of real facts and places, some more real than others. We hope that this adds to the fun of the story. If our version of these differs from accepted fact, this is purely literary licence.

Thanks are also due to all the friends who have read the manuscript and made suggestions which have led to a far better end product.

I dedicate *Dark Designs* to KMG, my rock in all things.

TPSG, London 2012

Dark Designs pays homage to the "snobbery with violence" genre and its heroes such as Bulldog Drummond, Lord Peter Wimsey, Simon Templar, Richard Hannay and Biggles. So thanks to their creators for many years of pleasure – and of course to George Sanders, Ronald Colman, Robert Donat, Michael Redgrave, Basil Radford and Naunton Wayne who brought them to the screen.

Historical characters and real locations have played their part in enriching the fiction, and we apologise unreservedly if anyone is offended in any way – apart from the odd traitor, assassin or Nazi collaborator, of course. The same is true if you share a name with one of the characters; please treat this as a sign of friendship.

Thanks to Tim, my collaborator and friend of 30 years. I wrote most of the words but he planned most of the plot, so this couldn't have happened without him.

Thanks too to Sir Charles Stourton and his colleagues who have given us so many ideas over the years: to Paul, Barney, Hilary and Neil, you know who you are, and to Sarah, without whom Gussie would not have been possible. To Iebe for his city tour, and to Tom and Aaron who saw that there really are many cats in Seborga. To Alan for laying down the challenge at my 50th birthday, to Melissa, John, Wendy and all the others who have helped throughout with support and advice, and to my late mother and father, for obvious reasons.

KB, London 2012

'High permisson of all-ruling Heaven
Left him at large to his own dark designs,
That with reiterated crimes he might
Heap on himself damnation, while he sought
Evil to others...'

Milton, *Paradise Lost, Book 1*

1

Monday 18th June 1928

Christopher Cushing ran his finger inside his clerical collar, easing it away from his neck. He was hot and bothered. It was a warm and thundery June day in London, the briefcase he was carrying was heavy, and the steak and kidney pudding he had eaten with his godson, Geoffrey Scott, at his club at lunchtime lay equally heavily in his stomach.

He peered through the glass door of the mansion block at the end of the mews. 'Come straight up,' Commander Ross had said. There was no sign of a caretaker but the door was unlocked. Cushing hooked his umbrella over his arm, took off his hat, mopped his brow, sighed and set off up the stairs to the first floor.

All day, he had been mulling over why on earth Ross had given him the briefcase in the first place. He had not seen him for ten years, not since the end of the Great War, when they served together in Naval Intelligence. 'Why me?' Cushing kept thinking. What had Ross said? "A matter of national importance"? Hardly the sort of thing to entrust to a middle-aged vicar. Perhaps it was some kind of elaborate prank? Never mind. He could just drop off the briefcase, then young Geoffrey could drive him back to the station.

Despite his scepticism, however, Cushing was already more than a little intrigued. 'Damn the man,' he muttered, as he saw an oak door labelled – as Ross had said – with the name of Samuel. 'More silly games.'

The door was slightly ajar and he pushed it cautiously. The large sitting room was a mess. Books had been pulled from shelves, drawers opened, papers scattered and cushions slashed open. He crept into the room and immediately could see a body slumped on the floor by the desk near the window. It was Ross, lying amid the wreckage of a broken chair. Hurrying over, he knelt down by Ross's side, but he had seen enough dead men during the War to fear the worst. There was a bloodstained rent in his white shirt and he felt for a pulse more in hope than expectation. Ross's wallet and keys were on the carpet next to his body; someone had already been through his pockets.

A noise and a muffled curse from behind one of the other doors in the apartment alerted Cushing and he quickly stood up as the door was thrust open. A thin man wearing a trench coat and with a scar on each cheek gave a start when he saw Cushing and swore loudly in German. As the thin man reached beneath his coat and pulled out a pistol, another man, wearing a policeman's uniform, came into view behind him.

'You! Stand very still,' ordered the man in the trench coat in thickly-accented tones. He spoke abruptly to his colleague. 'Horstmann, nehmen Sie seinen Aktenkoffer.' Then, again to Cushing, 'No games, please. Give the briefcase to my friend Mr. Horstmann.'

As Horstmann moved towards Cushing, he passed momentarily in front of the pistol, and Cushing saw his chance. The red mist he had felt twelve years before in France rose again behind his eyes.

'You're not a policeman,' he cried, and, grabbing his umbrella, he lunged forward and caught Horstmann hard with it in the pit of his stomach. The German dropped to his knees cursing and Cushing swung the heavy briefcase wildly, striking the other man a glancing blow and causing him to drop his pistol. Cushing did not wait for him to pick it up. Diving for the door, and dropping his umbrella as he went, he leapt onto the landing and down the stairs. Splinters of wood flew from the banisters near his right elbow. They were shooting at him. Here, in London! In broad daylight! He ducked frantically, keeping a firm grip on the briefcase, and as he burst through the doors into the mews he could have sworn he felt another bullet zip past his ear.

He ran out into the quiet cobbled street and bumped into a middle-aged woman coming out of a jeweller's shop, calling out an apology without stopping. The two men chasing him appeared round the corner. They too were impeded by the woman who was trying to gather her shopping bags and her clutch of small dogs, giving Cushing more precious seconds. He was conscious of a dreadful feeling of déjà vu. He had run from German bullets before, the weight of a wounded sergeant on his shoulder dragging him down. He was not going to let the Huns do any better this time.

Horstmann continued to chase him on foot but, as he looked back, Cushing glimpsed the man in the trench coat, now with no gun visible, jump onto the running board of a large black Lagonda parked outside a pub.

The clergyman was breathing heavily, and was regretting his substantial lunch. He was not in the best condition, and had not had to run at all since last summer's church fete. Horstmann was closing on him fast, and Cushing could hear the car behind revving up. He ran out of the narrow street towards the Berkeley Hotel, waving and shouting at his godson whose small green open-top Alvis sports car was parked outside. Geoffrey Scott was sitting waiting in the car, the engine running, his hat set at a jaunty angle, a cigarette between his lips.

He opened his mouth to abuse his godfather, then his face broke into a huge grin as he saw the pursuing policeman. 'What the...? Padre? Uncle Kit? What on earth?'

There was no time for pleasantries. Cushing opened the car door and fell unceremoniously into the passenger seat. 'Drive, man, drive!' he shouted, drawing great gulps of breath.

Glancing at the policeman, Scott needed no second bidding. 'Good show, Padre,' he chuckled, took a last drag from his cigarette, flicked it away and pushed the accelerator hard to the floor. Horstmann made a last despairing grab at the briefcase, but the tyres squealed as Scott drove away, leaving the German floundering. Hotel porters were moving anxiously to Horstmann's side and gesticulating at the Alvis.

Cushing could see the black Lagonda with the other German still on the running board nosing out onto the main road. 'That car. They're after me. Keep driving, quickly!' he shouted hoarsely, as Horstmann pushed his helpers away and he and the other man climbed into the back of the black car.

Scott swung the Alvis past the church and round the corner. 'So what's going on, Padre? On the run from the rozzers again?' He smirked. 'And at your age too!'

Cushing glared at his godson as he weaved expertly in and out of the light traffic, and then looked again over his shoulder. The black car was still in sight. 'Faster, man!'

Scott sped along the leafy streets of Belgravia, the Lagonda still on their tail. A noise like an angry wasp passed his left ear and the windscreen of the Alvis shattered. 'Hold onto your hat, Padre!' he called, punching a larger hole in the glass and driving twice round a quiet square as if it were the race track at Brooklands, the Lagonda following in close pursuit.

'They're shooting at us!' shouted Cushing, unnecessarily.

'I've worked that much out,' muttered Scott. 'Keep your head down!' On the third circuit, Scott overtook a slow-moving black taxi cab, and then pulled sharply in front of it. There was a squeal of tortured tyres as he swung his car into a side road. The taxi screeched to an abrupt halt, the driver shaking his fist at the Alvis before covering his face as Cushing's pursuers attempted the same manoeuvre. It was less successful, and the Lagonda skidded into a wall – one of the South American embassies, noted Cushing with some satisfaction, as he heard the crash. Scott drove nonchalantly on to join the traffic on Hyde Park Corner.

'Well that was fun,' he said, still grinning, as he hooted at a bus that was grinding its way slowly along Piccadilly. He leaned forward and knocked the remaining broken glass from the windscreen. 'So what's happening, Uncle Kit? I think you've got some explaining to do. Not to mention a few repairs to the car.'

Scott swung the Alvis through the gates of the In and Out Club on Piccadilly and gave the porter a friendly wave. 'Sort this out for me, Cherry, there's a good chap. Come on Padre, you look as if you need a drink.'

He was not wrong. As Scott sauntered up the marble staircase, stopping to check his appearance in the mirror at the top of the stairs, Cushing took an appraising look at his godson. At twenty eight, tall, well-built and well-dressed, Scott had lost a little weight since Cushing had last seen him playing rugby for the Harlequins. That had been three months earlier, when they had arranged today's lunch. Scott was not truly handsome, but rather fashionably ugly, with the rugged good looks of a natural sportsman, and Cushing suspected that he had already broken a few hearts.

They threaded their way through the thick haze of pipe and cigar smoke in the quiet bar, Cushing still clutching Ross's briefcase.

'Afternoon, Harrington,' said Scott to the elderly barman.

'Large brandy and soda please, and the same for the vicar.' He settled down into a comfortable armchair beneath a large portrait of the King, reached into his jacket pocket and pulled out a silver cigarette case. Flicking it open with a practised gesture, he proffered it to Cushing who accepted gratefully. The cigarettes inside were expensive and monogrammed: Scott couldn't remember whose monogram it was, any more than he could remember which regimental crest was on the case or to whom it had originally belonged.

Still looking shocked, Cushing took a large swig from his brandy glass as Scott leaned forward in his chair, his eyes shining. The scar on his cheek, a souvenir of his own short war career, gave a predatory cast to his smile.

'Now, Uncle Kit, spill the beans. Why were the rozzers after you?'

'They weren't real police, Geoffrey, not with German accents and guns.' Cushing drained his brandy and Scott signalled to the barman for another. 'Whoever they were, they are after this briefcase. They've killed Ross and were searching his flat when I arrived. I poked one of them with my umbrella and ran for it. They were shooting at me!'

'Whoa there. Why were they shooting at us? What on earth have you been up to? Who's been killed? This is serious!'

'I haven't been doing anything,' retorted Cushing angrily. 'I told you at lunchtime. James Ross asked me to bring him this briefcase, and when I went to his flat he had been murdered.'

'All you told me at lunchtime was that you had to drop off a briefcase. That's why I drove you to Wilton Place from the Athenaeum. But that's all, none of the whys or wherefores. Who is Ross? Or was, I should say, if he's dead?'

'Well let me try and explain. It's certainly all a bit strange. Ross was at Cambridge with me. I didn't know him well. He was a quiet, studious man, quite unusual for Buckingham.' Scott knew that Buckingham College had long been more renowned for sporting rather than academic achievement. 'He got a first and went to the Foreign Office. That was thirty years ago, before the turn of the century. The old Queen was still on the throne, and the Boer War had only just started...'

'Come on, Padre, get to the point, you're wittering,' interrupted Scott, impatiently.

'All right, Geoffrey, all right.' Cushing took a further mouthful of brandy and stretched out in the armchair as the spirit warmed and relaxed him. 'I met Ross again in 1917. It was after I had been – well, you know. You were at school at the time.' Cushing's eyes became distant for a few moments.

Scott knew full well that his godfather, then a regimental chaplain, had been wounded on the first day of the Somme and had been decorated. Scott himself had been on active service in France for just three weeks before the Armistice, and that had been enough for him. This time he did not interrupt.

'Anyway, I was seconded to Naval Intelligence, code-breaking. I wasn't really fit for the front line any more. Ross was running the unit at Room 40. A mixture of service people and civilians. The unit was disbanded after the war, and I didn't see him again until Saturday night.'

'Saturday night?'

'Yes, Geoffrey, I told you at lunchtime. It was a dinner back at Buckingham for old members of the college who had fought in the Great War. I don't really know why I went. I thought I'd see a few old faces I suppose. Many more that we'll never see again, of course, the ones who didn't come back...' Cushing saw Scott's impatient expression and cleared his throat. 'I bumped into Ross at Cambridge station, all very smart, very much the City gentleman, and we shared a taxi to the college. But we hardly spoke after that. He was on high table at dinner, next to the Master, and there were too many other people to see. Do you know, I was chatting to James Feldman? I haven't seen him since we were both in hospital in Albert. He was with the South Africans who got a pasting at Delville Wood.'

'Will you get on with it? I want to know why people are shooting at us, not who you had dinner with!'

'Sorry. Where was I? Oh yes. I didn't see Ross over breakfast either. I had a stroll round the college, chatted to a few people. They were still clearing up some of the mess from May Week. I took the train back to London at about lunchtime. I was having a bit of a doze, I must admit – too much port the night before, you know. Anyway, he just burst into my compartment. He looked a bit of a mess, too, I can tell you. He checked up and down the corridor, drew the blinds, pushed this briefcase into my hands and asked me to bring it round to his flat off Knightsbridge at three o'clock today. Well, not exactly his flat, he told me it was in someone else's name.'

'Kept a floozy there, did he?'

'I hadn't thought of it that way,' mused Cushing. 'No, he just described it as a "safe house".'

'But why you?' asked Scott. 'I mean, you're at least fifty. You're a vicar from Guildford, not some cloak and dagger merchant. No disrespect intended, of course,' he added hurriedly, and took out his cigarette case again to cover his embarrassment.

Cushing glared disapprovingly at his godson. 'I thought he was pulling my leg at first. But he was obviously still working for the government. He told me that "they" were following him, that the service had been "compromised", and that he didn't have anyone else he could trust. He couldn't go to anyone in the service and he said not to go to the police. He said he'd asked the Master for some names of possible – what did he call them? "Irregulars", that was it. People he could recruit who weren't part of the service.' Cushing frowned. 'Ross said that my name hadn't been on the list, though he knew he could rely on me anyway.'

'Recruit to do what? And who are "they"?' Scott was on the edge of his seat now, gazing intently at Cushing.

'Sorry, Geoffrey, I've absolutely no idea. He said that it was vital that they didn't get the briefcase. "National interest", he said. "King and Country". Then he got off the train at the next station. I looked out of the window and couldn't see anyone following him. I thought it was all a bit odd, but I didn't think it was going to end up with some Hun shooting at me.'

'At us, don't forget. Us.' Scott stretched out his legs and glanced round at the pictures on the walls of the dark wood-panelled room. 'And how do you know they were Germans, anyway? You know you see Germans hiding behind every bush.'

Cushing frowned again. He had spent too long in the Scottish hospital for Scott to joke about some of his deep-set fears. 'When I went to the safe house – you know, the flat – I saw Ross. He was dead. He'd been knifed, or shot – knifed, I think. And there were two men searching the place. The one in the trench coat spoke in German. He called the other one, the bogus policeman, "Horstmann".'

Scott snorted. 'Well he certainly wasn't one of our policemen if he was shouting in German and shooting at you, that's for sure. What did you do then?'

'What do you think I did?' snapped Cushing. 'I ran away as fast as I could. Mind you, I hit one of them round the side of the head with Ross's briefcase – it weighs a ton, by the way – and poked the other one with my umbrella.'

'Good show'. Scott looked impressed. 'So, we'd better open up the briefcase.'

'We can't do that!'

'Why not? Those Germans were after it, they've tried to kill you for it, and they've already killed Ross for it. Come on, Padre. What else do you think we should do?'

'Take it to the police, of course'.

'We can't. You just said that Ross told you not to trust anyone, didn't you?' Scott stubbed out his cigarette.

'But what about Ross?' asked Cushing. 'He's an old friend, and he's been murdered. I have to report that, surely. I'm committing a crime if I don't.'

'Stop worrying. All in good time.'

'And what about the car? They will have got the number. They could trace you.'

'Ah.' Scott looked embarrassed. 'Well, it's not exactly my car. Remember old Harry Tremadoc? I'm sort of – well, sort of borrowing it while he's in South America.'

'That's kind of him,' said Cushing, and then checked himself. 'Wait a minute. Does Tremadoc actually know you've borrowed his car?'

'Not exactly, no. But with Harry in Rio de Janeiro or wherever, at least they won't be able to trace us. Come on, let's get this briefcase open.' He drained his brandy glass, unwound his long legs and stood up. Cushing stood too, and brought his face close to Scott's.

'Not before we telephone the police. I can't bear the thought of Ross just lying there.'

'Fine. If you must. But do it from a public call box, not from my club. We'll walk round the corner to my rooms and open up the briefcase there.' Cushing hesitated. 'Come on, Uncle Kit,' he added, urgently. 'Let's move.'

They left the bar and walked down the stairs, Scott side-stepping the barman who was unsuccessfully trying to give him the bill. 'Just put it on my tab, Harrington, there's a good chap.'

2

Monday 18th June 1928

Cushing and Scott walked the short distance up Piccadilly towards Albany where Scott had his rooms. Stopping at a telephone box opposite the Ritz Hotel, Cushing dug some coins out of his pocket, looked nervously over his shoulder and went in, picking up the receiver while Scott held open the door to listen. He asked the operator to be connected to the police.

'Hello, yes,' said Cushing. 'Yes, my name is Smith, yes, that's right, Smith.' He spelled the name out and Scott rolled his eyes. 'I want to report a murder. Yes, a murder. Yes, it's a Mr. Ross and – yes, I said murder.'

Scott poked him in the arm. 'Hurry up, man,' he whispered. Cushing gave the address of the mews flat, and then continued to mumble answers to other questions. 'He's been stabbed, I said,' but that was the end of the conversation as Scott snatched the receiver from his hand and replaced it firmly on the cradle. 'Come on,' he urged, half-dragging his godfather out of the telephone box and up the street. The noise of the buses and taxis was overwhelming and the exhaust fumes made Cushing cough. 'You know I think I preferred the old horse and carriage,' he said, wistfully.

They reached Albany and strolled into the courtyard and

through the fine Georgian portico. They were greeted by the caretaker from behind his screen. 'Afternoon Mr. Scott, sir.'

'Afternoon, Clarence. All well I trust?'

'Yes indeed, sir. A gentleman from your tailor called for you earlier, but I told him you had gone to the country for a month.'

'Good man,' said Scott, smiling, and coins changed hands as he and Cushing took the newly-installed lift to the third floor.

Scott's rooms were comfortable enough but, his godfather always thought, somewhat spartan. There were few books or other personal effects, though several pictures of "Vanity Fair" cricketers and photographs of teams for which Scott had played over the years adorned the walls; though Cushing had played rugby and cricket for school and college, his godson was a much better sportsman than he had ever been. Cushing peered at a decorated oar commemorating the Oxford May races. 'I say, Geoffrey, you were at Lincoln. This oar is from Balliol.'

'Just one of my hunting trophies,' grinned Scott. 'I'm no oarsman – far too early in the morning. Rugger and cricket for me. I'm playing this weekend, as it happens.'

'I thought you said you weren't going to play this year?'

'I said I wasn't going to play for Surrey. Douglas Jardine has more or less taken my place in the side, damn him. I loathed the man even when we were at Oxford together. I have a drink with Percy Fender every now and then, though – he's a sound man. But I've played for I Zingari, and I'll be guesting for the odd country house team at weekends. I like going to country houses – it helps to pay the bills now the old trust fund has stopped paying out.'

'What? You play for money?'

'No, of course not, I couldn't do that.' Cushing looked relieved. 'No, I make the money playing cards.' Cushing's relief turned to dismay. 'Mind you, I'm quite flush at the moment. I borrowed twenty pounds and put a tenner each way on a tip I had for the Derby last weekend. It romped home at 33-1. I must pay Tom Wood his twenty quid back one day. Oh well.' He laughed. 'The girls tend to be prettier in the country as well. Do you know, there was a place we played in Hampshire where the daughter of the house...'

'Enough,' interrupted Cushing. 'Shall we have a look at this briefcase?'

'Bring it over,' said Scott, taking evident pleasure in his godfather's discomfort. He cleared piles of letters and other papers from the table. As he did so, a photograph of a girl fell from one of the envelopes to the floor. Scott glanced at it, then threw it into the waste paper basket. 'Pull up a chair, Padre, and let's get down to it. What have we got?'

Cushing lifted the heavy briefcase onto the table and tried the clasp. He frowned. 'It's locked. Perhaps we'd better go to the police after all.'

'Don't be ridiculous,' retorted Scott, picking up a paper knife. He leaned over and fiddled briefly with the small lock, and a few seconds later prised it open. 'There we are, Uncle Kit, you can do the honours now.'

'How did you...? Where did you learn...? No, no, don't tell me,' he said. He pulled out a loose sheet of paper and two large brown envelopes and handed them over to Scott, followed by two objects, each of which was wrapped in what looked like a pillowcase. 'These are what made the case so heavy.'

'Let's have a look then,' said Scott, a gleam in his eye.

'Wait a moment,' replied Cushing, 'there's something else.' He reached into the bottom of the briefcase and removed a small blue envelope. 'That looks like the lot,' he said, as he started to unwrap one of the pillowcases carefully. Scott leaned over and snatched the other, hurriedly unrolling the linen and revealing a scarf. Protected by the scarf was a block of dark clay, with strange markings inscribed on it. 'What on earth is it?' asked Cushing.

Scott looked disappointed. 'Well I was hoping that it might have been a couple of gold bars after all the trouble we've had, not some stupid clay tablets.'

Cushing finished unwrapping the other pillowcase; it was a second tablet. 'They look ancient. But what are they?'

Scott scowled. 'How the hell should I know?'

'Well you did read archaeology,' replied Cushing mildly.

'That's true, I did,' admitted Scott, looking at them more closely. 'They could be old. And the inscriptions aren't in English.' Cushing raised an eyebrow, and Scott continued, holding a tablet up to the light. 'Of course it's not in English, I mean it's not in the Latin alphabet. Not hieroglyphics either – I've been reading about Carter's expedition recently, and this is definitely not Egyptian. More linear. Like cuneiform. Hmm.' He paused. 'They could be valuable.'

'Perhaps there might be a clue in some of the papers?'

'Good idea, Padre.' Scott put down the tablet rather more carefully than he had picked it up, and looked at the piece of paper, stroking his thin moustache. 'Now, what have we got here? There's a list of names written on Buckingham College notepaper, some of them crossed out. Do you recognise any of them?' Cushing shook his head, then opened the first brown envelope.

'There's a typed note to Ross from someone called Hitchcock. And what's this?' He pulled out a white card, expensively embossed. 'It's an invitation to a charity ball. Looks as though someone's had a bath with it – it's in a bit of a state.'

He opened the second brown envelope which was bulkier than the first. 'A wallet, a set of keys, a pen, a pair of spectacles, some loose change.' He opened the wallet. 'Did you say the letter to Ross was from someone called Hitchcock? Look, here's some sort of identity card.'

Scott took the wallet from him. 'Major Gordon Hitchcock,'

he read. 'This has been in water as well.' He sniffed the leather and grimaced. 'And look at all this cash! There must be...' He stopped, glancing up, his face flushing. 'Well, not as much as I thought.' He slipped the wallet into his pocket. 'What's the blue envelope?'

'It's a letter, addressed to a D. Stockington Esquire at an address in Putney. Should I open it? It's sealed. I don't think I should, it's private.'

'Oh for heaven's sake!' exploded Scott. 'Open the wretched thing.'

After a moment's hesitation, Cushing slit open the envelope. 'Handwritten, on Buckingham College notepaper again, dated Sunday morning.' He flicked forward to the end of the letter. 'It's signed by James Ross. He must have written it just before he took the train.'

'Who is this Stockington johnny?' queried Scott?

'No idea,' replied Cushing. 'Let's see what he says.

"My dear Stockington," he read out loud. "'My apologies for writing to you at home, especially as I know that you will not receive this until you get back from France. I fear that I may be placing you in great danger by contacting you at all. I have evidence that the service has been compromised, possibly to the highest levels, and you are the only one left in whom I have complete confidence."

'Sounds like some awful penny dreadful,' interrupted Scott.

'Well whatever it sounds like, it was important enough for people to kill him,' retorted Cushing. He continued to read.

"'I am now in Cambridge. Last night, and again this morning, I spoke to the Master of my alma mater, Buckingham College, with a view to getting some ideas about a few sound men to help us, men that we can trust, "irregulars", if you like, whom the opposition will not be able to trace."'

'The list didn't include you, though, did it, Padre? The Master obviously suggested younger men.' Scott grinned at Cushing who glared back. Scott actually thought that his godfather looked younger than his fifty years; he still had most of his hair, though it had turned largely grey.

'Wait a moment! The list!' He picked up the sheet of paper with names on it. 'This is Ross's list! His irregulars.'

Cushing nodded calmly. 'You're probably right. But we can't do much with it at the moment. Let's carry on with the letter.' He continued to read. '"I dare not share this with anyone else in the service. I shall take cover in the flat off Knightsbridge that we used last year to interrogate the spy Cuthbert; that should be safe enough."'

'Very safe,' muttered Scott, sarcastically, as he paced round the room.

'"As you know, Hitchcock and I were working on the Horchdienst project, trying to crack the code."' Cushing interrupted himself. 'Aha! Horchdienst. Told you they were Germans.'

Scott raised his eyes to the ceiling and placed his hand on Cushing's shoulder. 'Yes, yes, you've made your point.'

Cushing read on. '"But Hitchcock has uncovered much more. I don't know enough detail yet, but he has hinted at a conspiracy that goes both high and deep – the police, the government, the City. It appears to be international too, and our old friends the Synarchists could be involved."'

'What are synarchists?'

'No idea, I'm afraid. Wait! Listen to this!' He continued to read. '"I'm afraid I have to tell you that Hitchcock is dead. His body was found by the weir at Shiplake, near Henley on Thames in Oxfordshire, on Tuesday night. He had been shot twice in the back, and his hand and wrist were also badly cut, but it doesn't look as if the bullets killed him. The poor man seems to have drowned, though we await the results of the autopsy."'

'Oh. So that's why his things were so wet.' Scott paused. 'Sorry. Poor chap.' He picked up the spectacles and keys that he realised must have belonged to Hitchcock, and shivered.

Cushing scowled. 'Just listen. "I have managed to hush things up, and at least he had no family to be concerned about him. Fortunately, the local beat bobbies recognised his papers as meaning that he was one of us, and they telephoned me."'

Scott interrupted again. 'The identity card. Of course. Must be for whatever branch of the service he was in.'

'"After I identified the body, I had a difficult hour with the Chief Constable, a decent enough fellow called Davies, but I was able to take charge of Hitchcock's personal effects. In the poacher's pocket of his Barbour jacket were two clay tablets; it's a good thing that the pocket kept them largely dry. I welcome your thoughts on the contents when we meet. They look very old and I need to talk to some of my friends at the British Museum. They may be priceless – of inestimable historical value, I mean. I cannot decipher the writing on them which appears to be in some form of code, but I sent a photograph to Joe Page in Fulham. He has largely retired now, so I think he should be secure."'

Cushing took off his glasses and looked at Scott who was transfixed, on the edge of his seat. 'I remember Page from when I worked in Room 40 during the War. A good man, a civilian, a teacher I think, but Bolshevik tendencies if I remember correctly. Welsh, too.'

'Get on with it,' urged Scott. 'I want to hear more about them being priceless. I could use a bob or two.'

'"Meet me at the French café on Villiers Street at 9.30 next Monday before you go into the office. Or contact me at the safe house if you get this message sooner. Keep your eyes and ears open. The safety of the realm may depend on it. And trust no one. With best wishes, etcetera etcetera." And it's signed by James Ross.'

'He's been on the sauce,' said Scott, emphatically. 'Totally barking. Or too much sun. Or that's what I would have said, I suppose, if we didn't know the poor chap had been murdered.' He picked up the official-looking memorandum from the first envelope and glanced at it.

'So what do we have to go on?' asked Cushing. 'A letter to this chap Stockington, who is obviously an agent and who won't be back in the country for a week. Another dead agent in Oxfordshire. And Ross, of course.'

'And this memorandum, which isn't a lot of help,' said Scott, and started to read. '"To Commander J. Ross, from Major G. Hitchcock. Re. Code Investigation Horchdienst." Whatever that may mean. It's dated 12th June – that's last Tuesday.'

'And the day Hitchcock was killed,' interrupted Cushing. 'What else?'

'"Your memorandum of 11th June refers."'

'Well that's not very helpful,' said Cushing. 'What else?'

'He says "Please refer to my reports of 5th June and 22nd May."'

'Where are they? What are they?'

'Whatever they have to say, they are probably rotting somewhere in a filing cabinet in Whitehall.'

'You're right, not a lot of use at all. What next?'

'"As we discussed earlier today, this seems to be bigger than either of us had thought. I shall investigate Jupiter further and search his property."' Scott looked puzzled. 'What does he mean by "Jupiter"?'

'It's common practice to give code names to key individuals, to save giving the game away accidentally. Stockington may be able to find out who they mean. Anything else?'

'"Expect further news at the end of the week",' read Scott.

'And he didn't make the end of the week,' said Cushing, staring into the distance. 'Poor man.'

'But what about the invitation card?' interrupted Scott. 'It's been water-damaged, so it may have been in Hitchcock's pocket. I mean, if he drowned.'

Cushing read it out. '"Sir Charles and Lady Sloane cordially invite" – and the name has been left blank – "to a Midsummer Ball at Longley Hall, Berkshire, at 8.00pm on Saturday 23rd June. In aid of the Empire Society for the Christian Education of Impoverished Children. Evening dress. Carriages at 2.00." Doesn't mean a lot to me, I'm afraid.'

'It does to me,' replied Scott. 'I've been to Longley Hall, and I vaguely know a girl who lives there. I went there for a cricket match last summer. And there's been news in the society pages about this Midsummer Ball for some time.' Scott rummaged on the floor and found a newspaper. 'Good job Mrs Duggins hasn't cleared the weekend papers away yet. Yes, here we are.'

He read out the article. '"Great excitement in anticipation of next week's Midsummer Ball. Sir Charles Sloane, who will host the ball at his estate, Longley Hall, near Sonning in Berkshire, refused to be drawn on the likely guest list. He told this reporter that "the most important thing was to raise money for the charity." His wife, Lady Sloane, was more forthcoming. "A real mix," she told us. "Politicians, actors and actresses, lords and ladies, famous sportsmen; all rubbing shoulders with local dignitaries and family friends. It's going to be a wonderful gathering." The Midsummer Ball will be held on Saturday 23rd June. Get yourself a ticket if you can. This reporter will certainly be there."'

'But why should Hitchcock have an invitation to this ball in his pocket?' asked Cushing.

'Good question. Maybe he was going.'

'Why is it blank then? There's something not quite right.' Cushing's brow furrowed. Suddenly Scott leapt up, looking aghast at the clock on the mantelpiece.

'Look here, Uncle Kit,' he said, 'I'm sorry, but I've got to get ready. It's almost seven o'clock and I'm meeting a girl tonight.'

'Isn't this business more important?' said Cushing, crossly.

'Well you can get on with saving the country, Padre. This girl is really important too. I mean she may not be a great looker or anything, but her father does own most of Dorset.'

Cushing spluttered, and Scott continued. 'Anyway, you must be exhausted, and it's too late for you to go back to Surrey tonight. Stay here if you like. I'll put some pyjamas and shaving kit out for you and I'll drive you home after breakfast.' He tossed Cushing a bunch of keys. 'Pop down the road to your club for supper. I'm sure the Athenaeum can rustle you up a chop or something. Help yourself to anything here, of course.' And with that he disappeared into the bathroom, leaving Cushing puzzling over the clay tablets.

3

Monday 18th June 1928

Later that evening, Cushing took himself off to the wood-panelled bar of the Travellers' Club in Pall Mall. The room was thick with smoke and the walls were covered with paintings of famous explorers and trophies from distant parts of the Empire and beyond. He had a large port on the table in front of him and his friend Peter Clifford was filling his own glass from the decanter.

Only fifteen minutes after Scott had left the flat, dressed to impress and with his thick dark hair heavily slicked back, Cushing had put down the tablets and poured himself a whisky and soda, brooding for a while over his godson's behaviour. Like so many young people, he lived a hectic, irresponsible existence – Cushing preferred not to go so far as to think of it as hedonistic – in a world that was rebuilding itself after the cessation of hostilities. Young Geoffrey had served in France only for two or three weeks, and been slightly wounded, and while Cushing was proud of the boy, he just wished that he would settle down and do something worthwhile with his life.

Cushing had been at Cambridge with Scott's father who had been killed in the Boer War, never seeing his only child. Cushing and his wife were close to the boy and to his mother, who died, still a grieving widow, when Geoffrey was only eleven. It had been Cushing who ensured that the young man went to a good boarding school and then, on his return from war-torn France, to Oxford. He smiled, thinking of the afternoons standing at the edge of a rugby field, cricket pitch or river bank, cheering the lad on and reliving his own sporting youth even while he had been recovering from his own injuries and mental scars, as well as the loss of his beloved wife. He had certainly done his best for the boy, but there was still that wild and disrespectful streak. He smiled again, thinking of Scott's father. He had been just the same, at Cambridge and then as a brave army officer.

Cushing sighed and reached for the decanter, then paused and replaced it on the table, realising that he needed company. Peter Clifford. Just the man. He picked up the telephone, gave the operator the number and found Clifford still at work in his rooms above his medical practice in Harley Street. 'Peter? Christopher Cushing here. I'm in London and I need to talk to you. Are you free? You're not going to believe a word of what I'm about to tell you.'

Clifford had invited Cushing to his own club, shared a meal and listened, chewing methodically on the end of his pipe and absorbing everything that Cushing had said. 'You're absolutely right, of course,' he said. 'You can't go to the police. But we've got to do something.'

'You said we,' said Cushing, raising an eyebrow hopefully.

'Well of course,' replied Clifford, enthusiastically. 'After all, you can't do this on your own, and young Scott sounds a bit unreliable.'

'Not unreliable. He's a good young man, just a bit headstrong.' Cushing looked at Clifford across the low table. The two had first met in France. Cushing had encountered Clifford, haggard, prematurely grey and covered in blood, working tirelessly in the field hospital as a never-ending stream of ruined bodies passed under his knife and needle. As regimental chaplain, struggling to keep his faith in the man-made hell of the trenches, Cushing had spent too much time in the hospital with the dead and the dying. Clifford, only a couple of years Cushing's junior, was now looking sleek and prosperous, several stone heavier than when the two were in France. 'Well, glad to have you on board,' said Cushing. 'Not that I know what ship we're on!'

'Wouldn't miss it for the world,' said Clifford, confidently. 'I have to say, though, that my immediate reaction when you went through the story was that I'd have to ship you back to Craiglockhart for some fresh Scottish air and some more rest. But it's too mad to have been made up, even by you.'

'Thank you – I think,' replied Cushing, leaning back in his leather armchair and glaring at the picture on the wall above him of a heavily-medalled and bewhiskered general who appeared to be glaring back.

His mind went back to the dark days of wartime and its aftermath. By nature a peaceful man, he had watched, frustrated, as many of his parishioners had marched off to France. He had grieved with the rest as the news came through of those who had died or been wounded at Mons and Loos, but he found it increasingly difficult to look their families in the eye, even as he was comforting them. Did they think him a coward? He was relatively young, fit and with no children of his own, and was becoming convinced that he could do more for his country in France than he could as a vicar in rural England.

And then his life changed overnight. It had become obvious that the war would not be all over by Christmas, and his wife had gone to visit her widowed mother in London to persuade her to join them in the safety of Surrey. His beloved Mary had been killed, along with her mother and dozens of others, in one of the first zeppelin raids on the capital.

He had struggled to conquer his own grief, questioning his pacifism and even his faith. His faith had survived the struggle, but he needed to make a decision. Should he desert his flock and leave the comforts of home for the unknown horrors of France? Was he driven by anger and revenge? It was to Mary he still turned for advice, and he fancied that she answered him in that amused, almost exasperated tone she employed when he was unable to make up his mind about the best way to couch a sermon. 'Stop tormenting yourself,' he heard her say. If you feel you should go, just go. You won't stop the fighting by staying here.'

And he had gone, leaving his church and parishioners. And for what? Had he been of any help? Certainly he had rolled bandages, carried stretchers and held up lights while the likes of Peter Clifford had struggled to save lives. As he battled to cope with the endless mud, the inadequate food, the penetrating cold and the lack of sleep, he had again questioned his own faith even as he tried to comfort the dying and boost the morale of the living.

Then there was that last dreadful day at the front. July 1st, 1916, the first day of the battle of the Somme on which the British army suffered sixty thousand casualties. Maddened by the horrors he had seen, half-blinded by smoke and deafened by the noise, he had followed the men of his regiment into a hail of bullets to try to rescue a young man from his own village who had, like many others, been mown down in the first wave of the assault. He had put the man over his shoulder and staggered back to the relative safety of the trench to find that the young soldier was already dead. Sobbing uncontrollably and wishing he were dead too, he had lurched back three times into no man's land, each time dragging back a wounded man. The third time he ignored the searing pain in his arm when a bullet struck, and was able to heave the unconscious body of one of his sergeants back into the trench before falling lifelessly on top of him. Found later by a stretcher party, he was patched up in a field hospital and shipped back to England.

His physical wounds had healed, but his mind had spiralled out of control. When an elderly colonel came to the hospital to present him with a medal, he began to weep again, and the nurses and doctors had been unable to stop him crying until sedation brought him merciful relief. That was when he was sent to the new-fangled hospital outside Edinburgh. The huge grey stone building at Craiglockhart had been only recently converted for the treatment of officers wounded in mind as well as body, rehabilitating them so they could be shipped back to the front line. Many civilians regarded the inmates of "Dottyville" with suspicion, pointing and sniggering at the men wearing their blue armbands in the streets as they worked to help in the community while they slowly recovered. As an officer, and a decorated officer at that, few could actually question his bravery, but there was no leeway for the hundreds of private soldiers who may have suffered similar symptoms of what was only just being called "shellshock".

When Cushing had eventually been discharged from Craiglockhart, he was, like many of the other patients, deemed to be medically unfit for further active service, but he had been eager to continue to contribute to the war effort. Transferring to Military Intelligence, he began working for Ross. And look where that had landed him. He began to laugh out loud, not realising that Clifford was speaking.

'And I'm sure some of the rest of the boys would be game for a bit of fun,' he said, unaware that Cushing's attention had wandered. 'What did your man Ross call them? Irregulars? Well we can be pretty irregular if we want to be. Now, the first thing we need to do is a bit of sleuthing. First thing tomorrow, you pop down to Putney and see if you can find out when this man – Stockington, did you say? – is back from his holidays. I've got patients all day, but I can join you in the evening. Why don't I pick you up in the car? We'll go and have a word with this decoder chap in Fulham.'

'Are you sure? About the evening, I mean? That's marvellous. Though I don't know how long I can stay in London. I need to get back home to Surrey sooner or later. I can't stay with Geoffrey forever, and I checked – the Athenaeum is full. No room at the inn.'

'That won't be a problem. You can stay at St. John's Wood with me. You were planning to stay over on Saturday anyway, after the Lord's test, so your room is all made up. The memsahib is down with friends in Dorset all week, and young Harry – you know he's at Trinity now? Just finished his first year. He's spending most of the long vacation with Molly's family in New York.'

'That will get a bit warm in a month or so.'

'Ten weeks with Molly's family would be far too hot for me at any time, I can tell you. Still, the place is empty, so you're more than welcome.' He leaned forward, conspiratorially. 'Now, what else do we need to investigate?'

'Well the biggest thing must be these old tablets.'

'Absolutely. I'm looking forward to seeing them. What more can you tell me about them?'

'Only that they look ancient, they are covered in some form of script or code, and they look like they are made out of baked clay. Sorry, I'm no expert. Young Geoffrey knows a bit about archaeology, though he pretends to be a complete idiot, and he didn't have any idea either.'

'I'll give John Grainger a call for you tomorrow. Do you know John? I was at college with him. He's an American, but very sound. He's at the British Museum now.'

'No, I don't know him, but splendid, thank you.' Cushing was impressed with Clifford's energy. 'Now there has been nothing about Ross in the evening papers, nothing even about gunfire in Belgravia, so they must have covered that up in the same way Ross covered up Hitchcock's death.'

'True. I would have expected to see something about a body in the Thames in the weekend papers, but nothing at all. Where exactly was the body found?'

'Ross said in the letter that it was by the weir at Shiplake. That's near Henley.' Cushing knew the area fairly well, and had been to watch the famous rowing regatta several times when he was younger. 'But I don't know the weir, of course.'

'Well, old man, we're in the best place in London to find a decent map. Finish up your port and we can pop along to the map room.'

Fifteen minutes later, the two men had made their way to the map room, stopping briefly on the way to admire a collection of shrunken heads brought back from Sarawak by Rajah Brooke. The map room occupied a substantial space, heavily curtained and with dark shallow-drawered map chests along every wall. At that time of the evening it was deserted, and the two friends were soon poring over a large scale Ordnance Survey map covering the area of the Thames where Ross had said that Hitchcock's body had been found.

'Now,' said Clifford, 'the question is whether he was shot at the weir, or further upstream. Pity I can't take a look at the body. There's no way of knowing for how long the poor chap was in the water. Oh well.'

Cushing looked up at Clifford, surprised at his apparent cold-bloodedness. 'There would probably have been too many people around by the weir for the murderer to have pulled a gun. Someone would have heard the shot, or shots. He must have fallen in further upstream. It can't have been far, or he would have been caught up at another weir.' Cushing peered over the top of his spectacles and spotted a name he recognised. 'Let me see that,' he said, abruptly. 'Look, here.' He stabbed at the map with his forefinger. 'Look, the next weir is here at Sonning. That's Berkshire. I hadn't realised that it was so close – the county boundary is the river. Look, look! Here it is. Longley Hall.' He paced round excitedly.

Clifford looked blank. 'I'm sorry, Christopher,' he said, 'I've absolutely no idea what you're talking about.'

'Ah,' said Cushing, apologetically. 'I didn't mention the invitation, did I?'

'What invitation?'

'In Ross's briefcase, among Hitchcock's things. There was an invitation to the Midsummer Ball. It had obviously been in water, so it must have been in Hitchcock's pocket.'

'And this is relevant, is it?'

'Yes! Longley Hall is where the ball is being held. Hitchcock must have gone to Longley Hall and taken the invitation from there.'

'You don't know that.'

'Of course not, but it has to be. It's what, only a couple of miles upstream from the weir at Shiplake? And it's only a little way downstream from the weir at Sonning. He could have been shot, fallen in the river and drifted down to the weir in a couple of hours.' Cushing prowled up and down the room, deep in thought.

'Conjecture, laddie, pure conjecture. What are you suggesting? That the belted earl who owns the place gunned the poor chap down in cold blood?'

'Well, maybe not. But we have to go there.'

'You can't just go and snoop round somebody's private house.'

'No, but I can go to the ball.'

'Can you? Why, have you been invited?'

'No, obviously not. But it's a charity do, isn't it? I can always ask Gussie.'

'Gussie? Who's Gussie?'

'Gussie? Oh, I'm sorry. Mrs. Augusta Gordon. She's an old friend, a widow, very much in the society circuit in London. She does a lot of charity work. She'll be able to help, I'm sure.'

'A widow, eh?' Clifford looked knowingly at Cushing. 'You old dog. Rich too, is she?'

Cushing coloured. 'It's not like that at all. I've known her for years. She used to live in Surrey when I was the vicar – she still has a cottage near me, though she spends most of her time in London now. She was very kind after Mary died.'

Clifford had never met Mary Cushing, but knew that his friend still felt the pain of her death in 1915. Cushing had told him once, in France, that he and Mary had been childhood sweethearts and were married even before Cushing had been ordained into the ministry. There were no children, perhaps explaining why he was so fond of his godson Geoffrey, but the two had been inseparable through Cushing's early curacy, his tenure in India and his return to the Surrey countryside as vicar. As a doctor, Clifford knew that Cushing had been devastated by his wife's death and that this had contributed to his decision to join up and to his eventual breakdown. He cleared his throat. 'So what does Gussie – sorry, Mrs. Gordon – do now?'

'As I say, she organises some of these big society bashes. She was left a fair amount of money when her husband died, poor girl.'

'Did you know him too?'

'Briefly. She met Archie during the War when he was in hospital – she had volunteered as a nurse, you see. He was badly injured. Gassed too. No one ever thought he'd make it. But he did – then the influenza took him. Tragic.'

Both men stood in silence for a few moments, their thoughts going back to France, then Cushing continued. 'Anyway, after Archie died, Gussie and I – well, we stayed in touch. I'll call her tomorrow and see if she can arrange a ticket.'

'What on earth would you do at Longley Hall, even if you can wangle a ticket?'

Cushing paused. 'We've got a few days to work that out, Peter. In the meantime, how about a nightcap?' The two men left the map room, satisfied with what they had learned, and returned to the bar.

'Cheerio old man.' Clifford waved from the back of his taxi as Cushing walked, a little unsteadily, down Pall Mall. He had refused Clifford's offer of a lift, preferring to stretch his legs in the warm evening air – it was, after all, only a short distance back to Scott's flat. His head was spinning, still overwhelmed by the events of the day, and not helped by several glasses of port. 'Goodbye, Piccadilly,' he hummed, and waved in a friendly manner to a passing policeman who acknowledged him with a brisk salute.

His thoughts wandered over the evening's conversation, and it was only when he returned to Scott's flat and saw the two clay tablets on the table that he could convince himself that it had all really happened. He picked up one of the tablets, but knew he could do no more that evening. He was exhausted. He pulled on a pair of Scott's pyjamas and lay down on the bed in the spare room, his mind still racing, but was asleep in minutes.

He was awoken by a loud crash and leapt up, his heart racing. He glanced at the clock and saw that it was past five. There was more banging from within the flat, then a low groaning as if someone was in pain, followed by a tuneless whistle and the splashing of water. With some annoyance, he recognised the sound – he had heard Scott singing before. He wondered whether his own family had disapproved of his own youthful exuberance back in the nineties quite as much as he now disapproved of Scott's, then rolled over and went back to sleep.

Five hours later, wearing one of Scott's shirts that was clearly a little too tight around the middle for him, Cushing was sitting at the dining table, looking again at the tablets and documents and starting to make notes. His godson had still not emerged from his bedroom. There was a rattle of a key in the lock and the door opened, admitting a large, florid-faced woman of middle age with startling red hair.

'Morning, dearie,' she said, walking straight past him, opening a cupboard, donning an apron and pulling out a box of dusters. 'I've not met you before.'

'Er... no,' said Cushing, as she advanced towards him holding a mop. 'I'm Mr. Scott's godfather. Christopher Cushing.'

'Nice to meet you, sir,' she replied. 'I'm Mrs. Duggins. Now I suppose Mr. Scott isn't up yet. Bless him. Such a nice young man.' She looked at the tablets in front of Cushing. 'Blimey,' she said, 'what have you got there then?'

Cushing covered them with one of the old pillowcases. 'Nothing important,' he said, hurriedly, 'but best not to touch them. They're a bit fragile.'

As the woman bustled into the kitchen, Scott appeared at his bedroom door wearing a splendidly ornate dressing gown.

'Ah, Padre, good morning,' he said, grimacing and rubbing his eyes. 'Morning Mrs D.' He yawned, and grinned at Cushing. 'Did you have a good evening?'

'Yes, thank you,' replied Cushing. 'And I don't need to ask about yours, seeing the time you came back this morning.'

'Splendid, splendid.' Scott ignored the jibe and called out 'I say, Mrs. D, how about some breakfast?'

'Oh Mr. Scott, you're such a one!' Her voice was affectionate. 'Kippers for two, dear?'

'No, not for me, thank you,' said Cushing quickly.

'Come on, Padre. We've got a busy day today. We have to start with a proper breakfast.'

'I did, about three hours ago,' replied Cushing, testily. 'And stop calling me "Padre"!'

'Oh well, please yourself. Just toast then, please, Mrs. D.' Scott picked up one of the tablets and juggled it from hand to hand.

Cushing winced. 'Put it down, Geoffrey, there's a good chap.'

Scott casually dropped the clay tablet back onto the table and strolled over to the window where he gazed out at the buses on Piccadilly. 'It really was an excellent show at Drury Lane last night,' he said, absent-mindedly. 'Don't know why I hadn't got round to seeing it before. How did that song go? "Tote that barge, hump that bale, get a little drunk and you land in jail." Plus ça change, eh Padre?'

Mrs. Duggins placed a rack of toast on the table and Scott sat down in front of it and reached for the butter. 'Thanks, Mrs D,' he beamed, and turned to Cushing. 'Pass the marmalade, Padre, there's a good chap.'

He then fumbled in his pocket and passed Cushing a small piece of paper, torn from a notepad. 'What's this?' asked Cushing?

Scott looked a little shamefaced. 'I was looking at some of the papers and things when I got home,' he said, unconvincingly, his mouth full of toast. 'I found this in Hitchcock's wallet when I was – er – looking. I thought it looked interesting. Help yourself to tea, old man.'

Cushing looked askance at Scott, then at the piece of paper. 'It says "Assass. Ital R. Thur 12." Then the word "Tranquil". Then two question marks. Then a second line: "Lapsit Exillis", with three question marks. What does all that mean?'

'Well, "assass" is pretty obviously "assassination",' replied Scott. 'Don't know about the rest.' Cushing pointed at the kitchen door, from behind which there was now an absence of noise, and put his finger to his lips.

Scott tapped the side of his nose knowingly. 'Aha! Pas devant les domestiques, n'est-ce pas? You're getting into the swing of this cloak and dagger stuff, aren't you?'

Cushing lowered his voice. 'Be serious for a minute, can't you, Geoffrey? Now "Lapsit Exillis" looks to be Latin. My Latin is pretty good, but it doesn't make sense. "It is fallen from them"?' He looked puzzled. 'No, it's nonsense. Perhaps Hitchcock just noted it down wrongly.'

'Well think about the rest, then,' said Scott, cramming the last slice of toast into his mouth and wiping the butter from his lips with the back of his hand. 'This part is obviously a date. Now when was there a Thursday 12th?' He checked his diary. 'Well the last one was in April.'

'So was there an assassination around then? In Italy, perhaps? If that's what "Ital" means.'

Scott looked blank and shrugged.

'We could go to the library,' said Cushing. 'They will have all the back issues.'

'Or I could save you the journey and phone my friend Brodders.'

'Who?'

'I play cricket with him every now and then. He writes for The Times. Does the obituaries. Great job. Leaves plenty of time for cricket.' He grinned. 'He could look it up for us, I'm sure.'

'Good man,' said Cushing, enthusiastically. 'Do you have his number? Find out if anything happened in Italy on or around 12th April involving an assassination.'

'Bit of a long shot,' smiled Scott, picking up the receiver and asking the operator for the number. He was put through and Cushing tried to catch the conversation. He heard Scott whistle softly as he made some notes. 'Thanks, old man,' said Scott. 'No, no, nothing in it for you, no scoop, I can assure you. Sorry. See you in Oxford.' He replaced the receiver and turned round to Cushing. 'Well well.'

'What? Tell me.'

'An attempt on 12th April to assassinate the King and Queen of Italy. They were driving through the streets of Milan in an open-top carriage and some Bolshevik threw a bomb at them. It missed, exploded in the street and killed loads of people. No one British, obviously.'

'So...'

'Patience, Padre. Apparently the assassin was a man called Romolo Tranquilli, a known agitator and a member of a dangerous international group called the Synarchists.'

'Synarchists?' repeated Cushing. 'Ross mentioned them in his letter, didn't he?'

'Absolutely. And Hitchcock scribbled the word "Tranquil". That's this man Tranquilli.'

'You're right. But what's so important about some Italian Bolshevik trying to blow up their king? It happens all the time over there.'

'Maybe Hitchcock was collecting information about a Bolshevik conspiracy. The last thing in the article that Brodders read out to me was that Prince Umberto spoke out against the Bolshevik threat to Europe.'

Cushing pondered for a few moments, and shook his head. 'Had we missed anything else in the wallet?'

Scott failed to look Cushing in the eye. 'No, nothing. I went through it all fairly carefully.' He coughed, pushed his plate to one side and called 'Thanks, Mrs. D.' to the kitchen, from where energetic cleaning activity could suddenly be heard again. 'Anything in the papers about your escapade yesterday? Or about Ross?'

'Not a dickie bird. But as I said to Peter Clifford last night, they covered up Hitchcock's death, so I imagine they would cover up Ross's as well. And the only people who saw me were those fake policemen.'

'Apart from the people in the street, and at the Berkeley, of course,' said Scott. 'Plenty of witnesses. Anyway, who's Peter Clifford?'

'He's an old friend. We served together in France – he's a sawbones. We had a couple of drinks last night at his club while you were out enjoying yourself.'

'Fair enough,' said Scott, breezily. 'So what do we do now?'

'You don't do anything,' barked Cushing. He fingered his collar. 'Look, sorry old man, but I mean, dash it, I'm going to Putney to check out when Stockington is back from his holiday, and then I'm going over to Fulham to see old Joe Page. And I'm going on my own. I've already put you to too much trouble.'

'Now I'm not having that,' said Scott, raising his voice. 'This is my show too. Some Hun shoots at us in the middle of Belgrave Square and you expect me to ignore it?' The sound of breaking crockery came from the kitchen.

Both men continued to argue, now whispering, and Scott was finally forced to relent. He had previously admitted that he was busy that evening anyway, and was secretly relieved to hear about Clifford and that his godfather was not embarking on his investigations alone.

'How about a lift to Putney then?' he offered.

'No thanks,' replied Cushing. 'That's kind, but I can easily take the train. I've borrowed your street map. And I want to walk over to Watts in Portman Square first and buy another couple of shirts. Yours really doesn't fit!'

Scott smiled. 'I've been thinking,' he said. 'I'm off to Oxford this evening – there's quite an important cricket match starting on Thursday. You can stay here, of course. But why don't I pop up early and see if my old archaeology tutor has got any ideas about these tablets?'

Cushing pursed his lips. He was uncomfortable with letting Scott take the tablets away. 'No, don't do that. Give him a call on the telephone first,' he suggested. 'Though if you're keen to help...'

'Of course I am!' interrupted Scott.

'Yes, quite. Thank you. It would be really helpful if you could try and find out a little more about these "Synarchists", and this "Lapsit Exillis" thingamajig. I'll work on a couple of other leads.' He felt guilty not telling Scott his theory regarding Longley Hall.

'Look here, Uncle Kit', said Scott, after a brief pause. 'I was thinking last night. If these people really are looking for you now – well, I think you should have this.' He opened a desk drawer and presented Cushing with a package wrapped in canvas. Cushing opened it and saw that it was a service revolver in a holster. He looked up at his godson.

'What's this?'

'Well it's obvious what it is, Padre. I brought it back from France ten years ago and – well, the next time some Hun takes a pot shot at you in Knightsbridge, I'd like you to be able to shoot back.'

'It's not going to happen, Geoffrey, but thank you anyway.' Cushing felt a new respect for Scott as he handed him back the revolver. He laughed. 'What would the bishop say if he heard that I had been picked up by the police for "packing a rod" in the West End?'

There was a noise from the kitchen, followed by loud ostentatious humming, and both men started guiltily. 'She'll be ringing all her friends later,' said Scott, smiling. 'On my telephone, of course. She's an incurable gossip. Not that anyone would believe a word. They'll think she's been at my gin again.' Cushing laughed.

'Mind you,' continued Scott, 'she's a good soul really. She's got an invalid husband and a huge brood of kids, and she works all hours to support them. If she fancies the odd pick-me-up, or uses the telephone now and again, so what? She probably deserves it.'

'Which reminds me,' said Cushing. 'May I use your telephone now?'

He flicked through the telephone directory and tutted when he found no entry for Stockington. He wrote down the address and number of every J. Page in south west London, then looked up Gussie Gordon's number. He gave it to the operator, and was surprised and delighted when Gussie answered the telephone herself. 'Christopher, darling,' she said enthusiastically. 'How lovely to hear from you. But you've caught me in a terrible rush; I'm just about to leave. Are you up in town? Wonderful. Would you be able to do tea at the Savoy tomorrow morning? Lovely. At eleven? See you there. Bye.' And Cushing was left spluttering 'Yes, Gussie, of course' to a silent telephone. He smiled affectionately and Scott gave him a knowing wink. 'Who's the girl, Uncle Kit?'

Cushing ignored the question. 'Well,' he said, 'it looks like I'm staying in London till tomorrow at least. Then I must get back to Surrey, I've got this wretched midsummer service on Sunday and I need to do some preparation. And I don't have a lot of time – I'm coming back up on Saturday for the test match.'

'Excellent,' said Scott. 'The West Indians, eh? It should be a good day. I'm sorry to miss it.'

'I'm surprised you won't be there,' smiled Cushing.

'Picked for an important cup match, I'm afraid.'

'Never mind. Still, I'll see you later. I'll be back this afternoon before you leave for Oxford, if I may.' Cushing carefully put Ross's letter and Hitchcock's memorandum in his pocket, and poured himself another cup of tea.

4

Tuesday 19th June 1928

Cushing looked out of the window as the train left Waterloo Station, the concourse still bustling even after the businessmen had dispersed to their offices. He watched the light drizzle falling on the river, and admired the Houses of Parliament on the far bank. His morning paper was on the seat beside him, largely unread; he had had too much to think about to bother even with the sports results.

The engine wheezed into Putney station and Cushing coughed as smoke came through the window. He quickly checked his appearance in the glass, having picked up new clothes on the way to Waterloo earlier in the morning and changed at the outfitters. He stepped onto the platform and climbed the stairs, nodding politely to the stationmaster. He crossed the high street, walking briskly past a line of neat Victorian terraces towards the road in which Stockington lived. It was many years since Cushing had been to Putney, cheering on the Cambridge eight, and as he moved further away from the station and towards the river he was conscious that some of the roads down which he was walking had then been market gardens and the old velodrome. He sighed, thinking of those happy days before the War.

'Afternoon, sir.' A ruddy-faced postman stood on a corner, sack over his uniformed shoulder. 'Good afternoon to you,' replied Cushing.

'It's brightening up,' said the postman, cheerily, and Cushing realised that the rain had indeed stopped. He shook the water from his umbrella and furled it. Having abandoned his own umbrella in Ross's flat, he had borrowed this one from Scott. It was an expensive make with a silver band; Cushing had not wanted to take it, but Scott had been insistent, admitting that it might not have been his in the first place.

Cushing left the postman to his duties and walked down a wide orderly street lined with trees in full leaf. A couple of cars were parked in the road. He stopped outside a smart semi-detached property with a tidy front garden, made sure that he had to hand both Ross's letter and a letter to Stockington that he had prepared earlier, opened the gate and rang the bell. He pulled himself to his full height and waited. A young woman in a black dress with a white apron and cap answered the door.

'Good afternoon,' said Cushing. 'I'm a friend of Mr. Stockington and I wondered if I could speak to him?'

The girl looked up at Cushing suspiciously, but relaxed when she saw his clerical collar. 'Sorry, sir – Reverend, I mean,' she replied. 'Mr. and Mrs. Stockington are on holiday at present. I don't expect them back until Sunday.'

'Ah, yes,' demurred Cushing. 'Mr. Stockington told me he was going to France, but I hadn't realised that he was on holiday and so I wasn't sure when he would be back in London. But Sunday is five days away, and this is rather important. Is there an address in France where I can write to him?'

'I don't have one, sir, Reverend. Sorry, sir.'

'How about a work address?'

'No, sir.' The girl began to look suspicious again, and Cushing realised he had gone too far.

'No matter, my dear, no matter.' He smiled at her, winningly he hoped. 'Can I leave a message for him?' He was disappointed not to find Stockington at home but, from what he had read in Ross's letter, he knew that it had only been a faint chance that he would be there. He had come prepared and took the envelope containing his own letter from his inside pocket. 'Perhaps you could make sure that Mr. Stockington gets this when he gets home? Sunday, I think you said?'

'Of course, Reverend,' she said, taking the letter. 'Who shall I say was looking for him?'

Cushing ignored the question. 'That would be most kind, my dear,' he said, 'thank you.' He left her standing at the door as he shut the gate. 'Goodbye,' he called, 'thank you again,' and started to walk back in the thin sunshine towards the High Street, silently congratulating himself for not having revealed his name.

He passed the postman who was still at the same corner, leaning against a pillar box indulging in a quiet cigarette. The postman grinned and gave a cheery 'Afternoon again, Vicar.' Cushing acknowledged the man, and then frowned. What if they were already starting to look for a clergyman, whoever "they" were? The girl may not have known his name, and he had signed the letter to Stockington only as "a friend", but she had seen his collar. 'Dash it,' muttered Cushing, and looked back over his shoulder at the postman. The same man, and he had seen his collar too. Maybe the man wasn't a real postman? Could they be following him already?

Cushing stopped abruptly and turned round, but the postman had moved down the street with his sack of letters. He realised that his forehead was damp and wiped it hastily with his handkerchief. A smartly-dressed woman walking a Labrador dog eyed him curiously, and a road-sweeper with a broom approached him. 'Are you all right there, sir? Looks like you're having a funny turn.'

'No, no, I'm fine, thank you,' replied Cushing, hastily. He retraced his path a few steps and took a road heading away from the station and into the maze of small streets leading towards the river. He was now sure he was being followed, and quickened his pace. He turned right, then left, then looked over his shoulder to see a man in a dark hat and lightweight overcoat. Could this be another German? Cushing doubled back on himself in front of the impressive façade of the Hippodrome and was breathing heavily when he saw the welcoming sign of the Duke's Head. He determined to cut in and out of the pub but, reaching the door, he saw the man in the dark hat greet another man and enter an adjacent building through an iron gate. Cushing stopped for a couple of minutes to recover. 'Pull yourself together, man,' he mumbled to himself, realising that the pub would be a welcome refuge in more ways than one.

He chose a table looking out over the river. Half way through his second pint, and having consumed an excellent roast beef sandwich, he was starting to feel far more comfortable. He had suffered regular bouts of chronic fear and black despair ever since his return from France, though since his stay at the hospital at Craiglockhart he had felt that he had been able to put them aside. He knew that it had been irrational to be concerned about being followed, though maybe this was small consolation. 'The men who killed Ross weren't real policemen,' he reasoned, 'and, even if they were, they couldn't have tracked me down this quickly. And I haven't done anything wrong.'

In truth, Cushing had not felt so alive in years. His continued spells of sickness after the War had left him unable to hold down any responsible position, and he knew that the Church had been kind to him in maintaining his current situation at the old church at Albury. Little more than a sinecure: a handful of services a year, with the occasional christening, wedding or burial; a small stipend (though with his own private income he was quite comfortably off); he was conscious of the comments about him whispered by younger men who did not understand. But now he was doing something important, for the good of the country, something of which he could again be proud. And there was something about being shot at that gave him clarity of mind and purpose.

He finished his pint and walked across the road to a telephone box where he asked the operator to connect him to the first of the possible numbers he had for Joe Page. A woman answered, and Cushing pushed pennies into the slot. 'Good afternoon. Is that Mrs. Page? Mrs. Joseph Page?' 'Mrs. John Page, if you don't mind,' came the reply, and with a quick apology Cushing replaced the receiver. There was no reply to the second number he tried, nor the third, but the fourth time he was lucky. As the man answered, Cushing recognised his voice and remained silent. Page's house was only half an hour away on foot, and it was enough to know that he was there.

In fact, Cushing was there sooner than that, having taken one of the new closed-top buses across the river and up the King's Road. Page's house was a little run-down, sitting at the end of a Victorian terrace next door to a smart new vicarage that backed onto a large church. Cushing pulled his hat down over his eyes – he knew the local vicar, or at least knew his name, and felt that he should be circumspect at least where he could.

He walked up to the door and knocked twice. After a short while, he heard steps and the sound of keys in locks, and the door opened slightly, held on a chain. Through the crack, Cushing recognised Page, a short and scruffy man with lank, thinning hair and round glasses. For the second time that day he was greeted suspiciously. 'Mr. Page?' he enquired. 'Don't you remember me, Joe? Christopher Cushing?'

'Well I'll be...' Page's Welsh accent was still noticeable. His expression changed from surprise, to pleasure, then to concern.

'Christopher Cushing. What on earth do you want after all this time?' -

'Well you could let me in,' replied Cushing, hopefully. 'It looks like rain.'

Page looked worried, then cross, but the chain rattled and the door opened. 'I suppose you had better come in then,' he said, unenthusiastically. 'I'll make some tea.'

'Splendid, splendid,' said Cushing, as he was ushered into a front sitting room. It was as messy as its owner, with overflowing ashtrays and dirty plates, cups and bottles scattered here and there among piles of papers and books. The room smelled of stale food, smoke and, as Cushing noticed with some distaste, Page himself. His attention was drawn to piles of leaflets and tracts, including advertisements for marches and Socialist League rallies. Some had Page highlighted as a prominent speaker, sharing platforms with Harry Pollitt, James Maxton and other rabble-rousers whose names were known to Cushing from their frequent appearances in the newspapers. He surreptitiously put one of the leaflets into his pocket, and started to flick through a copy of L'Humanité, noting that Page was half way through translating one of the articles from the left-wing French newspaper into English.

'Still supporting the old Bolshevik cause I see?' said Cushing, as Page entered, still in his carpet slippers, with two steaming mugs of tea. Ten years older than Cushing, the last decade had not treated Page well.

'And why not?' responded Page, defensively. 'Someone has to fight against fascism, and you and the likes of you might just as well be in league with them. You're just as bad as the Trotskyites. The whole country is riddled with corruption: revolution is the only...'

'That's all right, old chap,' interrupted Cushing. 'You don't have to impress me.' He had been impressed in the past, though, despite himself, with the fervour that Page had been able to express, both in writing and on a soapbox. He knew from his work as a code-breaker that Page was highly intelligent, but through the rant he also recognised the spark of a natural orator. A shame, Cushing thought, that Page's talents could not have been applied to a better cause. Page may have been an atheist and a communist, but Cushing knew from the man's work in Room 40 and from long conversations with him that there was no doubt that he was a genuine patriot. The two had had many lively debates in the past, often long into the night. Cushing always liked a good academic argument, perhaps a little too much, and Page had never been able to shake his faith, at least no more than it had been shaken during the War.

The two men exchanged guarded pleasantries for a while, trading memories of their time in Room 40 and the people they had known. But Cushing had noticed that Page was becoming increasingly nervous. He also saw the marks of bruises on Page's face. 'What happened there, old man?'

'Just fell downstairs,' answered Page, grimacing.

Cushing was not convinced. 'I would have taken a bet that you had had a run in with the British fascists at one of your rallies.'

Page grinned, and touched the bruises tenderly. 'Honourable wounds,' he said.

'Well I guessed it wasn't something that happened when you were teaching.' Cushing smiled, too, pleased that the ice was starting to crack.

'I haven't been able to teach much recently,' glowered Page. 'The school I went back to after our unit was disbanded – well, they didn't like what I stood for at the time of the General Strike and booted me out. I haven't had a teaching job since.'

Cushing was genuinely affronted by this, and felt sorry for Page. 'So are you still at the old code-breaking game?' he asked hastily.

'Every now and then, for the old firm,' replied Page. 'I'm

officially retired now though. Nothing for a while.' Cushing knew he was lying.

'Really?' he said, innocently. 'Nothing in the last few days? Nothing from Ross, perhaps?'

Page turned away. 'Don't know what you're talking about,' he grunted. 'Look, I've got lots of work to do. Nice to see you after all these years, of course. But I really need to be getting on.'

'My dear chap, absolutely,' said Cushing. 'But before I go, perhaps I could – er...'

'Oh yes, of course,' replied Page, and directed him through the greasy kitchen to the lavatory at the rear of the house. On his way back, Cushing quickly opened an adjacent door and saw a large and well-lit table covered with books and papers. He peered more closely at the desk and noted with satisfaction a prominent photograph with a picture of a familiar-looking tablet, along with a rubbing that seemed to be of the same object. 'That's not right,' thought Cushing. 'Ross sent him the photograph, so where did he get the rubbing from?' He silently closed the door and returned to Page's sitting room.

'Now Joe, if you were to hear anything from Ross about a particular code, why don't you give me a call? It could be important, you know. And I may be able to help. After all, you're not the only retired code-breaker that Ross might be in touch with, every now and then.' Cushing felt quite pleased with himself for that little touch.

The two men shook hands. Cushing knew that Ross had trusted Page, and, while he felt instinctively that he could do the same, he knew that there was much that Page was not telling him. Had he been in the same position, of course, Cushing would certainly not have revealed any information to a man he had not seen for ten years.

'Look, Cushing,' muttered Page, 'just in case, where can I find you?'

'Just leave a message at the Athenaeum,' replied Cushing, and then, almost as an afterthought, 'thank you.' He left Page standing at his front door, nervously twisting his fingers.

'A job well done,' thought Cushing as he stopped just beyond the church to make some notes in his pocketbook, then walked briskly and jauntily towards the underground station.

Back at Albany, he was stopped by the caretaker. 'Mr. Scott isn't in, sir. He's gone away for a couple of days, so he said, sir.'

'Damn the boy,' thought Cushing. 'That's all right,' he said. 'Mr. Scott gave me a key.'

'Ah well, sir, that would be more than my job's worth to let you go into Mr. Scott's rooms, sir, even with a key. You see, sir, I'm responsible for security here.' He sighed, theatrically.

Cushing was in no mood to argue, and pulled half a crown from his pocket. 'Clarence, isn't it? We met yesterday. I am Mr. Scott's godfather, you know,' he said, pointedly, holding the coin between his fingertips.

'Well that's different, sir,' replied Clarence, deftly pocketing the coin. 'Come to think of it, I thought I recognised you. Just let me know if I can be of any help to you, sir.' But Cushing was already half way up the stairs.

Letting himself into Scott's flat, the first thing he saw on the table was an envelope addressed to him. He slit it open and read the contents.

"I hope you've had a productive day," he read. "I've gone to Oxford early. As you suggested, I've taken one of those old tablet things – I know a man who may be able to help." Cushing spluttered. "Back later this week, help yourself to anything you need. Enjoy the test match if we don't speak before then. That package is still in the top drawer if you need it. Cheerio. Geoffrey."

'Damn the boy,' said Cushing, out loud this time. He found

a small case and packed his old clothes into it along with some of Scott's, adding a spare razor and toothbrush, and wrapping the remaining tablet carefully in the middle. He returned to the desk and dashed off a short note to Scott telling him of his movements, first at Clifford's, then at home in Surrey before returning to London at the weekend. He sealed the envelope, propped it up on the desk, and left, carefully locking the door behind him.

Sitting in one of Peter Clifford's armchairs with a large glass of port and a cigar, Cushing rehearsed his argument. The moment he had arrived at St. John's Wood, Clifford had told him enthusiastically about his conversation with John Grainger, the American archaeologist from the British Museum. Clifford had arranged a meeting with Grainger on Friday to show him the tablets. In return, Cushing showed Clifford his one remaining tablet, and chided Scott gently. Clifford was impressed, and possibly relieved that his old friend had not been imagining the whole thing.

Cushing told Clifford about his visits to Putney and Fulham. Clifford had been slightly disgruntled that he had gone to visit Page without him. But now it was time for Cushing to reveal his plan for the following night, and he was not going to let Clifford miss the fun.

'It's very simple, Peter. It looks as if Page is in the middle of decoding the tablets from the photographs that Ross sent him. I've seen them. He denied having any contact with Ross, but then again I would expect that. But listen, he's also working from a rubbing.'

'A rubbing?' asked Clifford, lighting his pipe. 'What do you mean?'

'You know, like people make rubbings of brasses in churches. Page was working from a rubbing as well as from the photographs.

47

And the rubbing looks like it's been taken from the same tablets.'

'So what?'

'So what? Isn't it obvious? Ross didn't mention a rubbing, so Page must have received it from someone else. And the rubbing must have been made before Hitchcock stole the tablets and was killed.'

'And how does that affect us?'

'Hitchcock took the tablets and was shot. But if Page was already working on a translation of the message on the tablets from a rubbing made before then, he is our link to the men who killed Hitchcock!'

'But Page may not be directly involved...'

'Of course not, but we need to know who he's working for. So I've got a plan. Look here, I picked this up from Page's house.'

'What is it?'

'It's a leaflet about some ghastly Bolshevik rally for the miners in South Wales tomorrow night. Somewhere called Merthyr Tydfil. Page is on a platform with that dreadful man Aneurin Bevan.'

'That Welsh windbag? He's pretty harmless, isn't he?'

Harmless? Bevan is a raving firebrand Communist, trying to stir up the workers for another General Strike. He's dangerous. We don't want troops on the streets again.'

Clifford had sympathy with Cushing's views, but was keen to get to the point. 'But what have these Bolshies got to do with us?'

'It's obvious that Page lives alone – the place is a dreadful mess. That awful smell of long unopened rooms.'

'Page, or the house?' inquired Clifford, drawing heavily on his pipe and breathing out a long plume of smoke.

'Both, actually.' He wrinkled his nose in distaste at the memory. 'But it means that the house will be empty tomorrow night. So we just break in and...'

'Break in?' Clifford jumped to his feet. 'Good heavens, man, you can't do that. It's illegal!'

'Not as illegal as shooting people in Knightsbridge. Come on, Peter, this is a matter of national security, as Ross said. You're not getting cold feet, are you? You were all for it last night.'

'You're starting to sound like your godson. The one you said was headstrong.'

'Not at all. After all, how difficult can it be? I've read a lot of detective stories and it's a matter of seconds to jemmy a lock.'

'That's if you have a jemmy, of course. But why do we need to break in? Can't you just go back and beard him in his lair?' Clifford collected the decanter from the sideboard and refilled Cushing's glass. He sat heavily back in his armchair.

'Thanks, old man. Well, first of all because he's in Wales. And second, because he's working for the opposition. We can't just turn up and ask him about that. And look,' continued Cushing, warming to his theme. 'I've already cased the joint...'

'You've done what?'

Cushing frowned at Clifford, who was clearly less well versed in the more lurid American fiction of which Cushing was an adherent. 'I've reconnoitred the place. All very easy. We cut through behind the church, and then climb into Page's garden over the wall of the vicarage. If we can't break in through the French windows, then it's up the drainpipe and in through one of the ones upstairs.'

'We?' exclaimed Clifford.

'Well I suppose you can keep a lookout if you prefer,' admitted Cushing, somewhat grudgingly. 'But I need you there – and I've been looking forward to your support. At the very least it would be good to have someone on guard. And I might need a leg up over the wall. Now, if you don't have a jemmy, do you have a chisel and a hammer? And how about a flashlight? Come on, man – as you said last night, it will be a bit of a jape.'

5

Wednesday 20th June 1928

The cold light of day had dampened Cushing's enthusiasm. The man in the hardware store in St. John's Wood had shaken his head and looked askance at a middle-aged clergyman trying to buy a jemmy. Which, thought Cushing, was perhaps no bad thing. Had he succeeded in purchasing one, he would have had to check it in at the cloakroom at the Savoy Hotel along with his hat.

He arrived slightly early for his meeting with Augusta Gordon, as he always did, though he knew she would be late, as she always was. He had been quite embarrassed by Clifford and Scott joking about his relationship with her. While he knew he always looked forward to seeing her, he had come to realise quite how close they had become. Having been drawn together through their shared grief, she had become one of the pillars of normality for him when he was ill, and now he was better, he had been coming to London to see her increasingly frequently. But certainly there had been no hint of romance – there was no way that she would ever think of him in that way, and nor had he ever considered such a thing himself.

He walked up the odd narrow cul-de-sac, where the taxis

famously drive on the wrong side of the road, and through the glass doors of the grand hotel. A uniformed doorman directed him to the Edwardian tea rooms, where he sat waiting for her to arrive, leaning back in a comfortable armchair, listening to the music being played on the piano and looking up at the fine chandeliers hanging from the ornate ceiling. He was on his second pot of tea by the time she arrived, clutching an armful of packages. Wearing a smart Chinese silk jacket, and with her dark hair fashionably bobbed, she looked every inch the society hostess that she had clearly become.

'Gussie,' he said, delightedly, standing up awkwardly with teacup in hand.

'Christopher, darling,' she purred, taking his free hand and kissing him fondly on the cheek. 'So lovely to see you.' She sat down and various waiters relieved her of her bags. 'What a morning. What a morning!' Cushing poured her some tea which she sipped, nibbling elegantly at a biscuit. 'So, darling, what brings you to London?'

Cushing had decided that it was probably better not to share any of the recent happenings with Gussie. 'I've been visiting my godson. You remember Geoffrey Scott?'

'You've spoken about him many times, but I've never actually met him.'

'He was packed off to boarding school before you moved to Surrey, of course. I knew his father at college. He was killed at Spion Kop before Geoffrey was born, and the lad's poor mother died young too, so Mary and I looked after him, sent him to school – my old school, in fact, only up the road from where I was the vicar so I could watch him play cricket and rugby – and then to Oxford after the War. He's done very well.' He beamed proudly, forgetting his misgivings about Scott's lifestyle, and Gussie smiled affectionately back at him.

'Yes, you've told me. You've been a good godfather, haven't

you? How old is he now?'

'He's twenty eight. Good heavens, that makes me feel old.' Cushing smiled again. 'And have you been busy?'

Gussie needed no encouragement to talk about her charity work, and Cushing was delighted to hear that she was involved directly in the organisation of the Midsummer Ball at Longley Hall.

'It sounds as if it's going to be a wonderful do,' he said. 'Perhaps I should come along?'

'Oh Christopher, you are a dear, don't you remember I invited you weeks ago? You said you didn't think you could make it. You're getting so absent-minded, you know. I'm going with Johnnie Gibson now. You remember Johnnie, don't you? He was in the RFC.'

Cushing frowned. 'Yes, I think so. Odd-looking cove, not a lot of conversation.'

'Christopher, you darling. I do believe you're jealous.'

'Not at all. Well, maybe just a little.' He smiled again. 'So could you arrange a ticket for me?'

'Darling, they are like gold dust. Just a little more expensive. But for you?' She opened her handbag and produced an invitation like the one he had seen in Ross's briefcase. 'Shall I make it out for you and a guest?' She arched her eyebrows. 'What's her name?'

'Just me, Gussie, just me. Unless I could bring my old friend Peter Clifford? He's got deep pockets and it would be good for the cause and all that.'

'Well they are double tickets, so I imagine you can bring who you like. Just save a dance for me, that's all. I'll just put it down as "guest". Do you have a pen? Now what makes you want to come to the ball all of a sudden?'

Cushing handed her his fountain pen. 'Just call it my charitable instinct,' he said. 'And to see you, of course,' he added hurriedly. 'Though I'd also like to meet Sir Charles and Lady

Sloane.'

She looked surprised, but finished writing the invitation and handed it over with a flourish. 'And your pen, of course. You'll need that for the cheque.' She laughed at Cushing's surprised expression. 'Well it is for charity, darling.' She tapped her fingers on the table as Cushing wrote, wincing when Gussie told him the amount. 'And don't forget, you'll have to dust down that old white tie and tails. I haven't seen you dressed up for years. Mmm, very dashing, I'm looking forward to it. Don't forget that dance. Anyway, darling, I must rush.' She stood up and kissed him. 'Thanks again for tea, and I'll see you on Saturday.'

As Gussie left the room in a waft of silk and perfume, Cushing gazed after her admiringly. Perhaps it was not only the excitement of the events of the last couple of days that was making him feel young again.

Later that evening, Cushing and Clifford stopped at the White Horse on Parson's Green for a spot of Dutch courage. They had travelled back to south west London on the underground and were hot and grumpy. Both were disguised in old coats and battered hats that Cushing had found in Clifford's garage and garden shed, and Cushing had covered his clerical collar with a thick scarf. He felt very uncomfortable and was increasingly concerned at how conspicuous they might look, dressed so heavily on such a warm evening. The coats were weighed down with a collection of chisels, hammers and screwdrivers from Clifford's house.

Cushing had not really wanted to risk being seen in the pub, and thought it a needless danger in case they were recognised later. On the positive side, however, the fact that people might overhear their conversation at least meant that Clifford could not continue to try to dissuade him from carrying out the break-in.

Furthermore, both men had been in need of a sharpener, but the boisterous atmosphere of the crowded bar had done little to relax Clifford. 'You said you were looking for some fun, Peter,' Cushing reminded him. He drained his whisky. 'Come on, let's go.'

Cushing strode briskly across the green, though he slowed down and turned his face away as they passed two policemen walking down the King's Road. Was it only two evenings ago that he had waved happily at a policeman in Piccadilly? Were they already looking at him suspiciously?

Clifford was still dragging his heels. 'We could always wait for a couple of other chaps to join us,' he said. 'I called old Jerry Sinclair today and told him that something was up. No details of course. No names, no pack drill. But he's game. And he's got a DFC. He'd be much more use to you than me.'

'Oh do give it a rest, Peter. Two nights ago you were game for anything. Look, we're here now.'

The two men stood outside Page's house. The gas lights in the street were beginning to emit a glow in the twilight, but there were no lights on in the house. 'Right,' said Cushing. 'Back round the corner, past the church, and over the vicarage wall into Page's garden. When you've given me a bunk up you can come back to the front of the house and keep an eye out for the police. Or anyone. If you see anything, hoot like an owl.'

They stood in the road outside the church, smoking, Clifford's pipe and expensive tobacco at odds with his appearance. Cushing had insisted that they waited, supposedly nonchalantly, for two more policemen he said he had spotted to pass them. Clifford cursed Cushing's fevered imagination as the pair came closer and were revealed to be a courting couple.

'Come on then, Peter. If it were done, t'were well it were done quickly and all that. Quick, there's no one in sight. Down the side of the church now.' They opened the side gate into the vicarage garden. There were no lights, either in the vicarage or in

Page's house.

Cushing paused between two small trees against the wall. 'Ready, I think,' he whispered. 'Give me a leg up here.' Clifford cupped his hands and heaved Cushing upwards. He scrambled up and over the wall, panting, and Clifford heard an undignified scrabbling noise.

'What's going on?' he called.

'Ssshh!' came the response from the other side of the wall, in a stage whisper that was perhaps louder than necessary. 'It's very slippery. I've just fallen into some sort of a bush, and I've split my trousers. Anyway, I'm over. Get round to the front and keep a lookout. I'll come out through the front door. I shan't be long.'

'Righto,' said Clifford, happy to get out of the vicarage garden. As he looked back, he grimaced as he saw the flashing of Cushing's light. But there was nothing he could do now but leave him to his task.

Cushing selected a screwdriver from one of his many pockets and jammed it next to the lock of the French windows. He exerted pressure, and the handle of the screwdriver snapped off in his hand. 'Damn it,' he muttered, deciding that smashing the large window would cause too much noise. He dragged a garden table towards the rear of the house, looking nervously around him as every sound the wood made as it grated along the paving stones seemed to be magnified. This really wasn't as easy as he had imagined. He climbed onto the table and, grateful for his heavy gloves, grabbed the rusty drainpipe, pulling himself up to the top of the small outhouse, snagging and tearing his coat as he did so.

He peered at the small window pane and the latch, then after a couple of minutes unsuccessfully fiddling with a chisel, he turned off the flashlight. 'It's a lot easier in the books,' he said to himself, and smashed the glass with a hammer. He looked round anxiously; he had not expected it to make quite so much noise. He cursed as he reached through to open the window and stabbed his hand on a piece of broken glass. But the window was now open, and he climbed through, switched on the flashlight again, and headed downstairs straight for the back room.

Balancing the flashlight on the corner of the desk, he started to flick through the papers. Out of the corner of his eye, he noticed that the photographs Ross had sent were still pinned up on the wall, along with the rubbing. He looked at the rubbing more closely; it seemed identical to the photograph. The desk was covered with notes and the floor strewn with pieces of paper. Page had been working hard. There were various books on Egyptology and other ancient languages, opened, with pages marked, and a file of newspaper cuttings marked "Ugarit". 'I recognise that name,' thought Cushing, and started to make notes himself, hurriedly copying down some of the words from Page's notes and from the newspaper cuttings.

Flicking through the overflowing papers on the desk, Cushing found a handwritten letter from Ross to Page, and then another letter to Page, this time on headed paper, typed and dated two weeks before. 'How odd,' he thought, reading quickly. 'It's from the Admiralty. Someone else asking for a translation of the inscription on an artefact, and enclosing a rubbing. Who is this man Domvile? "DNI NID"? That's Naval Intelligence. Maybe it's just the usual inter-service rivalry. No, it must be more than that. Why is he being so secretive? Meeting in St. James' Park? No, this isn't right at all.'

He was conscious of time passing, and continued quickly to note down more of the fragments and words from Page's notes, filling several pages of his little notebook and pursing his lips as he did so.

Clifford had been standing nervously under the streetlamp near the front of the house for a good half an hour. He was fiddling with his pipe, lighting and relighting it, when he looked behind him and jumped guiltily as he saw a policeman approaching. 'How many of these wretched people are there?' he asked himself. 'Evening, Constable. What a pleasant evening.'

'Indeed, sir,' replied the policeman. 'Can I help you?'

'No, but thank you,' said Clifford, aware that his dishevelled disguise did not match his well-spoken voice. 'I'm just taking some fresh air. A bit of exercise. That's all.'

'I see, sir.' The policeman came closer, and eyed Clifford up and down. 'Do you by any chance have any identification, sir?'

'Yes, of course,' said Clifford, then blanched as he saw the beam of a flashlight in Page's front window. 'Why didn't the idiot just turn on the lights?' he asked himself. As he froze, the policeman turned to see what Clifford was looking at and also saw the flashlight.

'Oi!' shouted the policeman, and pulled out his whistle, blowing it for all he was worth. As he did so, Clifford let out a loud hoot, less like an owl than a panicked gull, and hared off down the road.

Cushing's flashlight went out immediately, and the policeman was torn between chasing the escaping Clifford and apprehending a burglar in the act. He banged on the front door, shouting for the occupants to open up. Cushing realised that the game was up, put the notebook into his trouser pocket and fled straight out of the French windows. He dragged the table back towards the wall and heaved himself over, puffing and panting, back into the vicarage garden. He did not stop to retrieve his hat which had fallen off in the dark, but let himself out of the gate and ran back past the church.

He heard the thudding feet of the policeman behind him, but he had a good start. 'What am I going to do if they catch me?' he thought, as he pounded up the road and round the first corner. 'What am I doing? I'll be defrocked.'

He could hear the policeman's whistle blowing frantically

and, realising that he was unlikely to be able to outrun the law, he quickly dodged behind a hedge. Gradually the noise of pursuit disappeared down a side road and, feeling sick to his stomach, he abandoned his coat and tools in a dustbin. He took off his scarf, revealing his dog collar, and started to walk slowly and calmly back towards the King's Road, coolly wishing a polite 'good evening' to the red-faced policeman he passed on the way. 'No, Constable, I didn't see a man running. Sorry. Good night.'

'Come on, Christopher, it was a complete bloody shambles!'

Peter Clifford emptied his second large whisky and reached again for the decanter on the sideboard, refilling Cushing's glass as well as his own. The two men had made their way separately back to St. John's Wood, somewhat chastened. Cushing had waited on the doorstep for a quarter of an hour after a long journey on the underground before Clifford had arrived home. He stood up and lit another cigarette.

'Well we've certainly learned a few lessons about breaking and entering,' Cushing said. 'Next time we'll take some professional advice. I know just the man.'

'Next time?' roared Clifford. 'There isn't going to be a next time. Don't you realise we could have been arrested?'

'But we weren't, were we? And we found out so much more about what's been going on.'

'I don't care. I would have been ruined. Molly would kill me.'

'Two men are already dead, Peter.'

Clifford slumped back in his armchair. 'Forget Craiglockhart,' he muttered. 'You're beyond help.'

'Now look,' said Cushing, earnestly. 'Page had been sent the rubbing by a man called Domvile. He is the Director of Naval Intelligence. He was obviously known to Page. There was reference to a fee and to the fact that someone is going to pick up the translation.'

'So what?'

'It was dated two weeks ago. That means that this man Domvile definitely had access to the tablets before Hitchcock stole them. And these people are also using Page to do the translation.' He frowned. 'Maybe this Domvile chap is one of the people in Intelligence that Ross was talking about, the ones who have been compromised. That would explain why he was using Page. He's known to them.'

'That's a bit of a leap of faith. And what would the intelligence corps be doing messing about with old Egyptian artefacts?'

'They're not Egyptian,' said Cushing automatically. 'But that's a fair point. Whoever they are, they knew that Page was good at his job. Which he is, I know. And he's already made a decent start on the translation.'

'Really?'

'Absolutely. The photograph was annotated where he had had some success. The place was littered with scribbles, newspaper cuttings and books on ancient languages and things. From his notes, it's not a code, it's a language. Does the name "Ugarit" mean anything to you?'

'Not a dickie bird, old man,' replied Clifford.

'Not a lot to me either, really,' admitted Cushing. 'But Page had made a couple of notes about the place. Don't you remember reading about it in the papers recently? It's somewhere in the Middle East, I'm sure; there's a big archaeological dig going on, like Carter and Lord Caernarvon in Egypt a few years ago.'

'What, gold and jewels and things?'

'Now you're sounding like my godson,' observed Cushing, tartly. 'But if this tablet is in Ugaritic, it's hardly surprising that it's not easy to translate.'

'So it's like ancient Egyptian after all, then, is it? I thought that was all pictures. Birds and things.'

'Well, ancient Egyptian pictures are called "hieroglyphics", but they just translate into letters and words the same way that our alphabet does. This language, if Page is right and it is a language, of course, is linear. Like cuneiform.' Clifford looked blank. 'I know a little about it, and young Geoffrey would know a fair bit more. He read archaeology, after all.'

'You know a surprising amount about it all yourself.'

'Well, all the code breaking and translating I did in Room 40 may have helped, but the rest is just the benefit of a classical education. Look, I wrote down some of the translation that Page had made.' Cushing pulled his battered leather notebook from his jacket pocket. 'The first part is about Baal, with various expressions presumably used to describe him, like "the rider of the clouds" and the "son of El".'

'Baal?'

'Baal was a pagan god, worshipped by the Phoenicians if my memory serves me right.'

'So that would be about right for this place you mentioned in Turkey?'

'Absolutely. And he's mentioned in the Bible a few times too. Elijah came up against him, I know, and I'm sure there was something even earlier, going back to Moses. Do you have a Bible?'

'Yes, of course.' Clifford reached over to a bookcase and handed a Bible to Cushing who flicked through it for a few seconds. 'Yes, here we are. Book of Kings. I remember now. King Ahab, who married the infamous Jezebel, of course, worshipped the false god Baal, and was overthrown by the worshippers of the true Lord.'

'Yes, but…'

'Let me read you this, Peter. "They smote them with the edge of the sword; and the guard and the captains cast them out, and went to the city of the house of Baal. And they brought forth the images out of the house of Baal, and burned them. And they brake down the image of Baal, and brake down the house of Baal, and made it a draught house unto this day. Thus Jehu destroyed Baal out of Israel."' He rolled the words round his tongue, relishing the familiar cadences of the King James Bible. 'Beautiful language. They'll never improve on words as exquisite as these.'

'What's a draught house? Is it some kind of pub?'

Cushing laughed. 'More a public lavatory, I think. Like a field latrine in France – most unpleasant.'

'Well they were a bloodthirsty lot, that's for sure. So Baal is a god, or demon, then. Is he the same as Belial in Paradise Lost?'

'Probably, Milton picked up quite a few names like that. I think Baal is in there too, or his followers the Baalim. "The streets of Sodom" were where you found Belial, I seem to remember. But it's the same root as Baal, I think, and so is Beelzebub.'

'What, the old Lord of the Flies? But if it's a sacred text about some pagan god of some sort, it may all be very interesting to the academics, but...'

'No, there's more. It's all fragmented, but Page has made a note about something falling to earth. Look, here. It may be a stone, because later there is a scrap about a stone being held sacred, and being used to "crown our kings". Then there's something about the source of all powers, and bringing forth fire and demons. Page has translated it as being some sort of cup, or vessel. Or perhaps a weapon.'

'A weapon?'

'Yes.' Cushing frowned and then threw up his hands. 'Oh no, it's not some ridiculous Grail legend, is it?'

'What on earth are you on about?'

'Well, many people have written about the Grail and the Ark of the Covenant both having huge powers. This tablet seems to be writing about another artefact that is older even than the Ark, so predating Moses.'

'So it's real, is it? The tablet, I mean.'

'It's an amazing thing if it is. But there's no reason why it shouldn't be. I'm no expert, of course. Now where does Ugarit come into it?'

'Ugarit?'

'Yes, where they have been doing that archaeological dig. Page has made a few notes about the place. Of course – if these tablets really are from Ugarit, where they could well have worshipped Baal, they have been buried for years. And only dug up recently.'

'So this powerful artefact that the tablets refer to. It could be entirely unknown to modern scholars?'

'You could be right. Your man at the British Museum will know. Now, have you got Sunday's paper still?' Clifford went out into the kitchen and returned a couple of minutes later. Cushing rapidly leafed through it and waved a sheet of print in triumph. 'Here you are,' he cried. 'Look, here's the headline. "Further Archaeological Finds at Ugarit. In a statement made on Monday, Doctor Claude Schaeffer of Strasbourg University announced further finds at the archaeological excavations at the ancient Phoenician city of Ugarit, near Ras Shamra in Palestine. "There is new evidence that the site, previously thought to have been a new discovery and untouched since the Babylonian period, had been broken into sometime during the eleventh or twelfth century, most probably during or soon after the First Crusade," he said. "A number of Templar artefacts have been uncovered, and these will be exhibited in Berlin at an appropriate time," added Doctor Schaeffer."'

'So what?'

'So someone has robbed this archaeological site and stolen these tablets. They made their way to Domvile. Maybe he stole them, or he had access to them at least. We know he sent rubbings of them to Page a week before Hitchcock acquired them.'

'Stole them,' interrupted Clifford, grumpily.

'But he's a British agent, so he must have had good cause. Ross took them off Hitchcock's body and sent the photographs to Page to translate, so Page now has two versions of the same thing. We know the Germans killed Ross for the tablets, but he didn't have them. He had already passed them on to me. But why were they after them? Why are they so important? Why were they shooting at me?'

'Damn it all, Cushing. I don't think it matters why. The fact is that they were. We're in this too deep. Two men are already dead, as you keep on saying. You've got to tell the proper authorities tomorrow. Later today, I should say – it's already two in the morning.'

'But Peter...'

'No. You've got to be sensible. I was right behind you when you first told me about this. I'm sure I'll be laughing about running away from policemen this time next year, but I just don't care about the whys and wherefores any more. You're getting caught up in some wild conspiracy theory. I don't like it, and it's getting ridiculous. Good night.'

And he tapped out his pipe and stomped off to bed, leaving Cushing deep in thought.

6

Thursday 21st January 1928

Cushing willed the train to Guildford to go faster. Breakfast had been a frosty affair, though Clifford's temper had certainly improved from the previous night. He continued to exhort Cushing to go to the authorities, though he had been unable to suggest which particular authorities these might be. Cushing was becoming disappointed in Clifford who he had thought would have been more supportive. 'Young Geoffrey has got plenty of backbone, but isn't reliable,' he thought, 'and Clifford's the other way.' Clifford was, however, still happy to make arrangements to meet Cushing on the following day to go to the British Museum and, against his better judgement, to join Cushing at the Midsummer Ball. 'Though don't tell Molly!' had been his last word on that matter.

Cushing's urgency now was driven by something he had read in the newspaper on the train. A small item on page four had caught his eye, and for a while he could not place the name "Tremadoc" and why it was familiar to him. But all became suddenly clear. "A violent assault has taken place on an elderly servant during an attempted burglary at the house in Wiltshire of Mr. Henry Tremadoc, currently serving with H.M. Consulate in Buenos Aires. The burglars savagely beat the servant, a Mr. J. Benger, while quizzing him on the whereabouts of his employer and his car. One of Mr. Tremadoc's cars, a green two-seater Alvis 12/50, was indeed missing, though Mr. Benger was unable to say for how long it had not been in the garage. Police are now searching for this car, which is numbered MFR 50."

'Stupid boy,' muttered Cushing, to the concern of the two ladies opposite him in the compartment. 'They're on to us already.'

His own car was where he had left it on Monday morning at Guildford station. He drove the small "Bullnose" Morris the few miles back home over the downs to his old cottage, marvelling as he always did at the beauty of the rolling English countryside. He entered the village of Albury, admiring its beamed houses, ornate chimneys and tiled roofs. He passed the wooden road sign on the little green and raised his hand from the wheel to wave at people he knew going into the pub.

His cottage was set a way back from the centre of the village near the new church. This had been built in the old graveyard and was a Victorian brick construction that Cushing had always felt to be somewhat solid and ugly, even when he was the vicar there himself. The new vicarage, his former home, was a sprawling building, and as he parked his car he could hear the young vicar's four children playing in the garden. The old vicarage had fallen into disrepair, along with the original church, before the turn of the century, and the cottage was more than adequate for him. He got out of the car and looked towards his own church which was obscured by the thick greenery of the Surrey countryside, only the gothic chimneys of the mansion showing above the trees.

He let himself in, then grimaced as he saw the formidable figure of Mrs. Sturdy, one of his more venerable and indeed substantial churchwardens, striding towards his door in a substantial floral dress. He had realised as soon as he had seen the twitching of her curtain as he drove past that she had seen him return, but he had hoped she would have given him rather more time before knocking on his door. He tried to put her off politely, but she was persistent, removing her hat to reveal a pile of brightly-dyed hair. She made him a cup of tea, and he was forced to listen to what seemed to be endless prattling about arrangements for Sunday's traditional midsummer service, together with the flower show and village fete that took place on the same day. 'Thank the Lord,' he thought, 'that I don't have to do this every Sunday any more.' And then he felt guilty, knowing how much work was involved in organising the event and conscious that he was abandoning his team of helpers on Saturday when he was at the test match. He determined to listen to what the well-meaning woman was saying.

It had been seven years ago that the majority of Cushing's duties had finally been removed. His absence during the War itself, followed by his periods of sickness, had meant that he had been unable to serve the community as he would have liked. He had once had hopes of a far more senior position in the church than that of a country vicar, but those hopes had faded after he had, as he felt, been banished to Lahore. He loved India, where his father had worked for many years and where he had been born – in fact he had regarded his first visit to England to go to prep school as a journey to a foreign country. He had thought he would rebuild his career there, but Mary had been too sick to stay for more than a couple of years, and on his return to England he had repeatedly been passed over at the diocese before being put out to grass at Albury. But there were worse places to be – it was a delightful little village, he had come to love and respect his flock, and he had been well supported by his curate as well as by Mrs. Sturdy and his other loyal friends.

The new bishop was an old friend who knew both of Cushing's war record and of the shellshock from which he was still suffering. The old square-towered Saxon church in the grounds of the mansion had been in a poor state of repair for many years, and most of the services had been held at its newer and larger neighbour for some time. The bishop had taken advantage of changes in the boundary of the diocese to appoint the curate as vicar at the new church, giving him most of the parish responsibilities, and leaving Cushing with light duties at the old church which remained open only for special occasions. And while Cushing hated to be patronised, he was grateful for the extra time this had given him, not just to potter round the parish, but to raise funds for the restoration of the church, study his fine collection of rare books, and work on his monumental treatise on the Saxon churches of Surrey. Now he needed all the time he could spare to examine the tablets.

Some of his faithful parishioners, like Mrs. Sturdy, would never acknowledge that there had been any change at all. She eventually left, her duty done, and Cushing grabbed the telephone and asked to be put through to Scott's old college in Oxford. The Lincoln College porter answered, and Cushing left a message for Scott to call him urgently at home. He then tried to immerse himself in parish paperwork for an hour, but could not concentrate. How could he, when Scott was in danger, when two men had been murdered and when the safety of the realm was in peril?

He made himself another pot of tea, and looked around the cottage. It was thirteen years since his wife had been killed and the place lacked a woman's touch. There was a confusion of books everywhere, old paintings and prints on the walls, and papers scattered on every surface. Mrs. Sturdy had kindly left some fresh flowers for him in a vase, and he had noticed with some satisfaction that Leach, the estate handyman, had tidied the garden.

He opened his telephone book and looked at some of the names of people that he might call on for help. He grimaced.

Cushing's Irregulars? He didn't think so. This wasn't a John Buchan novel, and he was forced to agree with Clifford that it wasn't really a job for an amateur. Not that that would stop him, of course. He remembered saying to Clifford that they needed a professional, and so he turned to the page with Philip Brock's number on it. Sergeant Brock's was one of the first lives he had saved when, having followed the rest of the regiment charging out of the trench, he dragged the wounded man back to his own lines. He knew that Brock had been some sort of petty criminal before being called up, and this had been helpful when extra supplies were somehow diverted from the quartermaster's stores to the regiment's own kitchens. He had therefore been delighted when the ex-sergeant had written to him after the War to seek his advice on a change of career. Cushing picked up the telephone again and gave the London number to the operator.

He was put through, and a female voice answered. 'Good afternoon,' said Cushing politely. 'I wonder if I could speak to the Reverend Philip Brock. It's an old friend of his here, Christopher Cushing.' He heard a muttered conversation in the background and the tones of his old sergeant came across the line.

'Mr. Cushing? Good to hear from you, sir. How are you?'

'Very well, Badger, very well. How nice to speak to you after such a long time. How are things at St. Jude's?'

The two men chatted inconsequentially for a few minutes, mainly about the work that Brock was doing at his church in London's East End. Cushing apologised for calling the ex-sergeant "Badger", but Brock laughed. 'That's what the boys call me at the boxing club, sir. But is there anything I can do for you?'

Having initiated the conversation, Cushing was unsure how to continue. 'It's just a bit of research I'm doing,' he said, 'and I wondered if you could do me a favour. I think you've got some particular skills that I need. But I need to speak to you in person. I'm in Surrey now, but I'm coming up to London tomorrow.

Could we meet? I can easily come to you?'

The two men made their arrangements – Badger was insistent that Cushing should join him and his wife for dinner – and after the usual niceties Cushing replaced the receiver. 'That's something, I suppose,' he said to himself, 'though Peter won't be very pleased.'

He cleared his desk of papers about the midsummer service – a bizarre tradition for a Christian church, he thought – and the fete, not to mention the increasing number of weddings and christenings planned for the summer, and unpacked the clay tablet. He took his leather notebook from his pocket and a couple of clean sheets of paper from the drawer, and started to work on the puzzle he had been left.

Three hours, several cups of tea and most of a plate of biscuits later, Cushing's head was spinning. It had taken him this long to understand only a small amount of Page's thinking, and, even with a partial translation as a starting point, he had been able to progress it no further. He was just thinking he must be getting old when the telephone rang.

'St. Peter and St. Paul,' he answered automatically.

'Padre? It's Geoffrey. Can you hear me?' Scott was shouting down the line at him.

'Geoffrey, thank heavens. Are you all right?'

'Of course I am, dammit. I scored ninety this afternoon, so all's well with the world. Drawn a bit of a blank with that tablet, though. Anyway, why the urgent message?'

'Don't shout about the tablet! Look, Geoffrey, have you seen the paper this morning?'

'Just the racing results. Why? What's wrong? What's so urgent?'

'Someone has been round to your friend Harry Tremadoc's house and beaten up the butler. It must have been the two Huns. They have traced the car to Tremadoc and they're looking for it.'

'Well they won't link it to me here.'

'That's not the point! The police are looking for it now. Where is it?'

'Parked in a street in Oxford. I haven't used it since I got here, and there wasn't space to leave it at college.'

'Could the police, or the Germans, identify you from anything you've left in the car?'

'Well I've got my cricket kit in the boot. I'll take that out. I say, thanks a lot, Padre. What a lark. But what a pain, too. I've got rather attached to that car.'

'Look, it doesn't matter about that. I'm just glad you're safe. When are you coming back to London?'

'I wasn't planning to be back until Saturday, but I suppose I'll need to get hold of another bus. I've got plans for the weekend.'

'Well don't even think of using the Alvis. Don't let me keep you, this is serious. Off you go and empty the car of anything that they could possibly link to you.'

'Understood. Bye.'

'Call me later and tell me about the tablet...' But Cushing was talking to himself. At least Scott was safe. The Germans were clearly well-organised, though, if they could identify the owner of the car from the number plate and make their way to Tremadoc's house in just two days.

'This is dangerous business,' he thought, 'but, dash it, I have to admit that I'm starting to enjoy myself.'

Cushing had woken with a start and was pleased he had remembered to set the alarm clock. He bounced out of bed with a new energy, having slept like the proverbial log. He had decided not to attempt any further translation from the tablets after his initial failures. He felt that he could do little to add to Page's work, and in any case he had only one tablet to look at, for which he cursed Scott quietly. So he had focused on his Bible, and had found that Baal had been mentioned even more frequently than he had remembered. From Moses and Aaron defeating the Baal-worshipping Midianites through to Elijah, Zephaniah and Jeremiah, Cushing began to realise quite how close the Israelites had actually come to worshipping Baal rather than the true Lord. 'Thank heavens for Elijah,' he thought, as he cleaned his teeth, satisfied with his evening's research.

He remained puzzled, however, about how any of this related to the rest of the mystery, and was looking forward to meeting Clifford's archaeologist friend. After a quick bath and a hurried breakfast, he was soon parking his car at the station and buying a ticket for the train back to London. His bag was heavy. He had laid out his evening dress for Saturday's ball and was pleased that he was able to squeeze into it – if only just.

Scott had not telephoned him back, and Cushing was beginning to worry. Perhaps the Alvis had already been spotted? Perhaps his godson was already being questioned? Still, there was nothing he could do about that.

He took a bus across the bridge, admiring the dome of St. Paul's and the gothic intricacies of the Houses of Parliament sparkling in the morning sunshine, and walked to the British Museum where Clifford was waiting for him. Both men were early, and so Cushing brought Clifford up to speed with what had happened since they had last met. Cushing was not surprised at Clifford's response to the news about the car. 'He's in a funk,' thought Cushing, as they entered the museum's grand portico.

Clifford indicated a stout, greying man standing by the Rosetta Stone, one of the greatest treasures of the museum. 'There's Grainger. It seemed appropriate to meet him there, bearing in mind we have an ancient stone to translate.'

John Grainger was making his farewells to a thin-faced scholarly-looking man of about thirty, wearing darkened round glasses and carrying a large attaché case. They parted, shaking hands, and Grainger turned expansively to beckon Clifford over, revealing a brocaded waistcoat that was straining somewhat at the buttons. Grainger had been at Oxford with Clifford and was now Head of Near-Eastern Antiquities at a museum in New York. Clifford shook Grainger's hand warmly and introduced him to Cushing.

'Good to meet you, Reverend,' drawled Grainger in an accent that clearly hailed from well below the Mason-Dixon Line. 'I've been having an interesting sabbatical here, but Peter Clifford tells me that you may have something even more interesting to show me.' He ushered the two men past the spoils of an Assyrian temple, through a door marked "Private" and up a flight of narrow stairs into a large but very messy office.

After small talk with Clifford and the obligatory cup of tea brought in by a flustered-looking young graduate, Grainger fixed Cushing with a piercing eye. 'So what have you got to show me, Reverend?' he asked.

Cushing unwrapped the tablet and explained innocently that he thought the artefact was Middle Eastern, though not Egyptian. Grainger moved a bright desk light towards the tablet. 'Hmm, you're right, definitely not Egyptian,' he said. 'It's old, though, maybe even older than Egyptian. Three thousand years old, or so, I'd say. And it's in very good condition. But the language – well, it's not like anything I've ever seen before. It's linear, of course, more cuneiform, and these triangular shapes are a bit like early Hittite, but...' He put the tablet carefully down on the table. 'Where did you say you got this from?'

'I didn't,' replied Cushing. 'It belongs to a friend. What would you think if I suggested that it was from Ugarit?'

Grainger gave a start. 'Well I'll be.... I was speaking to a man about Ugarit only a few minutes ago. You saw me saying goodbye to him. A man called Claude Schaeffer, from Strasbourg. He's beginning to excavate the place now and is in London looking for more funding.'

'So could this be from Ugarit?'

'I guess it could,' said Grainger, peering closely at the tablet. 'Then again, I guess it might not be either. Schaeffer said that there had been some trouble at the dig. Some looting.' He looked suspiciously at Cushing. 'Where would your "friend" have got this?'

'I can't tell you that,' replied Cushing, nervously. 'But I can assure you that it is absolutely legitimate.' He hoped that Grainger could not see the rising colour on Clifford's cheeks.

'But if this really is from Ugarit – and I'm not saying that it is, for sure – then we should be linking up with Schaeffer. Can I hang onto this for a while and see if I can get Schaeffer back here?'

'If you don't mind I'd far rather I kept it in my possession. You see, it actually belongs to the Government and I wouldn't be at all comfortable leaving it.'

'How about if I were to take a photograph? I'd love to get to work on it myself.'

Cushing acquiesced – he could think of no reason why he should decline – and Grainger rummaged around for his camera equipment. Cushing thought it worthwhile to risk exposing his hand a little more. 'If this set of symbols here were to represent the word "Baal",' he said, slowly, 'would that be relevant?'

'What? How could you...?' Grainger looked closely at the tablet. 'I suppose the symbols here, and here – well they are similar to...How did you know?'

'There are some hints in an old ecclesiastical text,' replied Cushing, vaguely. 'Other than that, just a lucky guess. I may be wrong, of course.'

'Which texts are these? Where are they? Can I see them?'

'I remember them from some research I was doing in Cambridge many years ago,' lied Cushing. 'In the Divinity

School. I knew that reading about old pagan religions would come in useful one day.' He began to flush, and promised himself to plan a more convincing story for next time. 'Look,' he said hurriedly. 'If these symbols really do equate to Baal, could the next bits be some sort of honorific? I mean they always gave the full honorific, didn't they? Like the Egyptians. "Rider of the Storm", that sort of thing?'

'Rider of the Clouds,' replied Grainger, automatically. 'Strider of the Heavens. Walker of the Stars.' He looked up. 'Hey, they really give you a rounded education at Cambridge, don't they? Anyway, you could be right. Let me take those pictures and I can get to work. I could get an FRS for this!'

As Grainger fussed with his camera and lights, he talked about the ancient worship of Baal. 'Baal appears all over the Middle East,' he said. 'Phoenicia, Tyre and Babylon; the Canaanites and even the Carthaginians, though that was probably because of the Phoenicians.' Grainger drew the curtains. 'He started off as a fertility god, but was then more often depicted as the king of the heavens, wearing a huge crown. I'll show you a statue in a few minutes. And of course the Israelites had a big thing about Baal too.'

'I know,' said Cushing, pleased to be able to show off some of his biblical research from the previous evening. 'If it hadn't been for Elijah smiting…'

'Well I'm sure you know all about that, Reverend,' interrupted Grainger. 'But of course one of Baal's honorifics was "the Light Bringer". Just like Lucifer, eh?'

'Well Lucifer was only mentioned once in the Bible, you know, and then obscurely,' said Cushing, a little smugly. 'We have Milton to thank for making that name synonymous with Satan and his dark designs.'

'Well that's as maybe,' said Grainger. 'But some of the old legends say that Baal fell from heaven, just like Lucifer, or Satan.'

'Really?' said Cushing, interested again, and thinking of the notes that Page had made. 'What do you know about any of the ceremonies associated with Baal worship? Is there anything about a stone falling from heaven? Something powerful, used in a coronation or something?'

Grainger took the first of several photographs, leaving all three of them blinking from the flash of magnesium, and then looked at Cushing quizzically.

'There are certainly references to stones falling from the crown of Baal, but I've always read that as meaning shooting stars. Meteorites were highly prized and used in religious ceremonies.' He looked pointedly at Cushing. 'I think you know more about this tablet than you're letting on, Reverend. But let that go for a while. If you can give me any more help with the translation then I'll sure be in your debt. Just call me when you can.'

Grainger wrapped up the tablet reverentially and reluctantly returned it to Cushing. They strolled out past various exhibits and stopped at a Tyrian statue of Baal depicted, as Grainger had said, with a huge crown. They shook hands and Cushing and Clifford started to walk away, leaving the American among the collection of Middle Eastern artefacts. He called out to them. 'Hey, and don't forget to call if your "friends" find any more of those things! I want that fellowship!'

Later that evening, Cushing took the underground to Whitechapel and walked to the church where he was looking forward to seeing Sergeant – or rather, and more recently, the Reverend – Brock again. Cushing enjoyed the noise and flurry of east London, the hustle and bustle of people, cars, lorries and horses, the smell of cooking and the closing market stalls, and the rows of little shops run by the Jewish immigrants looking like something out of a tale by Dickens.

He consulted his map and knocked on the door of the vicarage where he was delighted to meet Brock's wife, Rachel. Badger had shown Cushing pictures of his sweetheart during the War, but Cushing had been unable to come to the wedding as he had been at the sanatorium in Scotland at the time. He had sadly missed Brock's ordination for the same reason. Rachel Brock was a charming woman; she had been a nurse during the War, and Cushing was surprised that she remembered Gussie Gordon from one hospital in which they had both served. She had a baby in her arms, and introduced her four year old, Sarah, for whom it was a special treat to meet her new "Uncle Kit".

Brock himself returned to the vicarage about fifteen minutes after Cushing had arrived. A wiry man with thinning dark hair, Brock enthusiastically started to talk about his church which he said was flourishing. The ex-soldier, originally from the neighbourhood himself, had a real affinity with the run-down area and many of its poorer inhabitants, and his robust and practical style went down well with his parishioners. He had set up boxing and association football clubs for the local youths, run on a daily basis by a combination of old soldiers and old lags, and the community was growing. Cushing smiled when Brock told him that he was known to many of his flock as "Father Badger".

Badger offered Cushing a drink, but declared that he had himself taken the pledge not long after he was ordained. The two men reminisced over dinner about their time in the trenches. Cushing had not expected that his own faith, however tested during the senseless brutality of war, would have had such a profound impact on Badger's life.

Cushing was keen to hear more about how Badger's new career had developed, and particularly the problems he was facing in the east end. Badger was particularly concerned about the rise of the British fascists, and explained how some of their thugs were starting to make trouble for the locals. Effectively,

Badger said, he and the fascists were looking to recruit the same young men, but for different purposes.

When the meal was finished and Rachel Brock had cleared the table and gone upstairs to feed the baby, Cushing was at last able to explain the real reason for his visit. He related all that had happened, starting with the murder of Ross and being shot at in Knightsbridge.

Badger was gaping open-mouthed at some of Cushing's improbable story, snarling at the mention of the Germans, though he was eager to pass quickly over the translation of the tablets and Cushing's discourse on the worship of Baal. He wanted to hear more of the action, but when Cushing gave the details of the embarrassment of the burglary at Page's house, Badger laughed out loud at the tale of ineptitude. A glint came into his eye. 'It's not really what a man of the cloth should be doing, sir, is it? I mean, bungling a break-in like that. Hanging around outside attracting the police, and all that. What you need, sir, is some professional help.'

He went to a bureau in the corner of his sitting room and pulled out a number of leather bags. He selected one and opened it, producing a black silk pouch containing a number of implements that appeared to Cushing to be almost surgical. 'A few souvenirs,' said Badger. 'Whenever I help any of the old boys to go straight, I always get him to hand over his tools of the trade to me. Now, let's start from the beginning...'

After a couple of hours and endless cups of tea brought by a frowning Mrs. Brock, Cushing had begun to get the hang of how the pointed and curved tools could be used to open the tumblers of a lock. "Scrubbing", Badger called it, and he made it look terribly easy. The more Badger talked about the dubious skills he had acquired, and the elements of field craft associated with the activity of breaking and entering, the more Cushing realised how lucky he and Clifford had been on Wednesday night not to have been apprehended.

'You're doing a grand job there, sir,' said Badger. 'We'll have you an expert in no time.' He grinned again. 'Just let me know when you're going to try out these new skills, and I'll come over and watch you in action.'

Cushing realised that he had to leave if he was to catch the last underground train back to central London, and he thanked Badger and Rachel for their hospitality, not to mention the lesson in crime.

'Now one thing, sir,' said Badger as he left. 'I owe you a favour or two, and this is for the good of the country after all. A bunch of toffs plotting, begging your pardon, and the Huns doing their dirty work. Well, don't forget, if you need me, I'm with you all the way.'

7

Saturday 23rd June 1928

The traffic in the narrow country lanes was already starting to build up as Cushing neared Longley Hall for the Midsummer Ball. It was a clear, warm evening, and the wide crescent moon shone brightly. As he drove closer, he could see the dome of the mansion lit by the beams of searchlights.

Cushing was driving Clifford's Rolls Royce, but Clifford was not in the car. Cushing was still ruminating about their last heated exchange.

The two men had spent the day as they had planned, at Lord's, enjoying the first ever test match between England and the West Indies. Both were MCC members, and were wearing blazers and their bright red and yellow ties. Lounging in front of the famous pavilion, Cushing had been intent on trying to forget the stresses of the previous days. He had caught up with a number of old friends and occasionally even watched the match, the white figures of the fielders on the perfect grass and the batsmen flickering to and fro. 'Half the General Synod appears to be here,' he laughed, introducing Clifford to some elderly churchmen and steering him away from others. 'More of a vicar's tea party than a cricket match.' He felt a twang of jealousy as he looked at the impressive girth of Cyril Garbett, his contemporary and once a fellow Surrey vicar, now Bishop of Southwark. The bishop was rumoured to be heading for greater things, and Cushing wondered briefly how his own career in the church might have developed had some of his early academic treatises not been so poorly received by the church authorities. Few could understand how he could have reconciled his high church leanings with his then controversial views on Darwinism.

Still, he thought, no point in getting maudlin. The sun was shining and cricket was being played. And a splendid day's cricket it had been, and a momentous occasion, with the crowd spiritedly welcoming the new tourists, cheering and throwing their hats in the air when the Lancastrian Ernest Tyldesley made a fine century. 'Well played, sir,' called Cushing, clapping energetically. He also applauded when Douglas Jardine, the man whom Geoffrey Scott disliked so much, came out to bat on his debut for England. He was pleased on behalf of his godson, though not for his country, when Jardine was out cheaply. 'If only Geoffrey were here to watch,' he thought.

His enjoyment of the day's cricket had, however, been marred by Clifford's continual griping. He had – at least when their fellow members were not listening or had nodded off in the afternoon sunshine – persistently returned to the subject of the murders. Particularly, he had tried to talk Cushing out of his plan to explore Longley Hall in search of proof that it was indeed there that Hitchcock had been shot. "Casing the joint", Cushing had called it, and was perfectly prepared to admit that his plans were, at best, fluid. This had annoyed Clifford, but what had really incensed him after they had walked back to his house, only a few hundred yards from the cricket ground, was when Cushing had shown him the tools that he had been given by Badger the previous evening. 'No, no, no!' he had shouted. 'Absolutely not. For heaven's sake, man, you'll just get arrested. Take the car if you like, but I want no further part of it.'

Clifford had mellowed as Cushing was leaving. 'Just be careful,' he had said. 'Look, I'm happy to help with practical matters in any way I can, but this is just too much. It's too risky. I'm sorry. But I don't need the car back till Monday, if you want to hang onto it. In fact I don't really need it till next weekend – I'm taking Molly down to the Riviera for a few days.'

Cushing should have left the conversation there, but could not resist making a last comment about his plans. This had been a mistake.

'Who do you think you are, Raffles?' Clifford's parting shot rang in Cushing's ears as he parked the car, straightening his white tie and tails which had become increasingly uncomfortable during the drive.

He joined a jabbering crowd that was being escorted up a boarded path lit by flaming torches towards the house. They were led to a group of marquees set out on the lawns that led down to the river; the sandstone and ivy of Longley Hall formed a perfect backdrop with the tall windows reflecting the lights from the lawns and formal gardens. It was certainly an impressive building, which Gussie had told him that Sir Charles Sloane had purchased only a few years previously. From the entry in "Who's Who" which Cushing had read earlier, it seemed that Sir Charles had made his fortune from munitions during the War, and he had clearly spent some of that fortune well.

The noise of music, conversation and the tinkling of glasses got louder as Cushing walked to the entrance where a liveried servant offered him a champagne cocktail. Silk, balloons, flowers, the dresses of the women: the marquee was a riot of colour.

He threaded his way through the crowd towards the dance floor in search of Gussie Gordon, absent-mindedly accepting a second champagne cocktail as he did so, and was shocked to see a familiar face.

'What ho, Padre.'

'Geoffrey! What in heaven's name are you doing here?'

'I could ask you the same question,' replied Scott, mischievously. He leaned forward and spoke quietly into Cushing's ear. 'I just saw that rather damp invitation going begging and I thought – well, it just seemed an awful waste. What are you doing here?'

'That's disgraceful,' spluttered Cushing. 'I can't believe...' He was interrupted by Scott who, placing a finger against his lips, took the arm of a very pretty blonde girl in a black evening gown who had joined them. 'Miss Fairfax, can I introduce you to my godfather, Christopher Cushing? Uncle Kit, this is Miss Phoebe Fairfax. Phoebe and I met at a cricket match here last year. It's her parents who are organising this do.'

'Charmed, my dear,' said Cushing in an avuncular fashion, attempting to smile at the girl and glare at Scott at the same time.

'Actually it's my mother who has been doing most of the organising,' said Phoebe. She had very large blue eyes which seemed to have difficulty in focusing. 'My stepfather just writes the occasional cheque.' She looked round at the marquee. 'The occasional very large cheque.' She giggled, and then started to tap her foot impatiently. 'I say, Geoffrey,' she said petulantly, 'weren't we going to have a dance?'

'Why not? Come on then, old girl. You'll excuse us, Padre?'

'Padre?' queried the girl? 'Are you a vicar? How absolutely priceless! Geoffrey, your godfather's a vicar!' She giggled again as Scott escorted her towards the dance floor, whispering in her ear. Scott stood more than a foot taller than the girl, and he winked at Cushing over her head without her seeing, tapping his nose in a rather vulgar manner as he did so. Despite himself, Cushing was forced to smile. He watched the couple glide elegantly across the floor for a while, and was interrupted by a tap on his shoulder.

'Christopher, darling! You made it. I'm so pleased.'

'Gussie. You look – well, you look wonderful.'

And she did. Her dark hair lustrous, Gussie was wearing a simple diamond pendant and a deep green gown. 'Thank you, darling. You don't need to sound surprised.' She kissed him on the cheek, and then turned to a disgruntled-looking man standing behind her. 'You remember Johnnie Gibson?'

The two men acknowledged each other, and Cushing thought he heard Gibson snarl beneath his breath. 'Yes, we've met,' said Cushing, as Gibson gripped his offered hand with needless force.

'Now darling, Johnnie had asked me for a dance, but there are some people you absolutely have to meet. Johnnie, why don't you run along and get us some more cocktails. I must introduce Christopher to Anne and Charles.' She laughed in a way that Cushing found far more pleasurable than the girlish giggling of Phoebe Fairfax, and looked him up and down. 'You managed to fit into your evening clothes after all this time then?'

Cushing had little time to frame a suitable retort, or even to compose himself properly, before Gussie had led him towards one of the groaning buffet tables. Standing there, with a small group of men who were conversing earnestly while helping themselves to food, was a tall, handsome woman. Gussie introduced her to him as Lady Sloane, the ball's hostess.

'Anne, darling,' she gushed, 'let me introduce my dear friend Christopher Cushing.'

'A splendid evening, Lady Sloane,' said Cushing, politely. 'You've done so much.'

'Not at all,' she replied, 'Gussie and her team have really done all the work. And they've managed to arrange a beautiful evening for us as well.' She smiled at Cushing, and he could see from where her daughter's good looks had come. She took his arm and approached the group of men by the buffet table. 'Let me introduce you to my husband. Charles, dear,' she said, interrupting the group, 'this is Gussie's friend, Christopher Cushing.'

A lean man in his early fifties with cadaverous cheekbones and receding fair hair, Sir Charles Sloane turned to speak to his wife and acknowledge Cushing. 'Ah, yes, of course, how nice to meet you', he said, automatically. 'Mrs. Gordon has told us so much about you.' Gussie arched a disbelieving eyebrow at this, but Sloane continued out of politeness. 'Have you come far?'

'Well, Sir Charles...'

But Sloane was not really seeking an answer. Lady Sloane courteously introduced Cushing and Gussie to the other two men in his group. Lord Parmoor, a patrician-looking man, was probably nearing eighty, but was still ramrod-straight, with bushy white hair around his ears surrounding his bald pate. He stared quizzically at Cushing, as if he remembered him from somewhere. Cushing knew where it had been. The distinguished politician – he had been Lord President of the Council in Ramsay Macdonald's administration – had also been chairman of the National Church Assembly. Cushing had attended an event at Lambeth Palace where Lord Parmoor had spoken. In favour of conscientious objection, Cushing remembered with some disdain. Gussie had met him before and politely asked after his wife, who it seemed was an old friend. Before Cushing could speak to him, however, Parmoor, who had clearly been in mid-sentence when Lady Sloane had interrupted, turned back to talk to Sloane.

The other member of the group, a ruddy-faced man with sandy hair, shook Cushing's hand warmly. When he introduced himself as Sir Edward Davies, the Chief Constable of Oxfordshire, Cushing struggled not to show that he recognised the name from Ross's letter. News of Ross's murder had, of course, still not reached the papers. When the two men shook hands, Cushing felt the tell-tale questioning of a Masonic grip. He had been initiated many years before by his late father, but had let his early interest lapse. Despite this, he was able to respond and the two men started to converse. Over Davies' shoulder, however, Cushing was dismayed to see Gussie crossing the marquee to greet more people.

Having come to Longley Hall to find out more information, Cushing was unable to quiz Davies on a subject about which he was supposed not to know. He was also struggling to think how he could engage Sir Charles Sloane in further conversation. While Sloane and Parmoor were standing right next to him, they were paying attention only to each other, and he was forced to listen to the Chief Constable who had started a lengthy diatribe against the British Communist party, the trade unions in general and Lord Parmoor's support of the unions specifically.

Cushing knew he could hardly accuse Sloane of anything – after all, his theory was based on only the flimsiest of evidence – but was still only half-listening to the policeman's tirade when Gussie returned to the group. With surprise, he recognised the man with her.

Portly, jowly and with receding hair, Winston Churchill was a familiar figure. Now back in the cabinet as Chancellor of the Exchequer, Churchill had served in France himself before becoming Secretary of State for War, from which position he had signed Cushing's own Mention in Dispatches.

'I've been monopolising Winston and Clemmie for far too long,' said Gussie. Churchill disengaged Gussie from one arm and his wife, a tall slim woman of about forty, from the other. He guffawed gently, his cigar firmly clenched between his teeth, and shook Cushing's hand energetically. 'Ah, so you're Cushing,' boomed Churchill in slightly slurred tones. He took Cushing's shoulder in a friendly fashion and his eyes twinkled as he looked at Gussie. 'Fine woman, that. Eh? Eh?'

Cushing, slightly tongue-tied, engaged Churchill in pleasantries, surprised at how short the man was. Davies, the Chief Constable, joined the conversation, and Sloane then joined the group. It was Cushing's chance again, but no sooner had he started to speak when Gussie bustled up to them, Lady Churchill with her.

'Now, Christopher dear,' interrupted Gussie. 'We simply must have a dance to this delicious orchestra.'

'But... but....' Clementine Churchill smiled at his embarrassment. 'Do come along, Christopher,' Gussie said, forcefully, as she took his arm and led him away. As he looked helplessly over his shoulder, he thought he heard Davies saying 'Cushing seems a sound man' to Churchill, and he felt several pairs of eyes boring into his back as he disappeared into the crowd.

Gussie indicated Gibson coming towards them eagerly, carrying more drinks, and looked up at Cushing mischievously. 'Come on, let's get on the dance floor before he catches up with us.'

Cushing was not a skilled dancer, but at least he managed to avoid treading on Gussie's toes. He began to relax, feeling very content as he and Gussie stayed on the floor for three numbers, talking easily and naturally as they danced. He had avoided catching Gibson's eye, and also ignored Geoffrey's leer as he and Phoebe Fairfax spun around them.

At last, however, the dancing had to stop. Gussie promised him a slow dance later in the evening, and she was almost immediately snatched from him and back onto the floor by the jealous Gibson. Cushing watched her for a while before he remembered what he was here for. He knew that he was running out of time if he was going to make his way into the house.

There was no sign of his godson, and Cushing could see Sloane still talking to Churchill, Lord Parmoor and others; now was the time. He strolled round the back of the marquee past a throng of bustling waiters and walked the few yards past trees and statues towards the bright lights of Longley Hall. He was not alone. As he ambled round the gravel path which ringed the whole house, looking in the windows as he went, he passed several small groups of partygoers smoking and chatting animatedly, along with couples sitting arm in arm on one or other of the stone seats under the colourful rose bowers.

The main door of the house was open and he confidently walked between the ivy-covered pillars and into the hall. No one stopped him, and he seized the moment. He had in mind that his best hope might come from a private study; he had guessed that this would be upstairs as he had seen nothing of that sort through any of the downstairs windows. He looked round, and then immediately took the broad stairs two at a time. Again he was not stopped, and, with his heart pounding, he paused before trying some of the doors leading off the darkened corridor. Bedrooms, bathrooms, dressing rooms, but not what he was looking for.

With a start, he heard light footsteps behind him: he had no time to try and hide, and bent down to pretend that he was tying a shoelace in the hope that this would at least mask his face. He chanced a look, and saw that it was Phoebe Fairfax. She marched determinedly past him, staggering slightly. In fact she ignored him completely and went straight through one of the doors. Cushing breathed a sigh of relief. All was silent in the corridor, though he could hear the noise from the ball outside filtering in through the windows. As he tiptoed past the door through which Phoebe Fairfax had gone, it opened abruptly and the girl reappeared.

'What are you doing up here, you naughty man?' she asked. Her eyes were glazed and a small trace of white powder was visible on her upper lip even in the gloom. 'I say, you're Geoffrey's friend.' She giggled. 'Just help yourself, it's on the dressing table.' She breezed past a shocked Cushing and vanished down the corridor, calling out Geoffrey's name loudly as she did so.

Cushing cringed, but there was no further sound. He tried

the door at the end of the corridor, which he reckoned would be the room at the front right corner of the building. It was unlocked, and, taking a deep breath, with his heart racing, he opened it. It was indeed a study. The shelves on the wall were lined with books and there were lights on over a tidy desk and a couple of well-stuffed armchairs. A pair of decanters stood on a small table. Feeling guilty, he shut the door behind him and swiftly looked at the books and papers, even opening a couple of desk drawers, but he could see nothing suspicious. Maybe Clifford had been right. What a hare-brained scheme! What on earth was he even looking for? What would the consequences be if he were caught? He had no evidence against Sloane, and he would probably be charged as a petty thief, if he were not dismissed as a lunatic.

Nevertheless, trembling somewhat, Cushing pressed on. He went to a pair of double doors in one of the walls and opened them. It was a small dressing room, with coats and jackets hanging up, and shoes and boxes on the floor. He froze as he heard footsteps outside the door of the study, and then began to panic as he heard the door handle start to turn and the sound of voices. With his escape route blocked, he quickly went inside the dressing room and pulled the doors shut behind him.

He heard the study door open and close again. He could hear at least two sets of footsteps, and was convinced that the noise of his breathing and his thumping heart must be audible through the door.

'What a wretched evening. However did I let Anne persuade me that this ball was a good idea? Take a pew, John. A glass of port?'

'Thank you.' Cushing did not recognise the second voice, though the first was that of Sir Charles Sloane. The second man started to speak again, in a slightly odd accent that Cushing could not quite place. 'So what is it that you needed to tell me in private? Everything seems to be under control after the break in.

You told me we had eliminated the problem, and, from what you said in your last report, everything is coming together nicely. We will soon be ready to act.'

'We have another problem. Just a small one.' Cushing could hear the nervousness in Sloane's voice.

'Well? What kind of problem?'

'That blasted idiot Page has got himself burgled.'

'Has anything been taken?'

'No, they were disturbed, but the burglars got away. The useless flatfoots caught them in the act, in fact, but they ran for it. It's probably just a coincidence, but what worries me is that our men checked the place and it seems that Page was also working for Ross. Maybe it is all connected.'

'Hmm. I told Domvile that we shouldn't have used a Bolshevik. Can't trust them. That fiasco in Italy was caused by a Bolshevik.'

'Tranquilli wasn't really a Bolshevik,' said Sloane. Cushing drew in his breath sharply, recognising the name from Hitchcock's notes. 'Tranquilli's brother is one of ours, as you know. Domvile was just trying to cast the blame on the Bolsheviks.'

'No matter,' said the foreign voice. 'I never saw Prince Umberto as a candidate for the true kingship anyway, though he has his uses. And in any case we now have a better option. But the time is right and the momentum is with us. It is imperative that we act now, and mobilise the order. Not because these people are starting to interfere, but because our people from Ugarit have such good news.'

'I wouldn't be too worried about these people getting in the way, John. Ross and the man I shot can't have had more than a slender clue about what we are doing. While these other people may have the tablets, they don't know what they mean. And they don't know anything at all about the relics, do they?'

'My dear Charles, you're right. We just need Domvile and

his men to get them back, that's all. You told the Council that the tablets can lead us to the correct ceremony after all these years, and I am sure you know what you are talking about.' Cushing could hear a silky menace in John's voice. 'Our men at Ugarit will be able to confirm the final pieces of the jigsaw, and I also understand that they have good news about the location of the relics in Europe. They are carrying out a full dig at the old monastery in Seborga. Leaving no stone unturned, as one might say.' Cushing heard clinking of glass as he presumed that more port was poured. 'We must get everything right, retrieve the objects and give a real signal to the world. Domvile and his security wallahs have hushed up everything to do with Ross, and the police are neutralised.'

'That's true enough. Davies, the Chief Constable – you met him earlier – is an honest fool. If it hadn't been for him we would have recovered the tablets before Ross got involved. But he knows nothing.'

'And what about the man at Ross's place, the one that that damned fool Gemp let escape?' Cushing's heart pounded again.

'No news, and no identification,' replied Sloane. 'He was disguised as a vicar, whoever he was. But we'll get him soon enough, and the tablets. We've already found the car that his accomplice was driving.'

'I just don't like the authorities sniffing about, for whatever reason. I don't like people making stupid mistakes.' Cushing could hear the venom in the man's voice.

'Just another small delay, that's all.'

'Still, better to tie up any loose ends. I'll have a word with Domvile about this man Page. Well, come on, Charles. We'd better get back to this damnable party, I suppose. We can carry on this conversation when you give a full report to the Council next week.'

Cushing could hear the noise of glasses being replaced on

the tray, and then footsteps as the two men left the room. He stretched and breathed again, exultant that his hunch had been proved to be correct, and then suddenly felt more than a little sick. 'I'm in a right pickle here and no mistake,' he muttered. 'Tranquilli. Murdering Ross. The tablets, and relics too, and some sort of a dig. This Domvile man. And who is this John. He's a cold fish. Loose ends?' He shivered. 'It really is a conspiracy. It's monstrous. He talked about mobilising an "order". How many people are involved in this? Not everyone at the ball, surely? Not Davies, obviously. And surely not Churchill....'

He opened the door of the dressing room with some trepidation to give himself more light, and then started to check the pockets of the jackets and coats, but to no avail. He spotted that one of the coats was jammed in the rear wall – not just snagged, but stuck, as if in a door. He tapped on the wall once, realising immediately that this may have been foolhardy. There was a hollow sound. Gently, he felt round the sides of the dressing room for a switch or handle. He found a switch and flicked it, and a light came on in the dressing room. He switched it off again hastily, hoping that no one had spotted the light from outside, and continued to prod and poke around for a means of opening a door.

Eventually, his patience was rewarded as a panel slid aside, revealing a button. He pressed it, and there was an audible click. Cushing gave a low whistle of anticipation as the rear wall opened a crack and he pushed it further open. He found himself in a narrow darkened room about a third of the size of the study. He could make out the drapes of a heavy curtain over each of the two windows. He went back into the dressing room, made sure that the door to the study was shut, and switched the light back on. This gave him enough light to see round the room properly: another large desk, a rail of weighty and outlandish robes, and more shelves of books.

There was a lot of dust, and Cushing sneezed twice, nervously waiting to see if he had been heard. After a little while he moved towards the desk, his mouth dry and his heart pounding, looking briefly at the robes: thick material, heavy cowls, inscriptions in gold thread, and a heavy smell of mothballs. 'Masonic, of some sort,' he muttered. 'Well, they would be, I suppose.' He fingered some odd-looking silk masks hanging from hooks by the robes. 'Hmm. I don't know whether they'd use these in any Masonic ritual that I've seen. There must be something more to them than that. And why are they kept in this secret study?'

He halted as his shoes made a slightly hollow sound as he stepped on a rug. He pulled the rug aside, causing more dust to swirl round the room, and found a large trapdoor. He pulled it up, surprised to find that it swung open easily and silently, on well-oiled hinges. He could just make out a set of stone steps leading downwards, but he was unable to find a light switch. 'An uncomfortable squeeze,' he thought. 'Some kind of priest hole. How appropriate. Or a passage between the walls. I wonder where it goes? It must go all the way down to the cellars.' He closed the trapdoor and replaced the rug as carefully as he could.

He looked at some of the books and was shocked at some of the rare and valuable titles he recognised. The subject matter was esoteric, and ranged from the deeply theological through the Masonic to the arcane. Cushing had some of the books in his own collection, and there were many others that he envied. Among the incunabula were a number of rare medieval texts, from illustrated gospels to demonologies. Cushing appreciated the hand of a true collector, but had little time for admiration. He needed to search the desk and filing cabinet, and knew he was running out of time.

Opening the drawers of the cabinet, he quickly looked at some of the labels on the files, and spotted the word "Ugarit" along with place names that he thought to be archaeological digs of the last twenty years and other sites of academic interest. Most of the remaining files were on people, and he recognised the names of prominent figures on the international stage interspersed with others that were unfamiliar to him. He particularly spotted a file marked "Churchill" and another marked "Umberto". The last few files were a collection of single words that would have appeared totally random, had it not been for the context of the translated tablets. Stone, crown, fire, falling stars; he quickly flicked through the file marked "Stone" but there was too much to take in.

On the desk he was thrilled to see yet another rubbing of the tablets. 'As if I didn't have enough proof already,' he thought. Next to it, and opened, he spotted a heavily bookmarked and annotated copy of "Morals and Dogma" by Albert Pike. He recalled as a child when he had found his father's copy of the Masonic text and was caught reading it; he had been soundly thrashed and sent to bed without any supper.

A book of ancient woodcuts was lying open, and Cushing grimaced at its harsh treatment. He sketched quickly the page to which the book was opened, a picture of what appeared to be a coronation ceremony with the king surrounded by horrific demons and a background of falling stars. The picture reminded Cushing of the Botticelli illustrations to Dante's Inferno, but clearly drawn by a madman. He wrote down some of the Latin inscriptions, and then scribbled down a few of the words from another paper on Masonic rites about King Solomon's Temple together with what appeared to be a specific ritual.

On top of a pile of papers was a copy of a lengthy typed letter, addressed to "Frater Secundus". The typewriter, a Woodstock, was pushed to the back of the desk. He flicked through the letter and his eyes opened wide in triumph. The writer, whom he assumed to be Sloane, was excitedly reporting on progress arising from the discovery of artefacts from a number of archaeological digs, some of which had been stolen. He was reporting on Page's initial fragmented translation of the tablets. "This seems to put everything in place," read Cushing. "The Templars discovered the truth. We need to take the important elements of these rites and unite them with real objects of power for the final ceremony. The most recent discoveries will enable us to use the Blazing Stone, the Lapsit Exillis. Then we can crown the True King." Lapsit Exillis? Cushing recalled those words from the scrap of paper in Hitchcock's wallet. He started to make notes, but there was more in the letter, much more. Was this the letter from Sloane to which the mysterious John had referred? What on earth were they up to?

Cushing thought of stealing the letter, then realised that this would be too obvious and would give away that somebody had been in the room. He stepped back from the desk and tripped over an object on the floor which clattered noisily. He waited, frozen, fearful that he had been overheard. Stooping to pick up the wastepaper bin, he was struck by a thought as he replaced its scattered contents. In his hand he was holding a piece of used carbon paper. He held it up to the light: it was the letter, and appeared to be mostly readable. He found two other carbons which he also carefully folded and placed in his pocket. No one would miss the contents of a wastepaper basket. He wiped his stained hands on his handkerchief. It was time to leave.

He turned off the light but, before leaving, he walked over to the curtains, opening the heavy drapes a fraction. The window looked to the east, so he could not directly see the marquee, but in the light of the searchlights he could see that the lawns led directly down to the river. The dust on the windowsill had been recently cleared, which seemed unusual, but there were a couple of dark droplets on the side of the window. Was that blood? Cushing's hands were sweating with a mixture of excitement and fear. Yes, he was sure that it was blood. Was this a trace of where Hitchcock had met his end?

He became conscious of a smell like that of a newly-oiled cricket bat. Linseed oil? No, it was fresh putty. He looked closely, and could see where glass had recently been replaced. He opened the window carefully and looked down at the thick ivy covering the walls, and started to picture the scene. Hitchcock, discovered by Sloane rifling the desk, just as Cushing was now, and then squeezing out of the narrow mullioned window to escape, smashing the glass in his haste and cutting his wrist. Cushing imagined Hitchcock climbing down the ivy with the tablets in his pocket, being shot as he made his getaway. Perhaps he was hit for the second time as he ran bleeding across the lawns. He would have dived for the safety of the water, but been dragged down by weakness from his wounds and the weight of the tablets. Cushing's blood ran cold.

'I have to get out of here,' he thought, wiping his hands clean again on the curtains and ensuring that they were carefully rearranged. He went back through the secret door at the back of the dressing room into Sloane's study, making sure to turn out the light. Walking cautiously to the door, he waited until he was certain it was quiet and then quickly came out into the corridor. 'I'll be shot if they catch me,' he thought, his earlier fears about being defrocked now paling into insignificance. He walked back towards the main stairs and only a few seconds later was stopped in the hallway by a large and imposing figure. A uniformed servant with the build of a prize-fighter blocked his path.

'Can I be of any assistance, sir?'

'Yes, I'm terribly sorry,' blustered Cushing. 'I was walking up by the house getting some fresh air and was suddenly – well, you know, I was caught short. I was looking for... The front door was open and.... Too many cocktails, what?'

'The facilities are clearly marked down by the marquees, sir,' replied the burly servant, taking Cushing's arm and escorting him firmly towards the door. 'This part of Longley Hall is private.'

Cushing kept up a patter of mindless apology and excuse as the butler took him to the front door and pointed him back towards the tented area. Apologising again, and hoping that he had given the right impression of innocence and idiocy, he strolled down towards the river, where a number of punts and rowing boats were now being propelled across the water by whooping groups of young men and women. Very different from the scene he had imagined when Hitchcock had been killed. He put his hand in his pocket for his cigarette case and started when he found the small bag of implements that Badger had given him. He had not had to use them, but what if he had been searched? Wasn't it a crime to be caught "going equipped"?

He was very much in need of a drink, and walked back to the marquee where a waiter was on hand with more cocktails. Cushing felt suddenly out of place: he was discomfited by the difference between the normality of the ball and the things he had discovered only ten minutes before. He felt a hand on his shoulder and turned abruptly.

'I say, Padre, I've been thinking.' Scott was loud and more than a little drunk. 'This place is only just upstream from where they found Hitchcock's body. I was wondering...'

'Not here, Geoffrey, for heaven's sake! Keep your voice down! Look, I was thinking the same thing, but let's talk later.'

'All right, Padre. Mum's the word, eh?' Almost immediately, Cushing saw Gussie Gordon waving at him and went over to take her arm.

'Darling, where have you been? I've been looking all over for you. We simply must have another dance.' She looked at him strangely. 'Are you all right? You look like you've seen a ghost.' Cushing was just about to reply when Scott reappeared at his side.

'I know what I've been meaning to tell you, Padre. I spoke to my old tutor about those tablets...'

'Hush, man!'

'What tablets are these?' inquired Gussie.

Scott ignored her question. 'Not the foggiest notion. So you can have it back if you like. It's in the back of Phoebe's car, in my cricket bag. But I've found out what synarch... Synarch.... What that bunch of revolutionaries are all about.'

'Geoffrey, please!'

'Excuse me,' interrupted Gussie, turning to Scott. 'You must be Christopher's godson.'

'I am indeed, madam. But I don't believe we've had the pleasure?'

'I'm Augusta Gordon. I remember you from Albury when you were a boy.' She smiled up at the well-built, athletic young man now standing bashfully in front of her. 'But what on earth are you two rabbiting on about? What tablets? What revolutionaries? Is that word you're hunting for synarchists?'

'I promise I'll tell you the whole story,' interjected Cushing. 'But not now. Please.'

'Then I insist you buy me dinner on Monday night,' she replied.

'Well, of course...'

'Geoffrey!' Phoebe Fairfax interrupted them, taking Scott's arm possessively. 'Hello, Mrs. Gordon. I hope you're enjoying the party.' Her eyes were still glassy, but she caught sight of Cushing and sniggered. 'I say, you're that man who was trying to get into my bedroom.'

'Surely not, Phoebe?' laughed Scott, as Cushing blushed deeply and Gussie glared at all three of them.

'That's becoming a very expensive dinner on Monday night, Reverend Christopher Cushing. But in the meantime, I think we'd better have just one more dance...'

8

Sunday 24th June 1928

Cushing arrived back at his home in Surrey in the small hours of Sunday morning, and slept late. He dressed hurriedly, but had regained a semblance of calm and normality by the time he had to officiate at the morning midsummer service which, along with Christmas and Easter, was one of the few regular celebrations at his little church. He was pleased that he had written the sermon a fortnight before, but his mind was wandering, and he suddenly felt guilty about the mechanical way in which he was repeating the familiar old words of the prayers. He pulled himself together – whatever was happening elsewhere in his life, he had realised long ago that his faith was paramount.

The old Saxon building looked lovely, though as always Cushing was embarrassed at its poor state of repair, even though he had worked tirelessly to raise money to support the restoration. At least, he thought, his efforts had left the place better than it must have been at the turn at the century. He took advantage of his early arrival to wrap the clay tablet carefully and conceal it in the crypt. Mrs. Sturdy had fulfilled her promise and the church was overflowing with flowers; Cushing placed his own fresh flowers on his wife's grave. The church service went smoothly, but, as he made polite conversation afterwards with the Lord Lieutenant and the Duke of Northumberland, he was still in shock at what he had discovered the previous night. It was true: the conspiracy about which Ross had written was real, and Sloane and the unknown John had referred to it as an "order". How widespread were the tendrils of this mysterious organisation?

He went to lunch at the mansion in whose grounds the church stood, an event which under usual circumstances he would regard as a pleasant interlude in his somewhat humdrum life. As he spoke to the local worthies and the other guests, including a young and ambitious clergyman sent from the diocese who seemed embarrassed to be seen talking to Cushing, he realised that he had been carrying out these midsummer services for twenty years. Where had his life gone? His youthful ambition had long faded, and he had fallen into a dull routine enlivened only by his books and by occasional trips to London to see his old friends. Old friends like Gussie Gordon, of course – what a splendid time he would have had at the ball, had he been able to concentrate on having fun as well as on his investigations. Even then, he had not enjoyed himself so much in years. And it was more than just dancing with Gussie – the whole experience of the last week had given him a new and fresh feeling of excitement that he had not felt for years.

At half past two he joined the Duke as he officially opened the annual fete and flower show on the wide lawns. The brick building with its Tudor chimneys dominated the scene, and as Cushing watched the local people enjoying themselves in the summer sunshine, the children running over the grass, he found it hard to believe what he had heard the night before.

As soon as he decently could after the prize giving, and grateful that there was no evening service over which he had to preside, he made his apologies and walked back to his cottage.

He paused on the way for a few minutes to watch a cricket

match on the village green, and marvelled at the tranquillity of the scene. Swallows swooped low over the pond and flitted in and out of the nearby barns. This was England, his England, and he was filled with a renewed sense of purpose. Germans in London, shooting at him in the streets? He would do everything in his power to stop this international conspiracy damaging all that he held most dear.

The cricket match finished and he returned home where he collapsed on the sofa and could not stop himself from dozing off. When he awoke with a start, it was dark. Exhausted, he crawled upstairs to bed.

The following morning he left the house in early light, having decided to take Clifford's car back to St. John's Wood before meeting Stockington. With the test match being played close by at Lord's on that day, he wanted to avoid getting caught up in the heavy traffic and the throngs of people that would be expected.

It was an easy drive into London, though Cushing was still very sleepy and, unfamiliar with London's streets, he got lost on more than one occasion. Eventually, however, he reached Clifford's house and parked the car, leaving the key with a maid as Clifford had already gone to work.

He walked to the underground station with his suitcase, joining the many smartly-dressed individuals with bowler hats making their way to work.

He hoped that Ross's colleague had read his letter and would be waiting to meet him. All Cushing had said in the note he had left with Stockington's maid was that he was a friend of Ross, that it was a matter of the highest importance, and that he would be "dressed as a vicar". He had proposed the French café in Villiers Street for their meeting as it had been the same one that Ross had suggested in his own letter to Stockington, the one that had never been posted.

He emerged from the underground in bright morning sunshine and found the café. He had made excellent time and ordered coffee and a pastry, wishing now that he had had a proper breakfast before leaving. He waited, dividing his attention between the morning paper and the people in the café. He turned to the sports pages and read the report of the cricket match he had seen on Saturday, but became conscious that an earnest-looking and youthful-faced man with reddish hair, aged about forty and wearing glasses, was watching him from behind his own newspaper from a couple of tables away. After a few minutes, the man came to his table.

'Excuse me,' he asked, 'are you a friend of Mr. Ross?'

'Yes. You must be Stockington. I'm Christopher Cushing.' He smiled. 'And this isn't a disguise. I really am a vicar. Please sit down.'

'What can I do for you? This is rather unusual, to say the least.'

'Well,' replied Cushing. 'I don't really know where to start. Probably by asking you to hear me out. It may be hard to believe – in fact I'm not sure if I believe it myself.'

'Go on.'

'I knew Commander Ross many years ago. We were at college together, then I worked in Room 40 during the War. I met him again just over a week ago and he gave me a briefcase to look after. I took it back for him as he asked, and found he had been murdered.'

'What?'

'Oh. Yes, I suppose you wouldn't know yet. It's not been in any of the papers. He was murdered by some Germans. But I got away.'

'Now look here…'

Cushing interrupted him. 'Look, this may sound far-fetched, but it's true. It's to do with Horchdienst and more. Your colleague Hitchcock is dead too.' Cushing stopped as Stockington gaped, and then recovered his composure. 'Ross told me not to go to any of the authorities, so I haven't. But he wrote you this letter.' Cushing reached into his pocket and gave Stockington the envelope. 'That's how I knew to contact you.' He started to speak again, but Stockington raised an admonitory finger.

Stockington read the letter in silence and put it back into his own jacket pocket. He looked suspiciously at Cushing. 'I'm going to have to go into the office and see how much of this is true.'

'Yes, of course, I understand. But remember that Ross trusted you. You mustn't let anyone know that he's left information for you, or they'll get rid of you as well. You and I are both "loose ends". And you have to pretend that you don't know about Ross and Hitchcock being dead.'

Stockington glared at Cushing over his glasses. 'Thank you,' he said, curtly. 'I had thought of that. But I'll need to meet you again. And can you make sure that you don't leave London?'

'I wasn't planning to,' he replied. 'I'm already starting to investigate some of the things from Ross's letter.' Stockington winced, and ran his fingers through his red hair. 'I'll tell you everything I've found out once you're convinced that I'm telling you the truth.' He passed over the memo from Hitchcock to Ross that referred to a number of previous reports. 'You should have this as well. You may be able to check up on some of these files. But where shall we meet? Here? Or would you like to come to my club? I'll be staying at the Athenaeum.'

'Here is best. I'd rather not risk us being seen at your club. Half past six?' Stockington stood up and the two men guardedly shook hands. 'By the way, where are these clay tablets?'

'They're safe, don't worry. And I've even got a little way on the translation.' Cushing decided not to mention that the translation had been done by Page, and certainly not to reveal that one of the tablets was in the case by his knees.

'That's good – keep them safe. I'll see you this evening.' He left Cushing sitting over his half-eaten pastry wondering whether he had done the right thing.

Cushing marched the short distance to the Athenaeum and through the impressive columned entrance, where he left his case with the porter. He walked round below the imposing staircase and squeezed himself into the club's uncomfortable telephone kiosk.

He took a handful of coppers from his pocket, lifted the receiver and spoke to the operator. His first call was to Clifford's practice in Harley Street. Clifford was, almost inevitably, busy, but at least Cushing was able to leave a message to let him know that he had returned his car. He then asked the operator to be put through to Scott's number in Piccadilly. This time he was successful, and Scott's jovial tones came through at the other end of the line.

'Hello, Mayfair oh-two-double-nine? Hello? Is that you, Padre? Splendid. Did you have a good time on Saturday? I didn't see you leave. You didn't go off with Mrs. Gordon, did you, you old dog?' Cushing was already beginning to regret the call.

'Where are you anyway?' continued Scott, airily.

'I'm at the Athenaeum,' replied Cushing. 'Now...'

'Good man,' interrupted Scott. 'It's almost eleven o'clock now. I'll see you there for lunch at about one. Bye.' Cushing was once again left mouthing at the receiver. He sighed, realising that he would be expected to pay for the lunch, and then picked up the telephone again, asking to be put through to Badger in the East End. As he spoke to Mrs. Brock, having discovered that Badger was down at the boxing club, he became conscious of the somewhat choleric face of one of the more venerable members of the club, Colonel McClelland, pressed against the glass. He finished the call and stood up, catching his trousers on a protruding nail as he did so.

'Thought you were going to be in there all morning,' muttered the Colonel as they skirted round each other in the narrow corridor. Cushing, feeling like a naughty schoolboy, wandered into the club drawing room and flicked through the newspapers – even the serious papers had covered the Midsummer Ball, he noticed – until Scott breezed in to join him.

'Funny thing,' said Scott. 'We were having lunch only this time last week. A lot of water under the bridge since then, eh?'

Sitting in the dining room over the club's excellent steak and kidney pudding, looking out over the gardens, Scott had listened carefully to Cushing's story of his discoveries at Longley Hall. Cushing noted, however, that even his retelling of the conversation between Sloane and the mysterious John, and his conjecture that Hitchcock had been shot from the window of the secret room, were not enough to dent the young man's appetite.

'So what do we do now, then?' Scott asked.

Cushing had no clear answer, other than to wait and see what Stockington's response might be. 'I hope you're around this week if Stockington needs us.'

'Well, I'm actually heading off to France on Wednesday. Deauville, don't you know. There's a Rolls Royce rally and it sounds like a lot of fun.'

'But you don't have a Rolls Royce.' Cushing pondered for a moment then, thinking of Tremadoc's Alvis, looked up suspiciously. 'Do you?'

'Not exactly. But Phoebe does. Or at least her old man does. That's Miss Fairfax, you know. You met her on Saturday night.'

'For heaven's sake, man,' interjected Cushing loudly, earning a loud 'tut' from the bewhiskered Colonel lunching alone on the other side of the room. He continued more quietly. 'You can't go to France with Miss Fairfax. I mean, dash it all, her stepfather is one of – well, one of them.'

'You're not suggesting that Phoebe is involved?' asked Scott mildly.

'Well, maybe not.'

'And if we are trying to keep an eye on Sloane, then being in with the daughter has got to be an advantage, n'est-ce pas?'

'That's immoral, Geoffrey.'

'Not at all. Anyway, I'm going. It should be a hoot. But I haven't had a chance to tell you what I have found out – well, other than when you didn't want me to tell you at the ball on Saturday. While you've been playing at Raffles and Bulldog Drummond, I've been busy.'

Cushing stayed silent, shaking his head warningly, while the waiter brought the stilton, then asked Scott to carry on.

'Well first of all, synarchists. No one knows much about who leads them, but they appear to be a radical group. They are a bit like the fascists in some ways, very different in others. They are certainly anti-Bolshevik, but otherwise really secretive. They crop up as a name all over the place: Europe, Mexico, the United States. Lots of blathering in the papers about them being a group of financial and industrial magnates. You know, a group of gnomes that run everything in secret. Though it's all hearsay, of course. But it would make sense for Hitchcock to be investigating them if he feels, or felt, I suppose, that there is some international conspiracy going on.'

'This doesn't take us any further.'

'No, but at least it's something. Now we concluded from that note in Hitchcock's wallet that he had had some sort of a tip-off that this chap in Milan, Tranquilli or whatever, was going to chuck a bomb at the King of Italy. The assassin was supposed to be both a bolshevik and a synarchist, which doesn't make sense.'

'Absolutely,' said Cushing. 'So in the conversation I overheard at Longley Hall they were talking about the "fiasco in Italy" and that Tranquilli was one of "theirs". They are trying to frame the Bolsheviks. Or the Synarchists? Or is Sloane a synarchist? Oh, Geoffrey, this is getting much too complicated.'

Scott signalled the waiter for another glass of port. 'This will make you feel better, Uncle Kit. Anyway, you said that Sloane and this John were talking about how Prince Umberto, he's the Crown Prince of Italy, of course, would become the "True King".'

'So are they trying to bump off the King of Italy and place his son on the throne? If so, why?'

'Well they must have a good reason. But whatever the rights and wrongs, I can't see what we can do about goings on in Rome.'

Cushing frowned. 'You're probably right,' he said. 'Though last time some European princeling was murdered we had the War to end all Wars...'

Scott nodded, then continued enthusiastically. 'Let me tell you a bit about "Lapsit Exillis". Once again, that was on Hitchcock's note.'

'And now I've seen Sloane's secret study,' said Cushing, 'I know where Hitchcock got the words from. It's a "blazing stone" used again to crown the "True King". So we're back to Italy.'

'Well I spoke to one of the old fellows at Balliol I used to know. I didn't go to many lectures as a matter of course, but his were great fun. He related archaeology to belief, cult and legend, especially medieval stuff. It's been his life's work, I suppose; he's at least ninety now, but still hale and hearty.'

'What did he have to say?'

'Well he gave me chapter and verse. Lapsit Exillis literally means "the stone that fell from heaven"...'

'No it doesn't.' Cushing raised his finger in disagreement, but Scott continued.

'Well, almost. And it's been associated with this for years by occultists and other crazies.'

'I've never heard of it.'

'Perhaps you're not crazy enough then.' Scott blushed. 'Sorry, I didn't mean it like that. No offence meant.'

'None taken. Carry on. I'm listening.'

'It is supposed to be the stone that fell from Lucifer's crown when he was pitched out of heaven. A ruddy great emerald, allegedly. Now that could be useful.'

'More Milton,' mused Cushing.

'What was that?'

'Nothing, nothing. Sorry. Just that I was looking up Baal, from Page's translation of the tablets, you know, and was led to Paradise Lost.'

'I haven't read it since school. Didn't like it much then. But the old boy I was talking to said that it was written about by a man called...' Scott paused to consult a grubby piece of paper in his pocket. 'Here we are, Wolfram von Eschenbach. And some people in the Middle Ages talk about this stone in the same way that they talk about the Holy Grail.'

'Oh no! I said to Clifford that this was probably some footling Grail legend.'

'Well there are enough people that are taking it pretty seriously. The old fellow from Balliol may have been on his fourth or fifth glass of port at that point, but he said that it was central to a lot of Masonic belief. Then he changed the subject. He stopped talking about the Masons, and went back to the Grail.'

'Stuff and nonsense,' said Cushing, angrily.

'Well did you know that there was a sort of Grail legend that went all the way back to the Garden of Eden? I didn't. Not until he told me, anyway.'

Cushing grimaced. 'So these people have got hold of this Lapsit Exillis thing and are planning to take over the world with it? Is that it? They're digging for the Holy Grail and other relics, are they?' He laughed mirthlessly. 'Clifford was right. It's crazy. I'm going crazy. And no, thank you,' he said, as he saw Scott beckoning for more port. 'I'm meeting Stockington again in three hours and I'm out to dinner after that. And I want to spend some time this afternoon transcribing those carbons.'

'Good show, Padre,' said Scott, jovially. 'I'll come along and help.'

In fact Scott was a lot more use than Cushing had anticipated, joining him in the high-walled and balconied library which was otherwise empty. He helped to work out words where the carbon paper had been used and reused and the meaning was unclear. In a couple of hours, they had the basis of a transcription that Cushing could at least recognise. The fragments of text confirmed much of what Cushing had overheard. Presumably written by Sloane to Domvile, the letter referred to the ruthless elimination of targets including the King of Italy and Commander Ross. The organisation to which they belonged seemed bent on retrieving artefacts they believed to have some ancient power, and there was more reference to Ugarit and other archaeological sites.

Scott read it through and whistled, to the continued annoyance of the librarian who had come in earlier and frowned at them for talking.

'This is one hell of a conspiracy, Padre,' he said. 'Domvile and Sloane are in it up to their necks. I don't think you should give any of this to Stockington yet though. Just in case.'

'Stockington! Good heavens, Geoffrey, it's almost six o'clock. I've got to get changed!'

'Tell you what, I'll come with you to watch your back. Just in case it's a trap. I say, did you take that revolver I left for you?'

'I did no such thing!' replied Cushing, vehemently. 'But yes, in case I'm arrested or something it would be good to have you knowing that they've taken me. Thanks.'

Scott went on ahead, and when Cushing arrived at the café he spotted him seated at a table near the window with an evening newspaper, smoking and with a large éclair in front of him. Stockington was already there, looking quite ashen and fiddling with the sugar cubes and tongs. Cushing, suddenly envious that Scott was reading about the day's play at Lord's, sat down opposite Stockington.

'Dreadful tea,' said Stockington. 'I don't know why Ross used this place,' but he waved at one of the waitresses for more.

Cushing was desperate to find out whether Stockington had any news. 'Did you check out my story?'

'I did. It's rather disturbing. As soon as I arrived at the office I was called into a meeting. I have a new chief. You're right – Ross and Hitchcock are both dead. But the chief wouldn't give me any details, and what's more I've been taken off the work I was doing with Ross. Horchdienst – you know the name. I'm being transferred, promoted, so they say. To personnel. Pretty damned suspicious. I'm being pushed away from this case completely. Frankly, I'm shocked.'

'So…?'

'So I didn't tell the chief anything about Ross's letter. I went to check the files that Hitchcock wrote about, and they have all been removed. I can't even find out who "Jupiter" was.'

'So what are we going to do?'

'Well I'm not going to do anything at this stage. I'm going to keep my head down. But I do have some ideas. Before that, tell me what you've found out.'

Cushing gave Stockington a brief summary, but something at the back of his mind still urged caution, so he kept back a lot of the detail. He told Stockington about his suspicion that Hitchcock had been shot at Longley Hall, and emphasised the fact that Ross had described it as an international conspiracy of synarchists, but did not speak of the conversation he had overheard, nor the secret room. He told him that he knew that Page had been working well on the translation of the tablet, but did not say that he had broken in. He mentioned Ugarit, but not his meeting with Grainger. And he did not mention Scott or Clifford at all.

'I've uncovered a few references from looking at the tablet and the translation, though,' he said, 'and I need to understand what they are all about. Some of them are more than just archaeological. They seem to be Masonic, even occult.'

'Occult? What do you mean?'

Again, Cushing was unsure how many cards to play. But after a few sentences about rites and rituals and the associated regalia, Lapsit Exillis, Baal and the like, he could see that Stockington did not understand a word.

'This mumbo-jumbo stuff isn't really my cup of tea,' said Stockington, 'but I know a man who might be able to help. Before that, though, where exactly are you keeping these clay tablets?'

'I've got them safe,' said Cushing. 'Locked away in a bank.' He hoped that Stockington would not spot that he was dissembling.

'Well, don't lose them. They could be the key to the whole thing. Look, I'm worried that Ross thought he couldn't trust anyone but me. And now you – I've got to trust you.' He scribbled rapidly on a piece of notepaper. 'Here's an address, it's safe, I think. Keep digging, and post me any further information that you get. If I need to speak to you urgently, I'll call you at the Athenaeum and leave a telephone number for you to ring me. I'll use the name "Gerald". I've given you a telephone number as well, but only use it if you really have to. Is that clear?'

'Of course. Is that your real name?'

'Gerald? No, it's David, actually. Tell you what, I'll use FitzGerald. I don't want the porter saying "Gerald who?" every time I ring. And use the same name when you write to me, or use the telephone. I'll be at this café every Monday at half past six in the evening if all else fails. Oh yes, and you'd better not use the name "Cushing" either. "Collins", perhaps? He's the only literary vicar I can think of offhand. All right? Understood?'

'Understood.' Cushing was mildly offended by Stockington's choice of alias.

'Now, the man who may be able to help with your mumbo-jumbo references is a strange cove. We've used him a couple of times in the past. His name is Crowley, Aleister Crowley. Ah, I can see that you've heard of him.'

Cushing had indeed heard of Crowley, an infamous trickster and supposed magician who had a dangerous reputation, and was shocked.

'He doesn't seem like the sort of chap that we should be dealing with.'

'Maybe not. He's just a bit of a crank, though. Mostly harmless, I should say. Or at the very least, I wouldn't call him conventionally dangerous.' Stockington paused. 'But he knows his stuff about the occult, witchcraft and all that. One of our men – well, let's just call him Dennis – is our main contact with him. Crowley has been a sort of double agent for us before now. But Dennis is out of the country, so I can't contact him. He runs a wine business in his spare time. It's a useful cover.'

'And the Secret Intelligence Service needs information about the occult?'

'Absolutely.' Stockington smiled at Cushing's surprised expression. 'Not every day, of course. It's not what you and I believe in, it's what the other side believes in that matters.' Stockington gave Cushing two addresses, one in Jermyn Street in London, the other in Scotland. 'I'm sure you'll be perfectly all right. But do be careful.'

'It sounds as if you think he's fairly dangerous after all.'

'Well, it's all stuff and nonsense. Shouldn't worry a man of God, eh? Don't mention me, of course. Just say a "mutual friend" gave you his address.'

'I shall. But isn't there anything else you can do, from the inside? I still don't know what I'm looking for.'

'Quite – and nor do I yet. But if you're right about this, I'm better placed keeping my head down and seeing what I can do on the quiet. I've been taken off Horchdienst and I'm not even allowed to investigate the death of my friend. And it's very worrying about those files going missing.'

'What is Horchdienst? Can I ask? I assume you can't tell me a lot.'

'It's one of those secrets that isn't really a secret. I can tell you a little, I think.' He steepled his fingers. 'The Germans have been trying to secure our naval codes. That's what Horchdienst was all about. Ross became involved because there was an indication that our own intelligence services had been compromised. Ross had put Hitchcock on the case, and he was following various links, but he seems to have stumbled on something much larger.'

Cushing frowned. 'So if you're off the case, what can I do?'

'Ross may have been right – it could well be that some "irregulars" really are better placed to help here. You and some other outsiders, if you have any friends lined up. I suspect you already have.' He looked pointedly at the table near the window where Scott was peering at them over his newspaper. 'I'll coordinate your activity. "Run" you, is the technical expression, don't you know. I think that's safest for all of us. It won't help the cause if I wind up murdered like Ross and Hitchcock.'

Cushing suddenly had an idea. 'Your new chief,' he said. 'He wouldn't be called Domvile, by any chance?'

Stockington jumped as if the table had given him an electric shock. 'How did you know that?'

'Just a guess. But from what I've found out, Domvile knew about these tablets before they came into the possession of Ross and Hitchcock. Your new chief is one of the ungodly, I'm afraid. I suspect you're probably in more danger than I am.'

'But that's crazy,' he said, his usual veneer and sang froid slipping. 'I've known Domvile for.... No, I suppose anything is possible now. Look, I must go. Call me when you can.' He rose and left the café quickly, tipping his hat at Scott on his way out.

Scott wandered over to Cushing's table. 'Sorry, I didn't think he had spotted me,' he said, apologetically. 'Never mind. What did he have to say?'

Cushing had wanted to impress Gussie Gordon and had selected Luciano's. He knew it only by reputation as a fine and fashionable restaurant in Mayfair, but was shocked and horrified by the noise and the crowd, even on a Monday night, and, he had to admit, by the prices. The maître d'hôtel had been patronising when Cushing had arrived, unfamiliar with the restaurant, but had melted totally when Gussie, a familiar customer, joined him. Cushing had begun to relax in Gussie's company and was starting to tell her parts of his story after she quizzed him about the tablets that Scott had mentioned at the ball.

Although he had been modest about his own accidental role in the affair, he had felt quite proud when he described his secret activity and what he had found out. But Gussie soon poured cold water on his discoveries.

'Now darling, that's just nonsense. You can't seriously be suggesting that Charles Sloane is mixed up in some way with this horrible murder? I mean, dash it all, he's married to one of my best friends. And are you really saying that Winston is part of it, just because he was speaking to Charles on Saturday?'

'Now I didn't say that exactly....'

'And being shot at in Belgrave Square? Breaking into people's houses? Now really, darling. I think you must be going potty.'

'I wish I were,' he replied. 'The trouble is that it's all deadly serious, and it isn't a game. Geoffrey Scott was shot at too, remember, and Stockington, the secret service man, has confirmed that Ross and Hitchcock are dead. So I didn't make it up.'

Gussie frowned at him as she selected an enormous cream concoction from the dessert trolley. 'And who is this mysterious "John" person? There must have been dozens of Johns at the ball.'

'I was going to ask if you could help me to find out,' replied Cushing. 'Is there any chance you could get hold of a list of guests?'

'Well I can do a lot more than that,' she said. 'Someone has to keep an eye on you, and it doesn't sound as if Geoffrey Scott is going to do that. If you're right – and I'm not saying you are, mind – then you need someone to do some digging around on your behalf, and I know some of these people. The least I can do is try and keep you out of prison.'

The waiter hovered again, raising an eyebrow. 'Two large brandies, please,' ordered Cushing.

'Now Christopher, you naughty man, are you trying to get me tipsy?'

Cushing blushed deeply. 'I say...'

'Well you could always take me to a night club after dinner.' She laughed at his discomfiture. 'Poor Christopher. Not really your sort of thing, night clubs, are they? Though you danced very well on Saturday. Now, tell me a little bit more about this Aleister Crowley. He sounds awfully exciting. From what I read in the papers...'

'He sounds an absolutely ghastly man. A charlatan with thoroughly evil ideas.'

'I'd love to be a fly on the wall when you meet him,' she said mischievously. 'Now, is there anything I can really do to help? Other than the list of Johns, I mean. I'm off to Scotland on Thursday and I'd like to do what I can before then.'

'Scotland? What are you doing in Scotland?'

'Archie's great uncle, the old Laird. The MacGlish of MacGlish, as we should call him. It's his ninetieth birthday'.

Cushing remembered Gussie's late husband, a thoroughly decent sort who had died in the flu epidemic not long after the War, never having fully recovered from his wounds. 'Good that you're still part of the family. Is it a big occasion?'

'Huge. The castle is in the middle of absolutely nowhere, but I gather there is going to be a massive feast, Highland games, tossing the caber and so on. And reeling, of course.' She looked at Cushing and laughed at his expression. 'Oh come on, Christopher, it won't be as bad as all that. They're not all covered in woad these days. Well, maybe some of them. And there may even be running water.'

'Is this a Gordon clan gathering?'

'No, the MacGlish is Archie's mother's uncle. He's a spritely old fellow. Still walks miles a day. He has an eye for the ladies too.'

'You'd better watch out for him, then.' They both laughed, comfortably, two old friends. 'It sounds like you'll have a super time.'

'I'm sorry to be leaving you, dear,' she said, patting his hand. 'I don't trust you not to do something stupid – as if breaking into my friend's house wasn't stupid enough.'

'Your so-called friend – sorry, I mean her husband, obviously – seems to have shot a British officer,' said Cushing, a little pompously. 'So I don't think it's wholly stupid. His German friends have killed my old colleague and shot at me.' He smiled. 'Don't worry, though. I'll be careful, and I'll tell you everything. Thank you.' She was the third person to express concern about his safety that day.

Cushing signalled the waiter for the bill, and the two left the restaurant and walked arm in arm through the quiet streets of Mayfair. She talked inconsequentially about her trip to Scotland,

and all too soon they were at Piccadilly. She hailed a cab to take her to her house in Chelsea and kissed Cushing goodnight. 'Now you take care of yourself, Christopher,' she said again, warmly. 'I don't want you getting hurt.'

Cushing watched the cab turn round and saw Gussie waving from the window. He could still smell her perfume, and he sighed as he walked slowly back down Pall Mall to the Athenaeum.

9

Tuesday 26th June 1928

Cushing slept late at the club before walking the short distance to Jermyn Street, fortified by a large breakfast and the news of England's victory at the cricket. Regent Street was already crowded, with a throng of buses and cars hooting at a slow-moving horse-drawn coal cart.

He found the address Stockington had given him, in the narrow street next to a large cheese shop with an inviting window and opposite a large church. He knocked on the door. It was opened by a sallow, shabby-looking man in a crumpled suit.

'I have come to see Mr. Crowley,' announced Cushing.

'He's not here,' responded the man curtly in a light Scots accent.

'Will he be returning soon?'

'I doubt that,' sneered the man. 'He's away.'

Cushing frowned. 'Away? Would that be at his residence in Scotland?'

'That's right.'

'And will he be there long?'

'Aye, he will.'

'Then I'll send him a telegram. Thank you.' Cushing turned

and left, the door slamming hard behind him. He took a short constitutional around Green Park, enjoying the summer warmth, happily acknowledging passers-by who tipped their hats at him with a cheery 'Morning, Vicar'. After a while, feeling refreshed, he returned to the Athenaeum where the porter accosted him.

'Post for you, sir. Second delivery, just arrived.'

'Thank you, Rafferty.' He opened the letter and smiled. Gussie had been very prompt with her letter of thanks for the previous evening. He strolled into the library and quickly wrote letters to Scott, Clifford and Badger, and then a telegram to Aleister Crowley in Scotland.

"Sir", he wrote. "I beg to ask for some of your valuable time to help me with some research on references of a potential occult significance. A mutual friend has suggested that you may be able to assist. I can travel to Scotland if that would be of convenience to you. Assuring you etc. etc. Cushing, Athenaeum, London." He frowned, and scratched out over half the words. If he was to continue dining with Gussie Gordon he would need to make economies somewhere. He gave the letters and telegram to Rafferty and returned to the library to continue with his study of the Sloane letter.

He began to nod off over the papers, despite the whirling of his thoughts, and was startled by the arrival of Rafferty with a telegram. Cushing read it anxiously. "Delighted to assist research stop. Suggest Thursday afternoon or Friday lunch Boleskine House stop. Intrigued stop. Crowley."

He put aside his paperwork and took a copy of Bradshaw's railway timetables and a large road map from the shelves. Getting to Loch Ness was going to be quite an expedition. The fast train to Edinburgh was easy, then a local train to Inverness, after which he presumed that he would be able to hire a car, or take a long taxi ride.

Taking the train would also have its own advantages, he

thought. He returned to the telephone kiosk and called Gussie Gordon, arranging to meet her at King's Cross station to join her on the Scotch Express on Thursday, then sent a telegram back to Crowley confirming that he would arrive on Friday lunchtime.

He strolled into the drawing room and fell into one of the large armchairs, and was astonished when he woke with a start and realised that it was almost three o'clock. He was clearly still exhausted. But he made another telephone call, arranging to return to Whitechapel to see Badger for supper, and then took two buses to the British Museum to spend a couple of hours carrying out more research.

The following day he returned to the British Museum, making sure that he did not bump into Grainger. He was becoming frustrated. His hours of research had been fruitless, continually finding himself at a dead end. He had used his church connections to enable him to access certain rare and obscure texts, but his studies raised more questions than they answered.

He consoled himself with the support he had received from Badger. He had been eager to hear the details of Cushing's discoveries at Longley Hall, and had offered his help. Cushing was delighted that his old friends were stepping up to the mark, and Badger was proving himself to be more energetic than Peter Clifford. But, later that evening, he was starting to regret accepting Badger's offer to join him at another visit to Joe Page, the old code breaker. Badger had a glint in his eye that indicated that he was hoping that Page would be out, so that he could practise some of his dubious skills with his old friend – in a good cause, naturally.

Against his better judgement, Cushing had arranged to meet his fellow clergyman at the White Horse in Fulham, where he had sat with Clifford the previous week. The two men finished their pints of beer and, one tall, one short, strolled openly in their clerical collars towards Page's house. They passed the church from which Cushing had fled before, and he grimaced as he remembered his stumbling departure through the vicarage garden, the shouts of the policeman ringing in his ears. They turned the corner, approached Page's house and rang the doorbell. There was no answer, and Cushing frowned as he noticed milk bottles on the doorstep and the morning paper still half way through the letter box.

'One bottle of milk I can understand,' he said, turning to Badger, 'but not two. I wonder if he's all right?'

'Well, sir, if you're thinking what I'm thinking, we ought to take a look, if you know what I mean.' He winked, knowingly.

'Be serious, man.' Cushing frowned again. 'But you're probably right. Oh damn it all, let's just get going.'

'Good man,' said Badger. 'After you, sir. Show me the way.'

They walked back round to the church, cocking their ears at the sound of the service being conducted inside, through the side gate and into the vicarage garden once again. 'Oh yes,' said Badger, in a detached tone of voice. 'Very good. Good job there's a service on. Very good.'

Cushing scowled, concerned that it was still broad daylight, but allowed Badger to give him a leg up over the wall, just as Clifford had helped him a week before. He turned and helped Badger down to join him in Page's garden.

Badger positioned a dustbin to make it easier for them to jump over the wall on the way back, and then walked nonchalantly up to the French windows, pointing out the closed curtains to Cushing. 'Why are they closed, sir? Seems odd to me.' He offered Cushing a black silk bag, and, although they assumed the house was empty, spoke in a whisper. 'Now, sir, do you want to have a go?'

'For heaven's sake, man. Just do it. You're the professional, after all.' Cushing's reply was also a whisper.

Badger shrugged his shoulders. 'Please yourself, sir. Though I thought you might welcome the practice. I haven't done this for several years myself. Oh well. May the Lord forgive me.' He extracted a small device from his black bag and fiddled with the lock for less than a minute before leaning back with a satisfied expression on his face. 'I always loved using this little beauty,' he said. 'Now, let's give this a go. It may be that the door is bolted, but that isn't very likely.' He pressed down the handle and leaned on the door, pushing it open against the curtain and easing his way through. 'There we are, sir. Thought so. In you come.'

The two men went into the room in which Page had been doing his translation work. Badger made sure that the curtains were properly closed and took a flashlight from his pocket. 'It's a lot tidier than it was last time,' remarked Cushing. 'And the rubbing isn't on the wall any more. No books. And look – all the papers that I saw on the desk. He's taken them away.' He flicked through the papers that were left, but saw nothing to do with the translation that had clearly taken up so much of Page's time in recent weeks. I say, Badger...'

But Badger had left the study, and Cushing was interrupted by a harsh call to attention. 'Psst. Quick, sir, come through here.'

Cushing turned off the flashlight and quickly joined Badger who was standing in the hallway looking into the kitchen. 'What is it?'

'Look, sir.'

Cushing looked down and saw the body of Page lying on the red-tiled floor, a pool of darker red visible around his head. His glasses lay smashed on the floor, a yard away. Flies were buzzing round the body. Cushing retched, and then pulled himself together.

'Good God. They've done for Page too. That man John at Longley Hall said that they would be dealing with loose ends. Oh, the poor man.'

Badger leaned over Page, checked his pulse, somewhat unnecessarily, and then swiftly searched his pockets. 'Look at his wallet. There's ten, fifteen pounds in here. No casual burglar would have left that behind. I think you're right, sir.'

'And they've taken every trace of the translation.'

'Yes, I heard you say, sir. I think, if it's all right with you, sir, that we ought to go.'

'But what about Page?' Badger rolled his eyes. 'Oh, yes. I see what you mean. Yes, Badger, I think you're right. And the quicker the better.'

The two men went back into the study. 'Hold on a moment,' said Cushing. 'Let me have one last look around.' He peered optimistically in some of the drawers, but was forced to admit failure.

Badger leaned over and pulled a couple of screwed-up pieces of paper from the wastepaper basket. 'What have we got here, sir?'

Cushing took the papers and straightened them out.

'What is it?'

Cushing gulped. 'I think it's the beginning of a letter to me. "Dear Christopher," it says. "I have been thinking since your visit, and I am concerned that things are a bit odd. You asked about Ross. Well, he asked me to translate some old Egyptian tablet that he had photographed. It's very strange, but..."'

Badger interrupted him. 'Perhaps later, sir? I suggest we leave. Now.' He turned to go, and Cushing had no choice but to follow. They hurriedly climbed back over the wall after taking the time to lock the French windows again. They went calmly out through the vicarage garden and past the church one more time, the sounds of a choir coming clearly through the stained glass windows.

'What do we do now?' asked Cushing.

'Well I don't know about you, sir, but I think I need a stiff drink.'

'I thought you'd signed the pledge, Badger?'

'This would be purely medicinal, sir.'

'I think I'll join you, then, old man,' replied Cushing. 'But we can't leave Page lying there any longer. I think there's a telephone box on the King's Road. I'm going to call the police.'

The two walked silently back to the White Horse. Cushing stopped at the first red telephone box he found and asked the operator to be put through to the police. He pretended to be a neighbour concerned about the milk bottles and newspapers on the doorstep, and hung up quickly before giving his name. He was conscious that this would be the second murder he had reported in a week.

Badger had a brandy and grimaced, but in fact it took Cushing a second one before he was sufficiently relaxed to talk, in whispered tones, in the corner of the public house.

'It must have been Sloane. Or the man Domvile that they spoke about on Saturday night. They called Page a "loose end". And they've done him in. Just smashed his head in. Will they stop at nothing?'

'Maybe it was those two Germans, the ones who killed Ross and shot at you.'

'Probably. Just like the Hun to sneak up on Page and bash him over the head. Poor chap. And they've taken all the evidence. All of it. Nothing left of the translation.'

'It's a good job you came round last week, then, isn't it sir? But what was in that letter in the wastepaper basket? They missed a trick there.'

'Yes, they certainly did. I think he was trying to warn me. And then maybe changed his mind, or was interrupted. Look, the letter doesn't go on for much longer. I read out the bit about him thinking something was odd. Listen.' And Cushing read out the rest of letter.

"'It's very strange, but I had already been approached by our old friends to translate the same thing, this time from a rubbing." Told you. "Anyway, I started thinking after your visit. Why is our secret service so interested in some old tablet? Why two different people, on the QT from each other? Why me?"'

'All fair questions,' interrupted Badger.

'Quite right.' He carried on. "'I'm out of my depth. I mean I've translated most of the words, I think, but I don't understand the implications. It's all about power, and the use of power. Now I'm no traitor, you know that, though we've had our differences. And I'm worried about giving any of my results back to…"'

'Well?'

'That's where the letter stops, half way through a sentence.'

Badger scratched his head. 'Maybe this was a first attempt. Maybe he wrote a longer letter afterwards and posted it.'

'He can't have done. Otherwise I would have received it by now. Look, Page must have been killed on Monday at the latest, only a day or so after I heard Sloane talking about him. There were two pints of milk on the doorstep, remember, and it's only Wednesday now. Or maybe…' Cushing suddenly turned white.

'What is it, sir?'

'Stop calling me "sir", Badger, please! Sorry, I didn't mean…'

'Don't mention it, sir. But what's the problem?'

'Well, what if he had already written the letter, and they have it? They could know who I am, and that I am at the Athenaeum? Oh God…'

'Hold on, hold on,' said Badger, calmingly. 'There wasn't an address on the letter, was there? And no name, apart from "Christopher"? What would the chances be of Page writing a new letter, addressing an envelope and not actually posting the thing before these ruffians came to murder him? There was a pillar box almost opposite his house, after all.'

'Was there? I didn't notice.'

'Well why don't we pass by Page's house again and take a look? We can see if the police have arrived too.'

'Good idea, Badger. I want to make sure that he isn't left lying there any longer than necessary. But won't it be risky?'

'For Heaven's sake, sir, no one will be worried about two middle-aged vicars!'

As they walked round the corner, they could see a small crowd forming, and the road was blocked by a number of vehicles. They got closer, and Cushing could see clearly that at least one was a police car, and that another was an ambulance. They hurried to join the crowd, then approached a large policeman standing in front of Page's house. Cushing thought that the silhouette of the policeman was familiar but, even if it had been the same one who had chased him from the house the previous week, he was sure that he would not be recognised.

'Good evening, Constable,' said Cushing. 'What's happening here?'

The policeman saluted. 'Well, Vicar, I shouldn't really be saying too much, but it looks as if the gentleman who lives in the house here has been murdered.'

Cushing and Badger both blanched. 'Murdered? How? Who?'

'I'm no detective, Reverend, but only last week the gentleman was burgled, and I almost apprehended the criminals myself. It's my belief that the thieves came back and that poor Mr. Page disturbed them.'

'But we did no such – I mean, poor man, how dreadful. But when did you find out that he had been killed?'

'A neighbour saw the milk and papers piling up and called us earlier this evening. I entered the premises myself' – he preened, proudly – 'and found the body.'

A seedy-looking man in a dirty raincoat and holding a notebook called from behind Cushing. 'What's your name,

Constable?'

'P.C. Benton, 1158.' The man wrote it down and pulled a large camera and flash from a canvas bag. He lined up a shot of the policeman and the front of Page's house, and Cushing and Badger were temporarily blinded by the flare of magnesium. The front door opened and a uniformed sergeant came out.

'What's going on here?' he yelled. 'Benton, what the hell do you think you're doing? Keep these damned people away from the crime scene.' He looked at the two clergymen. 'Begging your pardon, sir. Reverend. Reverends. But stand aside, please.'

Two ambulance men came out of the house carrying a stretcher with a shrouded form and took it to their vehicle, driving off. The shabby man took another photograph and the sergeant addressed the crowd. 'Now ladies and gentlemen, nothing more to see. Make your way home now, please. Unless anyone has any information that might help us?'

Cushing looked at Badger and shook his head. They started to walk away when the reporter barged past them. 'Hold on a minute, Sergeant. I'm White, Evening News. This man, Joseph Page. Constable Benton here says he was murdered. Tell me what happened. How was he killed? Was there anyone else in the house?'

'I can't say very much,' said the sergeant. 'The deceased was struck on the head with a blunt instrument by person or persons unknown. Probably some time on Monday. The doctor says he has been dead for about forty-eight hours.'

'Were there any signs of a break in?'

'Not that we have been able to ascertain.'

'And what's this about a burglary last week? Your Constable said that it was the same men that murdered Page?'

'We will be making a full enquiry, sir. Now come along, please. I've got work to do.'

The sergeant shut the door. The reporter grinned. 'Not

something you see every night in Fulham, eh?'

The two friends ignored the squalid newspaperman and walked disconsolately back to the underground station.

'What shall I do about this letter?' asked Cushing. 'I can't stay at the club. I shall have to move out. Though they might follow me. And I can't even go back to Albury? Can I? And Badger, they might even have followed me to your house. Oh Lord, what have I done?'

'Look, sir, I really don't think it's a problem. If they killed Page on Monday afternoon, or even Monday night, they would already be on our tails. And we haven't seen them. If it makes you happy, go to Scott's tomorrow morning, or move in with me and the missus if you like.'

'But…'

'But nothing.' Badger looked around and pointed. 'Look, no men in trench coats lurking on the platform. Look, I need to get home. Ask the porter at the club if anyone has been asking for you. And stop worrying.'

'All right. But I don't like to feel as if I am being hunted in my own country.'

10

Thursday 28th June 1928

Cushing had arrived early at King's Cross, having taken his bags to Scott's flat via a circuitous route of underground, bus and two taxis. He had found time for a good breakfast, but eyed everyone in the Athenaeum suspiciously as he ate. Rafferty had assured Cushing that no one had called for him, but he was still not wholly convinced by Badger's reassurances. On his way out he had slipped Rafferty a ten shilling note – an ostentatious expense, he felt, but a worthwhile one – to make sure that the porter would tell him whether anyone asked for him in the future.

He was at Scott's flat at Albany for no more than five minutes, but, having carefully locked the door on the way out, he reopened it and walked briskly to Scott's desk. He opened the top drawer and looked for several minutes at the service revolver that Scott had left for him. He made up his mind and, muttering a prayer, put the revolver and a box of ammunition into his case. He was not prepared to go down without a fight.

By the time Cushing reached King's Cross, he had cheered up. He loved the noise and bustle of a railway station and spent half an hour happily smelling the steam, oil and coal smoke. He walked up the platform to stare at the great green locomotive. He had forgotten that the old Scotch Express had been replaced with the new Flying Scotsman only the month before.

He had arranged to be on the same train as Gussie, but it was already past quarter to ten; the train would not wait, and she had still not arrived. He was starting to worry. He looked repeatedly at the large clock over the station concourse, and, with only five minutes to go, he was pleased to see her elegant figure threading through the crowd followed by a gaggle of heavily-laden porters. With her, carrying a small bag and pointing at the platform, was Johnnie Gibson, her erstwhile escort at the ball the previous weekend.

'Christopher, darling, why on earth are you standing around on the platform?' she said. 'Come on, quickly, or you'll make us miss the train. Hurry up.' She turned to Gibson. 'Johnnie, darling, thank you so much for the lift. Will you take care of the porters? You know Christopher Cushing, of course.'

'Ah, Cushing. Yes, we've met.' He glared at Cushing. 'I didn't realise you were going to the party with Mrs. Gordon.'

'No, no,' replied Cushing, colouring. 'I've got another appointment. Near Loch Ness. I'm not going to the party. No. Absolutely not.' He looked at Gibson who was clenching and unclenching his fists.

'I should hope not,' muttered Gibson, darkly, as Gussie hurried Cushing past the ticket collector and to their seats in a first class carriage. Again, Cushing was uncomfortable with the extravagance, but began to relax as the huge engine pulled out of the station and accelerated into the Hertfordshire countryside.

'Edinburgh in only a few hours, with no changes,' said Gussie, relaxing into her seat. 'That's progress for you.'

Cushing smiled affectionately at her. 'I hadn't realised you were so interested in trains.'

'I'm not, but I love travelling fast. Train, car, aeroplane, motor boat. I love it. Oh I say, here's the young man with some tea.' She waited until the man had poured the tea and left some biscuits. 'So how are you getting to this Crowley man tomorrow? Where are you staying tonight?'

'Well we get into Edinburgh at about six. There's a train to Inverness and I'll find a hotel near the station. I'll hire a car tomorrow morning, or take a taxi if I can find one at a reasonable price.'

'Oh Christopher, you are so sweet. Of course you won't. I'm being met by one of Uncle Alex's drivers at Edinburgh. The old Laird lives only about twenty miles from Inverness, and he must have at least ninety spare rooms.'

'But…'

'No buts.'

'But I don't have a kilt or anything. I don't even have my evening clothes.'

She laughed at his embarrassment, as she always did. 'Don't be so silly. No buts, I said. You come and stay at the castle, we can drive over to see this Aleister Crowley tomorrow, and I can put you on the night train back to London in the evening.'

'But Gussie, this man may be dangerous.'

'Just because he believes in devils? Surely you aren't going to let that superstitious nonsense get to you. It's going to be a jape. "The wickedest man in the world", isn't that what you said? Oh this will be fun.' She settled back into her seat and looked at the rolling green countryside while Cushing opened and shut his mouth like a goldfish.

It was a delightful journey. Cushing showed Gussie all of the documents, and she made several helpful observations on the implications of the mystery he was trying to solve. News of Page's murder had not had time to make the morning papers, but he told her what had happened. In return, she showed him the list of people called John who had been at the Midsummer Ball. It was a long list, ranging from John Jacob Astor, the newspaper magnate, to an Oxford don called John Tolkien whose name Cushing did not recognise.

'Our John's voice sounded foreign, though,' said Cushing, scratching his head.

'Well, Astor is as British as they come, or sounds it, though he was born in America. Tolkien could be anything. What do you mean by foreign?'

'It was just an undertone, a suspicion of an accent. I don't know, maybe I'm just expecting to see foreigners everywhere.' He flicked through the guest list. 'Hmm, very much the great and the good. No obvious candidate though.'

'He could have been a house guest, of course. Not actually on the guest list for the ball at all, I mean.'

'Maybe, maybe. Oh Gussie, this is so frustrating!'

The journey was over all too soon and the train arrived on time in Edinburgh at six o'clock. Cushing had felt a little like a character from a novel. Like Richard Hannay, he was a hunted man on a train to Scotland putting miles between himself and a corpse in London, but the more time he spent with Gussie the more relaxed he had become.

He tipped the porter who was struggling to load Gussie's voluminous luggage into the back of a large black Rolls Royce. The chauffeur, Hamish, a squat dark man in a smart uniform, acknowledged Gussie with a mumble and grunted through his beard when she told him that Cushing would be travelling with them. Hamish made no further sound as he steered the car expertly along increasingly narrow roads, and the evening light gave them both a fine view of the impressive scenery. Gussie became more and more animated as they drove north through the wild countryside. She had only been to the Highlands a few times, and had only met her late husband's great uncle twice before, at the wedding and funeral. Cushing had also been silent – his previous trip to Edinburgh had been to Craiglockhart, to convalesce after one of his several relapses following his shellshock.

It was late, though still light, when they arrived at the castle, following the long drive past a herd of white-belted cows. Eventually they reached a huge turreted pile. They were shown through to the library where a tray of sandwiches awaited them. A fire roared in the grate despite the heat of the day, and the walls were covered in swords, armour and the sad-looking heads of proud stags.

The door burst open and a small wiry man with an enormous white beard entered the room, followed by a servant. The MacGlish of MacGlish embraced Gussie in a huge bear hug. He then turned to fix Cushing with his piercing blue eyes.

'Good evening to you, sir. And you are?'

Gussie spoke for Cushing. 'This is Christopher Cushing, an old friend. He has an appointment up by Loch Ness tomorrow and I thought you wouldn't mind....'

The MacGlish turned his eyes towards Gussie and she faltered.

'Aye,' he said. 'You'll be having a dram with me.' It was a command, not an invitation. 'Jamie, see to the minister.' The servant poured enormous measures for Cushing and the MacGlish from the decanter on the sideboard, and added a little water. The MacGlish spluttered. 'What do you call that, Jamie? The gentleman has been travelling all day. He'll be wanting a proper drink!' Cushing winced as Jamie poured another inch of whisky into each of the glasses.

'Here's tae ye!' Cushing sipped his enormous drink while the MacGlish drained his. 'Come on, man, drink up. Jamie, another for the minister.'

Cushing woke with the morning sun pouring into his bedroom. He sat up suddenly and his head throbbed. He could remember little of the deep and meaningful theological discussion he had had with the MacGlish into the small hours of the morning, long after Gussie had gone to bed, but he certainly regretted finishing the decanter of malt whisky, excellent though it had been. He took a quick bath, successfully negotiating the castle's antique plumbing, and strolled downstairs.

There were at least a dozen people in the breakfast room. The MacGlish, dressed in a disreputable tweed jacket, was holding court over a huge plate of bacon and kidneys, and Cushing was able to make his way to the groaning sideboard without having to speak to anyone. He lifted the covers from the salvers and winced at the sight of kedgeree and eggs, contenting himself with a cup of tea. The MacGlish broke off from his story and addressed Cushing loudly. 'Ah, minister. You've wasted half the morning. What's wrong with ye?'

'Good morning, MacGlish,' said Cushing, through gritted teeth. 'You're looking full of the joys of spring.'

'The minister and I were putting the world to rights last night,' said the old clan chief to his admirers. 'And I can tell you he likes a drop of our special Scottish communion wine.' The other breakfast guests, to whom Cushing had not been introduced, laughed dutifully.

An arm linked into his. 'Don't mind him, Christopher,' said Gussie. 'He obviously likes you. In fact from what I hear about last night, you passed with flying colours. He's been out for hours already, of course, taking pot shots at poachers, or rabbits, or something.' She turned to the MacGlish. 'Uncle Alex, would it be all right if Christopher and I borrowed one of the cars this morning?'

'Aye, my dear. Just take the Rolls. Hamish will drive ye.' Then he turned back to the others and began a long and scandalous story about a long-dead relative, standing up to emphasise a point and revealing his tartan trousers.

Cushing and Gussie sought out the taciturn Hamish and pored over a map. Cushing had received directions from Crowley and pointed out their destination to the chauffeur. 'We go along the south side of Loch Ness, through Inverfarigaig...'

Hamish's eyes rolled and Gussie giggled. 'Oh Christopher, you don't pronounce it like that!'

'Well how do you pronounce the wretched place?'

'Inver... Inver... Well, it doesn't matter. What time do we need to leave, Hamish? If we're looking to get there at one o'clock?'

Hamish grunted incomprehensibly, but Gussie seemed to understand him. 'Splendid,' she said. 'See you at the front steps at eleven.'

Cushing and Gussie walked round the gardens for an hour, with Gussie talking happily and Cushing screwing up his eyes at the bright sunlight. They were back at the castle in good time to find the car waiting at the steps, with Hamish standing at its side. The MacGlish appeared at the huge wooden doors and called out to Cushing. 'Hey, Minister. Ye'll be staying for my birthday tomorrow.'

'Well, I, er...'

'Nonsense. Of course you're coming. What's more important than my birthday that you have to rush back to London?'

'I'm sorry. I mean, I'd love to wish you well....'

Gussie interrupted him. 'I'm sorry, Uncle Alex. Christopher really does have to go back to London. But I'm sure you can stay till Saturday morning, Christopher, can't you?'

The MacGlish grinned, and Cushing realised that he had never before resented having to conduct a christening service so much. He really wanted to stay in Scotland with Gussie, even if the mischievous old rogue MacGlish would force him to drink more and more whisky.

As the Rolls Royce bumped its way down the narrow lanes alongside Loch Ness, Gussie was again enthralled by the beautiful highland scenery. She admired the sun sparkling on the water of the loch, the dark fir trees and the distant mountains, and she cooed at the red woolly cattle. Cushing still felt somewhat ill from the previous evening, and was less enthusiastic. Even the brand new Silver Ghost was rocking too much for his own comfort, especially as the journey took a couple of hours.

Hamish pulled the car up at a gate house where a small and nimble man muttered 'Aye, the man will be expecting ye', and opened the gate. A tree-lined path opened to wide lawns and gardens, a little overgrown, with beautiful views over both the loch and a small and apparently ancient graveyard. Ahead of them was a low, white-painted house. A burly man in a beard was chopping wood at its side. He glared at the car, but otherwise ignored them.

Hamish drove up to the house and stopped the car, opening the door for Cushing and Gussie. He muttered something. 'I'm sorry?' asked Cushing. Hamish muttered again, this time more loudly, and pushed his whiskered face close to Cushing's. 'Ye be taking care of yourself here, sir. Ye won't remember me, but I remember you. I was in the Gordon Highlanders, sir, and we all remember you coming round the trenches and keeping our spirits up. Ye're a good man, for a Sassenach, sir. We raised a glass to you after we heard ye'd had a Blighty one. Glad to see you again, sir, if you don't mind me saying so. I'll be here if you need me.'

'Thank you, Hamish,' said Cushing, suddenly feeling very moved.

'That's all right, Hamish,' interrupted Gussie, blithely. 'Thank you. We'll call when we need you.' As Hamish returned to the car, Cushing saw him take a hefty spanner and place it on the seat beside him. 'Bless him,' said Gussie. 'He seems to be worried about us. Come on.'

'Actually...' But Gussie ignored him. She tripped up to the

door and, without waiting for Cushing, rapped the knocker twice. A young fresh-faced man, round-eyed and wearing a smoking jacket that was too big for him, answered the door. He waved a manicured hand and raised an eyebrow.

'We're here to see Mr. Crowley,' she said.

'Ah, yes,' said the young man, in a slightly foreign accent, looking her up and down and then addressing Cushing. 'Mr. Cushing and – and a friend. Aleister is expecting you.' He looked at Hamish and called to the bearded man. 'Rory. I say, Rory. Could you give Mr. Cushing's man a cup of tea?'

He showed Cushing and Gussie into the house, stepping over a heap of climbing gear that had been abandoned in the hallway. The house was dark, with many old pictures and hangings, and smelled strongly of stale incense and something unpleasant that Cushing could not identify. The two were taken into a drawing room with old gilt mirrors on the walls, and lit by guttering candles. The wide windows that would have given a stunning view over the loch were heavily draped. It was disagreeably warm.

The imposing figure of a man stood in a bay window with his back to them, as if he was staring out of the curtained windows. He was completely bald, with a thick, fat neck, and was wearing a heavy brocaded dressing gown. Cushing peered through the gloom at the designs embroidered on it, which seemed in the candlelight to be moving and swirling. The smell of incense made him feel heady, and again he regretted the Laird's hospitality.

Crowley addressed them, without turning around. 'Mr. Cushing? Delighted. You hadn't told me that you were a priest.' Cushing automatically put his hand to his collar. 'And you have brought a guest?' He spun round, revealing a fat, pasty face with multiple chins and a pair of bright staring eyes. He came towards them and appeared to shrink as he did so. Cushing saw that he had been standing on a stool. 'Thank you for seeing us, Mr. Crowley,' he said, and introduced Gussie. He turned his gaze on her and she tittered like an embarrassed schoolgirl. 'I've heard so much about you,' she said, lamely. And then 'I love the view of the loch from your garden.'

Crowley licked his lips, and invited them to sit. 'Thank you, my dear. It took me many years to find the house. It has a power, a thelemic power.' Cushing winked at Gussie. 'The Aeon of Horus, though I don't expect your sort to appreciate what I mean. It is the centre for all of my followers, the whole order.' He stopped. 'But I am being inhospitable. Sebastian, some Madeira for our guests.' The effeminate young man poured glasses for Gussie and Cushing, and then one for himself.

'Thank you Sebastian, you may leave us.' The young man looked offended and stalked towards the door, taking an angry kick at a large black cat that yowled and slunk behind a sofa. 'Sebastian, please, leave poor Mathers alone.' The youth scowled and left the room, taking his glass with him. 'Poor Mathers. Sebastian is so jealous of him. Incidentally, Cushing, a church used to be on the site, but it burned down. Most tragic.'

'Yes, I'm sure....' Cushing was not sure about what to say, but Crowley spoke over him.

'We have a mutual friend, I understand. No names. I can guess. It is very convenient for the government to consult me when they need advice on matters of the occult. Don't look so offended, Father Christopher. You know you believe in the occult yourself, or you wouldn't be here.'

'Well, yes, I mean no...'

'And we may occasionally be on different sides.' Crowley laughed. 'But the differences between our two religions are less than you might think. Now.' He clapped his hands. 'Let us see if you can excite me with your question.'

Cushing had prepared what he had thought was a more convincing story than the one with which he had struggled at the British Museum, but he wilted under Crowley's scrutiny. Within a few minutes, he found himself blabbing all the information he had – which, he realised, was not very much: the tablet from the Middle East, the Masonic rite that needed objects of power to complete it, the possible role of the Templars, and the crowning of a king with the Lapsit Exillis. He even showed Crowley a small fragment of a rubbing he had made of the tablet. Whenever he faltered, Gussie enthusiastically filled in the gaps he had left.

'Congratulations,' said Crowley. 'You have aroused my interest.' His voice had originally been high-pitched, almost bird-like, but had gradually become more sonorous. Cushing found his posturing somewhat pretentious. 'Let us have lunch, and I shall explain.'

Over lunch of a strongly-flavoured but indeterminate game stew, served by the bearded man, Rory, Crowley started to piece together some of the elements of the story.

'You have said you are not a practising Mason yourself any more, but I believe you will be aware of some of the ceremonies associated with Freemasonry. Many low-level Masons never achieve power. But power there is. Ritual and ceremony bring their own power, just as the power in your church lies in its ritual. Those fools who seek to trivialise those rituals do not understand.

'There are many different Masonic groups, and their rituals are different, incomplete. You ask about a "Frater Secundus". In several sects, he would be very senior. Secret societies tend to be divided into cells with different responsibilities, and a "Frater Secundus" would lead one of the cells, looking after finance, logistics, research and the like. Secrecy breaks down when members of the society know one another socially, of course. But the faith is fragmented. The Rosicrucians hate the Skull and Bones, the Germans hate everybody, and the Ordo Templi Orientalis – well, let me just say that we have our own views. But the rituals are key to all of us.

'The history of the Masons ostensibly goes back to the

founder of the Temple of Jerusalem, but it was during the Crusades that the Templars found some of the real secrets. They discovered that ritual transcends the basic capabilities of man. They have hidden the power for many years, and though some of it has been lost, they have kept most of the great secrets for themselves.

'Many died to protect them. Philip the Fair of France wanted them for himself, and wiped out many of the Templar leaders, but others went into hiding. A few years before the mass murder of the Templars, a crusade was preached against the Cathars in southern France, for the same reason. And again, the secrets have been hidden and passed from generation to generation.

'This rite of which you speak must be one of those secrets. A king will be crowned, with all due ritual and sacrifice. The ritual will need words of power, jewels for the crown, and the stone. The Lapsit Exillis.'

'Surely this is all just.....' interrupted Cushing, rudely, but Crowley continued.

'You do not have to believe. They believe. And belief brings more power. And power is what this is all about. As I say, you have interested me.'

'So the tablet is…?'

'Ah, the clay tablet. That must be original. I am sorry you did not bring it so I could examine it. If what you say is true, it dates back to the time of Baal. Three thousand years before your Christ, perhaps. The tablet sets out part of the ritual, the detail of the rite that your rivals now seek to recover.'

'So how do they know…?'

'When the Frankish kingdoms fell, the Templars took the artefacts of power and hid them. Your archaeologist, Schaeffer, has said that the ruins at Ras Shamra were compromised. They were. We know that the crusader castle at Ras Shamra was built over the site of ancient Ugarit. That must be when the Templars took the crown and the gems. And the Lapsit Exillis, of course.

But who knows where they took them?'

'Why is that so important?' asked Cushing, slowly.

'Because, my dear man, it is core to the ritual. The Lapsit Exillis is supposed to be the stone in the crown worn by Lucifer when he fell from heaven.'

'But...'

'Don't interrupt, Cushing! Whether it was or not doesn't really matter. As I said, it is what they believe that counts. But it is core to unlocking the true power behind the ritual. It will control, even unite the different groups, and it will have worldwide significance. There have been groups and organisations seeking these artefacts for many years – the Germans have always been keen – and I have been aware of more activity recently. But this is new to me.'

'So what on earth do we do?'

'Well the simplest thing would be to find the artefacts that the plotters are looking for before they find them themselves. Yes, they would certainly merit investigation. That is what I would do. But I fear our time together must come to an end.' Crowley clapped his hands again and Rory entered the room. 'Please escort our guests back to their car. Father Christopher, Mrs. Gordon, it has been a delight.'

Cushing and Gussie were led to the car, blinking owlishly in the daylight. Hamish looked relieved to see them. As they drove away, Cushing fancied he could see Crowley's face visible in the window, clear until they turned the corner and the whole house was lost to view. Both Cushing and Gussie felt tired, muzzy and confused.

'What a charming chap,' said Gussie, yawning.

'Honestly, Gussie, how on earth could you be charmed by that repulsive, balding little man?'

'Well you can talk, darling. All this talk of keeping secrets and you told him everything you knew.'

'Of course I didn't. Only a blithering idiot would tell Crowley everything. I couldn't have done.' He shook his head to clear it. 'I didn't. Did I?'

11

Saturday 30th June 1928

It was with much regret that Cushing left the castle the following morning. It had been a splendid evening, one in which he had been more careful about how much whisky he had consumed.

He had watched the preparation for the Highland games for a few minutes: people were arriving from all directions, food and drink was loaded into the marquees, ropes for the tug of war and the large wooden cabers were delivered. The pipers were practising early. Cushing had always hated the sound, recognising bagpipes as weapons of war rather than musical instruments. He had wished the old Laird well for his birthday celebrations and kissed Gussie goodbye. Hamish drove him through the morning sunshine to Inverness, and was less taciturn than usual, reminiscing about the Great War.

As Cushing sat on the train heading back to London, he would much rather have shelved all of his responsibilities. Not only the christening the following day – why did the parents have to pick this Sunday of all Sundays, he thought, guiltily – but also the work that he had to do to resolve the conundrum that Ross had left him. 'Why me?' he thought, not for the first time.

All he wanted to do was return to Scotland to join Gussie at the MacGlish's birthday reeling ball. Not that he could reel, but he had started to enjoy himself so much. He had not even reached York, and he was starting to miss her.

That reverie made him think more widely about what he was doing. Middle-aged, overweight, hardly a man of action. What on earth was he up to, getting caught up in this conspiracy? Surely he should just call Stockington and hand the whole thing back to the authorities? But he realised quickly that this would be a waste of time. There was no one else. But what would Mary have said? What would Gussie say if she thought he was wavering? How could he even consider such a thing? He put his head in his hands and tried to think.

The whistle of the stationmaster at York woke him with a start. His head had cleared and he knew what he had to do. He forced himself to concentrate on his next tasks. He would follow up on Crowley's suggestions and spend more time in the reading room at the British Museum – he knew that he was more suited to books and research than to action. He also wrote letters to Scott, Clifford, Brock and Gussie setting out everything that he knew: a worthwhile precaution, he thought, in case Page had indeed addressed an envelope to him and made him the next target for the murderous Germans.

He arrived back at Guildford late, having crossed London by underground and taken a train to the country from Waterloo station, but for once was pleased to pass Mrs. Sturdy in her front garden, whistling for her cat.

'I say,' he asked, 'has anyone been looking for me? Any strangers, I mean?'

He was more than happy to hear that she had seen no one. He had been concerned that the Germans could easily trace his location in Surrey through any copy of Crockford's, the book that lists all Church of England clergymen, their parishes and other information: a "Who's Who" of the clergy. But he felt safer having loaded Scott's revolver and placed it under his pillow before falling asleep.

He slept late, something he normally never did, and had to rush through his parish business before the long-planned christening. He was preoccupied and the organist looked at him strangely as he made mistakes with the service. He declined a drink with the christening party and returned to the vicarage.

He packed several bags and loaded them into his car. He had decided to drive back to London in time for an early start at the British Museum on Monday morning. Before he left, he went down into the cellar and took a case of wine to the car, the least he could do for his friends who had been so hospitable, then had a thought. He opened his locked gun cupboard and looked at the shotguns, but decided that they would be too noticeable. He returned to the cellar and uncovered a large tin box. He pursed his lips, then opened the box. He unfolded some cloths and revealed his souvenirs of the Great War which he had promised the doctors at Craiglockhart that he would destroy. He had broken that promise, but now felt pleased that he had kept them: two German pistols – one Luger, one Mannlicher – a bayonet, and three German stick grenades. He carefully folded them back into the cloths and gingerly carried the box to the car. He hoped that the grenades particularly were going to be safe after all this time. 'I can give Geoffrey his revolver back now,' he thought. 'They shot at me first. Let's see how they like this.' He laughed mirthlessly to himself, wondering what the doctors would be saying now. 'What am I doing?' he asked himself. 'I'm not a soldier, I'm a vicar. Is this really me? They'll probably lock me up and throw away the key.'

A voice from close behind startled him. 'Father Christopher?'

Cushing spun round, the box in his hands. 'Mrs. Sturdy, you gave me a terrible shock. Don't creep up on me like that!'

After further pleasantries, he explained that he would be in London for a few days. He got into his car and drove back to London, taking his bags up to Scott's flat and returning Scott's revolver to the desk drawer. Scott had removed the second tablet from his cricket bag and left it propped up on his table with a note. Cushing spent half an hour wrapping the tablet carefully and finding a safe hiding place for it in a wardrobe, then sat in a comfortable armchair planning his research the next day, a large glass of whisky in his left hand and his pistol in easy reach of his right.

The reading room of the British Museum had been a familiar haunt of Cushing's in his younger days when he was carrying out research for the learned academic and theological papers that had got him into so much trouble all those years ago. He had become a regular visitor again while researching for his ever-expanding – and uncontroversial – tome on Saxon churches, a mission he had thrown himself into and which he knew that friends like Gussie and Clifford were convinced he would never actually finish. Would the same be true of the mission he was now embarking on?

As he joined the queue to sign himself in the following morning, Cushing was horrified to see Grainger, the American archaeologist. Grainger had spotted him, and there was no escape. Grainger dragged Cushing to the Museum tea rooms and begged him for further information about the tablet. Luckily, Cushing was truthfully able to say very little, though he knew enough about Baal, especially after his meeting with Crowley, to keep the conversation going. In fact, the excitable Grainger told Cushing far more about Ugarit and about Claude Schaeffer's investigations.

Schaeffer had told Grainger a lot about the progress of his dig. Grainger was able to confirm to Cushing everything that Crowley had mooted. The ancient Ugarit citadel, itself long covered by Ras Shamra, had been built over by the Templars after the First Crusade. The building known as "Saladin's Castle" had been built close to the ruins of the Templar fortress a hundred years later.

Grainger said that Schaeffer had told him that his investigations had been limited, partly because the dig had not received full government funding and support, and that artefacts had been going missing. In all honesty, Grainger admitted, he suspected that Schaeffer himself might have been selling priceless treasures on the black market to fund his continued work, or even passing them secretly to the people who were funding him and just claiming that they had been stolen. 'The man is French, after all!' he said.

Cushing asked about the implications of the original site being "compromised" by the Templars.

'Well,' said Grainger, 'it's a complicated site, with one civilisation on top of another and all. But the interesting thing is that he found both Templar and ancient Ugaritic artefacts all mixed up.'

'Which means…?'

'I'd guess that the Templars were doing their own excavations there too.'

'So what might they have found?'

'Impossible to say in any detail, especially as the Templars may have removed anything some eight hundred years ago. But I'd hazard a guess at grave goods of various kinds. The Templars would have been interested in treasure, obviously, but anything left in a tomb could have been of huge value.'

'Gold, you mean,' asked Cushing.

'Well, yes, but I meant of scientific value, obviously. More tablets, religious images. Anything.'

'And the Ugarits – is that the right word? Phoenicians, of course. Were they Baal worshippers?'

'Exactly. Just like you said the other day. That was a damned good call, Reverend. I've made pretty good headway with that tablet, by the way. It's all around the ceremony for crowning the king. Details of the ritual. The stones, the crown, the orb, the sword, and a sacrifice or two. In fact it's funny how little has changed between prehistory and your coronation ceremonies here and now. Apart from the sacrifice, I guess.'

'I suppose so. But what are these stones? Just big jewels, like in our modern crowns? Or do they have some part to play in the ritual?' Cushing thought for a moment. 'Are we talking about the "Lapsit Exillis"?'

'You're joking, right? The stone from heaven? No, that's a load of nonsense.' Cushing, remembering what Crowley had said about belief, and also conscious that Sloane's gang was in the process of carrying out a series of archaeological digs, was not as convinced as he might have been. 'But I'm not really sure. The ritual on the tablet seems to be just an instruction manual for the coronation ceremony, with an indication of the power and control over the king's subjects that follow. If I can get proof that this tablet is genuine, it will be an entirely new spin on the worship of the old gods, and the whole meaning of kingship. I mean, it dates back to when Moses was parting the waves in Egypt.' Grainger laughed.

'I'll tell you one thing, though,' continued Grainger. 'It's a good thing that both sides of the tablet have survived as well as they have.'

'What do you mean?'

'Well, there's only half the ritual on each side. I mean, if the high priest of Baal followed the instructions on one side only, without what's on the back, well, who knows what would have happened. There are some pretty dire warnings about doing the ceremony wrongly. I can guess he would have wound up sacrificed himself.' The two men laughed together, Cushing rather more nervously than Grainger.

'So what about the Templars, then?' persisted Cushing. 'If they had taken away all the stones and the crown and that stuff?'

'Fairy tales,' scoffed Grainger. 'Stuff and nonsense.'

'What if the Templars had tried to follow the rite, seven or eight hundred years ago, I mean.'

'Well, the Templars aren't really my area of expertise. You should speak to Miss Longhurst in the reading room.'

'Which one is she? All of the ladies, and gentlemen, that I've met have been very helpful.'

'But Miss Longhurst – she's one of the curators – is a bit of a specialist on the Crusades. She might be able to point you at some obscure Templar tomes. But take care, you hear? There's something of the night about her.' He laughed at his little joke, though Cushing failed to see why it was so funny. 'Good luck. And me? I'm going to carry on translating your tablet. You're sure the real thing is safe?'

Cushing blushed. He knew that one tablet was wrapped in an old gardening jersey in the crypt of his church at Albury and the other in a cricket sweater at the bottom of a wardrobe at Scott's flat at Albany, but he wasn't prepared to admit that to the archaeologist.

As the two men parted, Grainger urged Cushing to keep any of his discoveries secret. 'I want to get my name on the bottom of this paper.'

'I know,' laughed Cushing. 'You want to be an FRS!' The two men shook hands, and Cushing was confident that his secrets would be safe with Grainger, at least for a little while longer.

He returned to the reading room and asked for Miss

Longhurst. A severe-looking woman dressed in black, her grey hair in a tight bun, came out to see him.

'Miss Longhurst? I'm Christopher Cushing. Professor Grainger said that you might be able to help me with regard to some information about the Templars.'

She looked at him dismissively over her pince-nez. 'You don't look like the normal sort of treasure hunter we get in here.'

'Well, I'm not. I'm just interested in some old Babylonian artefact thingies and...' He wilted under her stare. 'I mean, if the Templars had taken any of these stone tablets with writing on, not gold or anything, I mean...'

'You mean where in Europe they might have hidden anything of value. Here we go again. Men!' She stalked round to his side of the counter. 'Come on, follow me. You can read Latin, I suppose. How is your medieval French?'

'Actually,' said Cushing, a little pompously, as they passed galleries of shelves and went up two narrow circular metal staircases, 'it's not that bad. Maybe a little rusty now. But I used to muddle through my Roman de la Rose and my Chrétien de Troyes when I was at Cambridge.'

She sniffed. 'I've been digging information out for these wretched treasure hunters for the best part of twenty years. I know exactly where to look. Here we are. This is where I always start.' She came to a chest with large shallow drawers, put on a pair of white gloves and opened one of the drawers, pulling out some sheets of parchment. Cushing reached out and she slapped at his hand, passing over another pair of gloves. 'Written by Thierry d'Armentières,' she said. 'He was one of the last crusader knights to leave the Holy Land. This document describes the siege of the last fortresses, and the boat packed with treasure that left Acre. That would have been in 1291 when it fell to the Mamelukes and the Frankish kingdoms came to an end.'

'Hmm.' Cushing looked hard at the document. 'I'm

surprised it isn't in Latin. Whoever wrote this was a Hospitaller, not a Templar. Look at the cross. The Templars wore a red cross, the Hospitallers a black cross with shorter arms.'

'I know that,' she said, pityingly. 'That's why I said crusader knight rather than Templar. Sorry, I was trying to make it simple. But I can see that you're serious, though. Almost a scholar. I'm sorry to have been so abrupt. I do get so many time wasters.'

'So,' said Cushing, scanning the document and feeling rather pleased with himself, 'Thierry writes that the treasures of Acre were placed on a boat and sent back to France.'

'Yes,' she replied. 'And no one knows what happened to the boat. It may have stopped off in Cyprus, which would have been the most obvious place for it to go, but there are no records. We can safely assume, I think, that if it did get back to France and didn't sink, most of the treasure wound up in the hands of Philip the Fair after he effectively wiped out the Templars in 1307. 13th October, to be precise. Which is the origin of the superstition about Friday the thirteenth.'

'Yes, as you say,' said Cushing, absent-mindedly, continuing to read.

'Of course the French kings were somewhat single-minded about money and power,' continued Miss Longhurst. 'They were in league with the Pope and were able to justify doing whatever they wanted. It was only a century before they turned on the Templars, you know, that the Pope preached a crusade against the Cathars, the Albigensians, in the south of France. And the French kings jumped on the bandwagon. They finally wiped out the Cathars in the middle of the thirteenth century. Very closely linked, the Cathars and the Templars, of course.'

Cushing remembered that Crowley had also mentioned the Cathars, but was concentrating on the document. 'What's this here?' he asked, interrupting her. Thierry refers to other Templar treasures, the "treasures of the north", that had been sent home by the Prince of Antioch after the fall of Jerusalem in the care of a man called Fulk de Montfort. Thierry calls him "The Guardian of Lebanon". Very grand. But where did he take them to? I can't make this out.' He spelled out the letters. 'P, Y, L, M, Y, R, E. Where's that?'

'Rather strange, I know. Yes, that's Palmyra. About 150 miles east of Damascus.'

'That can't be right, surely.' Cushing spotted that Miss Longhurst was glaring at him, presumably for contradicting her. 'I mean, begging your pardon and all that. But if these treasures were being sent home, why would they go east?'

'Maybe they were treasures originally from the east that were being sent by the Prince of Antioch as some form of payment to Saladin, and Fulk was the emissary. Jerusalem fell in 1187, a hundred years before the fall of Acre, and that triggered the Third Crusade. Maybe the Prince of Antioch thought he could save his own skin by paying some sort of tribute.'

'Or maybe Fulk was intercepted by the Saracens and robbed. Then it would have been the Saracens who took the treasures to Palmyra. It just seems unlikely that someone called "The Guardian of Lebanon" would take whatever he was guardian of and hand it over to the Saracens. Is there anything else about this Fulk de Montfort? Do we know anything about him? Where else can I look?'

'I've got all day,' said Miss Longhurst. 'Where shall we start?'

After five hours, with a break where Cushing bought the curator a cup of tea and a toasted teacake at the Museum tea rooms, they had got no further. The only de Montfort who kept cropping up in their investigations was the Simon de Montfort who led the Albigensian Crusade. Though having checked a map, Cushing could see that the Templar castle of Ras Shamra was indeed near Antioch, and so may well have been the one from which Fulk had taken the treasures of the north. He was sure that he was on the right track.

'Can we go back to the first manuscript?' he asked, by now thoroughly fed up with the whole process. She obliged, and he stabbed with his finger angrily at the page. 'Why Palmyra? It doesn't make sense.'

'Reverend Cushing!' she exclaimed angrily, and snatched his hand away from the document. 'Look at your finger. Look what you've done!' And sure enough, on his index finger was a mark, as if ink had come off the page.

'Wait a minute,' he said. 'It's all right. That's not ink. That's mouse droppings.' He looked at the page again through his glasses, and saw that one of the aged letters had changed. Whether or not it actually was mouse droppings, and he was not prepared to test his theory more closely, the "L" of the word that he had assumed to be "Palmyra" had been altered. Something had come off the manuscript, and the word now read as "P-Y-R-M-Y-R-E". 'Sorry and all that. Look, take it back, I think we've done enough today.'

As Miss Longhurst huffily replaced the precious manuscript, not noticing the difference, Cushing continued to apologise, though his mind was whirling. Where was "Pyrmyre", if not Palmyra? He needed to look that up, without arousing the suspicions of Miss Longhurst.

'I say,' he said, nervously looking at his watch. 'You've been terribly helpful. It's only four o'clock now, but would you by any chance care for a cocktail when you have finished? Just as a way of saying "thank you", I mean.'

She preened. 'Well, Reverend, that would be delightful. Though I have to work late tonight, and I won't be free till about eight o'clock?' She simpered alarmingly, but he gritted his teeth and smiled.

'Excellent. I'll see you outside the main gate, then, at eight.'

She escorted him down the stairs and into the main library. 'A bientôt,' she said, pressing a note with her telephone number into his hand.

Cushing shuddered, and immediately went back to his books. He was looking for a place called Pyrmyre. And two hours later, he was sure that he had found it. Parmoor, in Oxfordshire, between Henley and High Wycombe and only an hour from London. Parmoor had been known as Pyremere in the fourteenth century, and had been owned, at least from the reign of Henry VI, by the Knights of St. John of Jerusalem – the Hospitallers. And in the garden of Parmoor House was a huge cedar tree, reputedly grown from a seed that had been brought back from Lebanon at the time of the Crusades. So, he mused, Fulk de Montfort could have taken treasures from Ras Shamra, which was just to the north of Antioch, to England, and planted the cedar tree when he arrived. 'Tally ho!' he shouted, and was quickly hushed by a barrage of hissing from affronted readers and librarians.

Parmoor. Now where had he heard that name recently? Of course. Lord Parmoor, the prominent socialist politician who had been at the Midsummer Ball with Sir Charles Sloane. Was this coincidence or something more sinister? A bell rang, announcing the impending closure of the library. He packed his papers into his briefcase, returned the books and went out, blinking, into the daylight.

He had planned not to meet Stockington until he had more information. He was struggling to work out how to explain developments, especially the death of Page, when he had only given Stockington half the story in the first place. While he would have preferred to keep his cards close to his chest for a little longer, however, he felt that he owed the man an update, especially as he was now concerned about his own safety.

He arrived at the café in Villiers Street shortly after half past six and found Stockington finishing his coffee. Cushing thanked Stockington for the introduction to Crowley, and told him of some of his findings.

'This seems to have become some sort of archaeological wild goose chase,' demurred Stockington. 'You're supposed to be investigating why two people have been murdered, not hunting buried treasure.'

'Three, actually.'

'What?'

'Three people. Murdered.' Cushing explained about Page, and gave more detail about his concerns about Domvile, for whom it seems that Page had also been working. 'And I'm actually worried that they may be on to me.'

'Why so?'

Cushing showed the red-haired Stockington the letter, and explained his fears.

'I don't think you have anything to worry about,' replied Stockington. 'But let's walk a while, and see if anyone follows us.'

They did, for about twenty minutes, before Stockington pronounced that he was sure that it was safe. As they walked, Stockington explained that his investigations were all hitting brick walls – suspiciously so, he thought. Having been taken off Horchdienst and moved to a staff job, he had not even been able to pursue any more investigations into the Synarchists.

'Well you be careful too,' said Cushing. 'One hint that you are on to them and Domvile could get rid of you as well.'

'Thank you,' replied Stockington. 'I hope I can look after myself. But that's good advice. I try not to make it obvious that I am asking questions.'

'Keep in touch,' he said, as Cushing hailed a taxi back to the British Museum. He was only slightly reassured, and the added weight of the German pistol in his briefcase gave him further comfort.

Waiting for him at the Museum gate was Miss Longhurst. He groaned inwardly, and escorted the elderly blue-stocking to a nearby pub. It was a small price to pay for serving his country.

12

Tuesday 3rd July 1928

On Cushing's return to Scott's flat after drinks with Miss Longhurst – he had made his excuses and fled before feeling obliged to invite her to dinner – he had looked up Parmoor on a map, and noted that it was less than ten miles from Longley Hall. Lord Parmoor and Sir Charles Sloane were practically neighbours. Maybe it was more than coincidence? Cushing was beginning to hatch a plan, and knew that he needed to be careful, just in case.

Suddenly fearful, he telephoned both Rafferty at the Athenaeum and Mrs. Sturdy, and was pleased to find that no one suspicious had been looking for him. He then called Badger, and the two men agreed to meet for lunch the following day at the Lyons Corner House in Shaftesbury Avenue.

He poured himself a whisky and grappled with his conscience for a while, then made his mind up and lifted the telephone receiver once again. He sent a telegram to Gussie wishing her well and inviting her to join him and Badger for lunch, then knocked back the rest of his whisky and went to bed.

He slept poorly. Not just the thoughts whirling round his brain, nor his fears that the Germans were on his tail; when he did fall asleep, he was also plagued by hideous nightmares. He blamed this on his meeting with Crowley, and guessed that the vile images he could not shake off had come from that loathsome little man.

He woke early and paced around the flat, struggling to find the right words to describe his plan to Gussie. The phone rang and he jumped nervously.

'Hello, Mayfair oh two double nine. Geoffrey Scott's residence.' It was Gussie responding to his telegram, and despite his careful planning he became tongue-tied. Not that he needed to speak at all: Gussie enthused about the Laird's party so much that he could hardly get a word in edgeways. He was delighted, however, that she confirmed that she was able to join him for lunch.

He walked up the damp London streets towards the bustling restaurant and found Badger already there. Cushing began to pour out his theories. Badger was excited, though for a while he seemed to be more concerned about Miss Longhurst. 'She'll have you for breach of promise, if you're not careful,' he laughed. But soon he became fully attentive, listening to Cushing's conjecture about how Fulk de Montfort had taken certain Templar treasures from Ras Shamra, via Antioch, to Parmoor.

'Of course the house is all brand new – well, last century, anyway,' said Cushing. 'But the connections with the Hospitallers are clear. We have to go there.'

Gussie arrived, fashionably late, and Cushing introduced her to Badger. The two immediately chatted warmly before she spent a quarter of an hour gushing about the ninetieth birthday of the MacGlish, much of which Cushing had already heard on the telephone. 'Oh Christopher, you should have been there.'

Cushing sighed, but let her continue. He wished he had been there, of course. But after Badger cleared his throat noisily and the cheerful uniformed waitress had come twice to take their orders, he brought the conversation back to his findings about Parmoor.

'So what's your plan, darling?' asked Gussie. 'You can't just walk up to the front door and ask to search the place.'

'Well,' said Cushing, a little shiftily, 'I wondered whether you might be able to help.'

'Me? What can I do?'

'Well, I know you chase people for money on behalf of charities. And I think you know Lady Parmoor. Is there any way in which you could contact her and say that you are raising funds for some charity or other? If you say it is for bringing the gospel to darkest Africa, or something like that, then Badger and I could come with you.'

'Well I suppose…. I mean of course I know Marian – Lady Parmoor, I mean – but….'

'Good girl. We'll go back to Scott's flat after lunch and you can give her a call.'

Gussie was shocked at Cushing's cheek and muttered crossly into her pudding, though gradually began to smile. The two men began to concoct a suitable story which they could use to justify asking Lady Parmoor for a donation.

They strolled back to Albany and Gussie, rather against her better judgment, telephoned Lady Parmoor. She insisted that the two clergymen did not listen to her conversation, but called them back into the room when she had finished.

'You're in luck,' she said. 'Marian is leaving for Paris tomorrow – she's meeting her husband there – but she is at home this afternoon. So if you have your car with you, my dear man, we can be there by teatime.' She banged her hand onto her forehead with a theatrical gesture. 'How did I let myself be talked into this? She's my friend, damn it.'

'Now, Gussie, dear…'

'Don't you "Gussie dear" me, Christopher Cushing! And

you're just as bad,' she said, as Badger tried to interrupt. 'You pair of rogues.' And she started to laugh. 'Oh stop looking like a couple of guilty schoolboys. Come on, tell me about this "charity" that we're going to represent.'

'We?' asked Cushing.

'Absolutely. I'm part of the team, aren't I?'

With a wide grin still on his face, Cushing drove his two friends to Oxfordshire in his elderly Morris car. The rain had lifted; it had become a lovely afternoon and the English countryside was at its finest.

Before leaving, Cushing hastily scribbled a letter to Scott in Deauville: he felt guilty about staying in Scott's rooms without specifically telling him. He had also pestered Rafferty and Mrs. Sturdy once again. There was nothing abnormal to report, and Cushing was becoming reassured that Page's letter to him had not got into the hands of the enemy.

As they drove through Marlow, Gussie started to tell Badger all about the Midsummer Ball, but Cushing shivered slightly as he recalled how he had found the secret room, with Hitchcock's blood on the windowsill, and how Sloane and the mysterious John had casually planned the murder of Page.

They continued through the pretty hamlet of Frieth and eventually up the ample drive of Parmoor House. The house, a fine brick building, was dominated by a vast cedar tree that stood only some thirty or forty yards from it. Cushing parked the car and the three walked up to the door and rang the bell. Gussie looked askance at Cushing, and queried why he was carrying a walking stick. He winked knowingly, but did not have to answer as a severe-looking butler answered the door and took them past a massive oak staircase to the drawing room.

While they waited, Cushing gazed through the window at

the huge cedar, then at some of the paintings on the wall. Among various pictures of the family, some captioned as Sir Alfred and Lady Cripps – Cushing recalled that their host had been ennobled shortly before the War – were a few of the house and its predecessor, a more modest brick building with expansive Tudor chimneys. Cushing called the others to look more closely at one of the paintings.

'Look at the legend here,' he said. 'The picture is dated 1806 and it shows the cedar tree. It calls the tree "The Guardian of Lebanon". That's what Fulk de Montfort was called. This must be it.'

But the others were unable to comment as the door opened and Lady Parmoor entered. 'Marian, darling,' said Gussie, kissing Lady Parmoor on both cheeks and introducing Cushing and Badger. Cushing vaguely recognised her from the Midsummer Ball, though they had not spoken; she showed no sign of recognising him, for which he was grateful. Lady Parmoor was a fine-looking woman, obviously somewhat younger than her husband, and Cushing recalled Gussie telling them that she was the second Lady Parmoor. She welcomed the two churchmen and offered them tea.

Under the guise of making polite conversation, Cushing could not stop himself from asking Lady Parmoor about the history of the house.

'There has been a house on this site since before the Domesday Book,' she said. 'Not the same house, of course – it's been knocked down, rebuilt and added to many times over the centuries. My husband's late father did a lot of research on the history, and the owners of all the different properties all seemed to in the wrong place at the wrong time. The Yorkists were persecuted by the Lancastrians, the Lancastrians persecuted by the Yorkists, the Catholics by the Protestants, the Templars – well, we never seemed to get it right.'

They laughed politely, though Cushing blushed slightly at her mention of Templars.

'My husband's family also carried out a lot of restoration work, as I gather the old place had gone to rack and ruin. The main building is all in good order now, though the old Dower House and many of the outbuildings are still just piles of rubble.' She smiled mirthlessly and poured more tea. 'Maybe we should get to work on rebuilding the Dower House for me before my stepson inherits everything.'

'Plenty of time for that, Marian,' said Gussie, tartly, and Cushing sought to change the subject a little.

'And the tree, Lady Parmoor,' he said, pointing out of the window. 'The cedar that appears in so many of the paintings. It's a fine specimen.'

'Ah, well, there are lots of stories about that tree,' she replied. 'It is supposed to have been grown from a seed planted by a knight who returned from the Holy Land.'

'I see from that picture that it is called "The Guardian of Lebanon". Why is that?'

'Just because of the old crusader who planted the seed, I imagine,' she said. 'It's always been known as that. Cedars of Lebanon, you know. Like the ones they used to build the temple in Jerusalem.'

'Fascinating,' said Cushing, a little hurriedly. 'You did mention that the house belonged to the Knights of the Temple.' After his conversation with Miss Longhurst, Cushing had hoped that Lady Parmoor might have made a reference to the Hospitallers.

'That was several houses ago. Ancient history, I'm afraid.'

'So is there no crusader history left at all, Marian?' interrupted Gussie. 'In the house, I mean?'

'Well, as I say, there has been so much rebuilding work there is nothing left, apart from some of the old cellars. The old Tudor house was apparently riddled with tunnels, priest holes and what have you. It was the Catholics who had to a lot of hiding, of course, back in the sixteenth century. Some of the tunnels were built even earlier, dating back to the Wars of the Roses. Apparently there was one old tunnel that went from the cellar below the kitchen all the way to the Dower House. It was all far too dangerous, of course, and falling down, so Charles's father had the lot blocked off.' She put down her tea cup. 'Now, why don't you tell me a little more about this charity?'

Cushing blushed and started to explain the need for aid to support church schools in Northern Rhodesia. Badger gave splendid support and, though the two stumbled a little about some of the detail of their imaginary venture, Lady Parmoor was happy to go to a small desk and write a cheque for a hundred pounds.

'To whom shall I make the cheque payable?' she asked.

Both men looked horrified – they had forgotten to attend to this particular detail in their planning. Gussie made signs at them from the other side of the room behind Lady Parmoor's back, and stabbed her finger at Badger.

'To me, please,' said Badger. Gussie shook her head and Lady Parmoor turned round with a quizzical expression on her face. 'No, no, I mean to my church. That will be best. St. Jude's, please. Thank you, Lady Parmoor.'

'Yes, thank you, Marian,' said Gussie, glaring at Badger. 'Now, Marian, you must have so much to do if you're taking the boat train for Paris tomorrow morning. Gentlemen, shall we leave Marian to her business?'

'Yes, of course,' said Cushing. 'But I'm terribly sorry, Lady Parmoor, I'm afraid I'm not feeling very well. A touch of malaria when I was a lad, and then a spot of bother during the War. I think I've just got a little too warm. Would you mind if I just got some fresh air before we leave? Perhaps a little stroll round the grounds for fifteen minutes or so?'

Lady Parmoor immediately gave her consent, looking concerned, and brushed aside Gussie's protestations that he would be "absolutely fine once we get into the car". 'You poor man, of course.' She pointed out of the window at a bench and table on the lawns. 'Go and sit outside for as long as you need. I have to go, but I'll send Hipson out with some cold lemonade. Off you go.' She turned to the others. 'Reverend Brock, how nice to meet you, do let me know how the school project develops. Gussie, darling, I am sure I'll see you soon in London.' The two women kissed again and Cushing, playing up his frailty, walked gingerly out of the front door and towards the gardens.

A few minutes later the three were sitting on the bench sipping their lemonade. 'Are you all right, sir?' asked Badger.

'Of course he is,' barked Gussie. 'What are you up to, Christopher?'

'I'm a little better now,' he said, and smiled. 'Yes of course, I'm absolutely fine. But I couldn't think of a better way to take a closer look at that cedar. The Guardian of Lebanon indeed. I wish we could have access to those old tunnels Lady Parmoor mentioned.'

'She's my friend, damn it,' said Gussie, angrily. 'I'm not having you trespassing on her property.'

'We're not trespassing. She said we could have a stroll in the fresh air,' replied Cushing mildly. 'And that's all we're going to do. Promise.' He limped off, leaning on his stick in case anyone was watching from the house, and Badger followed. Gussie, rolling her eyes, joined them at the tree, which was in fact quite close to the house. It was a splendid specimen, tall and old, some of its heavy dark branches bending almost to touch the grass.

They walked round the tree, then bent below the low branches which partially shielded them from observation from the house. Close to the trunk was a huge badger sett and evidence of recent activity from its occupants. Fresh earth had been turned over and Cushing absent-mindedly rooted through the spoil with his stick. Suddenly he knelt down, regardless of the mud on his trousers. He picked something up, and started to clean mud from it with his handkerchief.

'What have you got there, Christopher,' asked Gussie, sulkily.

'It's just an old coin, I think,' he said. 'A very old coin.' He stood up and poked around more with his stick, then shrugged his shoulders. 'Come on, I think we have overstayed our welcome.'

Gussie agreed and walked out from under the shade of the cedar, Cushing chivalrously lifting the low branches to make sure that she did not snag her hat or jacket. She started to walk back towards the house and realised that Cushing had stopped. She watched him staring at the coin he had found through his reading glasses, and then walking energetically the other way. She tripped after him. 'Christopher. Christopher! Where are you going?'

Cushing stopped to wait for her and Badger to catch him up and pointed. 'Look over here. Just down there, in that dip. Those ruins. That will be the old Dower House.'

'Yes, I know. Marian said so.'

'But don't you see,' said Cushing, walking closer towards the ruins, the others following. 'We know that Fulk de Montfort was called the Guardian of Lebanon, just like the tree. This coin...'

'What about it?

'It's a silver penny from the reign of King John. 1199 to 1216.'

'Which would be exactly right for Fulk de Montfort's arrival in England,' mused Badger.

'Exactly,' enthused Cushing. 'Fulk de Montfort's artefacts – the ones that everyone seems to be looking for. Maybe they were buried at the same time as this coin was lost. The old tunnels have to be the answer. Lady Parmoor said that a tunnel led from the house to the Dower House. The ruins are only a couple of hundred yards away from the main house, and the cedar tree is on a direct line between the two...'

'Now look here, Christopher Cushing. We are not imposing on my friend for one moment more.'

Cushing's shoulders slumped. 'Fair enough, Gussie. Come on then, let's go and get the car.' He grinned boyishly. 'We passed a nice-looking pub in Frieth. I think we deserve a pint.'

'We're going to have to go back,' said Cushing, cheerfully, as he and Badger waved goodbye to Gussie outside her Chelsea home.

'I know, sir,' replied Badger, phlegmatically. 'But Mrs. Gordon is going to be really unhappy.'

'We'd better not tell her then,' grinned Cushing, and the two drove back into the centre of London.

'So what exactly are we looking for?'

'I'm not sure, obviously. But it makes sense to me that whatever it is – and we think that Sloane and his gang are looking for it too – was buried at the same time as the tree was planted.'

'Then we will need to get down those tunnels as quickly as we can and take a look.'

'Good man. That's what I thought. Lady Parmoor is away tomorrow, so we could probably sneak in after dark...'

'We could do that, but I've got a better idea,' said Badger, encouragingly. 'Let's just walk through the front door. Well, drive through the gates, I mean.'

'What's your plan?'

'Well, we think there's a tunnel going from the big house to the Dower House, as near as dammit under the tree. We can't break into the house or dig up the tree, so we'll just have to find the entrance to the tunnel from the ruins of the Dower House. Lady Parmoor said it was an escape route for the Catholics, didn't she?'

'Exactly. But we can't just march in and start digging up the Dower House.'

'We won't be digging it up. We'll pretend to be from the local council, shoring up the unsafe ruins. We can work out the details later. Don't worry, I know just the people who can help us. Tell you what, sir, would you mind dropping me back in Whitechapel? I need to call in some favours and it's starting to get late.'

'How long will you need?'

'Well as long as I can get hold of Lennie and his boys before midnight, and Donald is around to knock together some decent documentation – well, sir, how about if you have your car ready to leave at six in the morning?'

'Six in the morning? For heaven's sake, Badger, I thought you meant weeks, or days. Who are these people?'

'Old friends. Don't worry, sir. I'm in your line of work now, not theirs. Trust me.'

Badger was as good as his word. To avoid waking the prying Clarence, Cushing was standing in Piccadilly next to his car as a large and elderly lorry, clearly of Great War vintage, wheezed into view and pulled up alongside. Badger jumped out, followed by the driver and two more men from the cab of the lorry, which Cushing noticed was freshly painted with the words "Oxfordshire County Council". They were immediately joined by two others who uncurled themselves from the tarpaulin-covered piles of equipment on the rear. Badger introduced Cushing as "Father Christopher" and the men greeted him enthusiastically and shook hands.

'This is Lenny,' said Badger, indicating a lean young man wearing a flat cap who had been driving the lorry. 'And these are Maurice, Jim, Chalky and Fred. Would you mind giving some of the lads a lift?'

'Not at all,' said Cushing, a little bewildered, 'but…'

'Thank you, sir,' said Maurice, squeezing his bulky frame into the back of Cushing's small car. 'It's a bit uncomfortable in the back of that lorry.'

Cushing turned to Badger. 'But how did you…'

'Just called in a few favours, as I said I would,' grinned Badger.

'That's right, sir,' said Lenny. 'But it's nothing to do with favours. Anything me and the lads can do for Father Badger, he only has to ask. Shall we get going, sir?'

Badger and Jim crammed into the car and a bemused Cushing followed the lorry through the suburbs of London. Jim pressed an enormous sandwich into his hand as he drove, and Maurice produced a flask of hot sweet tea. 'Just like old times, sir,' he said, dusting sandwich crumbs from his enormous beard.

'What do you mean?' asked Cushing, swigging tea as he drove.

'Well, sir, Father Badger said there was going to be some digging in an old tunnel. I used to be a sapper in the last lot.' He shivered. 'Mind you, I never thought I'd be going down any more holes after that.'

All of the men were silent for several minutes, their minds back in wartime France, before Cushing cleared his throat.

'So what's the plan?'

'Simple,' said Badger. 'Lenny and the boys are going to be from the local council, you see. The story is that there have been complaints. Some local kids come and play in the ruins of the Dower House, and one of them is now in hospital. So the council have to make it safe, cordon it off, that sort of thing. Repairs. Just like I said yesterday – though we've got some excellent authorisation papers now.'

'But how?'

'Well a friend of mine called Donald was up all night doing

the paperwork. One of the best in the business, Donald.' Badger whistled, casually.

'But surely Lady Parmoor...'

'Will have left to catch the boat train by the time we get there. The domestic staff may have seen you and me yesterday, but they won't have seen Lenny. And Lenny has a way with words, if you know what I mean. One of the best old school con artists...'

'I don't think you should be telling me,' interrupted Cushing.

'Don't you worry, sir,' grunted Maurice from the back seat, stuffing another sandwich into his mouth. 'We'll see you right.'

It was eight o'clock in the morning when they pulled into the side of the road in Frieth and Jim and Maurice returned to the lorry. Badger and Lenny exchanged a few words and Lenny steered the coughing lorry up the drive of Parmoor House. Cushing parked outside the separate entrance to the Dower House and waited, smoking nervously.

'I wouldn't worry,' said Badger, calmly. 'Though you might want to lose the dog-collar before too many people see us.' Cushing hurriedly wrapped a scarf around his neck as the lorry drew up next to them. Lenny leaned out of the window, beaming expansively, and gave the two clergymen a thumbs-up sign. 'Piece of cake, Father Badger,' he said. 'Donald done us proud. Let's go.'

After donning overalls, Cushing and Badger joined the other five in the ruins of the Dower House. They could see the roof of the big house a couple of hundred yards away, the enormous cedar tree directly in front of it. Jim and Chalky – a tall black man – were immediately put to the task of cordoning off the area, as the spurious council authorisation had said they would do.

'So where do we start, sir?' asked Lenny, as Maurice and Fred started to unload digging equipment.

'Well,' said Cushing. 'I imagine the tunnel from the cellars of the big house would have led to the cellars of the Dower House. So that's our first target, the cellars. Now the best place to start would probably be the kitchen. Where on earth do you think that have been?'

It was clearly going to be a difficult task. Some of the remaining walls were above head height, but stone and brick had collapsed and been picked over by scavengers for a hundred years, and the whole area was overgrown. A rough bothy had been created, presumably by workmen on the estate to shelter from the weather over the years, and empty beer bottles and traces of discarded food were still present. 'Look for the fireplaces and chimneys,' said Cushing. 'They are most likely to have survived.'

It took more than an hour before they were agreed on which part of the ruins had been the kitchen, and then Maurice, the former Royal Engineer, took charge. Another hour and a half of intensive digging, and then Maurice went back to the lorry and returned with a heavy box. 'Give me some room here please, gentlemen,' he said, and Cushing observed Lenny and Fred moving quickly to crouch behind a thick wall. 'Come on, sir,' called Lenny, and Badger took Cushing by the arm and led him to join the others. Maurice joined them, a metal box with a small plunger in his hands. 'Ready?' he asked, and pressed the plunger.

There was the muffled crump of an explosion and a shower of earth and small stones fell around them. Maurice peered over the wall. 'That should have done the business,' he said, happily, and walked back to inspect the results of his work.

'We're into the cellars,' he called. 'Careful now. Bring some light.'

The former sapper checked to make sure that the roof would not collapse on top of them, and then carefully lit lanterns as the group of men, also carrying flashlights, came down the ladder. The air was stale and thick with dust from the explosion, the floor covered with the detritus of ages, and the men had to cover their faces with scarves and handkerchiefs to enable them to breathe.

'We're looking for a door to the tunnel,' said Maurice, but

there was clearly nothing to be seen. 'Are you sure we should be looking in the cellars?'

'Well that's the obvious place for an escape tunnel to be,' replied Cushing, a little defensively. 'Unless...'

'Unless what?' asked Badger, his face ghostly with dust in the beam of the flashlight.

'Well, not "unless", but the tunnel might run straight to a chapel.'

'What chapel?'

'There would have to be a chapel of some sort. If this tunnel dates back to the Reformation, after the dissolution of the monasteries, you would expect the Catholics to have had a secret place to worship. Maybe...' He faltered, conscious of Maurice glaring at him. 'Maybe the chapel is underground, part of another cellar. You keep looking down here. Badger, you and Fred come with me and we'll see if we can find any trace of it at ground level.'

They left Maurice methodically tapping at the cellar walls and emerged into the sunlight, Cushing rubbing his eyes. They continued to search, but, after only fifteen minutes or so, they were conscious of another small explosion. Lenny's head popped out of the hole into the cellar and he beckoned them back down.

Maurice was standing in front of a hole in the cellar wall, grinning. 'You were right, sir. There's another part to the cellar, through here. It would be your chapel.' He waved the flashlight negligently. 'Looks like a statue, at least, from what I can see. Give us another hour and we'll be through.'

Cushing and Badger could hardly contain their excitement when Maurice announced that the chapel was safe. They returned underground and squeezed their way through the enlarged hole in the wall to find a substantial room that could easily have taken thirty or forty worshippers. The roof had been propped up at strategic points, and the room was lit with flickering lanterns. Cushing pointed out where the faces of the various statues had long ago been chiselled off.

'What's that all about?' asked Lenny.

'Part of the Reformation,' said Cushing. 'Removing the idolatry associated with Catholic imagery. The reformers wanted to simplify everything: the bible, the statues, the style of worship...'

'Quite barbaric really,' said Badger. 'They were able to strip out a lot of gold and jewels as well, of course.'

Cushing looked at him oddly. 'Well at least it shows we're in the right place for the tunnel to be a proper escape route. Well done, Maurice. Now, how about finding us a door into the tunnel from here?'

Maurice beamed proudly. 'Take a look here,' he said, pointing at where two or three stones had been removed from the wall. 'This is newer than the rest of the building. This was the entrance, see, and it's been bricked up.' He prised another stone from the wall and pushed it. 'Now what have we got here,' he asked, as the stone fell to the floor. He shone the beam of his flashlight through the hole. 'Looks like – yes! That's a result.'

'What is it?'

'This is your tunnel alright, sir,' said the sapper.

One by one Badger, then Cushing, then the others peered through the hole. Cushing looked at the remnants of the ancient vaulted roof of the tunnel. 'We've found it. Well done, Maurice. Well done, lads.'

The men felt that they had earned some lunch, though Maurice had to be torn away from his work. They left Jim and Chalky to keep an eye on the dig – Cushing could not help but think of it as a dig, their efforts being like those of a proper archaeological excavation. He recalled the newspaper coverage of Lord Caernarvon and Howard Carter in Egypt and those of Schaeffer in Ugarit.

Cushing and Badger made an attempt to tidy themselves and dress more appropriately, then drove to the Yew Tree in Frieth.

Over well-earned beer, lemonade and sandwiches, they agreed to take a couple of rooms in the pub, not knowing for how long they would have to stay. Maurice and Lenny were anxious to leave as soon as they could and, taking bottles of beer for Jim and Chalky, drove back to the Dower House. Cushing and Badger were not long behind them, but as they inched down into the cellars they were met by Maurice.

'I think you had better leave us to it,' he said. 'Off you go, sir. Mind you, some tea would be nice.'

For the next few hours, Cushing and Badger were reduced to making tea on a primus stove as the others worked in shifts, and taking mugs and packs of sandwiches down the ladder. They paced impatiently around the ruins of the Dower House, trying to anticipate what the men below were doing, and smoked all the cigarettes they had while they were waiting. They were jealous of Fred and Jim who calmly snatched forty winks in the sunshine when they came up for a rest.

'I'm glad Mrs. Gordon doesn't know we're here, sir,' said Badger. 'She would probably find some good reason why we shouldn't...'

'Why we shouldn't break in to one of her friend's houses and blow up the old Dower House? Frankly she might have a point.'

At about half past five, the muscular figure of Maurice reappeared. 'Proper council workers would be knocking off soon, sir,' he said. 'It will look suspicious if the lorry is here for much longer. We need to unload the rest of the pit props, then could you drive it somewhere safe for us?'

When Cushing and Badger returned, Lenny was on sentry duty. 'It might be worth taking a look downstairs now, sir,' he said. 'Maurice is doing a grand job.' Leaving Lenny, they went down the ladder and cautiously edged down the tunnel. It was nearly head height, and Maurice and his colleagues had cleared fallen debris and propped up the ceiling at regular intervals. Lanterns flickered and Cushing could admire the worked stone of the walls and ceilings. 'These walls are old – medieval,' he breathed. 'Pre-Reformation, I think. Much older than the chapel.'

As they picked their way along the tunnel, Cushing began to shiver again, thinking of the work that Maurice and his fellow sappers had done under enemy trenches during the War. He could hear voices and, after only a hundred feet or so, his flashlight picked out the huge figure of Chalky lifting a prop to support the wall while Fred and Jim pulled rock and brick away.

'Hello there, sir,' said Maurice, cheerfully. 'Slow progress, I'm afraid. We're in for a long night. Look, you two go back to the pub. We'll join you by and by when we need a break, and otherwise just keep at it.'

Cushing tried to dissuade him, but Maurice was adamant. 'Don't worry, sir – we'll come and get you if we find anything.'

After a well-earned bath, Cushing and Badger sat in the bar of the Yew Tree, Cushing nursing a half pint of beer and Badger a lemonade. Both men were largely silent, frustrated at their inability to contribute. Maurice, Lenny, Fred and Jim had come in for a drink and given them updates, and taken more provisions for Chalky who had again been left on guard. Night fell and, as the clock moved towards closing time, Badger shrugged. 'We might just as well try and get some shuteye,' he said.

Cushing lay on his bed, unable to sleep, listening to the ticking of the clock, hoping that any moment he would be summoned to the dig. Eventually he did fall asleep, fully clothed, only to wake with a start on hearing an unexpected noise. Immediately alert, he heard the sound of another stone coming through the open window and rattling across the floor. He leapt to his feet and leaned out of the window, just in time to dodge a third pebble. He could see Fred crouching by the hedge. 'What's happening?' he asked, in a stage whisper.

'We're all the way to the big house, sir.'

'I'll be down in a moment.' Cushing quickly washed, then checked the clock and was surprised to find that it was almost two o'clock in the morning. He crossed the landing and woke Badger, and the two men crept downstairs. They passed the old black labrador snoring gently by the bar and quietly left the pub. Greeting Fred, they decided to drive to the Dower House where they met Jim who gave the three of them a thumbs-up sign. The ruins glimmered in the ghostly moonlight. They changed back into overalls and descended into the underground chapel and along the tunnel.

Though it was only perhaps a couple of hundred yards down the tunnel, the uneven floor and the need to duck regularly made it seem longer, and Cushing and Badger were impressed at what a masterful job Maurice and the others had done in such a short time. They finally reached the end to find Maurice, Lenny and Chalky, filthy and dog-tired, sitting by the last set of pit props drinking tea. Cushing silently offered them a half bottle of brandy he had bought at the Yew Tree and they accepted it gratefully.

'This is as far as we go, sir,' said Maurice. 'By my calculations we are right up next to the big house. There's been a big fall from the roof. We've cleared it, but you can see all this new brick.' He flashed his light towards it. 'You said as how it had been closed up a few years back because it was unsafe. So nothing – just one big red herring.' He spat expressively towards the new wall and took another swig of brandy.

Cushing's shoulders slumped in sympathy with the exhausted men. 'And nothing on the way? No forks in the tunnel?'

'Nothing we've seen,' piped in Lenny, and Chalky shook his head in agreement.

'Never mind,' said Maurice. 'All in a day's work, eh? Anyway, we'd better get back so we can close the entrance properly. We don't want to leave the place so kids can come down here and really hurt themselves.'

'Hang on,' said Cushing. 'Can I check something? The Guardian of Lebanon.'

'What do you mean?'

'We found the coin under the roots of the tree. If this tunnel goes under the tree, or at least close to it...'

Maurice jumped up excitedly. 'That's an idea, sir. Go on up and pace it out, or measure it exactly if you've got some string.'

'There's a ball of string in the car, I think, but not enough.'

'Then take a couple of the lads and pace it out. Get back as quick as you can. It should still be dark.'

Cushing and Badger left the others carefully checking the walls one more time and, along with Jim, paced out the distance from the chapel to the cedar tree as accurately as they could, then repeated the process. Cushing realised that it would have been easier to measure a shorter distance from the house to the tree, but preferred not to risk being seen, even though only the faintest light of dawn was beginning to appear in the sky. As they returned, they saw Lenny's grinning face. 'Blimey, sir, you should see you all. If I didn't know what you were up to I'd think you'd all been drinking.'

They chuckled, and Cushing led them all back down the ladder. He started to pace out the distance he had measured, which was a difficult task on the uneven floor. When he eventually stopped, Badger passed him and continued by a few feet, and Jim carried on for several yards. 'Right,' he said. 'We're within a few feet of one another. Look carefully around here.' The others came close and Cushing raised his flashlight to the ceiling where some roof supports had been positioned and pointed at an area where the bricks were bulging. Maurice carefully prodded the spot and there was a worrying shower of dust and brick fragments. Again, Cushing recognised the fear of being buried alive that Maurice had faced every day during the War. As the dust settled, the men could see a large root visible where the masonry had fallen away.

'We must be close.'

Maurice continued to tap the walls, and Cushing inched along after him. He stopped, noticing a different pattern in the brickwork. 'Look here. These bricks are different, newer, laid in a different pattern.'

Maurice drummed the wall again. 'You may be right. Here, stand back.' Fred passed him a crowbar and he began to prise some of the bricks away. He then leaned back and picked up a sledgehammer which he handed to Chalky. 'Here we go, mate, you have a stab at it.' The big man took a swing at the wall and brick splinters flew in all directions. Suddenly there was a hole, and bricks fell in through it. Cushing took his flashlight and peered through.

'What can you see, sir?' asked Chalky, breathlessly.

Cushing swallowed hard. 'Beautiful, beautiful things,' he muttered. 'There's another vaulted ceiling, or what's left of it. And it looks like a statue. This must have been bricked up by the Tudors, or the Catholics, or the Hospitallers, or someone. It would have been...'

'Careful, sir,' interrupted Maurice. 'Those roots will have played merry hell with the ceiling. Let's shore it up safely, then we can look properly.'

The next half hour felt as long as any that Cushing could remember in his life. Maurice and Chalky widened the entrance and supported it with strengthening props. Cushing tried to flash his light past them to see more, but without success. Finally, having gone through the entrance to check, Maurice pronounced himself satisfied. 'All right, sir. Steady as we go. The ceiling is well made but the roots have damaged it, and it looks like badgers have been down here.' He looked round at Lenny. 'Badgers for Father Badger. That's a good one.' He was unable to see the pained expression on his friend's face. 'Other than the roots, though, and all the badger – er, droppings – it's just like the crypt at St. Paul's.

Your area of expertise, sir. Over to you now. I think you've found what you're looking for.'

Cushing thanked him and hurriedly took his flashlight. He wriggled through the gap, brushing spiders' webs from his hair and jacket and joining Lenny who was already placing lanterns around the chamber. Badger and Maurice joined them.

They were standing on a small area of flagstoned floor, covered with earth and brick from the fractured wall and ceiling. None of them, however, was looking at the ceiling. Cushing quietly pointed the beam of his flashlight down towards the stone effigy of an armed knight resting on a carved stone tomb. 'Look, the helmet, sword and shield. And the cross on the shield is a Hospitaller cross. His legs are crossed too. That means he went to the Holy Land, I think.' He went closer, reverently, and read the inscription that was still visible on the side of the tomb.

'Hic iacet – here lies...'

'Yes I know,' muttered Badger.

'Sorry. Here lies Fulk de Montfort, Knight of the Hospital of St. John of Jerusalem, Guardian of Lebanon. Died MCCI – that's 1201. He rests in death in sight of the relics he swore to guard in life.'

The men looked at one other and Lenny was the first to speak. 'So where are these relics then?' he asked. All flashed their lights around the floor, and could see nothing, until Badger played his light along the wall and gave a low whistle.

'Look, sir. On the wall, behind the tomb. It's another Hospitaller cross carved into the wall. No, it's not carved into the wall. It's on a piece of carved stone, like a tombstone set into a church wall. And the inscription is just the year again.'

'No it's not, it's a different year – it's MCCVIIII. That's 1209. What happened in 1209?'

'But look,' said Badger again. 'The stone has come away from the wall where the roots have come through the ceiling.

The cedar must have been planted to mark Fulk's grave. But look at the stone. There's something behind it. Here, lads, give me a bunk up.'

In fact it was Maurice who lifted Lenny and helped him to prise the stone gently from the wall. Lenny, sweating heavily and sitting uncomfortably on Maurice's shoulders, reached in and started to drag out a chest, about two feet long. Lenny teetered and looked as if he were about to drop the chest, but, before he could do so, the rotten wood began to fall apart. It was held together with ancient and rusted metal bands, and Cushing and Badger were able to take it safely before it fell to the floor in pieces.

Cushing could easily pull bits of wood away to reveal the contents: a package, wrapped in oiled silk. He unwrapped the silk carefully, Badger and the others leaning over his shoulder, and could see that it was a small box, about nine inches long. Its metal surface was still bright. He wrapped it again. 'Is there anything else here? We need to get away before the ceiling caves in – and open the box.'

'There's a lot of broken stone,' said Badger. 'A couple of old cressets, an old oil lamp. I can't see any other inscriptions. Nothing else here.'

'I'm sure I saw the glint of gold in the beam of my flashlight,' said Cushing. 'Candlesticks, perhaps?' The others shrugged, and Cushing could not see Lenny winking broadly at Maurice behind his back and giving him a thumbs-up sign.

Maurice interrupted. 'Wishful thinking, sir. I think we should go sooner rather than later. I'm worried about the ceiling.' As if to emphasise his point, there was a small fall of earth and stone.

'Then let's go,' concurred Cushing.

'But what about Fulk?' asked Badger.

'I'm not going to start grave-robbing. He's had a Christian burial, and that's the way he is going to stay.'

'Yes, of course,' agreed Badger. 'Come on, lads, give me a hand.' The men crawled back through the opening and an anxious Chalky risked a good look at the tomb himself. As he pulled himself out, there was a rumbling and another fall of earth and stone from within the crypt.

'Come on, lads, let's go, now,' urged Maurice, and the others needed no further encouragement. Picking up tools and lanterns as they went, they were soon out in the fresh air once again, shaking hands as Cushing passed round his bottle.

Dawn had broken while they were in the tunnel, and Maurice frowned. 'All right lads. We need to conceal all of this. Let me set one more charge and blow the entrance shut. The rest of you, just try and camouflage where we've been. Father Christopher, would you mind taking Lenny back to wherever you've left the lorry? We need to load up and get out of here before anyone sees us.'

Cushing wrapped the metal box and its silk cover in an old sack and placed it carefully in his car, jumping at the noise of another explosion behind him. When he returned, he had a suggestion.

'Let's take the box back home. I know you all want to see what's inside, but there's no point trying to open it here, or in the pub.' The others agreed, and after loading up the lorry and leaving payment at the Yew Tree, they all drove excitedly back to London.

Cushing had had to give another couple of shillings to the suspicious Clarence who had commented on the disreputable and dishevelled state of the seven men, as well as their arrival time. Cushing and Badger covered Scott's dining table with sheets and slowly and carefully unwrapped the silk to take a good look at the box.

Maurice looked longingly at the fine array of bottles and

decanters on Scott's sideboard. 'How about a stiffener, sir?' he asked.

'It's a bit early in the morning, isn't it?' replied Cushing, automatically, and then checked himself. 'No, I think you all deserve it.' He stopped and poured a couple of fingers of spirit into glasses for each man.

Badger looked disapprovingly at them, but smiled. 'Medicinal, of course,' he laughed, and went into the kitchen to put on the kettle.

Cushing continued to unwrap the silk and looked closely at the box under a bright light. 'It's like a reliquary,' he said, turning it round gently in his hands.

'What's one of those, then?' asked Chalky?

'They made them in the Middle Ages to house relics of saints. The toe of Saint Peter or a piece of the True Cross. It's beautiful.'

'Is it – is it gold?' asked Lenny, quietly.

'Plate, I think, but yes, I would say so,' replied Cushing. 'Look at the designs.'

They looked closely at the outside of the box, remarking on the Hospitaller crosses interspersed with intricate designs of swords and the rays of the sun.

'We're going to have to open it,' said Cushing. 'It contains the relics that Fulk brought back from the Holy Land.'

'There are so many fake relics, though,' said Badger. 'I mean, there were enough pieces of the True Cross around to build an entire church.'

'Well whatever is in here was obviously important to the Hospitallers. And it could be the things that Sloane and his gang of bully-boys are looking for, too.' Cushing reached for a paper knife on the desk, and Badger interrupted him.

'Actually, sir, would you mind if I did that? I've got a bit more – well, a bit more experience than you at this sort of thing, in a manner of speaking.'

Cushing happily stood up and let Badger open the box. 'Fair enough,' he grinned. 'What would the bishop say?' It was an easy job for the former cracksman, and the two men were soon looking at another package of oiled cloth. Badger slit it open to reveal a roll of parchment, which he gently unfurled. The fragile document bore a heavy seal at the bottom and the writing, though clearly very old, was clear.

'No relics,' Badger said, sounding disappointed. 'But your Latin is better than mine, sir. Why don't you take a crack at it?'

'I'll have a go,' said Cushing. 'It's not in Latin, though. It's in medieval French.'

'Either way, it's more your cup of tea than mine. I wouldn't mind another hot bath, if I may. I'm filthy.'

The other men left Cushing and Badger to their tasks and, after much shaking of hands, Cushing reached for his pocket to give the men something for their services.

'Don't worry about that, sir,' said Lenny. 'Anything we can do for a friend of Father Badger.' The others nodded in agreement.

Cushing looked nonplussed, but Badger agreed with Lenny. 'I think you'll find the lads will be happy to get their reward in heaven,' he said, pointedly.

Lenny and Maurice blushed, to Cushing's confusion. 'That's right, Father Badger,' said Lenny. 'Absolutely. Come on lads, we'd better be getting on.' The men shuffled out.

Some hours later, Cushing had worked out the ancient script and completed the translation. Both men had had quick baths – though they wished for a longer soak and a long sleep – and Badger had made a plate of sandwiches and another pot of tea. Cushing thanked Badger for the tea, but also poured himself another small medicinal whisky from one of Scott's decanters. He started to read, a little haltingly, from his notes, while Badger paced round the room.

'In the year of our Lord 1209, by the grace of God I, Amalric de Montfort, Knight of St. John, write this for those who may follow me, for my undertaking is fraught with danger.

'The French armies, led by my cousin Simon who has turned from the true path, wage bloody war on our brothers the Cathars.

'We have agreed to use the sacred relics to protect them. I have taken the treasures of the north to join their fellows.

'My father Fulk was entrusted with the crown and the stones, and we brought them from Ras Shamra to England. His brother Tancred took the sword and his brother Godfrey the orb. Now the treasures will be reunited and their power used to protect our comrades.

'The Grand Prior, King Peter of Aragon, fears the motives of Pope Innocent and has called the Guardians to Castrum Sepulchri. I will join the leaders of the free men at the castle. I will meet my brother knights at the chapel of the Christians on the slopes of Mount Caius. There the treasures will be brought together once again, and by God's will may fulfil their prophecy at the great battle. Thereafter they will rest in sanctity in the secret tomb in the chapel.

'It is my dearest wish that I will arrive in time to save the lives of our Cathar brothers.

'By my seal I, Amalric, son of Fulk de Montfort, Guardian of Lebanon and Knight of St. John, certify this.'

Cushing leaned back. Badger had stopped his pacing and was gazing enthralled at Cushing and at the ancient manuscript. 'That's amazing,' he said. 'Fulk de Montfort. The relics. It's all true. But what do we do now?'

'I'm not entirely sure,' replied Cushing. 'First of all I have absolutely no idea where this place is. Castrum Sepulchri? The castle of the Sepulchre? Maybe it's Jerusalem?'

'It can't be,' said Badger. 'Jerusalem had fallen by then. It's got to be somewhere in the Kingdom of Aragon, hasn't it? That's northern Spain, if I remember. And that's fairly close to where the crusaders were knocking hell – sorry, sir – tormenting the Cathars in the south of France. Anyway, that's your department.'

'Yes, back to the British Museum for me later. As soon as possible, in fact.' A pained expression came over Cushing's face. 'But the other treasures. That relates back to the writing on the tablet. The crown, the stones, the sword and the orb needed to crown the king. These must be the original Phoenician relics that Grainger told me about. That's just wonderful. To think that they might still be there, in Castrum Sepulchri. Together.'

'Well we don't know what happened in 1209, do we, sir? I mean, Amalric and his brothers may have met up for this council of war and all that, but what about the Cathar Crusade? They were supposed to be using the relics to fight on behalf of the Cathars, heaven alone knows how. I can't see them carrying sacred relics in front of them.'

'But that's exactly what they would have done. Like some sort of mystic talisman. And remember your Bible. Carrying the Ark of the Covenant in front of them, and all that.'

'Maybe. But the Cathars were soundly beaten. Weren't they? I mean, if there had been some huge battle, it would have been in the history books. Even at the school I went to. And Amalric makes it sound like Armageddon. So the odds are that the crown and sword and whatever are scattered to the four winds.'

'But if they're not, they will be at Castrum Sepulchri, in the chapel. So we'd better find out exactly where it is. And just as Crowley said, we have to find them before the opposition does. We know they are already on the hunt, even though we don't know why. Come on, Badger, let me drive you home. It's nearly lunchtime and Rachel must be worrying.'

'That's kind of you, but she'll be fine, honestly. I telephoned her earlier, while you were having a bath. And I can just take the tube – or even a taxi.'

'Are you sure?'
'Absolutely. You need to get off to the British Museum.'

13

Thursday 5th July 1928

Cushing was worn out, but knew that he had to keep going, and he was eager to find out more about the details of Amalric's document. As soon as Badger had left, he pulled out the telephone number that Miss Longhurst had given him and called her at the British Museum. She simpered down the telephone and, before he knew what he was doing, Cushing had arranged to meet her for lunch in the museum café.

Aware that Mrs. Duggins would be unhappy about the mud left all over the flat, Cushing tidied up as best he could. He also concealed the gold-plated reliquary from Parmoor carefully at the bottom of the wardrobe along with the tablet.

With a jaunty step he strolled to the British Museum, and before long he had found what he wanted. Despite being hurried over lunch, Miss Longhurst had been wonderfully helpful once again. It did not take long for her to show that a monastery had been founded at a place called Castrum Sepulchri and that Bernard of Clairvaux, founder of the Cistercian order, had himself been there to consecrate it along with Hugh de Payens, the Grand Master of the Templars and the other eight original members of the order.

'Unusual that they would all have come back from the Holy Land for that,' said Cushing. 'What made the consecration of a monastery so important?'

'I thought you said you weren't a treasure hunter,' said Miss Longhurst, archly.

'What do you mean?' asked Cushing, innocently.

'Castrum Sepulchri is rumoured to hold some great secret.' Cushing tried hard not to catch her eye. 'The castle has all become linked to the legend of the Holy Grail. And so I get these treasure hunters coming in and asking for information.'

'The Grail is just a legend,' answered Cushing, earnestly. 'I'm not interested in that. But this Castrum Sepulchri. Where is it?'

'Its modern name is Seborga. It's a little place in northern Italy, just over the French border.'

'Seborga?' Cushing recognised the name as being the place where he had overheard Sloane and John discussing an archaeological dig, and felt deflated that the opposition were so far ahead of the game. 'In Italy, you say?'

'Yes, Seborga. Of course, when it was founded it would have been in the Kingdom of Aragon. It's quite a pretty place. I went there when I did the grand tour, some twenty – I mean ten – years ago.' Cushing was sure that her original number was correct, especially as ten years ago Europe was at war, but was too polite to say so. She patted her hair and continued. 'Seborga trades on its past which is, after all, really rather limited. Cheap tin swords, that sort of thing.' She dug around in another section of the library and pulled out some detailed maps of the village to show him, still reminiscing about her travels as a young girl.

Cushing bought Miss Longhurst another cup of tea and a bun before leaving the museum. She was keen to meet him again after work, but he found a credible excuse about some charitable commitment – he did not want to admit that he was taking Gussie to a show. Miss Longhurst was clearly disappointed, and he began to feel a bit of a bounder. 'This is war,' he thought, in an attempt to justify his caddish behaviour.

He walked quickly to the nearest bookshop to buy some maps. He located the tiny village of Seborga quite easily, a few miles from Monte Carlo and just north of Ventimiglia. But what could he do? What could any of them do?

Drifting slowly back to Scott's flat through the teeming streets, he decided to take a diversion through Trafalgar Square. He looked up at the statue of Nelson for inspiration, then decided to seek that inspiration from a far higher authority. He turned and walked up the steps through the pillared entrance of the glorious church of St. Martin-in-the-Fields, where he had spent some time during the War comforting soldiers as they arrived back from France to the nearby Charing Cross station. So many had looked immediately to the church for comfort, and Cushing now found a haven of peace in a quiet side chapel. He prayed for a while, then talked softly to Mary. He looked at the stained glass in the chapel window and then suddenly jumped to his feet.

'The chapel!' he exclaimed, out loud. 'Christopher Cushing, you blithering idiot!' People stared at him as he strode purposefully out of the church, still muttering to himself.

Back in Scott's flat, he immediately started making telephone calls. The first was to Badger, and he rushed out a torrent of explanation.

'Castrum Sepulchri - it's in Italy. It's the same place that John and Sloane and that lot are digging, looking for - well, whatever they are digging for. But John said they were digging in the monastery. But Amalric said they were hiding the relics in the chapel. It's different. They're digging in the wrong place!'

Badger eventually calmed down the excited Cushing and pulled together a coherent sense of what his friend was saying.

'So you're saying you think that the opposition are on the hunt for the same relics as Amalric writes about in his letter? The Phoenician ones, you thought? Which we know he was planning to hide in the secret tomb in the chapel? What makes you think that the chapel isn't part of the monastery, where they are digging?'

'Because Amalric specifically says that the chapel is on the slope of Mount Caius. And Miss Longhurst showed me a map of the village – that's nowhere near the castle or the ruins of the monastery.'

'Fair enough, but what do you expect us to do about it? Stockington is hardly likely to interfere with some archaeological dig in Italy, is he?'

'We'll just have to go there ourselves!'

'What? We can't...'

'We must, Badger. For the first time, we are actually ahead of the opposition. We know where the relics are. They don't.'

'It's seven hundred miles away. And we're not archaeologists or anything.'

'Young Geoffrey is. Well, a bit.'

'But...'

'No buts, please. Come on, man. If we don't solve this, no one else will. No one in any sort of authority will act. They won't even believe us – look at Stockington, after all. We're on our own here.'

It took Cushing half an hour of cajoling to persuade Badger that he was right, and more time to convince him that they had to move quickly. Though still sceptical, Badger agreed to make arrangements to clear his diary and devolve his pastoral responsibilities to others.

Cushing then sent a telegram to Geoffrey Scott in Deauville, and another to Peter Clifford on his holiday in Menton – by fortunate coincidence, Menton was a mere thirty miles or so from Seborga.

Then a call to Jerry Sinclair, another old friend from the War years to whom Cushing knew that Clifford had already spoken. Sinclair ran a small charter airline service out of Croydon, and Cushing knew that flying would be the quickest way of getting to the Riviera. He arranged to meet Sinclair for a pint of beer at the George in Southwark before meeting Gussie at the theatre.

And, finally, Cushing sent a short letter to Stockington – using the alias of Collins – asking him to meet at the café the following morning.

The reply from Scott, an hour later, was typical. "Cushing care of Scott Albany London. See you in Menton stop. Send details of where and when to meet stop. Suggest there is always a Hotel de Gare stop. Plan to leave this evening stop. Most exciting stop. Re previous telegram if you get murdered please do not leave blood on my new carpet stop. Tally ho stop. Geoffrey." Cushing found a blue-bound copy of the Guide Michelin on Scott's shelves and sent a return telegram to confirm the rendezvous – unusually, there was no Hotel de la Gare – and, in anticipation of a positive response from Clifford, to give Clifford's address to Scott.

Clifford's reply came later, with the telegram interrupting Cushing's well-deserved doze. He was happy to meet Cushing, Badger and Scott, to help plan their expedition, and to arrange a hotel for them. Cushing felt, however, that he could hear a certain amount of reticence between the curt lines of the telegram.

Jerry Sinclair was delighted to be of assistance. A squat, balding man with a large moustache, Sinclair did not look like a hero as he lurched into the pub. As Clifford had pointed out, however, Sinclair had served in the Royal Flying Corps and won a DFC before being shot down in France. His dragging left leg was a constant reminder.

'Well, Padre, looks like you're in a bit of a pickle,' said Sinclair, downing his beer and immediately calling for more. 'Shot at by Germans, you say? In Knightsbridge? Well I'll be damned. Some sort of international conspiracy? Bolsheviks, I'll be bound. And Peter Clifford said you want to take the fight to them. Well I'm your man. What can I do?' He took two enormous cigars from his pocket and offered one to Cushing, who declined. Sinclair lit his and puffed foul-smelling smoke into the air. 'I get these from Algeria,' he said. 'I've got quite a taste for them now.'

'Well, Jerry,' said Cushing, looking around anxiously as his old friend's voice boomed round the pub. 'First of all I need a lift. I wonder if you might be able to arrange one of your planes to drop me and Badger – sorry, Philip Brock, he's my old sergeant and a vicar in Whitechapel now, you don't know him – down in the south of France? We need to get to the Riviera in a bit of a hurry. We're meeting Clifford and my godson, Geoffrey Scott.'

'Well now, that should be easy enough,' said Sinclair, thoughtfully. 'Dash it, it's a regular little private army you're getting together. Look, I'll fly you down myself if you like. It should only take four or five hours. I can even spend a couple of days down there with you. I was thinking of going to an air show in Toulouse next week, and I could use a bit of a holiday beforehand. When do you want to go? Saturday? Perfect. Send a telegram to Peter Clifford and he can meet us.'

'Well you're not going to the Riviera without me, and that's final,' said Gussie, emphatically. The show had been excellent, and Cushing's fears that he might nod off in the warmth after his recent exertions had not been realised. He found himself humming the same tune that Scott had been singing tunelessly a fortnight earlier as they walked towards a restaurant that Gussie had chosen.

'But Gussie, dear, it's far too dangerous.'

'Nonsense. And don't you "Gussie dear" me.'

He had told her, somewhat guiltily, about their surreptitious return to Parmoor House. Gussie was initially incandescent, accusing him of stealing.

'It's not stealing. I mean, we're doing this for the good of the country.'

'Tell that to the magistrates, vicar!'

After a while, though, she had calmed down and become intrigued. She asked many questions about Cushing's discoveries, the tomb, the letter and the conclusions that Cushing and Badger had drawn. And she would not now accept no for an answer.

'I'm coming, Christopher, and that's all there is to it,' she repeated. 'I love the idea of going down to the Riviera. The weather will be lovely. I'll start packing and you can pick me up on Saturday morning. We'll see if you can manage the flight without telling me how good it was in the "good old days".' She leaned over and kissed him on the forehead.

Thoroughly browbeaten, Cushing put his head in his hands. He knew when to give in gracefully.

The following morning, Cushing met Stockington in the café in Villiers Street as arranged. Cushing first of all gave Stockington Hitchcock's personal effects that had been in Ross's briefcase, for which Stockington was very grateful. He then enthused about his discoveries linking the tablets to the trail left by the Hospitallers, and his plans to travel to France and Italy.

'I said only a few days ago that I feared this was becoming an archaeological wild goose chase,' said Stockington. 'Swanning off to the French Riviera isn't going to help solve who killed Ross.'

'But don't you see, Stockington?' said Cushing, heatedly. 'Hitchcock took the clay tablets from Longley Towers, we think, and was shot for his pains. Domvile knew that Ross had the tablets, and Ross was killed. Page was killed working on the tablets. Now thanks to our friends at the British Museum we have found a link between Ugarit and the "treasures of the north" taken from the area by the crusaders. And we have traced those back to this place Castrum Sepulchri. So if we can only get hold of them, we may be able to understand exactly what the enemy are up to. And, more importantly, get to these treasures they are after before they do!'

'That's a fair point,' admitted Stockington. 'I'd normally insist that you didn't leave the country. But let me tell you something. It may be a coincidence, but it's a rather curious one. There was a burglary at the British Museum last night, and a few Middle Eastern and Egyptian artefacts were stolen. A couple of guards were chloroformed and some American professor bopped on the head. Everyone's fine, just a bit shaken. But you may be onto something with this archaeological route after all. Let me know when you get back.'

Cushing sat next to Professor Grainger's bed in St. Bartholomew's Hospital. The American was sitting up with a large bandage round his head, absent-mindedly picking at the box of chocolates that Cushing had brought.

'But damn it all, Cushing. Those robbers must have known what they were looking for. They came straight in and made for the photographs. One of them stuck a gun up my nose and asked where the tablet was, and I could truthfully say that I didn't know. They snatched the photographs and a load of my notes. Then one of them hit me over the head and I woke up in an ambulance.'

'Dreadful,' soothed Cushing. 'But this is important. Did you, er, did you mention my name at all?'

'No, not at all. They must have got the information about me having the photograph from Claude Schaeffer.'

'Schaeffer?'

'Yes. I showed a photograph to him, in strictest confidence, of course. I thought he might be able to help.'

Cushing smacked his hand into his forehead in exasperation. 'It was supposed to....'

'Yes, I know, I know. But don't worry. They never asked where I got it from, so I didn't have to mention you or Clifford. They won't be after you too, never fear.'

Cushing tried to pretend that this had not been the purpose of his question, then hurriedly changed the subject. 'I know you've told the police everything you know,' he said, 'but these burglars. They weren't by any chance German, were they?'

'No. One was English, one might have been Irish. That's as much as I was able to tell the police, anyway. Why do you ask?'

'Just a hunch. I had heard that some Germans were looking for these tablets too, that's all. No matter. But look, have you lost everything?'

'Actually no. I have copies of the photographs and of most of my notes. But if these guys publish first...'

'I don't think these people are trying to beat you to publishing a paper,' laughed Cushing.

'Well I'd welcome another look at the tablet itself when I can. Without that, the Royal Society won't be convinced that the whole thing isn't just some elaborate forgery.'

Cushing smiled. 'Don't worry, old man. I'll bring you both tablets when you're out of hospital. I promise.'

14

Saturday 7th July 1928

Shortly before lunch the following day, Cushing, Badger and Gussie found themselves at the bleak little airfield at Lympne in Kent, on the edge of Romney Marsh. Jerry Sinclair had been as good as his word, and was checking over his aeroplane with a mechanic.

During the drive down, Badger had, like Cushing, tried to persuade Gussie not to come, but she was adamant. Cushing realised when he was beaten, and helped to load Gussie's luggage into Sinclair's aeroplane. There was a lot of luggage. 'Don't worry, there's plenty of room,' said Sinclair. 'Actually, she's an old bomber. Quite a big payload.'

'What a dreadful place,' said Gussie, shivering. 'The wind off the Channel is biting, even in July!'

'You should have been here last month,' replied Sinclair, grinning. 'That mad old bat the Duchess of Bedford took off for India. Seventy if she's a day, and daft as a brush. She was supposed to be back in eight days, though there hasn't been a dickie bird from her since. But she threw a proper leaving party.' He grinned again. 'Come on, all of you. Wrap up well and make yourselves comfortable.'

'By the way, Jerry,' said Cushing. 'How rigorous are the customs in France if you come by aeroplane? I've got Geoffrey's revolver. I thought it might come in useful.' He had packed it earlier, but felt it advisable not to mention that he had also packed his own war souvenirs.

'I wouldn't worry, old man,' laughed Sinclair. 'They've got better things to do than pester us. They see me going to and fro all the time.'

It was the first time Cushing and Badger had flown, and neither enjoyed the experience. From Sinclair's first 'Chocks away! Tally ho!' to the wheels touching down in a French field, Cushing only opened his eyes for a short time. The plane lurched and bounced through the air and he was pleased he had not eaten since breakfast, especially after Sinclair had lit another of his vile cigars. He heard Badger groaning behind him and tried to shut his mind to where he was. Eventually they landed, and Sinclair and Gussie were both cheerful. 'Lovely smooth flight,' said Sinclair. 'It would have been a lot bouncier in one of my racing crates. Oh well. I think a celebratory drink is called for. Welcome to France!'

Cushing gratefully took a swig from Sinclair's hipflask to settle his nerves, but Badger felt too ill even to consider the medicinal properties of brandy.

'I was expecting to see the sea,' said Cushing. 'Where are we?'

Gussie laughed. 'Christopher, darling, we're not at the Riviera yet. I think we're somewhere near Paris. Jerry just stopped to refuel or something.'

'What, what? Refuelling? Yes, that's the ticket,' said Sinclair enthusiastically as he rejoined the group. 'Off in a couple of minutes. Done the paperwork, showed the passports, all that sort of thing. Ready?'

Cushing and Badger endured three more hours of hell

before Gussie poked them and encouraged them to open their eyes. Sinclair was making a wide looping turn and the whole Riviera coast was beneath them, sparkling under a cloudless sky. She ooh-ed and aah-ed, and Cushing and Badger had to be impressed, despite the way they were feeling.

Finally they touched down, not a moment too soon as far as Cushing was concerned. It was six o'clock, French time, and they were delighted to find Geoffrey Scott waiting for them.

'I've been down for a couple of hours,' said Scott. 'I sent a telegram to your chum Clifford last night from Beaune – had a splendid dinner, by the way – and he told me your plans. So I've had time to pay homage at William Webb Ellis's grave, and thought I'd pick you up.'

Sinclair secured the aeroplane while Cushing and Badger loaded the luggage into the enormous Rolls Royce to which Scott directed them. Scott was full of bonhomie. Cushing already knew from a postcard that Scott's motor race had been successful, but it was his luck on the gaming tables that had meant that he could afford to stay in Deauville with Phoebe Fairfax and her set for longer than he had expected.

'I've found our hotel too,' said Scott. 'It's a bit shabby, very French if you know what I mean, but it will do for us. Phoebe hated it, of course. It isn't exactly at the fashionable end of town. Anyway, she has booked herself into the Royale. She's having a swim, but we can meet her for dinner later. Then perhaps a little flutter?'

'Phoebe?' asked Cushing. 'You mean Miss Fairfax? She isn't here, surely!'

'Well of course she is. This is her car. Or her father's, at least. Don't worry, I'll look after her.'

'This isn't a holiday, Geoffrey. We need you because you're an archaeologist. Or you're supposed to be. Not as a chauffeur, and certainly not as some gigolo.'

'Oh Uncle Kit, don't be such an old prude. Phoebe's a sweetie. And as I say, it's her car.'

They assembled at a restaurant on the front near the Royale, able to sit outside in the warmth of the evening gazing at the sea. Clifford arrived and introduced his wife to the rest of the group. Molly Clifford was a small, bird-like woman, utterly charming, an American from a rich New York family. Badger, Scott and Sinclair seemed to be getting on well, and Scott's fund of scurrilous stories soon had them laughing. Sinclair was totally engaged by the quest.

Phoebe Fairfax, however, looking ravishing in an expensive cocktail dress, drifted in and out of the conversation. She was bored and would clearly have rather been in the company of her group of "bright young things".

'It's going to be a huge adventure,' said Gussie, happily. But Cushing was frustrated about not being able to speak in front of Phoebe. Even the fine dinner did not raise his spirits, and as the evening wore on, all the newly-arrived members of the group were becoming fractious and tired.

They arranged to meet at Clifford's villa the following morning. 'I've told Molly a bit about what we're doing,' said Clifford, after giving them directions through the winding narrow streets. 'Only very vaguely, of course,' he said, hurriedly, as Cushing frowned. 'But she's happy enough. So you might just as well use the villa as a sort of HQ. We can bomb over to Italy tomorrow lunchtime if you like. It shouldn't be too busy.'

The group went their separate ways: Clifford and Molly back to their villa, Phoebe to the Royale, with Scott walking her home, and the rest to the discreet pension into which Clifford had booked them. It was not the Royale by any stretch of the imagination, but it was comfortable enough. And there was time for a nightcap, though none of them wanted a late evening on the gaming tables.

'You're going to have to tell Phoebe some of what we're up to, you know,' remarked Gussie. 'After all, she'll find out soon enough when you start digging up the Castrum Sepulchri, or whatever it is.'

'You're probably right,' Cushing admitted. 'But not the real background, just that we're after buried treasure.' As Scott joined the group, having returned from seeing Phoebe to her hotel, Cushing ordered him a brandy and explained to him what he should tell Phoebe about their expedition.

'Oh I've already told her all of that,' said Scott, breezily. 'After all, I had to spark her interest somehow, or we wouldn't have got her car. And it's what we're all here for really, isn't it? Buried treasure and all?' Gussie laughed as Cushing spluttered and stalked off to bed in high dudgeon.

The weather was wonderful the following morning as they sat on the terrace of Clifford's villa, a small building perched on the hills above Menton towards the Italian border, surrounded by mimosas, oleanders and cypress trees. Cushing thought wryly how well Clifford's Harley Street practice must have been flourishing over the past few years to enable him to acquire such a lovely spot: diseases of the rich had clearly been a lucrative business. Phoebe had joined them by taxi, and they were all in high spirits. Looking down over the sandy roofs and turrets of the old town and the sparkling sea, they were able to relax and discuss Seborga. Or that had been the plan, but the party atmosphere overtook them all. Cushing had been to the Riviera once before the War, on his honeymoon; Badger had never been to France except in uniform, and was as excited as a schoolboy. Gussie, Phoebe and Scott were old hands and talked incessantly about the beaches, the casinos and the yachts.

Cushing, ever practical, tore himself away from the holiday

spirit and turned his mind to the issue of crossing the border into Italy. Sinclair was eager to be of as much help as possible before he had to leave on the Tuesday – he had taken advantage of being in the south of France to go on to an air show near Toulouse. The two finally herded the group into two cars; Molly was more than happy to stay at the villa while Clifford drove their car to Seborga.

The cars were spacious, especially as the luggage had been unpacked and taken into the hotel, but Cushing had loaded the boot of one of the cars with picks and shovels that Clifford had previously procured. Gussie carried a substantial picnic basket that Molly had prepared for them. 'I wouldn't want you to go hungry,' she said. 'It's a long time until supper.'

The border was only a couple of miles up the coast from Menton, and Cushing had been right to be concerned about crossing it. Both French and Italian border guards were officious, sneering at the British number plates and making an ostentatious check of the car and its contents and insisting that the boot was opened. It was at least half an hour before their passports had been verified – Cushing was glad that they had remembered to take them back from the hotel receptionist with whom he had left them the night before – and they were able to drive on into Italy along the coast.

'Was that normal?' asked Badger? 'They didn't have border controls last time I was in France.'

The road followed a sweeping curve along the coast, and then began to rise and fall. At one moment they were on an unfenced cliff two hundred feet above the sea, the next they were descending to pass a beautiful inlet.

'It's lovely,' said Phoebe. 'Can't we stop and have a swim?' She sulked when Scott refused.

They soon reached the bustling little port of Ventimiglia. The cars crawled through the crowds of locals who had brought in fruit, vegetables and animals for market day, and they were able to leave the coast road and head up the valley into the mountains to Seborga.

It was getting uncomfortably warm in the cars. 'Mad dogs and Englishmen, eh?' remarked Clifford as they got the first sight of the hill on which Seborga sat, the orange tower, tiled roofs and cypress trees of the village commanding a beautiful outlook over the Mediterranean. As they drove up the hill, twisting and turning along a seemingly never-ending series of hairpin bends, they had views of the ancient terraces which dated back to the Etruscans and miles and miles of lemon and olive groves. A large but tatty sign in several languages announced that they were entering the Principality of Seborga, and a blue and white flag flew proudly from a sentry box. A guard in a comical chocolate-soldier costume with a feathered hat saluted the car as it drove past. Gussie laughed out loud.

Clifford turned the corner and drove into an open square, from which there was no further exit, at least not one that could take a Rolls Royce. He parked his car in front of a shabby but nonetheless inviting café. Scott pulled up close behind and all the passengers got out. 'I thought it would be a bit grander,' said Scott. 'You know, city gates, a drawbridge and all that. Not just a dingy bar and a random statue of some Italian with a big moustache.'

They bought a local guidebook, somewhat hampered by the fact that none of them had more than a smattering of Italian, and had a welcome coffee and cold drink. A church bell further into the centre of the little town was ringing, and they established from the guidebook that a castle was close to the church. The monastery of San Bartelemeo, in ruins, was about a mile to the north east. Monte Caggio – presumably the mountain which Amalric had called Mount Caius in the parchment they had found in Fulk de Montfort's tomb in Parmoor – was towards the north, but there was no reference to a chapel on its slopes. And they had already driven straight past the ancient little church of

St. Benedict without noticing it sitting in a small grove of trees at the far end of the square.

Gussie, in search of a mirror, was the first to wander inside the café when she saw a large and poorly-executed mural of a crusader knight in armour. She called in the others to take a look, and Cushing recognised the name of the subject. It was Hugh de Payens, the master of the Templars, but strangely, as Cushing remarked, depicted wearing a Hospitaller cross.

The two black Rolls Royces had generated a fair amount of interest and, while they sat on the café terrace, they received the persistent and unwelcome attention of keen volunteer guides whose English was, despite their claims, rather worse than the party's Italian. Most were little more than boys, but one of them, a lean middle aged man, did speak reasonable English. 'I speak English good,' he said. 'I learn at Olympics in Antwerp. I fight with sword and my brother in Italian team. Many English my good friends. Now I guide my friends round Seborga, si? Where you want to go? I show you church, maybe? Big sword of crusaders in castle?'

'Well I don't see why not,' said Cushing. 'Get our bearings, and all that. And certainly worth having a look at the castle.'

The guide, whose name was Emilio, turned out also to be the local policeman. He gave them chapter and verse on the history of the area, very proud that Seborga was technically still an independent principality. 'We saw the border guard,' giggled Phoebe. As they walked the short distance to the castle, they were conscious of the number of stray cats in their way, some of which came scurrying up looking for food and wrapping themselves round Gussie's silk-clad legs. She shuddered audibly, and Emilio kicked them away. 'There are many cats in Seborga,' he said.

As they walked through the steep narrow streets of the town – more like alleys rather than streets, in fact – Cushing saw many manifestations of the Hospitaller cross, including one forming the whole paved area of a small square in front of the church. Emilio was proud of the church of San Martino, but it was clearly relatively new and a quick exploration showed it to contain nothing of interest. Emilio was reasonably knowledgeable about the history of the place. He expanded on the limited information that Miss Longhurst had given Cushing, explaining that St. Bernard had consecrated both church and monastery and that Hugh de Payens, master of the Templars, had come specifically from Jerusalem for the consecration. 'He die here,' explained Emilio, helpfully. 'Come, I show you his sword.'

The narrow streets were pretty, with stone buildings and low arches, though the cats were by now becoming a real nuisance, and the noise subsided as even the locals attempting to sell souvenirs to tourists began to slump in the midday heat. The smell of people and rubbish was becoming stronger. The town was really quite primitive and it was clear that the plumbing had not significantly improved since the death of Hugh de Payens.

The views over the terraced hills down to the sparkling sea were wonderful, and they could see the wide sweep of the bay in the distance. The bell tower they had seen from the road dominated the village, and the old houses were adorned with flowers. The blue and white flags that had been visible at the "border" were everywhere.

The party were, however, disappointed at the "castle". It may have been a castle once, but it had been built on many times and was now no more than a grand house. 'It is the Prince's palace,' said Emilio, extracting a few more lire from the grudging party for an entrance fee. The limited number of items on display did include a rusted medieval sword, lying sadly in a dust-covered case. 'Hugh de Payens,' said Emilio, enthusiastically, but with little actual confidence.

Above the case was a faded fresco showing crusaders attacking a city. 'That is knights attacking Jerusalem,' said Emilio.

Cushing indicated that the crusaders were wearing a mixture of Templar and Hospitaller crosses on their surcoats, and then rather patronisingly pointed out that the orders were created only after Jerusalem had in fact been captured by the crusading armies.

Emilio shrugged. 'You want see something else? I take you to church of St. Bernard and monastery of San Bartelemeo. We go in your car, yes?' He grinned like a schoolboy.

'Where is Monte Caggio?' asked Phoebe, innocently. The rest of the party winced.

'Is three, maybe four kilometres to the north, between here and Negi,' replied the guide. 'Why you want to go there? Is nothing good to see.'

'Are there no ruins there? A chapel, perhaps?'

'Maybe, but it is – how you say – fa schifo. Rubbish. Too small. And car not go there, road no good. You want ruins, you go to monastery like I say. Big ruins. Many people digging there. Americans, English, Germans.'

'Germans?' Cushing, Scott and Badger spoke as one.

'Yes. They all digging up old monastery. Very exciting. Lots of work. They our friends too.'

'Well,' said Cushing. 'Let's go and take a look.'

They squeezed Emilio into the back of one of the Rolls Royce – he was thrilled about being given a ride in such a grand car – and drove back out of town towards the north east. As they neared the ruined monastery, they were surprised to see that it was cordoned off. Two guards raised their hands to stop the car. Emilio got out and jabbered in Italian to one of the men, and turned back to the party. 'He say the monastery is closed. No tourists.'

The second guard, thick-jowled and sweating, joined the conversation in thickly-accented and broken English. 'Closed. Schlossen. Understand? You go now, English.'

'That's all right, Fritz, keep your hair on,' replied Scott, and then muttered something in German in a low voice. The guard shook his fist at the departing Rolls.

'What did you say to him?' asked Cushing.

'I think I heard,' replied Badger. 'And I don't think you really want to know, sir. Not bad, though, Mr. Scott. Very good, in fact. That told him. Where did you learn to swear in German like that?'

'It's another German,' said Cushing. 'They seem to be all over the place.'

'He's only a guard,' said Scott. 'Emilio said there were German archaeologists there, as well as English and American ones. Stop worrying.'

They drove back into the square at the edge of Seborga and parked the cars again. Emilio took them to the tiny thirteenth-century stone church of St. Bernard, originally built and consecrated by the founder of the Cistercians. 'It was all rebuilt a few years ago,' said Emilio, helpfully, and sure enough the inside was largely bare.

'Back to Monte Caggio, I think,' said Cushing. Looking at one another, and then at Emilio, they thanked the guide and left him protesting by the café at which they had met him. He looked at them suspiciously, but was mollified by a handful of lire. Phoebe waved farewell as they drove out of town in the direction that Emilio had indicated. The triangular shape of Monte Caggio was distinctive, and Cushing recognised it as forming part of the background to the mural in the café.

After about twenty minutes of hair-raising driving alongside steep and unprotected drops, the road narrowed even more uncomfortably and then became a dirt track. Clifford, who was in the lead, pulled up. 'No point risking the car axles on this surface,' he said. 'Emilio was right about the road. I'm afraid we're going to have to walk.'

They left the car and walked several hundred yards up

the green lower slopes of the mountain, taking what appeared to be a sheep track. They were already puffing and panting in the heat, by the time they reached the building they had first spotted, and were depressed to discover that it was a collapsed and overgrown shepherd's hut. Cushing, his fears dating back to his early childhood in India, was moving gingerly through the undergrowth behind the others, until Scott had convinced him – perhaps mendaciously – that there would be no snakes lurking. Twenty minutes later, they had uncovered another building. This time at least it was stone, but again it was a ruined house.

The party were starting to argue. 'The wretched place must be here somewhere,' cursed Scott. 'Emilio said so.' He took out his field glasses and scanned the slopes. Any one of a number of lumps and bumps could have been a ruined building.

Tripping through the scrubby and aromatic vegetation, they had two more false starts before they found the tumbled and heavily overgrown ruins of what they thought could have been a small chapel. Some of the surviving walls were still at head height, but they were hidden in a dip by a small stream and the party almost stumbled upon the remains of the building.

They scoured the ruins of the chapel. It was Badger who, pulling ivy and other vegetation from the remnants of the thick walls and frightening a number of lizards that quickly scuttled away, revealed a Hospitaller cross carved into the stone.

'Those people at the old monastery,' remarked Gussie. 'You're absolutely right, Christopher. If they really are looking for what we're looking for, they're…'

'They're digging in the wrong place!' chorused the others, laughing.

'Come on, Geoffrey,' giggled Phoebe. 'Aren't you going to dig?' Cushing helpfully offered him one of the shovels which he had brought from the back of the car. Scott, looking uncomfortably first at the two women, then at the four middle-aged men gazing expectantly at him, and then at the hot sun, removed his shirt and began to dig up the floor below the cross.

The others continued to search the remnants of the walls and flagstones and stripped away ivy from the ancient altar. All were hot and sweaty, and removed their jackets and waistcoats.

'Damn,' Gussie grumbled. 'I've torn my skirt on this wretched scrub. Oh well, it's been uncomfortable all day.' Taking a penknife from her bag, she proceeded to make an elongated slit in the skirt, much to Cushing's alarm. She shooed away the lizards that had taken advantage of the freshly-cleared altar, enjoying the new spot to bask in the heat, and began to lay out the picnic that Molly had prepared and that Sinclair had carried for her up to the chapel.

'That's so thoughtful, my dear, thank you,' said Clifford, who did not appear to see anything wrong with her outfit.

Scott continued to sweat in the afternoon heat, and began a second hole in front of the altar. His digging uncovered a number of small artefacts: pieces of metal, pots, the occasional coin, a ring and a small silver cross. 'Hospitaller,' panted Scott, tossing the cross to Clifford. 'Clean this up, there's a good chap.' Phoebe looked at the cross after Clifford had cleaned it, and attached it to her own necklace. 'Geoffrey's found buried treasure,' she sang, skipping round the site like a thing possessed.

After three hours – and the other men did eventually take their turn as well – they had uncovered a couple of rusted sword hilts, one with a gem set into it, along with a host of more minor finds.

'This is no good,' said Scott. 'I'm bushed. We'll have to come back tomorrow.'

They cleaned themselves as best as they could in the cold and fast-flowing stream and, taking only the more obviously valuable artefacts with them, drove back to the centre of Seborga for a well-earned drink, then back through the border posts.

After a day in the hot sun, the guards were less keen to conduct a proper search, but Cushing was concerned that they would need to be careful if they were to smuggle any larger finds into France.

Cushing was desperate for a bath, but Gussie and Phoebe were emphatic that they wanted a swim in the sea.

'I'll join you,' said Scott. 'We passed a nice little cove about half a mile back up the coast road.' Stopping to collect towels, the three walked back towards the border.

Cushing, Badger and Sinclair were relaxing in front of their hotel with a cool drink when the swimmers returned, still damp-haired and laughing.

'I'd have loved a swim,' said Cushing, ordering drinks for the newcomers, 'but I didn't bring my bathing costume.'

'That's all right, Padre,' said Scott, happily. 'Nor did we.'

Cushing looked at Scott in horror, then at Phoebe who was also grinning broadly, and then at Gussie. He turned brick red and found something important to examine at the bottom of his glass.

They felt they had earned their dinner, which was excellent. All were in high spirits, and, dressed up to the nines, decided to try their luck in the casinos. They clustered round Phoebe who was amassing a huge pile of chips in front of her on the roulette table, taking risks that all seemed to be coming off. 'My new cross is my lucky charm,' she said, and Cushing noticed that she was wearing it at her throat. She really was rather pretty after all, he thought, and then caught sight of Gussie at the other side of the table, poised with a cigarette and flushed with excitement. He gazed at her for a full minute, but was interrupted by a waft of smoke from Sinclair's cigar and the pilot's hand on his shoulder. 'A bit warm in here, old man. Fancy going outside for some fresh air?' The moment had passed.

15

Monday 9th July 1928

Cushing was up before breakfast, eager to continue with the excavations, but the others appeared to be in no rush. 'Don't panic, Padre' said Scott, tucking into a plate of eggs prepared by Molly Clifford. 'I mean, what we're looking for has been there for seven hundred years. Another half an hour isn't going to make a lot of difference either way, is it?'

Eventually they piled into the two cars and drove to the Royale to collect Phoebe. Scott went into the hotel but came out soon after, shrugging his shoulders. 'She's gone for a walk,' he said, apologetically.

Cushing's angry response was tempered when he heard Gussie. 'It's all right, Christopher. Here she comes.'

As Phoebe flounced prettily towards them, Cushing stuck his head out of the window. 'Come on, Miss Fairfax, we're in a hurry.'

'Sorry, Padre,' she replied. 'I had to send a postcard.'

'Postcard?'

'Oh yes. I always send postcards to my mother. I bought one in Seborga yesterday, but they didn't have a stamp.' She smiled charmingly and got into the car with Scott and Sinclair.

Cushing was apoplectic. 'We think her father is one of the people behind this whole escapade, and she's sending postcards telling him where we are!'

Despite the late start and the inevitable delays at the border, they were still able to start digging shortly after eleven o'clock. This time all the men dug extensively, below the Hospitaller cross and around and under the altar. They uncovered a few more small coins of little value, another ring, a comb and more pieces of weaponry. But it was several hours later when, tired, exhausted and after considerable bickering among the party, Scott leaned on his shovel and addressed his friends.

'Wait a minute. When Cushing and Badger were at Parmoor, the treasure was behind the cross, wasn't it? Or at least it would have been if you had gone in from the crypt rather than down the hole.'

'Yes,' said Badger. 'Though we didn't...'

'Well we're going to now.' And Scott took a pick in his hands. 'Stand clear,' he called, and despite Cushing's remonstrations swung it at the corner of the Hospitaller cross. Chips of stone flew in all directions, but after the third swing it was clear that there was a space behind the stone. Suddenly all the party were there, giving contradictory advice, but with more application of chisels, hammers and the pick, the stone was removed.

'What have we got here?' asked Scott, panting. 'It looks like a wooden chest. Come on, chaps. Give me a bunk up.' Sinclair and Badger eagerly supported Scott as he pulled the old wooden chest from its hole. Like the chest at Parmoor, it collapsed quickly into pieces, the decayed wood and rusty iron bands falling apart.

'Stop, man,' called out Cushing. 'You're destroying it.'

'That's alright, Padre,' puffed Scott. 'Look at what's inside. Ye Gods, that's heavy.' And from the remnants of the chest he pulled down a package wrapped in tarred cloth. He stood there holding it, Sinclair and Badger breathing heavily beside him from their exertions. He started to pull at the cloth.

'Careful,' urged Cushing.

'It's only some old shroud,' replied Scott, putting the package on the ground and continuing to rip at the material. He revealed a small metal box, similar to the one that Cushing and Badger had found in Parmoor, but a little larger.

'Is it big enough for the relics?' asked Badger.

'It's beautiful,' said Gussie, admiring what she could see of the ornate metalwork.

'It's gold, I think,' said Sinclair.

'It's locked,' said Scott, picked up a shovel and brought it hard down on the hasp as the other members of the party winced. 'There we go.' He leaned forward and opened the top. 'Hmm, no crown.'

There was a package wrapped in oiled linen, which Cushing opened carefully. 'It's a tube with another manuscript,' he said, 'and a map. Medieval French again. And with a seal. It's the de Montfort seal. They're in dreadful condition – be careful.' But the others were paying no attention. They were more excited by the package that Phoebe had opened. It was a bag of gold coins. She and Scott began to cavort around the old church, joined by the others, until Badger spotted a car parked next to theirs at the bottom of the hill. He reached for Clifford's field glasses, and was shocked to see a man in the passenger seat of the car looking straight back at him through a similar pair of glasses. 'We've been rumbled,' he said. 'Let's get out of here.'

The other car and the watchers sped off soon after being spotted, and the party packed up their belongings and loaded the cars as quickly as they could. Scott and Clifford drove quickly towards the border. It was approaching six, and a number of vehicles were already queuing at the crossing.

'Geoffrey, stop here,' ordered Cushing. 'Put the box in a rucksack. You and I can carry it over the hills to avoid the border crossing. Badger, you'd better come with us.'

And so they did, with Phoebe driving her father's Rolls back over the border with Sinclair, and Clifford driving Gussie. Cushing watched through the field glasses as their cars were clearly ordered to the side of the road and subjected to a detailed search. 'Come on,' he said. 'Let's get moving. It's only a few hundred yards.'

But several hundred yards through the maquis, rough terrain covered in thorn bushes and spiky herbs, was a major effort, especially as Cushing trod slowly and carefully, confessing a fear of snakes. It was over an hour before they were able to carry the reliquary chest over the hill and down to the road on the French side where the cars were waiting. 'They gave us a bit of a going over,' said Clifford. 'And I'm sure that the car we saw was parked by the back of the customs post. Still, here we are. In you get, we've got some celebrating to do.'

When they returned to Clifford's villa they cleaned some more of the minor finds, concealed the gold, and Cushing started to work on the fragile and yellowed documents. The rest of the party, apart from Badger, were drinking champagne, and there was much discussion of what to do with the treasure trove. After a couple of hours Cushing called them together.

'I haven't had a proper look at the map yet,' he said, 'but the letter is definitely another one from our friend Amalric de Montfort, as I thought. You remember that he took the relics to Seborga...'

'So where are they then?' interrupted Scott. 'Still in the chapel? Not more digging, surely?'

'Let me finish. As we said in London, it's all linked to the Cathars.'

'Who are the Cathars?' asked Phoebe.

Cushing rolled his eyes pityingly. 'A religious group. This part of France wasn't under the control of the French king, and he wanted it. The Cathars were very tolerant of the Moors, and they had access to all sorts of knowledge and learning that was unknown to the rest of Christendom at the time. The king got the Pope to denounce them as heretics and preach a crusade against them. It was called the Albigensian Crusade, because it was against people who lived near – well, near Albi.'

'Well it was easier for them to get to than the Holy Land, I suppose,' said Sinclair.

'Of course they were rich, and Philip II and later Saint Louis IX, the kings of France, and all the other hangers on, wanted their treasures.'

'And maybe these treasures, too?' said Badger. 'I mean the ones that Amalric took to Castrum Sepulchri?'

'Well from what Amalric writes, they were of huge value to the Cathars as well as to the Templars and Hospitallers. Let me read. "I, Amalric de Montfort, by the grace of God Knight of St. John and Guardian of Lebanon after the death of my father, God rest his soul, write this in the year of our Lord 1209.

'"I have travelled to Castrum Sepulchri with the crown and stones to reunite them with the other treasures of the north. The other Guardians are here – my uncle Godfrey who holds the orb and Hugh, son of my uncle Tancred, who holds the sword.

'"The Grand Prior has ordered us to take the secrets to Montségur where she who is the purest of the pure, the light of the world, will wield them to defend our brothers the Cathars against the false knights of France and he who calls himself Pope. The cities of Beziers and Carcassonne have already fallen..."' Cushing interrupted himself. 'That's a known historical date, the fall of Beziers. Simon de Montfort massacred all the defenders.'

'Nasty,' said Gussie. 'Who's this woman, though, the light of the world?'

'I haven't got a clue, Gussie, sorry. Anyway there's only a little more.'

'Get on with it, then,' urged Scott. 'What did he do with the treasure?'

Cushing glared at Scott and continued to read. '"Though we may die in the attempt, the secrets have the power to bring destruction to the armies of my cousin Simon. Should we, the Guardians, be unable to bring the relics back to Castrum Sepulchri, then she, the purest of the pure, whom I love, will become their Guardian. By God's grace the enemy will never discover her secret stronghold. I, Amalric, son of Fulk de Montfort, Guardian of Lebanon and Knight of the Hospital of St. John of Jerusalem, give my seal to this."'

'Whom I love?' queried Gussie? 'Isn't that romantic?'

'So what happened?' asked Scott. 'To the Cathars, I mean.'

'Well, there was a long and bloody war. The Cathar forces – and perhaps this is where Amalric and his men came in – forced the French armies back, but they still lost huge amounts of land. Simon de Montfort became Count of Toulouse and the French king annexed most of what is now the Mediterranean coast of France.'

'But what happened to the Cathars?'

'It was all very unpleasant. Huge amounts of death and destruction. It was the beginning of the Inquisition, you know, vile torture by the Dominicans in the name of God. The final Cathar defences, places like the great castle of Montségur, didn't fall until about 1245, I think. Most of the Cathars in France were put to the sword. Though they continued in Spain and Italy for a while.'

'I remember Montségur,' said Scott excitedly. 'This is more of the basis for the Grail legend. Sir Perceval and all that.'

'So are you saying that this crown that has gone from Ugarit to Parmoor to Seborga and then to Montségur is the Holy Grail?' asked Gussie.

'No I'm not!' retorted Cushing, angrily. 'Why does everyone

keep going on about the Holy Grail?'

'But the relics never came back to Seborga,' said Clifford. 'So if they survived this apocalyptic battle that he keeps talking about, they must be in Montségur. And maybe your map shows her secret stronghold.' He relit his pipe.

'And they will be worth a fortune,' said Scott. 'Off to Montségur, I think. It's either that or more digging here. Come on, off to dinner and we can decide what to do.'

Cushing did not stay long at dinner. The party had, despite Scott's objections, agreed to spend one more day digging at the chapel on Mount Caggio, and Cushing wanted to continue his studies of the map in his own room.

Only six of them drove to Seborga the following morning; Clifford had decided to avoid another day digging in the hot sun and elected to stay in the villa, "working on cleaning the artefacts", as he put it. Sinclair had agreed to delay his journey to Toulouse until the evening, so joined the others. Cushing had been concerned that there might be an issue because some of their passports had not been stamped the day before, but the border officers failed to notice.

When they arrived at the chapel, however, they found it cordoned off, like the abbey further down the valley had been.

'I told you, we've been rumbled,' said Badger.

'Never mind,' said Scott. 'At least we don't have to dig any more. How about a quick glass in the café and then back home?'

The journey had given Cushing the opportunity to tell them of the research he had done far into the night, and he continued this over a coffee in the café in Seborga. 'The letter and the writing on the map seem to confirm that this Amalric de Montfort was both a Hospitaller and a Cathar.'

'He had implied that when he talked about his Cathar

brothers,' said Badger. 'But is that possible? Can he be both a Hospitaller and a Cathar?'

'Unusual. But he is either in love with, or married to…'

'Or even both,' interrupted Scott.

'Do be quiet, Geoffrey. He writes about this "pure" woman in Montségur. Now the "pure" are equivalent to priests within the Cathar heresy, or faith if you prefer. And the Cathars were happy to have female priests, unlike us and the Catholics. So whether or not this "pure" woman, who seems to be a Cathar, wielded the relics, they may be in Montségur. What I don't understand, though, is this map. It points to a cathedral and to a "room of glass", but there isn't a cathedral in Montségur or anywhere near there as far as I know. I was wondering whether it might be some network of catacombs or caves, but the scale is wrong. You can't have a cave the size of a cathedral.'

'Maybe she was due to meet Amalric there, wherever it is, if all went wrong with the battle,' suggested Scott optimistically. 'Maybe that's where the treasure is?'

'It makes sense,' replied Cushing. 'And there's a mark on the map next to the glass room thing. Let's take a look at a road atlas. I think there's one in the car.'

A Michelin guide was swiftly procured, and Cushing pointed out Montségur on the map. 'It's about twenty or thirty miles south west of Carcassonne,' he said, 'fifty miles south of Toulouse, right up towards the Pyrenees. We could be there by this evening if we drove hard.'

'Well let's go,' said Scott. 'We've got a few days on the opposition, at least.'

They continued to plan over another leisurely coffee, then drove back to Menton and straight to Clifford's villa.

'Bad news, old man,' called Cushing, as they strolled through the front door. 'They've rumbled us. Hello, Clifford? Are you there?'

He was interrupted by a piercing scream from Phoebe as she entered the open living room. The others rushed to join her and found the body of Molly Clifford prostrate on the floor, blood caked on a wound in her head. Badger immediately knelt by her, checked her pulse and shook his head.

'Clifford? Clifford!'

Scott went into the kitchen and shouted back to the others. 'Oh my God! Cushing, Badger, don't let the women in here.'

'What on earth…' Cushing burst past Scott into the kitchen and saw Clifford lying on the floor tied to a fallen chair. There was blood on his face and hands.

'He's been tortured. And beaten,' said Scott. Cushing checked his pulse – Clifford was dead too.

Scott picked up Clifford's pipe from the table. 'It's not been out for long,' he said. 'This must have been very recent.'

Cushing looked up from his friend's body. 'You're right. I'd say that Peter and Molly have been dead for no more than two, maybe three hours. But it looks as if Peter had a heart attack or something. It doesn't look as if any of these wounds actually killed him.'

Badger came downstairs. 'The place has been thoroughly searched, but whoever did this has gone.

Scott was looking round. 'They have taken the letter and the chest.' He looked into the bread bin where the bag of coins had been concealed. 'And they've taken the gold too.' The sound of sobbing came from the hallway. 'Badger, keep looking round. Whoever did this may still be here. Phoebe, it's all right.' And displaying an unusual tenderness, he went out to comfort the weeping girl. Cushing followed, and hugged Gussie who had tears streaming down her cheeks, while Sinclair, cursing like a trooper, covered the two bodies with blankets.

'Come on, what do we do?' he said. 'We can't stay here.'

'Well, we have to phone the police, don't we?' said Cushing.

'We can't,' said Scott. 'We'll be implicated. We're the only ones who can stop whatever this conspiracy is. National security, remember? We've got to get to Montségur.'

'But Peter and Molly...'

'Let's get on the move. Ring the police, and our embassy people. I'm sure there's a consul in Nice. Then send a telegram to Stockington, get him to sort us out. Whoever killed Clifford and Molly has probably already fingered us too.'

'He's right,' agreed Sinclair. 'If the French police get hold of us we'll never be able to...'

'But we can't just leave them!' Phoebe and Gussie spoke together.

'I'm sorry,' said Badger, 'but I think we have to. The authorities are compromised, I think we know that, and they can trace us from the border crossings. It's dreadful, and we all feel guilty, but there's nothing we can do for Clifford and Molly now. We have to leave them.'

'Absolutely right,' agreed Scott. 'Come on, Padre. This is awful, but we've got a job to do. We owe it to Clifford and Molly.'

Cushing looked painfully up at his friends and drew his hands across his face. 'You're probably right. Geoffrey, you and Badger make sure that there is nothing to trace us in the villa. You'd better take the blankets off the bodies too.' He turned to Sinclair. 'Jerry, we will have to leave Clifford's Rolls behind. It's two o'clock now. Can you fly the girls to somewhere convenient near Montségur? The rest of us can drive. I'll go and clear out his car now.'

'Absolutely, old boy. I'm your man. This is more important than some wretched air show.'

Scott and Badger returned to join the others. 'The house is clear.'

'Right,' said Cushing. 'Let's go back to the hotels. We need to check out.' Gussie and Phoebe were still crying. 'Geoffrey, take

Phoebe back to the Royale. The rest of us, as quickly as possible. Pack and meet in the reception of our hotel. Then Geoffrey can drive Sinclair and the girls to the airfield and pick up Badger and me after dropping them off.'

'But Christopher, I don't want to leave you...'

Cushing hugged Gussie again. 'You'll be safe with Jerry. Trust me. But I need you all to be airborne before we call the French police. Please, dear.' He took out his handkerchief and mopped her cheeks.

'Can't we just go home now?' Phoebe was also still in tears.

'No, we can't,' said Scott, just as kindly. 'Soon, though, I promise. It's not safe for you at the moment.'

The group had agreed to meet in Carcassonne, where Sinclair had identified a suitable airstrip, in a hotel that they had selected from the Michelin guide. He and the girls had left by aeroplane, and Scott started to drive Cushing and Badger away from the coast. They knew it would be after dark by the time they arrived.

The three men were morose and racked with guilt about the death of Peter and Molly Clifford and about leaving the bodies so callously. All were accustomed to sudden death, but this seemed much worse. Cushing was concerned about how to get the news to Clifford's son in New York, while Scott muttered for a while about revenge.

Cushing made telephone calls to report the murders before leaving Menton, first to the British consul in Nice and then to the French police. Both messages were made from a telephone box and delivered in an appalling French accent, but at least Cushing had not had to leave his name. As they drove out of Menton they could hear the sound of clanging bells from what they assumed to be the French police cars heading towards Clifford's villa.

As they drove, they were all convinced that the police bells would soon be chasing them, but they arrived safely in Nice on the way to send a telegram to Stockington. "Two of our party gone west from Menton suspect courtesy alleymen stop. Returning soonest as continuing presence may lead to extended French leave stop. Can you help query. Reply Hotel de la Cité Carcassonne end. Collins." He hoped that Stockington could pull sufficient strings with the French police to stop the party from being wanted for the murder of the Cliffords.

'Are you sure you trust this Stockington johnny?' asked Scott. 'After all, whenever you tell Stockington anything, someone gets hurt. Look at Page. Grainger. And now the Cliffords.'

'Ross trusted him,' said Cushing, simply. 'And I can't see who else can help us.'

There were no police in pursuit, though they also feared that their escape would be dogged by the men who had killed the Cliffords. Cushing realised that they needed to be prepared.

'I brought your revolver with me,' he said to Scott, grimly. 'I've been meaning to give it to you for a couple of days now. I think you would make better use of it than me. I didn't think we would need it, but...'

'Thanks, Padre,' replied Scott through clenched teeth, and they lapsed into an uneasy silence.

They eventually arrived in Carcassonne shortly before midnight, safe but exhausted, with their fears of pursuit unfounded. They easily found the Hotel de la Cité, a fine hotel near the battlements of the hilltop fortress.

The others had arrived some time before and booked rooms for them all, and this time Cushing was in no mood to quibble at the expense. The hotel manager was grumpy about their late arrival, but had been persuaded by Gussie to open a couple of bottles of wine and arrange some bread and cheese for the hungry drivers.

'They may have taken the letter,' said Cushing, 'but we still have the map. First thing tomorrow we can find out more about the Cathars.'

16

Wednesday 11th July 1928

News of the death of two English holiday makers in the Riviera was on the front page of Le Figaro in the morning.

'They refer to it as a burglary that went wrong,' said Cushing, over a breakfast that none of them really wanted. 'No mention of us at all.'

All remained very depressed. As they walked round the fortifications in the glorious summer sunshine, Scott sneered at the array of massive towers rising above the apparently cyclopean walls. 'It's a fake, you know,' he said. 'It looks impressive, but most of it was rebuilt sometime in the middle of the last century.'

'I thought it looked too new,' said Phoebe. 'It's like a Hollywood film set.'

Cushing and Gussie searched bookshops, museums and tourist guides for references to the Cathars, and it was not long before they had found a name that might have been the "purest of the pure". Esclarmonde de Foix, a famous Cathar "parfait", was rumoured to have taken and hidden certain Cathar treasures at the time of the crusade against them.

'And look, Gussie, the word Esclarmonde actually means "light of the world". It must be her.' He continued to flick through the books. 'She was involved in the great debates between the Catholics and the Cathars and then built up the fortifications of Montségur.'

'What a woman,' said Gussie. 'A warrior, a politician and a priest. No wonder Amalric was in love with her.'

'But where did she take the treasures? I can't find anything about any cathedral either, you know, like it says on Amalric's map, and in any case the Cathars didn't really have cathedrals at all. The cathedral here in Carcassonne wasn't even built when Esclarmonde was alive, I checked.'

'Let's at least go to Montségur then. Maybe what you're looking at isn't a map of caves at all. Or perhaps the cathedral on the map is just the name of a cave below Montségur? And if Esclarmonde is from Foix, perhaps we should go and look around there as well?'

'That's a good point, Gussie,' replied Cushing. 'Come on, let's look at a map back at the hotel. I suppose we'd better buy one of these books, too. I think the shopkeeper is getting a bit cross with us.'

While Cushing and Gussie were carrying out their investigations, the others were hiring a couple of smaller and less ostentatious cars. Scott particularly had been anxious that the Rolls Royce could be traced, and after some negotiation was able to rent two small black Citroens that were rather less conspicuous and procure a garage for the Rolls. He had been concerned at Phoebe's reaction, but she was sanguine. 'It's only a car,' she said. 'My stepfather does have quite a few, you know. And if we're going to fly back to England, we will have to leave the car anyway, won't we, so why not here? He can always send a man to pick it up later.' She thought for a moment. 'Perhaps I should send him a letter telling him to send someone over now?' Scott was easily able to dissuade her from this plan.

They met again at the hotel at lunchtime. 'The place may be

a fake, but it does look great,' said Phoebe.

Cushing read a telegram he had received from Stockington. 'Strange,' he said. 'Stockington says that "our little problem", as he calls it, was being attended to before he made any enquiries.'

'What's strange about that?' asked Scott.

'My guess,' replied Cushing, 'is that the people who killed Peter and Molly reported to their masters. They included this Domvile man who has got to the French police in some way. I thought it odd that the morning paper only reported the murders as a burglary that went wrong.'

'Sounds feasible,' said Badger. 'But either way, we ought to get away from here.'

They agreed to drive to Montségur and then to Foix. Gussie and Phoebe, still in shock, were disappointed to leave such a luxurious hotel after so little time, but the men were adamant. 'And it was your idea to go to Foix, Gussie,' said Cushing.

They left the walls of Carcassonne behind them that afternoon and, as Scott drove through stunning scenery, south to Quillan and then west on country roads towards Montségur, Cushing spent most of the time in the passenger seat scanning the books he had bought. 'There's definitely a legend here,' he said, as the car bumped along the uneven roads – it was certainly less comfortable than the Rolls Royce. 'Esclarmonde is reputed to have taken the Cathar treasures from Montségur before it fell, but we're talking 1244, at least thirty years after Amalric de Montfort brought his treasures to her from Seborga.'

'Poor man,' said Phoebe. 'I wonder what happened to him? That was such a romantic story.'

'Well if the crusaders got hold of him he was probably hacked to pieces and burned to death,' said Scott. 'Though not necessarily in that order.' Phoebe and Gussie pulled faces. 'Sorry,' he apologised.

'And this book keeps bringing it back to the Grail legend, too,' continued Cushing. 'This writer equates Montségur with Muntsalvaesche.'

'What?' exclaimed Gussie and Scott together.

'It's the Grail castle in Parzival. You know, Geoffrey. Wolfram von Eschenbach. Or Wagner, if you prefer. We were talking about it just the other day. The thirteenth century poem.' Scott continued to look blank. 'Where the legend said the Grail was hidden. Oh for heaven's sake!'

'I'll think about the Grail in good time,' said Scott, grimly patting his pocket that contained the revolver Cushing had returned to him the day before. 'I just hope we get a chance to catch up with the people who did for Clifford and Molly.'

Cushing was quiet for a moment. 'They mean the same thing, too.'

'What do?'

'Montségur and Muntsalvaesche, or Montsalvat. They all mean "safe mountain".'

'If Esclarmonde took the treasures from Montségur,' interrupted Gussie, 'surely there is no point going there?'

'Well we don't know whether she did. And if nearly contemporary legend is mixing up the Templars, the Cathars, Esclarmonde and Montségur with this Grail nonsense, who knows what treasures we are talking about. I mean, Amalric writes about taking a crown and some stones, while his uncles and cousins brought a sword and an orb. There's nothing about a cup.'

'The Holy Grail is a cup, is it?' asked Phoebe.

'It's supposed to be the cup that Christ used at the Last Supper. Anyway, we have to go to Montségur and see if we can match up this map with caves or a cathedral.'

The ruins of the fortifications at Montségur were visible

from many miles away, proudly topping a rocky peak which rose abruptly from the arid scrub of the surrounding hills. Scott pulled into the side of the road to let Badger and Sinclair in the other Citroen catch them up.

'That's amazing,' breathed Gussie. 'How on earth did the crusaders manage to break down their defences? Those walls! That hill is so steep...'

'Starved them out, most probably,' said Scott. 'Or poisoned the water. Or maybe they were betrayed?'

'The survivors were all burned to death,' said Cushing. 'Over two hundred of them, and it took ten thousand crusaders to lay the siege.'

'Well let's get into town and take a closer look,' said Sinclair. 'I could use a drink.'

They drove into town, which was, in fact, no more than a small village strung out along the twisting road and centred on a small square at the foot of the peak. They parked the cars under the lime trees. As they walked towards one of the small bars, Badger drew their attention to a large black car parked opposite. 'I say, wasn't that the car that we saw in Seborga?'

'You could be right,' agreed Sinclair. 'We got a pretty good look at it as we drove back through the border. You know, when you went over the scrub to avoid the customs post.'

Scott flexed his fingers. 'I'm looking forward to meeting them,' he said, and sat down outside the bar which appeared to be deserted other than two elderly Frenchmen wearing berets and overalls and smoking cigarettes over two glasses of pastis. The waiter brought beer, wine and fruit juice, served in glasses that had apparently not been cleaned since the Armistice.

'Je cherche la cathédrale,' said Cushing to the waiter, somewhat optimistically. The waiter shrugged – there was no cathedral within a hundred miles. 'Nous avons un château.' He pointed up at the walls perched on top of the steep-sided mountain that loomed over the village. He cracked a joke with the two blue-clad locals who pointed at the party, snickering.

Cushing tried again. 'Peut-être on trouve des caves sous le château?' The waiter sneered again. He had cellars below his bar, he said, but he knew of none below the castle.

'Damn the man,' said Cushing. 'Why can't they speak proper English?' He turned back to the waiter. 'Pas les caves. Les cavernes. Les grottes. Souterrain.'

The Frenchman shrugged again disdainfully, having no knowledge of caves under the castle either, and Phoebe put her hand on Scott's arm as he started to rise, looking murderous. 'Steady on, Geoffrey. You can't hit him. He's only a stupid waiter.'

'I'm not looking at the waiter,' he said, angrily. 'Look. Over there.'

And across the small square the party could see four men walking up to the black car.

'Sit down, Geoffrey,' said Cushing, hoarsely. 'Look. That's the man who shot at me in London. The German, Gemp. And the other one – the one who was dressed as a policeman.'

'I know,' said Scott, moving his hand threateningly towards his pocket.

'No, Geoffrey, we've got to be careful,' insisted Cushing. 'We've got the girls with us.' The party watched impotently as the men they suspected of the murder of the Cliffords drove away, not noticing the group of English men and women in the bar opposite.

'Let's follow them,' said Sinclair.

'No, Jerry, we can't,' said Cushing. 'They will be armed.'

'So are we,' muttered Scott.

'Don't be silly, Geoffrey,' said Cushing. 'Now where were they coming from?'

'Maybe the hotel across the square?' said Gussie. 'It looks nicer than this bar, at least.'

'Let's take a look,' said Badger. They paid the surly waiter and crossed the square. The tables in front of the hotel were empty, but a sign over the door stated that the hotel was full. Next door, a tatty board announced a local museum.

'Gussie, you go in and see if this is where they are staying,' said Cushing. 'Badger, keep an eye on the cars. Jerry, you stay with him in case they come back. The rest of us, let's check the museum.'

An elderly man sat in a comfortable chair reading a book and charged Cushing, Scott and Phoebe a few francs to look round the grubby room. They peered at pictures of the castle, poorly-executed paintings of battles and people in medieval costume, dusty copies of Parzival, and various rusted bits of weaponry. Cushing drew their attention to a scene of men in armour with Templar and Hospitaller crosses on their surcoats, and then to one of the typed notices on the wall.

'It says here that the crusaders destroyed the walls entirely,' he said. 'So these ones must be more modern. Like Carcassonne.'

'This is more boring then Seborga,' moaned Phoebe.

'Seborga,' interrupted the elderly man in a croaking and heavily accented voice. 'You have been to Seborga? And you know about the Templars? Very interesting.'

'What do you mean, Monsieur?' asked Cushing politely.

'The Templars guarded the Grail, you know,' he replied, his eyes twinkling. 'They fought with the Cathars against the Pope's men. They came from Seborga and fought alongside our heroine, Esclarmonde. So this is why Parzifal is pictured as a Templar knight, you see.' He glared at them. 'But you are English, yes? Not German?'

'Definitely not,' replied Scott and Cushing, almost in unison.

'Good,' said the elderly curator, running his hands through his shaggy grey hair. 'Both my sons were killed at Verdun by the Germans. And you,' he said, looking at Cushing, 'you are a priest?'

'Yes, Monsieur,' replied Cushing.

'So am I, so am I. C'est parfait.' The old man laughed. 'Now, you have come from Seborga to Montségur. Tell me, what are you looking for? The treasure of the Cathars? Or the Holy Grail? Just the same as the Germans and Americans who have just left?'

'Well, sort of, I suppose,' admitted Cushing. 'But perhaps slightly different. Are there any caves under the mountain? And is there a cathedral in the area? And what happened to Esclarmonde?'

The elderly man looked flummoxed for a while. 'I know of no caves under the mountain,' he said, 'and no cathedral. There are caves all round this area of France, though. They discovered some old paintings by men from the Stone Age near here, just a few years ago.' He sighed. 'But I know what you are asking. There are no caves close to here associated with the Cathars. And Esclarmonde, well, some say that she took the treasures with her. But where she went, who knows? No one has ever found her tomb.'

'This Esclarmonde,' asked Phoebe, 'did she ever marry a man called Amalric de Montfort?'

'I have not read that she did, my dear,' he replied, 'but then again, our Cathar priests, our parfaits, both men and women, were allowed to marry. A strange name, though. It was De Montfort who led the Pope's men.'

'A different de Montfort,' said Cushing. 'It is his story we are following. He is a knight of the Hospital, not the Temple. We have seen an old document that said that he was in love with Esclarmonde.'

'Then maybe she did marry him, maybe she didn't. Perhaps you should try in Foix? Ask for my son, Bernard Buisson, in the museum there.'

'That's where we are going next,' said Cushing. 'Thank you.

We will.'

'I say,' said Scott, 'just what were these other people after?'

'The Grail, of course,' replied the curator. 'They are digging up at the castle. But I think that our secrets will stay hidden a little while longer.'

The three made their farewells, and met Gussie having a glass of wine in front of the hotel. 'Absolutely full,' she said. 'Ten rooms or so, all taken. A large party, it seems, an Englishman, a pair of Americans, a Frenchman, a Spaniard, at least two Germans. Archaeologists, investigating the castle. I think we should be on our way before they all come down.'

'Well I wasn't planning to go up to the castle anyway,' said Cushing, 'not in this heat.'

'And especially not now that we know the place is crawling with the opposition,' agreed Scott. 'It's a real international conspiracy, just as Ross said.'

'One thing I didn't understand,' said Phoebe. 'The curator man said he was a priest. How can he be? He's got children.'

Cushing frowned. 'I suspect he regards himself as a Cathar priest, or parfait. Mind you, I'm surprised to find anyone practising Catharism these days. But just as Esclarmonde can marry and have children, I imagine he can too, if he styles himself as some sort of parfait.'

Scott snickered. 'So the Cathars are just like the good old Church of England, then.'

'Not at all, they're heretics. We were...' He looked round and saw the others grinning at him, teasingly. 'Oh come on, let's get a move on. We need to pick up the others and find somewhere to stay in Foix. Gemp and his friends are on our tail – in fact they will be ahead of us by now.'

The drive to Foix as they wound down the road that hugged

the Ariège river was, if anything, even more spectacular than the route they had taken earlier in the day. The mountains were steeper and the river sparkled in the sunlight. They drove into Foix, admiring the medieval castle with its three towers again perched on a rock in the centre of town, and found a small hotel in the old town.

'I'm surprised that Simon de Montfort didn't raze this place to the ground as well,' observed Badger, over a lemonade.

'He tried, I think,' said Cushing. 'Then he struck some kind of a deal with the Comte de Foix and carried on south.' He turned to his friends. 'Anyway, look, I'm a little bit worried about money. I'm getting short of French cash and, even if we aren't front page news any more, I don't think I want to go to a bank. How much do we have between us?'

The others checked wallets and bags, and it was clear that they had enough francs between them to last for a few more days. 'I was lucky at the tables,' said Phoebe.

'And if all else fails,' said Scott, conspiratorially, 'perhaps these might help.' He took from his pocket a small number of gold coins.

Cushing spluttered. 'They are the ones we found in Seborga,' he exclaimed. 'What are you doing with them?'

'I just took my share for safekeeping,' admitted Scott, nonchalantly. 'Just a few of them. Just my share, you know.'

Cushing found it hard to keep his voice down and avoid the attention of the staff, but began to abuse Scott for what he had done.

'It's a good job I did, though,' said Scott, defensively. 'Otherwise they would all have been taken, wouldn't they? And Phoebe has her share too, of course.'

Phoebe blushed prettily and Cushing snorted again. 'It's a disgrace,' he muttered.

Sinclair looked around shiftily, and took some coins out of

his pocket and placed them on the table. 'Sorry, Padre,' he said. 'But I took a share as well.'

Badger looked uncomfortable, and then he too produced a handful of gold. 'I though that just in case anything happened...'

'Oh for heaven's sake!' exclaimed Cushing again. 'You should all be ashamed of yourselves. Am I the only one? Gussie? Surely...' He looked over and saw that she too was holding out a handful of coins.

Scott and Sinclair started to laugh. 'Come on, Padre. I think this calls for some champagne.'

17

Thursday 12th July 1928

The following morning, after an early breakfast, the party went straight to the museum at the foot of the castle and asked to speak to M. Buisson. Buisson, a middle-aged man with a shock of greying hair and a drooping moustache, bore a strong resemblance to his father.

Buisson was happy to help, especially after they said how his father had sent them to him, but was unable to give them much more information, though he added to their confusion with more muddling legend. 'According to the story, the forces of Satan, or the Pope, you know, came to take the Grail from Montségur and restore it to Satan's crown. All the other defenders perished, but Esclarmonde flew to the east in the shape of a dove.'

Scott muttered something under his breath that sounded suspiciously like 'stuff and nonsense', and asked about what happened to Esclarmonde after she turned into a dove. 'No one knows,' replied Buisson, stiffly, 'but her grave has never been found'.

When Cushing asked about the caves, Buisson told them of the caves beneath the castle hill in Foix which were already being prepared for the annual medieval pageant, but he knew of no cathedral. Cushing pressed him, though, spelling out some of the names on his map of the caves. 'Aha!' exclaimed Buisson. 'Lombrives, you say? Yes, that is familiar. Many Cathars died at the caves at Lombrives. It is less than twenty kilometres from here.

'My son explores the caves all the way down the river,' he continued. 'Every year or so we find new cave paintings. He will be back at lunchtime. You can ask him then, if you like.'

The group, now filled with enthusiasm, left the archivist at the museum and headed for the caves under the castle of Foix. They joined a guided tour and were shown prehistoric cave paintings and mammoth tusks by a grinning Frenchman dressed in medieval garb. Cushing surreptitiously confirmed that the caves bore no resemblance to those on his map. Groups of labourers continually walked past them, bringing electrical equipment to prepare for the medieval pageant.

'What is this pageant, anyway?' asked Cushing.

A tall, thin, clean-cut young man with fair hair in the tour party turned round and addressed them in accented English. 'You see, the pageant is about the crowning of the new king. It happens every year in Foix. They burn effigies of Moors as well, so you see that it is a good thing.'

'A good thing?'

'Why yes, of course. It represents the old conflict between good and evil, the black and the white, the new and the old, the masculine and the feminine, the holly and the ivy as they are shown in our northern pagan background. And of course it is a lot of fun for the peasants.'

'I'm sorry,' interrupted Scott. 'Have we been introduced?'

'No, no,' said the man. 'My name is Otto Rahn. I am a student from the University of Giessen. I am studying medieval history and I am here on my holidays. I am particularly interested in the Cathar religion, you see.' His eyes shone in the reflected light.

'Well it certainly is most fascinating,' said Cushing, torn between natural politeness and an unwillingness to share their names with the young German. He made up his mind and introduced the party to Rahn. 'So, have you been here long?'

'Only a few days,' replied the student.

'There are quite a few of your countrymen in this part of the world,' said Scott.

'Really?' inquired Rahn, innocently. 'I have not met any. I spoke yesterday to an American man who was helping to organise the pageant – he works for the Count, I believe – but I have met no Germans.'

'We came across them in Montségur,' said Scott, suspiciously. 'They are archaeologists, I believe.'

'Ach, well, perhaps I have not met them because I have not yet been to Montségur,' said Rahn. 'I was planning to take a car one day this week, maybe this afternoon. But I came to Foix by train, you see.' He consulted his watch. 'Perhaps you gentlemen, and ladies, would care to join me for a coffee? The tour is ending.'

Cushing was anxious not to tell the affable young German any more, despite the fact that he seemed to be exactly what he said he was, but they had another half hour to kill before returning to meet Buisson and his son. Rahn was clearly a knowledgeable student. He had begun his studies looking entirely at the military campaign of Simon de Montfort and the associated development of the Inquisition, but what he had seen in the area was sparking his interest in the Cathar religion and the legend of the Holy Grail. The conversation with the party, however guarded, served only to fan that spark.

They left Rahn at the café and returned to the museum, with Scott reminding Cushing not to be so single-minded about Germans. 'This conspiracy, it really isn't just German, you know. These are the international Synarchists, we think, remember.'

The museum door was shut and the sign marked "Fermé",

but Cushing knocked and Buisson welcomed them in. He took them through the museum to the house at the rear and introduced them to his son, Vincent, a dark muscular young man. Vincent looked at them in a surly manner and carried on eating his lunch, served by his mother, a stout, smiling woman, while the party fired questions at him.

Vincent remained unresponsive, and eventually Cushing was forced to pull out the old map. The archivist was immediately enthralled at the document itself, but his son looked only at the depiction of the tunnels. 'Ah yes', he said. 'La Cathédrale. This is it, yes?'

'La Cathédrale?' His father was as surprised as the party.

'Yes, this is what the spéléologistes – the cave men – call this big cave. It is part of the Grottes de Lombrives. And here, I know these tunnels. These ones, here, leading to La Cathédrale. They are all at Lombrives. But I do not know these ones, shown at the back of La Cathédrale. La Chambre de Cristal – the room of glass.' He stood up, excited. 'These caves, they have not been found. This is wonderful. Formidable.' He rattled on in a fast exchange in French with his father, who quietened him down.

'Vincent says that he would be honoured to guide you gentlemen to these caves. They are only twenty kilometres or so to the south, by the river near Tarascon. He suggests that you should go when there are no tourists. Perhaps tomorrow morning, very early?'

They arranged to pick up Vincent from the house shortly before four the following morning, when dawn would be breaking. He agreed that he would bring rope, flashlights, overalls and helmets for them to borrow.

'Why, are the caves dangerous?' asked Scott.

'In bad weather, yes, when it floods, otherwise no more so than other caves,' said Vincent, 'but if we are exploring new tunnels then I will wear a helmet. It is most exciting to have a new map.'

'And are they all locked up, if we are in the tourist season?' asked Gussie.

'Maybe,' he replied, shrugging his shoulders in a typically Gallic manner. 'But there is always a way into the caves.'

The party were frustrated to be wasting the best part of a day before their early start. 'What are we waiting for?' asked Scott. 'I mean, the place is open for tourists. And we passed Tarascon yesterday; it's less than an hour away. Come on. Let's take a look now.'

And they jumped into the two cars and drove excitedly to the Grottes de Lombrives. Parting with a few francs entry fee, they were ushered as part of a group of about a dozen tourists through an artificially-widened cleft into a twisting maze of tunnels. Cushing was able to sneak surreptitious glances at a copy he had made of the map, and recognised the route they were taking. The floors were damp and slippery, but the flickering electric light and the ropes attached to the walls of the tunnels made it easier than it might have been, even though they were wearing their normal shoes. Most of the tunnels were high enough to take a man walking, but Cushing and Scott were both tall and, despite the admonitions of their guide, kept banging their heads on the roof.

The guide stopped occasionally on the way and pointed out some of the exotically-shaped stalactites and stalagmites as well as some primitive cave paintings. About forty minutes after they had entered the cave system, Cushing whispered to Scott and the others. 'We're coming up to the Cathedral. Just like on Amalric's map.'

The guide warned the group to grasp the rope as he wanted to surprise them with the view of the Cathedral. The lights went out suddenly and, despite the guide's warnings, there were a number of female screams. The group shuffled forward in pitch darkness, hanging onto the rope, and Gussie was certainly hanging onto

Cushing as if for dear life. 'Attendez,' called out the guide, and the lights came back on.

The Cathedral was vaster and more beautiful than any cave that any of the party had seen before. Shards of crystal glittered in the lights, and the array of stalactites some hundred feet above them left them awed.

'It's wonderful,' said Gussie. 'And it's huge. It must be twice the size of the Albert Hall.'

The guide started to give his prepared tale of the five hundred Cathars who were murdered in the caves – the beginning of the Inquisition. Meanwhile, Scott and Badger followed Cushing as far as they could to the back of the Cathedral where his map showed a tunnel leading off. There was no tunnel visible, but a large area of the wall had been smoothed and carved into the shape of a huge cross, with an inscription in Latin etched into the wall next to it.

The guide came over to them, and spoke rapidly in French. Cushing translated. 'This is where the Cathar bishop, if that's the right word, Amiel Aicard, died after the fall of Montségur. This is why they call it the Cathedral.'

As the guide went away, Cushing started to look more carefully. 'I can't see another tunnel anywhere,' he said. 'I hope that Vincent will know where to look.'

The guide called the party back to rejoin the group and they trudged back to the surface, shivering now in the cold. They returned to the cars and started to drive back to Foix. As they left the car park, Cushing gawped out of the window as the large black car that they had seen in Montségur swept past them. 'That's him again. Gemp. The German. The man who killed Ross. They seem to be trailing us.'

'It's all right, Padre,' said Scott, calmingly. 'Again, they haven't seen us.'

'But they're here!'

'Yes, dear,' soothed Gussie. 'But we have the map, remember. They don't. And we're coming back in the morning.'

That evening, the group ate sparingly in the restaurant in the hotel, planning an early night. Cushing was insistent that Gussie and Phoebe should not join them. 'It's going to be dangerous,' he said. 'The tunnels won't be safe. And I'm worried about those Germans.'

'That suits me,' said Phoebe. 'It's cold and wet and slimy down there. You men go and have your fun. I'll meet you after breakfast.'

'Good girl,' said Scott, approvingly.

'Wait a minute,' interjected Gussie. 'You're not getting rid of me that easily. I'm coming with you.' And again, Cushing and the others were unable to dissuade her.

As they climbed the stairs to their rooms, they met the young German student, Otto Rahn, coming the other way. 'Good evening,' he said. 'I did not know you were in the same hotel as me. I have taken your advice and I went to Montségur this afternoon. Most fascinating. Though I did not find the German archaeologists of whom you spoke. I shall go again tomorrow.' He seemed genuinely disappointed that the party made their excuses and left him to his own devices.

18

Friday 13th July 1928

They were all tired some few hours later, though ready for action, wrapped up warmly and wearing stout boots. 'Phoebe is fast asleep,' said Gussie, glumly and probably a little jealously. Unlike the men, she was looking stylish in coat and jodhpurs. But like the others, her excitement was tangible as they saw Vincent waiting for them.

As they loaded the caver's equipment into the back of the cars, they could not understand why he was looking downcast. 'I was in the bar last night with my caving friends,' he said, mournfully, 'and two Germans came in. They said they were archaeologists, and they wanted a guide to the Grottes de Lombrives.'

'No!' shouted Cushing.

'But yes. I ignored them, and so did most of my friends.' He spat on the road. 'But Jean-Pierre took their money and left with them.'

'What time was this,' asked Cushing?

'About half past seven,' replied Vincent. 'That Jean-Pierre, he will take money from anyone.' He spat again.

'So we may have company,' said Scott, tapping a bulge in his jacket pocket.

'Good stuff,' said Sinclair, approvingly, and Cushing and Badger nodded in agreement.

'Hold on,' said Gussie. 'I've said before that we can't go round shooting people.'

'Why not?' asked Cushing, mildly. 'These two have shot at me already.'

'Well apart from anything else, Christopher, you're a vicar. It's just not right.'

'They started it. They killed Ross. Well if we bump into them I've got a little surprise waiting.'

The others did not understand what he meant, and they drove to Lombrives, the morning light starting to break through the gloom.

'I've just remembered,' said Cushing. 'It's Friday the thirteenth.'

'Unlucky for some,' muttered Scott.

'Exactly,' said Cushing. 'It's supposed to be unlucky because it was the day that the French king Philip the Fair turned on the Templars.'

'And it will be unlucky for those Germans if they get in our way,' emphasised Scott, and Cushing agreed. Gussie rolled her eyes in disbelief.

But when they arrived in the car park, there were no other cars there, and the party breathed a collective sigh of relief. They pulled on overalls and donned helmets, and unloaded lights, rope, and the picks and shovels they had brought back from Seborga. Badger walked up to the locked cave entrance and less than a minute later an impressed-looking Vincent waved to the others to join them. They roped themselves together, switched on the lights, and followed the route through the tunnels they had taken the previous day.

Half an hour later, and with fewer bangs on the head thanks to their helmets, they were all in the Cathedral. Cushing showed

Vincent the map and he agreed that it seemed as if the unknown tunnel started from the huge cross of the Cathar bishop. Cushing had noticed a number of what looked like Masonic marks on the map, and pointed these out to the rest of the group.

Gussie knelt down at the foot of the cross and beckoned the others to look at a mark close to the floor – a circle in a square that matched the one on the map. She then looked closer at the inscription. 'Look,' she said, 'there's a little carving of a dove here. Didn't you say that a dove was the symbol of the Cathars?'

'That's right,' said Cushing. 'And now you mention it, the Cathars wouldn't have used a representation of Christ on the cross. That's not right.'

'This whole area with the inscription looks as if it's covering something up,' said Gussie.

Scott walked over and tapped on the wall with his crowbar. 'You could be right,' he said. 'It sounds hollow,' and impetuously swung the crowbar hard at the base of the cross. Cushing stepped forward with a cry of anguish, but two strikes later and Scott had exposed a hole. 'Good thinking, Gussie, Padre,' he said, breathing heavily.

Vincent peered down with the flashlight. 'It is a tunnel,' he said. 'Magnifique. Widen the entrance.' Smugly, Scott continued to expand the hole until there was enough space for them all to crawl through.

'Keep roped together,' said Vincent, and led them through. After about ten yards, they were able to stand. Vincent was in awe. 'No one has been here for hundreds of years,' he said. 'I am honoured.'

They followed the map, Cushing noting more Masonic-type marks where the passages forked, and following them. Scott, keeping up the rear, marked the route in the event that they needed a quick getaway. Vincent urged them to be careful – he pointed out one area where the roof had collapsed, and they clambered over the fallen rock – and stopped at a sluggish stream. The rocks on either side were black and slippery. 'The water must be much higher when it rains,' he said. 'And we don't know how deep it is.' Cushing identified the stream on the map, and then they entered a cavern, where a huge stalagmite and stalactite were nearly connected in the centre, virtually filling the whole space.

'This can't be right,' he said. 'The map shows a pillar here, but nothing of this size.'

'The map is seven hundred years old, Padre,' said Scott. 'The stalagmite has had a lot of time to grow.'

They edged round the pillar, still roped together, and up a steep and narrow passage. As Vincent led them carefully round a corner, he brought them to a sudden halt, and indicated that they should be silent. 'Turn out the lights,' he whispered.

As the rest of the party rounded the corner of the passage, they could see a flicker of light. Vincent switched one light back on and covered the beam with his hand, and the party inched forwards. Scott reached into his pocket and took out his revolver, and peered round the corner. They could see him waving them on to join him. As they entered a small chamber they were silent.

Lit by guttering oil lamps, the ceiling sparkled with white quartz. 'The room of glass, perhaps,' said Cushing. The room was beautiful, but there was much else for them to look at. At one end of the chamber was a sarcophagus, and beside it was lying a figure, cross-legged, wearing chain mail and holding a sword. A dark passage led from the other side, and near it on the floor was slumped the figure of a bearded man in overalls, blood caked on a wound in his head. 'Jean-Pierre,' whispered Vincent, and checked the man's pulse. 'He is alive.' Gussie immediately went and knelt beside the injured man to treat him.

'They've beaten us to it,' muttered Cushing. 'And they've tried to kill their guide.'

'That's as maybe,' said Scott. 'But they must be coming back, or they wouldn't have left these lamps lit. There must be another way in.' He waved his flashlight. 'Look, that passage over there. They must have taken a load of stuff already and...'

But Cushing wasn't listening. He was looking at the body of the man in armour. It was more than a skeleton – the dryness of the air in the chamber had desiccated the body which seemed almost mummified – and it appeared to be the figure of a man aged about sixty. 'It's Amalric,' said Cushing, reverently. 'Look at his signet ring. It's the one he used to seal the documents.'

He moved over to the sarcophagus where the lid had been removed and placed on the floor. He looked at the body inside, clearly that of a woman, and then read the letters on the side. 'It's her,' he said. 'Esclarmonde de Foix. There's an inscription in Latin and Occitan, the Provencal language. We've found it. And Amalric has stayed with her in death for seven hundred years.'

Scott joined him and started to remove the ring gently from Amalric's finger. Cushing laid a hand on Scott's arm. 'Leave it, Geoffrey.'

'Look, Padre, if we don't take it, the others will.' He looked around. 'Bastards. Look, they've smashed open the chests over there, and piled up a load of swords and things. And they've broken Esclarmonde's grip on whatever she was holding. They must have taken all the good stuff, but they'll be back for the rest. We'd better move fast.'

Badger and Sinclair were looking at piles of equipment and documents that had been roughly sorted and placed on the floor. 'You're right, they must be coming back for this lot,' said Badger, frantically loading handfuls of ancient books and parchments into his backpack. He stood up, waving a pair of clay tablets similar to the ones that Cushing had found in Ross's briefcase. 'They missed these, though.'

Cushing allowed Scott to remove Amalric's ring, and looked more closely at the two bodies. Scott was right. The corpse of

Esclarmonde had obviously been roughly handled to access whatever else had been in the sarcophagus. Her hands, where the grip of death had tightened on some unknown object, had been roughly pulled back, and a finger broken, presumably to remove a ring. He looked down again at Amalric's body. There was a gash in de Montfort's mail shirt, and some of his ribs were broken. 'It looks like he was badly wounded,' he said, and felt inside the remnants of the padded leather jerkin inside his coat of mail. With a gasp, he pulled out another oiled package. 'It's another letter.'

Suddenly Vincent, who was standing at the end of the other passage, gestured wildly. 'They are coming,' he whispered. 'Allez, allez.'

Badger and Sinclair started to pick up the unconscious body of Jean-Pierre.

'What the devil are you doing?' asked Scott, abruptly.

'Well we're not going to leave him, surely,' replied Badger, taking the man's legs. 'I mean, that's what the Synarchists and their German friends did. We're British, after all.'

Scott shrugged. 'Get on with it, then.' With Gussie fussing over them, the two men and their burden made their way out slowly, squeezing down the steep passage and round the chamber with the giant stalactite and stalagmite. Vincent followed, then Cushing, but Scott was still inside the chamber loading things into his rucksack when a man appeared in the opening of the passage opposite. The two faced each other, the newcomer clearly shocked, and Scott started to hurry backwards. 'What the hell...?' exclaimed the man, in what seemed to be an Irish brogue. 'Was ist das?' heard Scott, as another man entered the cavern, passing the Irishman.

It was Gemp, the man who had shot at Cushing and Scott in London. He drew a pistol and aimed it at Scott who was retreating fast, encumbered by rucksack and flashlight. But Scott already had his own revolver in his hand, and fired it wildly. The noise of the shot was deafening in the confined space. He missed Gemp by feet and the bullet ricocheted round the chamber, knocking chips from the quartz ceiling. Gemp rolled to the floor and fired as Scott fled for the tunnel. Gemp's shot nicked Scott in the shoulder as he scuttled, cursing, to join the others.

'Hurry up,' he shouted. 'They're on my tail.'

The group were held back by the need to carry the unconscious Jean-Pierre, and a volley of pistol shots followed them as they limped down the tunnels, the opposition hard on their heels. 'Vincent, get the others to safety,' called Scott. He crouched down at the entrance to the cavern with the stream through which they had passed earlier, and turned his light out. He could see the lights of his pursuers and fired three times. There was a scream from the darkness and a splash, and he turned and ran. Around the corner he could see a light – Cushing had waited for him. 'I told you to go, Padre,' he shouted. 'Get a move on. I think I hit one of them. That should hold them for a bit.'

Breathless, the two men scrambled again over the pile of fallen rock and took cover. Undeterred by Scott's earlier shooting, their attackers were gaining on them. They had crossed the stream and were approaching, under the cover of aimed fire. More shots flew over the heads of the Englishmen, to which Scott replied in kind. Cushing pulled a pistol from his pocket and fired a couple of shots blindly into the darkness while Scott was reloading. Scott jumped a mile, then turned and looked admiringly at his godfather. 'Where did you get that pistol?' he exclaimed. 'It's an old German one, isn't it? You old dog.' Cushing smiled grimly in the beam of the flashlight, a strange glint in his eyes, and fumbled in his rucksack. 'I said I had a surprise for them,' he said. 'Murdering swine. They are the ones who tortured Clifford. Come on.' He fired two more shots from his old Luger, Scott followed suit and the two men rushed for the tunnel, pleased at

Scott's foresight in marking the route.

'Off you go, Geoffrey,' said Cushing. 'Run, now.'

'Don't be ridiculous, old man,' retorted Scott. 'You go. Or we can both hold them off here while the others get clear.'

'I've got a better plan,' said Cushing, ducking as a bullet ricocheted past his head. 'Let's see how they like this.' He revealed two more of his old souvenirs: the German stick grenades.

Scott winced. 'Have we been carrying those things around on all those bumpy roads? You must be mad! We could have been blown to bits. I hope they're safe.'

'I hope they're not,' replied Cushing, and, exposing himself to the risk of being shot, tossed the two grenades into the pile of fallen rock. 'Come on, run!'

The two men fled as fast as they could down the tunnel. A few seconds later they were thrown to the floor by the force of two loud explosions, and clouds of dust followed them up the tunnel. Choking and spluttering, they got to their feet. More large chunks of rock had fallen from the ceiling behind them, and they were blinded and deafened by the noise. 'Good work, Padre. Let's go. Come on.'

Scott half-dragged the stumbling Cushing down the corridor and helped him crawl out through the hole they had made back into the Cathedral.

'Thank heavens you're safe,' cried Gussie, throwing her arms around Cushing, who looked at her blankly.

'What happened?' asked Vincent. 'What was that noise?'

'I think the tunnel collapsed,' replied Scott. 'You said the roofs weren't safe, and you were right. Come on, let's get out of here.'

Filthy and exhausted, they stumbled back into bright sunshine. Vincent was anxious that they should leave before any of the staff arrived, but Gussie was emphatic that she should do the best she could for Jean-Pierre before taking him to hospital.

'I used to be a nurse, remember?' she said, and took control. She cleaned and dressed his wound properly, and, after prompting from Sinclair, did the same for Scott, whose injury from Gemp's bullet was minor and would heal in good time. He and Cushing still had ringing in their ears from the blast of the grenades.

Badger was concerned about Cushing who was wandering round the car park, distracted, talking to himself. 'I've seen him like this before,' he said to Scott, anxiously. 'You say he threw two grenades at the Germans? Where did he get them from?'

'Heaven knows,' replied Scott. 'But the shooting and the explosions may have sent the old boy over the edge again. They call it shellshock now, and he spent ages recovering up in Scotland after – well, you know...'

'After he saved my life. Yes, I do know.'

'Still, at least Cushing's bombs meant that the Huns couldn't follow us. He did a grand job. Come on, let's get packed up and back to Foix while we can.'

Gently they loaded Jean-Pierre's inert body into one of the cars, and coaxed Cushing into the other. They were interrupted by the noise of an explosion from the side of a hill half a mile away, and a cloud of dust and smoke slowly dissipated in the light breeze.

'They must have blown up the entrance they used,' said Vincent. 'I wonder if we will ever find the chamber again now? But we must! We have found the tomb of Esclarmonde. The legends, they are true. My father – he will be very proud.'

They drove slowly back to Foix, and, despite their concerns, did not see the car belonging to the opposition following them. As they drove, Jean-Pierre regained consciousness and, from what he could tell Scott and Sinclair, they were able to piece together what had happened. The other archaeologists, if they were all archaeologists, which Cushing doubted, had a very old map of the caves. Jean-Pierre had been able to use the map to find an entrance in the hills.

'The one they blew up afterwards,' said Scott, glumly.

'So where did they get their map?' asked Sinclair?

'Who knows?' replied Scott. 'Maybe from Schaeffer, or from their own digging in Ras Shamra. It doesn't matter now.'

Jean-Pierre revealed that they had indeed found the chamber shortly after midnight and had spent hours searching through their finds. The archaeologists were particularly thrilled about the contents of Esclarmonde's tomb. She had been holding a crown studded with thirteen jewels, and by her side were an orb with a huge gem set into it and a large sword.

'That's it then,' said Scott, darkly. 'They've got the treasure of the Cathars. After all that we've been through.'

Jean-Pierre told them, haltingly, that the group of archaeologists had smashed open the chests and sorted through piles of armour and weapons, selecting the choicest items, and started to take the first load back to the cars. Jean-Pierre recalled two of the Germans muttering to each other, then one of them pointed a gun at him. There was a noise from behind, a pain in his head, and nothing else until he woke up in the car.

'We're taking you to the hospital,' said Scott. 'You'll be fine.'

They followed the other car, driven by Vincent and with Gussie anxiously caring for Cushing in the back, to the hospital in Foix. Vincent was able to tell the staff that Jean-Pierre had been injured in a caving accident. He returned, driving through heavy pedestrian, motor and animal traffic – the pageant was starting that afternoon – to drop off all his equipment, and they were met by his father. 'Nous l'avons trouvée,' announced Vincent. 'Esclarmonde!'

The older Buisson was beside himself with excitement. 'C'est vrai? On a trouvé?' He was anxious to hear more, but the party excused themselves, promising to return and tell him everything after they had all had a hot bath.

An hour later, Cushing was still looking glazed, and his movements were mechanical, but Scott had helped him downstairs where he discovered Phoebe having breakfast with the German student, Otto Rahn.

'Ach, Herr Scott,' said Rahn. 'Your charming friend has been telling me that you have been to the caves at Lombrives where the Cathars were massacred.'

Scott looked daggers at Phoebe who smiled innocently back at him. 'Yes, we went there yesterday afternoon,' he emphasised.

'And she has told me also about your interest in the legend of the Holy Grail. I too have read my Parzifal, you see. And about the priestess Esclarmonde. Most fascinating. I came here because of my study of the crusade against the Cathar heretics, but I am encouraged to study this aspect of history much more.' He stood up. 'I am grateful to you all. I must go now, I have a car waiting. I hope that I will see you later, perhaps?'

And he left the party, who were coming down one by one, to their breakfast. Phoebe had finished, but the rest tucked hungrily into bread, croissants and jam, washed down with pots of strong coffee.

'We've got to get out of here as soon as we can,' said Scott, forcefully. 'Back to England, if we can get to Carcassonne and Jerry can fly us all home.'

'Fine by me,' said Sinclair. 'This show is more important than what I was planning to do in Toulouse. It won't take long for me to get the old kite up and running, and there's plenty of daylight.'

'Why do we have to go so quickly?' asked Phoebe, petulantly.

'The French authorities will have found out about the caves by now, and we don't know what the Germans are up to,' replied Scott. I don't trust this man Rahn much either. If we see the Buissons again we'll be stuck here for days if we're not careful. So we just have to go.'

'That's really unfair, Geoffrey,' said Gussie. 'After all, Vincent risked his life.'

'We have to,' repeated Scott. 'Look, we can come back later – next week, or next month, or something. But we've got to leave while we still can. The Padre is in no state to do anything much, and we need him back to normal to work on some of the documents.' Badger and Sinclair agreed.

'I'm all right, Geoffrey,' interrupted Cushing, haltingly. 'I can read. I can read perfectly. Why? What do you want me to read?'

'Don't worry about it now, sir,' said Badger, gently. 'Let's get back to Blighty and we can sort it all out there.'

The party hurriedly packed, and the men loaded the bags into the car. Gussie insisted on leaving a letter for the Buissons at the hotel, promising faithfully to return and enclosing some large banknotes for Vincent, and then joined the others in the car.

As they drove to Carcassonne where Sinclair had left his aeroplane, Cushing, despite Gussie's admonitions, started to try to read the parchment he had taken from inside Amalric de Montfort's chain mail shirt. But within a few minutes his head nodded forward and he began to breathe heavily and regularly.

'Let him sleep,' said Gussie. 'Too many bad memories bubbling up to the surface when he was being shot at, I think.'

It was early afternoon by the time they reached Carcassonne, and Sinclair spent an hour carefully checking his plane before completing the paperwork with the French authorities. Gussie thoughtfully made some sandwiches and Scott dashed a note off to the owners of the cars he had hired. 'We may not get our deposits back,' he muttered, 'but it's worth a try.' He also took advantage of Cushing's daydreaming, and removed the third stick grenade from his rucksack. 'I'm not going up in the plane if I know that lunatic has a bomb in his bag!' he exclaimed.

Soon they were airborne, but the flight back did little to calm Cushing's already frayed nerves. 'You're not keen on the old bus, are you, Padre?' laughed Sinclair, and Cushing and Badger could not disagree. Again Cushing was too sick to look at the documents they had saved from the burial chamber of Esclarmonde and Amalric. Scott flicked through some of the documents, and had a closer look at the clay tablets that Badger had discovered, but was none the wiser. 'Off to see Grainger at the BM again in the morning, I think, if he's out of hospital,' he said.

Finally they landed and made their farewells to Sinclair, who professed himself desperate to remain involved. 'Take my car,' he said. 'You won't all fit in Cushing's little Morris. I'll sort things out here and stay over, and I'll come and pick the old bus up tomorrow. Where from? Badger's?'

The two cars drove in convoy back to London, and it was dark when they arrived. First of all they said farewell to Badger, who had driven Sinclair's car, in the East End, and the friends agreed to meet at Scott's flat the following day. The others then all squeezed into Cushing's car and Scott drove them back to his flat at Albany for a nightcap. After he carried all the bags upstairs, Clarence assisting with lighter items, he made sure that the gold reliquary chest was safely stored under his bed. He then poured a large glass of brandy for each of them. Cushing, exhausted, fell asleep on the sofa after a few sips.

Gussie suggested that she gave Phoebe a bed for the night, an offer that she gratefully accepted. Phoebe acknowledged, though, that she would have to return to Longley Hall the following day, and that consequently she could not join the others. 'I suppose I'll have to face the music about the Rolls Royce sooner or later,' she said.

Cushing started to snore gently, and Gussie tenderly laid a blanket over him and kissed him on the forehead as he slept. 'Come on, Phoebe,' she said, 'we'd better take a taxi back to Chelsea. Look after Christopher, Geoffrey, won't you? See you tomorrow.'

19

Saturday 14th July 1928

By the morning, Scott thought that Cushing looked to be largely back to normal, though he was very subdued and his eyes occasionally twitched. Scott had got up early, at least for him, and brought breakfast. Cushing picked at it desultorily, and sipped his mug of tea mechanically.

Scott put down his plate of toast and waved a hand in front of Cushing's eyes. 'Hey, Uncle Kit. Padre. Pull yourself together. We've got a lot to do today.'

'No, no,' replied Cushing. 'Just let me go back to bed. I don't even know what day it is.'

'It's Saturday. 14th July 1928. Remember? Now look. We've got to get on with things.'

'Saturday?' Cushing still looked dazed. 'Yes, you're right. It's Saturday. I've got a christening to do tomorrow, I think.'

Scott rolled his eyes and snapped his fingers in front of Cushing's face. 'Well we can forget that, for a start. I'll call your verger or whoever and tell them you're ill. They can get someone else to do it instead.' He looked kindly at his godfather. 'Look, maybe you're right. Go back to bed for a couple of hours and we can get to work when you're feeling a bit better.'

Cushing was woken by the sound of the doorbell ringing. He looked at the clock by the bedside and realised that it was nearly noon and that he was fully dressed, though a little crumpled. He wandered out of the bedroom, rubbing his eyes, and saw Scott talking animatedly to Gussie. She rushed over, flung her arms around him and gave him a huge hug.

Scott came over and hugged him too. 'You look better, Uncle Kit.'

'Better than when? Last night? I think we were all pretty tired then.'

'You mean you don't remember breakfast?' asked Scott. Cushing looked blank. 'No, never mind.' He winked at Gussie. 'Come on, take a pew. I'll make some more tea and we can get stuck in. Your Mrs. Sturdy hopes you get better, by the way.'

Gussie raised an eyebrow, and Scott continued to talk from the small kitchen. 'She's Uncle Kit's verger, or churchwarden, or something. I called her to say that the old boy was too ill to do this christening tomorrow and that he'd come down on Tuesday or Wednesday.'

'What? What?' Cushing tried to get up from his chair, and Gussie laid a hand on his shoulder.

'Never mind,' said Scott, soothingly. 'It's all sorted now anyway.'

Cushing slumped back in the chair, and Scott brought in the tea. 'We've got to keep Stockington in the picture,' he said. 'Do you want to write him a letter, or send him a telegram? I think we need to meet him.' He passed Cushing some writing paper and a fountain pen.

'Probably a good idea,' murmured Cushing, and dashed off a letter. 'It's Saturday, though. Maybe we'd better send a telegram too.' He stretched, cracked his knuckles and gulped at his tea. 'That's better. Now, what else do we need to do?'

'Well, we have to see Grainger, I think, and show him some

of these new tablets. And perhaps recover the old ones. Where are they, anyway?'

'One is in your wardrobe,' smiled Cushing. 'The other is in the crypt of my church in Surrey. I'll pick it up next week, as long as you're sure I don't...'

'Yes, I'm sure, you really don't have to worry about that christening,' confirmed Scott, reassuringly.

'Where's the reliquary chest, the one that we found in Seborga?' Cushing asked. 'The one from Parmoor is in your wardrobe with the tablet, but...'

'Don't worry, Padre,' said Scott, hurriedly. 'It's quite safe. The most important thing for you to do now is to translate the document we took from Amalric de Montfort's body in the cave.' He took the package carefully from his bag, unfurled the parchment and laid it deferentially on the table. 'Over to you.'

Cushing, the light returning to his eyes, started to work on the document, while Scott turned to Gussie. 'We'll give him an hour or so and then I think it will be time for a spot of lunch. I'll get this telegram sent. Would you like to call Badger and Sinclair and get them to join us? And where's Phoebe?'

'She's gone back to Longley Hall. I tried to get her to stay for a little longer, but she felt she needed to get back.' She looked at the horrified expression on Scott's face. 'Don't worry. She may be a little airhead, but she won't let on what we've been doing.'

Gussie insisted on checking the dressing on Scott's wound, and then started to sort out some of the other papers they had brought back while Cushing pored over the letter. Scott picked up the week's papers and flicked through looking for any news on the murder of the Cliffords, and was surprised to find only a small mention of the story. 'Stockington was right,' he said. 'Looks as if it has been hushed up. No mention of us, at least.'

Lunch at the Athenaeum was shared by just the three of them. Badger had too many church administration and family commitments, and was unable to join them until at least that evening, and there was no reply from Sinclair, who they assumed was still on the train on his way back from the aerodrome. Fortified by the club's steak and kidney pudding, a welcome change after the foreign food they had eaten over the past week, Cushing was back to his former self. He had had significant success with the translation, and was beginning to enthuse about de Montfort's letter.

Scott was pleased to find out that other than a few calls from "FitzGerald", Stockington's alias, there had apparently been no one else looking for Cushing. He was more concerned than he had admitted that they would be sought by the French police, or by Gemp and his associates. Gemp would easily have been able to get at least Cushing's name from the passport he used when making hotel bookings or going through the border crossings, or – and Scott shuddered to think this – direct from Clifford before he was killed.

Cushing immediately returned to Scott's rooms to continue to work on the letter, while Scott and Gussie made a diversion to the hospital to check on Grainger. They found that he had been discharged. 'That's all right, though,' said Scott, 'I think the Padre has his home address.'

An hour after they returned, when Scott was toasting a muffin to go with the interminable cups of tea that he was making for the vicar, Cushing let out a sigh. 'That's it,' he said. 'I think that's all.'

'What does it say, dear,' asked Gussie attentively, walking over to the table and peering at the parchment.

'Keep your buttery fingers off,' snapped Cushing, and then apologised profusely for his sharpness, pressing her hand. 'I'll read it. It's in medieval French again. "I, Amalric de Montfort, by the grace of God Knight of St. John and Guardian of Lebanon, write this in the year of our Lord 1244. The castle at Montségur is doomed to fall, and I am sorely wounded. My beloved Esclarmonde is dead, and so we have brought her body to this place to lay it to rest. My cousin Hugh is also dead and his son Yves now leads the defenders.

"'We have also brought the treasures we hold most sacred: the crown, the stones, the orb and the sword, and the stone from heaven. They were reunited at Castrum Sepulchri, but they have failed us in our fight. No, they have not failed us: we have failed them, as we have been defeated by the forces of the Pope and the King of France. But by keeping them here and guarded under the rock of ages…'" Cushing looked up. 'Rock of ages? Can that be right?'

'Get on with it, man!'

'Sorry.' He continued. "'By keeping them here and guarded under the rock of ages, we will keep them safe so that the Inquisition will not find them and defile them.'"

'What's all that about?'

'Let me finish.'

'Sorry, Padre.'

"'I have not much time to live, so I shall stay here with my love and the treasures she fought so hard to defend. I know that my friends will already have concealed the entrance to this cave. Her grave is honoured, but I shall have no memorial. Let this letter affirm to all my love for her that will live after me, in the true and certain knowledge that those who follow will know how to use these things for good, and crown a king on earth to bring the true word of our Lord to the people.

"'The candles are burning low, and the pain increases. May the good Lord have mercy on my soul. I, Amalric, son of Fulk de Montfort, Guardian of Lebanon and Knight of the Hospital of St. John of Jerusalem, write this. Now I seek rest for the last time.'"

Cushing looked up, a lump in his throat, and saw Gussie blowing her nose. He saw the tears in her eyes, walked over and put his hand gently on her shoulder. She took it and squeezed it tightly.

'And there the Cathar treasures stayed, the relics of power or whatever, for the best part of seven hundred years,' said Scott. 'And now the opposition have got them. But what are they going to do with them?'

Cushing squeezed Gussie's hand again. 'Well,' he said, 'we know that Sloane and his gang have been looking for treasures, along with this Lapsit Exillis thing. Crowley said they would give power to whoever wields them, and that's obviously what Amalric thought too. And now they have them.'

'It's not just about wielding power,' said Gussie, sniffing loudly. 'Amalric says too that they should be used for good, to crown a king in the name of God, not for their own foul purposes.'

'You're right,' said Scott. 'What is the purpose of these things? Are they a force for good, or are they to help this bunch take over the world.'

'Or Italy, at least,' said Cushing. 'We know they tried to kill the king there, and I heard Sloane and John speak about Prince Umberto. Or "another candidate". So now they've got the relics, they can have another shot at the assassination.'

'Well I don't know,' said Scott, frowning. 'I mean, it all sounds pretty far-fetched. People aren't going to think any more or any less of a king just because he's been crowned with gems that are three thousand years old. Are they?'

'Didn't Crowley say that it's not what you believe in, it's what they believe in?' asked Gussie.

'I think that's right,' said Cushing. 'If Sloane and the others believe that they will help their own plans, perhaps they will. If Amalric and Esclarmonde believed that they will help to bring the true word of the Lord to the people, perhaps that is true as well.'

'Which Lord?' asked Scott, mischievously. 'Sorry, never

mind.'

'That's a fair question, Geoffrey. The crusaders believed in Christ and our God of the Old Testament. Baal was diametrically opposed to him. And the Cathars, of course, were heretics and didn't believe in Christ. So the relics are important to all these conflicting faiths.'

'That's as maybe. The question is that even if Sloane and these synarchists, if that's what they are, control the new King of Italy, where does that leave them? I mean, with the best will in the world, Italy isn't really that important to the rest of Europe. But what I want to know is what we are going to do now?'

On Sunday morning Gussie came by taxi to join the men and Cushing drove them to Badger's church in the East End of London. The service was not to Cushing's liking. There was too much modern glory and hallelujah for his taste; he preferred order and tradition. The church was packed, nevertheless, and Cushing was able to introduce Maurice, Lenny and the others who had worked so hard in the tunnels under Parmoor House to Gussie and Scott. Badger gave an excellent sermon, and as he spoke about friendship and sacrifice, the friends were sure that he was referring to Clifford.

Sinclair, who had called round at Scott's the evening before and consumed an inordinate amount of Scott's best brandy, joined them. 'I'm not really a churchgoing man, Padre,' he apologised, 'but I needed to pick my car up.'

They stood around after the service drinking tea, and Badger joined them.

'I hope Jerry's car is still where he left it,' joked Scott.

'The local villains know better than to touch anything left in the vicarage,' responded Badger, warmly. 'Even the car. In fact two of the young lads from Sunday school have been keeping an eye on it for you. They'll have polished it, given half a chance. And they'll be glad of sixpence for doing so.'

Sinclair laughed, and they strolled round to the vicarage where Rachel Brock had prepared a large tray of chops for lunch. They brought Badger up to speed with the translation of the de Montfort letter, and he whistled. 'So where does that leave us?' he asked.

'That's just what I asked yesterday,' said Scott, 'and I don't think we've got a clear idea. I'm all for going down to Longley Hall and putting one over on Sloane, but the Padre doesn't think it will do any good.'

'Let me speak to Stockington first, at least,' said Cushing. 'Even if I don't hear back from him beforehand, I can meet him at the café. And when we've finished here, I'd like to go and see Grainger.'

They left the Brocks to their family responsibilities, reminding Badger to be careful and to be on the lookout for anything or anyone suspicious, and drove to Grainger's house at the edge of Regent's Park. Sinclair, pleased to have his car back and more than happy to pay sixpence to each ragamuffin for the privilege, drove back to his office to catch up on his air freight business.

The three friends knocked on Grainger's door and the archaeologist answered suspiciously, only opening the door after Cushing had identified himself through the letter box. He ushered them inside nervously, and carefully locked and chained the door behind them.

The American was looking drained and, for such a large man, thin and drawn in the face. He was no longer wearing bandages, but still showed traces of bruising.

'It's not too early for a drink, I hope,' he said, after Cushing had introduced Scott and Gussie. He sloshed amber liquid from a decanter into glasses and handed them round.

There was no easy way to break the news about what had happened, and so Cushing came straight to the point, telling Grainger how the same group that had attacked him in the British Museum had murdered Peter and Molly Clifford in the south of France. The corpulent archaeologist was shocked; he had not seen the news in the paper. He drained his glass and refilled it, and slumped heavily into his chair.

'Poor guys,' he said. 'When's the funeral?'

Cushing was embarrassed. The funeral was not something they had even considered. 'We'll find out in due course,' he said.

'So what's happening?' asked Grainger. 'What are the authorities doing? Are the murderers in custody?'

Cushing looked embarrassed again, and Scott took over. 'Look, we'd better tell you a little more about what's been going on.'

'I think you'd better.'

'Well first of all, you were right. The first tablet we showed you must have been stolen from Ugarit. Not by us, of course, but it did come into our possession.'

'How…'

'Sorry, I can't tell you that. But we recovered some more tablets from the south of France, where the crusaders had left them with Esclarmonde de Foix.'

'We found her grave,' added Gussie, helpfully.

'You found the grave of Esclarmonde de Foix? Really? That's amazing! It's not my area, of course, but what a discovery. Where is it?'

'All in good time,' said Cushing. 'Geoffrey, let's have the tablets.'

Scott opened the cricket bag he was carrying and brought out the tablets and some of the other parchments that they had found in France.

Grainger stood up and peered closely at the tablets. 'Hey

now,' he said. 'These look to be very similar to the one you showed me a fortnight ago. I'd be honoured to get to work on them.' He looked suddenly ashen. 'And you say that Peter Clifford was killed for these?'

'These, and the secrets of the Templar treasure. It's an international plot. We think they are planning to use the relics they stole from the tomb to crown a king. Probably in Italy.'

'You're kidding me,' laughed Grainger, and then realised that the three were deadly serious. 'You mean the bad guys are looking to use the rites of power from three thousand years ago – Baal and all that – to crown the King of Italy? No, you're mad.'

'It's what they believe. We think so, anyway.'

'Well, the priesthood had control of the kings in Phoenicia and Tyre, just as they controlled the Pharaohs in Egypt, so there's plenty of precedent. But we're in the twentieth century. Surely...'

'Look, why don't you just take a look and see if there are any more clues in what we've given you. When shall we see you again?'

'How about coming to the museum at about half past three tomorrow?'

'Splendid,' replied Cushing. 'I'm seeing – well, the authorities, tomorrow evening, and every little will help.'

They left Grainger who called out his thanks as they walked back to the car, and they could hear the sound of the locks being shut behind them.

20

Monday 16th July 1928

Cushing was relieved to get a note from "FitzGerald" confirming their meeting later on the Monday, and was in surprisingly good spirits when he and Scott walked the few hundred yards to the Athenaeum for lunch. His bonhomie evaporated as Rafferty accosted him.

'Good afternoon, Reverend Cushing, sir. Sorry to bother you, but you wanted to know if anyone came in asking for you.'

Cushing blanched. 'What? Who?'

'Earlier this morning, sir. Two foreign gentlemen, they were.' He emphasised the word "foreign" with a curl of his lip. 'Came in as bold as brass and asked for you. I said as how you'd not been in for a couple of weeks.'

'Good for you, Rafferty. Thank you. What did they look like?'

'One tall and thin, one shorter and fatter. They didn't take their hats off, but the tall one had what looked like a bandage on his head. If were a gambling man, sir, I'd say they were Germans.'

'Gemp and Horstmann,' muttered Cushing to Scott, who was smiling at the thought of the bandage, presumably the result of Cushing's grenade.

'They left a number to call in case I saw you, sir,' continued Rafferty, groping in his pocket for a scrap of paper, 'and they gave me ten bob.'

'Then I thank you even more,' said Cushing.

'Oh no, sir,' said Rafferty. 'They may be foreign gentlemen, but you're an English gentleman, if you know what I mean. I'll take their ten bob and have pleasure of it, but they can go hang.'

Cushing grinned, and another ten shilling note appeared almost magically in his hand. 'I suppose they're not hanging around now, Rafferty?'

'No, sir. After all, they aren't members, so I moved them on pretty sharpish.'

'Excellent,' said Scott. 'We can enjoy lunch after all.'

But Cushing did not enjoy his lunch. 'They've found me,' he said. 'And what about you, and Gussie, and Badger? Sinclair, and even Phoebe? Is anyone safe?' He left Scott at the table and went to the lobby to make some telephone calls. He came back looking distressed. 'I can't get through to anyone,' he said. 'I mean I spoke to Rachel Brock, but I didn't want to scare her. Look, I don't want any pudding. Let's pop over to the BM and see how Grainger is getting on. And at least we have a telephone number for Herr Gemp. Perhaps Stockington can trace it.'

They decided to walk to the British Museum, enjoying the sunshine and making faster progress than the traffic on Shaftesbury Avenue. They passed a broken-down brewer's dray which had blocked Cambridge Circus, and Cushing tipped his hat at the policeman who was trying to sort out the problems. All the way, both he and Scott continually looked over their shoulders in case they were being followed, but all seemed to be well.

They arrived at the museum and threaded their way past the ancient exhibits, walked nonchalantly to the door marked "Private" and up the stairs to Grainger's office. The American had again locked his door, but was pleased to see the pair and welcomed them inside. The room was warm and Grainger was down to his expansive waistcoat and shirtsleeves.

'Well, boys, we've got something here,' he said. 'I'm pretty sure now that the two tablets are from the same source as the first one that you showed me. The message is consistent. They give more instructions for a priest to crown a king under the rule of the god Baal. Just as we said yesterday, they show how priests can control kings if they are crowned using a certain ritual, and in particular a crown with thirteen gems in it.'

'The crown that was in Esclarmonde's tomb, the one the Germans stole.'

'I guess so. It also talks about another stone, a larger and more significant one. It fell from heaven as a gift from the gods, and this stone can control not only the king but the whole people.'

'The Lapsit Exillis?'

'Hey, Reverend, don't get carried away with all that stuff again. It's all a load of mumbo-jumbo, as you know. But all the elements do link Ugarit, the Templars and the Cathars. It's magnificent. What a find.'

'And what about any of the parchments,' said Cushing, hopefully.

'They seem to be copies made in the early middle ages of other tablets. They are in pretty awful condition, but some of the larger fragments make some kind of sense. There's a mixture of Latin, medieval French and Occitan: you know, the language of the Cathars. If it hadn't been for these translations, I wouldn't have been able to piece together so much of the tablets.'

'What do they say?'

'Well there's a mix. More stuff on crowning the true king and all that. But there are some interesting pictures, crude pictograms if you like, of a coronation actually happening. This one here seems to show a priest controlling the king using some kind of device. It may be the large gem I mentioned earlier. And this picture shows a priest...'

'How do you know it's a priest?' interrupted Scott.

'From the headgear. Look, it shows a priest wielding this device and rays coming out it. So it may be depicted as a weapon of some kind.'

'So the whole kit is used for controlling the king and the masses? If it works, a group of priests using these things could control a whole country.'

'Well you may say that, Reverend,' said Grainger, grinning, 'but there's only one flaw in your argument. It's nonsense. It's all mumbo-jumbo. It isn't real.'

'But there is power in the ritual. Crowley said so.'

'Who?'

'Never mind. The important thing is that if the priests, and the king, and the people – if they all believe it, then maybe it could happen.'

'Yes, but they won't. This isn't a primitive Middle Eastern culture. This is 1928. It's just not going to happen.'

Cushing was more than a little disgruntled when they left, and he and Scott bickered all the way back to Villiers Street where Cushing was to meet Stockington.

'We must be missing something, Geoffrey. I know you all think I'm barking...'

'No, not at all,' interjected Scott, possibly a little too hastily.

'Barking up the wrong tree, I was going to say. I know it all sounds impossible, but if it isn't true, why are the opposition going to such an effort? It sounds as if their plot has been going on for years. It's about them taking control. And they are running an international network, and killing people to get the relics. Even to stop people finding information about the relics. Ross, Hitchcock, Page, the Cliffords, Lord knows who else. Oh for heaven's sake. Can't you see?'

They arrived at the French café and continued to mutter

darkly to each other until Stockington arrived. They stood, and Stockington looked up at Scott and shrugged before shaking his hand. Cushing introduced Scott, and Stockington smiled.

'Yes,' he said. 'We nearly met a couple of weeks ago. You were sitting over there, reading the newspaper, if I remember.' He stopped smiling. 'Now look. Can you tell me what the hell you bumbling amateurs have been up to? Getting two of you killed, for a start. I told you to be careful...'

'We were,' said Cushing, defensively. 'And it hasn't been a complete failure.'

'Really? You could have fooled me. Tell me a little more about Peter and Molly Clifford. That's what I call failure. I get a telegram from the south of France asking me to cover up your tracks, and I discover that tracks have already been covered up. What are you up to?'

Cushing took a deep breath. 'Right. We were looking for these archaeological relics...'

'I said I didn't want you going on some sort of ridiculous wild goose chase or treasure hunt.'

'Not at all,' said Cushing, haughtily. 'Just listen. We traced these relics from England to Italy to the south of France. We know that there is another group after them, but I'll come onto that later. We are pretty sure that they tracked us to Italy, and that they killed Peter and Molly in Menton. We saw them again in Foix, and I recognised one of the Germans who shot at Geoffrey and me in London. The ones who killed Ross.'

'Well that's something, I suppose.'

'Yes. He's called Gemp, we think, and one of his accomplices is Horstmann. And there are a whole load of others, Irish and French at least. Anyway, Gemp and Horstmann have been looking for me in London. They turned up at the Athenaeum and tried to bribe a porter for information about me. They left this telephone number. Perhaps you could trace it?'

'Thank you,' said Stockington, taking the piece of paper without looking at it. 'They must have tracked you down pretty quickly.'

'Well I am a vicar,' said Cushing. 'I must be pretty easy to trace. After all, they got to Geoffrey's car in a couple of days, and all they had to do to find me was look my name up in Crockford's.'

'Fair point,' admitted Stockington. 'Carry on.'

'We are sure that the conspiracy, and it's a big one, includes your chief, Domvile.'

'You said that the other day. Do you have any evidence?'

'Only that I have heard some of the conspirators use his name. And of course it seems more than a coincidence that someone from London was covering up the murder of the Cliffords before you even became involved.'

'Hmm.'

'Now, this conspiracy. We think they may all be synarchists, or masons, or both. They called themselves an "order". They are led by Sir Charles Sloane and a man called John, and we know what they were trying to do. I worked this out from Hitchcock's note, and then I overheard a conversation. They tried to murder the King of Italy and blame it on the Bolsheviks.' Stockington raised an eyebrow and shook his head, slowly. Cushing started to talk even faster, realising that Stockington was not convinced. 'It all makes sense. They plan to use these relics that we have found to crown Prince Umberto and take over Italy. That's why they broke into the British Museum.'

'I see.' Stockington was looking calmly at the somewhat wild-eyed Cushing. 'And these relics that you found. Where are they?'

'Well we have some. But the powerful ones – well, we don't … er...'

'The opposition took them from a cave,' interrupted Scott. He glared at Stockington. 'Stop looking at me like that. It's true, damn it.'

'We've not met before, Mr. Scott,' said Stockington, 'but I'm sure you won't be offended when I mention that Mr. Cushing here has a long track record of delusion. He sees things, I understand.'

'That was a long time ago,' shouted Cushing, and one of the waitresses turned round in alarm.

'Now I'm not saying I don't believe you,' said Stockington, 'or at least that I believe that you think what you're saying is true...'

'But they are here, in London again, looking for us.'

'I believe that, certainly. Sit down, Reverend, you're drawing attention to us again.' Cushing, breathing heavily, sat down on the hard-backed chair. 'Now I haven't been exactly idle, and there are some people in our service whom I can trust, whatever Ross said. You're right. It was Domvile who gave a direct order to hush up the murder of your friends. The French police had an anonymous call...'

'That was me!'

'Yes, I imagined it was. But that took place after our people had already started the ball rolling to keep things quiet.'

'So...?'

'So I think you gentlemen, and your other friends, should keep your heads down. Leave it to the professionals. This stuff about relics is patently nonsense – sit down, Reverend! It's patently nonsense, but I'm quite prepared to believe that the Synarchists could have tried to kill the King of Italy. Prince Umberto has fascist sympathies, and his father doesn't. And the same people could easily have killed Ross, and Hitchcock. Killing Page I don't understand, but I suspect he just got caught up on the edge of the whole thing.'

'He was translating the tablets. He knew about crowning the king.'

'Maybe. But I am now concerned about you. You say that the Germans know your name and have already been looking for you. This may be because they got your name from Clifford, or from anywhere frankly. I think you should leave London, all of you. Keep your heads down, as I say. You've done a lot more for your friend Ross than he could possibly have expected, or at least you've tried. Why don't you pop up to Scotland? You may feel better after one of your little rest cures.'

'Damn the man.' Cushing was still fuming about Stockington on Tuesday morning. 'Keep our heads down indeed. He's a patronising idiot. There's a huge plot afoot, and he wants us to keep our heads down.'

'He's right, though, in some ways,' said Gussie, soothingly. She had sat through Cushing's ranting the previous evening, and had no wish to continue the argument. 'They know you are a vicar, they must know your parish, and they know enough to trace you to the club. It's not safe. In fact it's not safe for any of us.'

'Well I'm damned if I'm just going to sit around,' said Scott, who had been cleaning his revolver on the table in his apartment.

'Nor me,' agreed Cushing. 'I just feel so useless. And I still can't get hold of Mrs. Sturdy. I called her last night and again this morning, and got no reply. Even she might be in danger.'

'Well give her another call, Padre, and let's pop down to Guildford and see. We need to go there anyway and pick up that tablet you left, if we are going to give it to Grainger.'

Cushing lifted the receiver again and gave the number to the operator. He started to speak and gestured to the others that he had got through. There was a high-pitched agitated squawking from the earpiece. Cushing's face darkened, and he spoke calmly and authoritatively down the line. After about ten minutes he hung up.

'What's happened,' burst out Gussie and Scott, together.

'They've been down there. At least I assume it was Gemp

and Horstmann. Two "foreign gentlemen", apparently, asking questions about me at the pub. The gardener told Mrs. Sturdy.'

'And?'

'And the vicarage has been burgled. Last night. They have made a real mess.' Cushing laughed mirthlessly. 'Not my vicarage, though. The new one. The young vicar. He and his family weren't in, fortunately. Poor Mrs. Sturdy is in such a state. She has been helping to clean up now the police have left.'

'Right,' said Scott. 'That presumably means they haven't got the tablet. Yet. Let's go down to Guildford now.' He put his revolver in his pocket, and turned to Gussie who was starting to fiddle with her handbag. 'Not you, Gussie. I think this definitely shows that Stockington was right. You need to keep your head down too. Is there anyone you could stay with for a few days?'

The engine of the little Morris struggled and whined as Cushing pushed the accelerator down to the floor. Cushing and Scott had dropped off Gussie at her flat in Chelsea, making her promise to find somewhere else to stay, then drove on over the downs to the village of Albury.

Cushing pulled up the car round in front of the memorial cross, and drove through the gate of the new rectory.

'I've not been here for a fair while, Padre,' said Scott, looking round and gazing at the new church. 'It's not a patch on your old place, is it?'

'It's not as attractive a building,' agreed Cushing, 'but at least it has a roof.'

They rang the bell, and Mrs. Sturdy answered the door. She flung it open when she saw Cushing, and a small army of local ladies was visible behind her.

'Oh Father Christopher, what a mess. What a day. Thank you for coming down, I know you've been ill.'

After a while, Cushing was able to get a word in edgeways, and he raised the subject of the foreigners who had been asking questions about him.

'Well I only thought about it when Mr. Leach mentioned that there were these two gentlemen in the pub asking after you, by name. You'd asked me if anyone had been looking for you, you remember, and I thought to myself, well, there's a coincidence…'

'But do you know where they are now?'

'Sorry, Father, no idea.'

'Never mind,' he said. 'I mustn't keep you, though. You've got so much to do. It's very kind of you to help. Presumably the police didn't catch the burglars?'

She shook her head, and Cushing and Scott left them to their tidying. They drove the short distance to Cushing's own cottage. Cushing had a strange feeling that he was being watched, and said as much to Scott.

'Don't worry, Padre,' he replied. 'We've got their measure.' And he tapped his jacket pocket, knowingly. Cushing had his German pistol in his pocket too, but was not planning to use it.

They walked up to the front door of the cottage and Cushing opened it with his key. He checked the downstairs rooms, and was comfortable that there was nobody else in the house. 'Keep cave,' he said, and headed upstairs. A few minutes later he gave the all clear, and Scott joined him. Cushing found a couple of suitcases and began to pack various clothes, books and other belongings.

'Hurry up, Padre,' said Scott.

'I'm not likely to be back here for a while, am I, Geoffrey?' Cushing said. 'And I can't leave some of the books downstairs. They're irreplaceable, and Gemp and his people might damage them. I mean, they'll be bound to be here sooner or later.'

'Just get a move on then,' said Scott. 'And don't forget we've still got to go and get the tablet. That's what we've come for, after all.'

'It's at the church. Don't panic, I'll be quick.'

Cushing finished his packing and they drove back through the village and up the narrow tree-lined lane to the old church.

'I wouldn't leave the car by the church,' said Scott. 'Can you park it by the manor house, or in those trees?'

Cushing thought that Scott was being over-careful, but acquiesced. The two men walked back to the little church and Cushing, as he always did, made directly for his wife's grave, pleased to see that Mrs. Sturdy had placed fresh flowers there on his behalf. Scott removed his hat. 'She was a good lady, Aunt Mary,' he said, gripping Cushing's shoulder supportively. They stood in silence for a few seconds, then Scott looked up at the church and whistled. 'The old place is still in a bit of a state, though, Uncle Kit, despite you touching everyone you know for donations to repair it.'

'Well that's why they built the new church fifty years ago. The roof here was unsafe, particularly the dome. That coincided with when they built all the new houses in the village, of course. People don't mind coming down here now for the odd special occasion, but no more than that. The new chap looks after the new church.' He pointed out some of the damage as they entered the building. 'Look. The roof of the chancel has completely fallen in.'

'It's a shame,' said Scott. 'You would have thought that they would keep a church mentioned in the Domesday Book in decent condition, not just let it go to rack and ruin.' He peered at the ancient brass on the floor and the faded painting of St. Christopher on the wall.

Cushing was impatient. 'I hid the tablet in the crypt. Do something useful and keep a lookout while I go and get it, will you?

Cushing took his hat off and fiddled with his keys, then went down into the crypt, lighting a lantern to see his way. Scott wandered back to the church door and suddenly called back. 'Padre! Back up here, quickly.'

The two cautiously peered out, concealed by the porch. 'Keep your head down,' warned the younger man. 'Now, be careful, take a look. There are four men coming up the lane.'

Cushing peered out, and the red mist that he had felt in Ross's flat a few weeks earlier descended upon him again. He hissed at Scott through gritted teeth. 'That's Gemp. And Horstmann. I don't know the third man. And the fourth, that's my gardener, Leach.'

The two men watched, horrified, as the quartet in the lane neared them. It seemed as if money changed hands, and Leach returned up the lane.

'Quick,' whispered Cushing. 'I'll go down into the crypt and get the tablet. You get out of the side door and sneak away beneath the ha-ha.' He tossed Scott his bunch of keys and entered the crypt, pulling the door closed behind him. He did not, however, have time to retrieve the tablet from its hiding place before he heard rustling and the noise of footsteps. He froze, struggling to hear what the men upstairs were saying. He thought they were talking in German, but could not be sure. Suddenly he heard an excited yell. 'Damn it,' he whispered to himself. 'They've found my hat.'

As he heard louder and more guttural orders, he extinguished the lantern and shrank back into the corner of the crypt. The door opened, and he could see daylight. There was the flick of a cigarette lighter, and a shadowy figure came down the stairs holding a naked flame in one hand and a pistol in the other.

Cushing took hold of a heavy candlestick and lashed it down hard down upon the man's wrist. The gun spun noisily off onto the floor. Cushing swung the candlestick again at the man, who screamed and fell, dropping the lighter. In the darkness, Cushing kicked him hard in the side of the head, and he went limp.

Another silhouette appeared at the top of the stairs and an accented voice called down. 'Horstmann? Wie geht's?' Cushing drew his pistol. Suddenly there was noise from upstairs. 'Hands up!' shouted Scott, and Cushing saw the figure spin round. Cushing heard a shot, then the distinctive thump of Scott's service revolver. The man fell heavily back and crashed down the stairs towards him with a scream.

Cushing heard Scott shouting 'Stop!' and there were further shots, including one from Scott's heavy revolver, then silence. Breathing smoke and cordite, Cushing carefully made his way up the stairs, his gun in his hand. As he came into the light he found Scott lying on the floor, his head covered in blood.

Horrified and sickened, he ran to Scott's side. Dropping his gun and muttering a prayer, he checked to make sure that his godson was alive. Mercifully, the young man was still breathing, and Cushing sighed with relief. A cursory examination showed that a bullet had creased Scott's skull, and that while there was a lot of blood, the wound was not fatal. Cushing had seen dozens of similar wounds in France, and was sure that Scott would be fine. Quickly he checked the door, and saw a figure in the distance running up the lane. He returned to Scott. Pulling out a handkerchief and realising immediately that it would be insufficient, he grabbed a surplice and ripped parts of the edge into strips to make bandages.

Scott stirred. 'What happened?'

'Geoffrey, I thought you were dead. Keep still. Let me fix up this bandage.'

Scott moaned in pain. 'Ouch! That hurts. What happened to Gemp?'

'I saw one of them running up the lane.'

'Shame. I think I winged him, though. The other one nearly got me as well, but I think I cooked his goose.'

Cushing went back down into the crypt to find the body of

the man that Scott had shot crumpled on the floor. He checked the man's pulse. 'He's dead. You killed him.'

'They fired first,' said Scott, who had crawled painfully to the top of the stairs and was calling down. 'It was self defence. What about the third one.'

'I hit him in the head with a candlestick,' said Cushing, who had relit the lantern. 'It's Horstmann, the one who was dressed as a policeman. So it must have been Gemp who got away.'

'Good work, Padre. Shame about Gemp though. How is Horstmann?'

'He's breathing, but he's still unconscious,' replied Cushing.

'Well let's make sure he stays that way. And tie him up.' Cushing followed Scott's suggestion, and bound the unconscious Horstmann with his own belt and shoelaces.

'Right, said Scott again. 'You'd better go and get the car. I'll keep you covered in case Gemp comes back. And we'd better hurry. Someone from the manor house is bound to have heard the shots and called the police.'

Cushing dodged towards the car and drove it back, as close as he could to the door of the church, then manhandled the heavy body into the back seat. He returned to the crypt with a case into which he packed the tablet that he had taken from its hiding place. When he came back again, he found Scott, white-faced and ill-looking, slapping Horstmann round the face to wake him.

'All right, Horstmann. We have a few questions.'

The man growled and spat. 'Ich kann nicht Englisch.'

'He doesn't speak English,' said Scott. 'Righto, I'll just shoot him.'

'Nein, nein!' Horstmann struggled in his bonds.

'Excellent, so you speak a little,' grimaced Scott. 'Now, first of all, I want to know. Who was it who killed Clifford in France?'

'It was Gemp, not me. I swear. And we didn't kill him. He died, while we were asking him questions. Before he told us anything. Aararggh!'

The shout was one of pain, as Scott kicked him hard again. 'I'm in no mood for games. And Molly? Mrs. Clifford?'

'That was an accident. I promise. Nein!' Horstmann hunched up as Scott pointed his revolver at his face and began to squeeze the trigger.

'You can't kill him in cold blood, Geoffrey,' shouted Cushing. 'Stop it. Now.'

Scott lowered his gun and staggered.

'Are you alright, Geoffrey? Look, that wound is worse than I thought. Let's get you back to London. And we need to take Horstmann to Stockington. He's the evidence we need.'

'I've had worse from Harold Larwood when I was batting last year,' said Scott, with false levity, but Cushing was not convinced.

The two men forced the recalcitrant Horstmann into the car at gunpoint, and sat him next to the corpse of the other man. Scott was swaying dangerously, and Cushing urged him into the passenger seat. He started the engine and drove off, his pistol on his knees.

Horstmann spoke from the back of the car. 'You will not get away with this. Let me go, and it will be the better for you.'

Scott leaned round unsteadily, and callously cuffed the German in the face with his revolver, drawing blood. 'Shut up,' he muttered, faintly.

'Come on, Geoffrey, keep your chin up,' encouraged Cushing, and they drove out of Albury and back onto the London Road. As they did so, a familiar-looking black Lagonda pulled out and followed them. Over his shoulder Cushing could see the contorted face of Gemp in the passenger seat. An unknown man was driving. 'It's Gemp,' he yelled, but Scott's head was lolling sideways.

He drove on, but the larger and faster car drove up beside them. Gemp leered in at the window and raised his pistol.

Cushing swung the wheel, but the driver of the Lagonda was an expert and kept alongside him. Gemp pointed the pistol, and suddenly Cushing could see that it was not aimed at him. He groped for his own pistol that had fallen on the floor, but a terrified yell from the back seat showed that Horstmann had also realised what was happening. The side window smashed behind him as fire burst from the barrel of Gemp's gun. Red gore splattered on the inside of the windscreen as the Lagonda sped away. Hastily Cushing looked over his shoulder to check, but Horstmann was collapsed on the seat against the other body, a gaping hole in the side of his head.

'Another loose end sorted,' muttered Cushing darkly to Scott, who was lapsing in and out of consciousness, and drove back to London as fast as he could, stopping only on the London Road at a telephone box to place a call to Badger.

His actions when he arrived at Badger's had been mechanical. Fearful that his car would attract suspicion as he drove to the East End – there were broken windows and three bodies in the car, after all – he was relieved when he arrived safely at the vicarage and nearly collapsed into his friend's arms. He was vaguely conscious of Lenny and Maurice, and the words of the larger man ringing in his ears. 'Nice to see you again, Father Christopher. Exciting having you around, sir.'

A small group of men, one of whom Cushing was sure was Chalky, took the car into a garage, and Lenny and Maurice supported Scott into the house where a man whom Badger introduced as Doctor McAlister was waiting. Rachel Brock had given Cushing a large mug of tea, then taken it back and tipped in a generous slug of liquid from an unlabelled bottle. Cushing choked, then felt grateful for the warmth that flowed through his veins.

'Off to bed, old man,' ordered Badger. 'You're all done in. Scott's going to be fine, and my boys will sort out the rest.'

21

Wednesday 18th July 1928

When Cushing woke, it took him some time to work out where he was. He was in a strange bed, and the noise from outside the window was unfamiliar. He stretched out in the bed, and all too quickly the memories of the previous day's events rushed back to haunt him.

He washed and dressed quickly, and found Badger and Scott talking over a huge plate of bacon and eggs. Rachel Brock was sitting next to them at the table feeding the baby. Scott was sporting an outsized bandage around his head.

'Morning, Padre,' said Scott, his mouth full. 'Glad you're up and about. I slept like a log, I must say, but the doctor has already been and bandaged me up again. Head hurts like nobody's business, but the doc says I'm fine.' He stood up a little unsteadily. 'Thanks again for bringing me back.' He extended his hand, and Cushing shook it warmly.

Cushing looked at Badger. 'Are you sure the doctor won't let on?'

'He's a good man and owes me a favour or two,' said Badger, reassuringly. 'Don't worry. And I'll get the lads to get rid of the two bodies some time later this morning. You know the lads.

Always happy to help out. There's a building site up the road with a convenient hole.' Scott looked shocked at Badger talking so openly in front of his wife, but Rachel smiled at her husband, while making cooing noises to the baby. Badger winked and gave a thumbs-up sign. 'She's a good lass,' he whispered.

'But surely we should at least tell Stockington? I mean Horstmann is the man who killed Ross. It's evidence.'

'A dead body isn't really evidence of anything, Padre,' said Scott. 'I think Badger's right. We can sort out Stockington later.'

'But…. But…..'

'And what about the car?' continued Scott.

'Lenny and Maurice are cleaning it up. It will be better than new by lunchtime, if I know those two.'

'Digging up a few tunnels is one thing, but won't they ask about the bullet holes and the bloodstains?'

'Nothing they haven't seen before. There was a big fascist march up the road a couple of months ago, and we used this place as a sort of field hospital. It's how things work around here. All the lads are ex-soldiers, or ex-cons. Not so "ex" in some cases, or at least they haven't been caught so far.' Cushing was still stunned at Badger's matter of fact tone. 'They are also keeping an eye out for me and Rachel and the kids. I told some of the lads that we might be being threatened, and they weren't having that. Safe as the Tower of London here, we are, I'd say. Anyway, we sorted out the bodies last night and went through their pockets. Just the usual stuff: identification, wallet, money, and so on. Both were based at embassies, one German, one Argentine.'

'Well we should definitely tell Stockington that!'

'It's too late to get them deported now,' grinned Scott, cruelly.

'The money was interesting,' continued Badger. 'Mostly English, but also some German marks and some Dutch guilders. That fitted in with the fact that Horstmann had a ticket in his pocket for the boat train on Friday. He was planning to go to

Holland.'

'Holland?'

'Yes, Amsterdam to be precise. And he even had a diary in his pocket – not a lot in it, frankly, or at least nothing I can make head or tail of. But there is a note for Friday saying "Nach Holland", and then a line through the following week, so I assume he planned to be there for that length of time. Oh yes, and a big asterisk for the following Saturday, that's the 28th.'

'What happens then?'

'Search me. Still, he won't be using his ticket.'

Cushing scratched his head. 'I really do need to speak to Stockington again. And look, Badger, would you and Rachel mind if we stayed here for a couple of days? After all, if they have traced me, they've probably traced Geoffrey and Gussie as well.'

'Fine by me,' said Badger. 'Rachel? We can put a couple of guests up for a week or so, can't we?' His wife nodded in agreement. 'That's sorted then.'

'Thank you. Both of you. So we'd better go back to Geoffrey's place and pick up some clothes and things. Geoffrey, are you well enough to travel?'

'I should say so. The car won't be ready though, will it?

Badger went outside and returned a few minutes with Lenny, who shook Cushing's hand earnestly. 'Lenny says that it will be another half an hour.'

'That's right, Father Badger,' said the young man. 'Just fixing the glass in the windows now, and we'll give it a good polish. Half an hour should see you right.'

'Thank you, Lenny,' said Cushing, again searching in his pocket to give the young man something for his trouble.

'I've told you before, sir, you don't need to worry about that,' said Lenny. 'Anything me and the lads can do to help a friend of Father Badger. Anyhow, we were well sorted last time.' He cleared his throat noisily. 'Look sir, if you want your car back I'd better be getting on. Cheerio.'

It was closer to an hour when they were able to use the car, but it was spick and span, with no sign of the broken glass or the blood that had covered the inside of the vehicle when they returned the previous evening. Cushing had written to Stockington asking him to contact Badger at the vicarage, and a new shirt and jacket had magically appeared from a local tailor for Scott to replace the clothes that were stained with the blood from his head wound the night before.

They drove through the City and parked off Piccadilly, cautiously approaching Albany and meeting the ubiquitous concierge, Clarence. Clarence inquired about Scott's bandages, which he dismissed as a cricketing injury, and declared that no one had been looking for him. Scott was, however, suspicious. 'He'd sell his own mother for a couple of bob,' he said. As they approached Scott's door he took his revolver from his pocket.

'Geoffrey, for heaven's sake, this is Piccadilly,' said Cushing.

'Look, Padre,' said Scott, abruptly, 'Gemp has plugged me twice. If I see him again I'm not going to give him a third go.' He opened the door carefully, and the two men entered the apartment. Warily they checked the rooms and found the place to be empty, and there was no sign of anyone having searched the place. 'Clarence must have been telling the truth,' said Scott. 'We live in strange times.'

Scott hurriedly packed some clothes and valuables, including a pack of ammunition for the service revolver, and they went back downstairs where Clarence was waiting.

'Away for a few days, Mr. Scott?' he asked, in an ingratiating manner.

'Yes, just off to the country,' replied Scott, nonchalantly. 'Yorkshire. Oh yes,' he asked, as an afterthought. 'Is there any post for me?'

Clarence gave him a handful of letters and they walked

back to the car, keeping a watchful eye out as they did. Scott squeezed himself into the passenger seat and, as Cushing drove back towards the east, started to open his post.

'Bill, bill, cricket, bill. Hang on, what's this one?' He held up an expensive envelope. 'That's Phoebe's handwriting.' He ripped open the envelope and read the letter, then gave a low whistle.

'What's wrong?' asked Cushing.

'It's Phoebe. She went back at the weekend and told her father she had left the Rolls in France and he's locked her in her room. She has had to bribe the girl who brings her food to take this letter.'

'Well she'll be safe there, surely.'

'Not when he finds out that we were all in the Rolls with her. We've got to get her out of there.'

'Steady on, man. You're in no state to do any rescuing.' He drove back to Badger's vicarage, firmly ignoring Scott's pleas to turn the car round.

'I don't like to admit it,' said Badger, over dinner, 'but I think Mr. Scott is right. The moment Sloane finds out that Phoebe has been connected with us, who knows what he'll do?'

'His own daughter? Surely not,' said Cushing.

'Only his stepdaughter,' said Scott. 'And we know he's right up to his neck in this conspiracy, and he's the one who shot Hitchcock, remember?'

'We don't actually have evidence of that,' responded Badger. 'And Stockington told us earlier...'

Cushing blushed. Stockington's tirade down the telephone had made him feel again like a naughty schoolboy, though admittedly telling the story of a gunfight in Surrey and two dead Germans may have been enough to tax the man's patience.

'Damn Stockington,' said Scott.

'Well he told us to stop interfering,' said Cushing, 'and that's one piece of advice we're going to ignore.'

'Absolutely,' said Scott. 'Look, we know that Sloane is one of the ungodly. And Stockington said earlier that he had traced the number Gemp left with Rafferty to the German embassy. So if he's in league with the Germans, Sloane must be a traitor as well as a murderer.'

'I'm with you,' said Badger. 'So what are we going to do?'

'Well what's wrong with taking a ladder and climbing up to her window?'

'Very heroic, helping the damsel in distress, and all,' said Badger. 'But we'll have to do it after dark.'

'And it's the right thing to do,' said Cushing. 'Gussie is safe with friends in Hampshire, though she's pretty unhappy about being stuck down there and missing all the fun. Sinclair is in France again. We're all safe here, so we can't leave Phoebe.'

Lenny pulled the familiar lorry, now freshly repainted with the legend "Badger and Sons, Window Cleaning", to the side of the road near Longley Hall. They had, in Cushing's words, thoroughly "cased the joint", and Cushing was pleased to find that Lenny clearly shared his love of detective fiction. The ladders, borrowed along with the lorry from Lenny's uncle, stopped rattling as he turned off the engine.

'I think this is about as close as we can get, sir,' he said. They had established that an easy hop over a wall would take them to the side of the building where Phoebe's window overlooked the ornamental gardens.

'It's a long way, though,' said Cushing. 'I'm just worried that they'll spot us.'

'In for a penny, Padre,' said Scott, grinning. 'Anyway, it's dark, and they won't see us from the front of the building. I wish

Badger were here, though. He'd be helpful if we needed to break in.'

'Well we couldn't all fit in the lorry, could we,' replied Cushing, tartly. 'But while we're here I want to have another look at Sloane's secret study, if I can.'

'Good man,' said Scott. 'I'm game. But let's get Phoebe first.'

The three manoeuvred the long ladder over the wall and left a small ladder on the other side in case they needed to make a quick getaway.

Longley Hall was far less ostentatiously lit than it had been at the Midsummer Ball almost a month before. The men were able to make their surreptitious journey with the ladder through the extensive grounds under cover of darkness, though Cushing was concerned that the white bandage round Scott's head might show up at a distance.

They cowered at the edge of an ornate hedged French garden, and Scott pointed at a window on the first floor. 'That's the one,' he whispered.

'Are you sure?'

'Of course I'm sure, damn it.' He glared at Cushing. 'Stop looking at me like that. I happen to know where her bedroom is, that's all. She pointed it out to me from the garden. Come on.'

'Wait a minute,' said Cushing, nervously. 'Look at all the other lights, and the cars parked. Sloane has got company.'

'Then he'll be occupied when we get Phoebe. Get a move on.'

They carried the ladder to the base of the wall and extended it to its full length, comfortably reaching the windowsill. 'Thanks, Lenny,' whispered Scott, and Lenny scurried back to the lorry to wait for them. 'Hold the ladder steady and I'll make my way up.' Cushing held it while Scott climbed to the window and tapped on it, several times. He grimaced as the window was flung open and could hear Phoebe's delighted squeals that he was sure would be audible in the rest of the house.

Scott climbed through and Cushing waited for what seemed an eternity. While he stood there, he heard a commotion from the front of the house and peered carefully round the corner. He could see people getting into cars and hear the hum of conversation, and quickly drew back to avoid being seen. As a convoy of cars made their way down the drive, he flattened himself against the wall, hoping that no one would spot the silhouette of the ladder. Once they had gone and he could hear no more noise, he gave a quick whistle and Scott stuck his head and arms through the window, a bag in his hands. 'Catch!' he said, in a stage whisper, and dropped the bag which landed noisily next to Cushing. 'Idiot!' hissed Cushing, and Scott stuck his head out again. 'She won't be long,' he said in an undertone. 'She's just packing.'

Cushing muttered darkly and climbed up the ladder, hauling himself into Phoebe's bedroom to see Scott standing in a corner tapping his foot. 'Hello, Padre,' said Phoebe, breezily. 'I'll only be a moment. Isn't this romantic?'

'For heaven's sake, girl,' said Cushing, turning to Scott. 'Look, you get her out of here as quickly as you can. Take her to Lenny and then come back and wait at the bottom of the ladder.' He moved closer to Scott and whispered so that Phoebe could not hear. 'A whole load of guests have left and I'm going to see if I can get into Sloane's secret room and see what is at the bottom of those stairs.'

He walked over to the door and turned the handle. 'It's locked.'

'Well of course it is,' said Phoebe. 'I've been locked in by my wicked stepfather. That's why you've come to rescue me. My poor little wounded soldier.' Scott looked thoroughly embarrassed. Cushing pulled Badger's little silk bag from his pocket and, after about ten minutes, heard a satisfying click.

'Well done, Padre,' whispered Scott, impressed. 'Good old

Badger, eh?'

Cushing opened the door and peered out down the long corridor. 'Go on,' he commanded Scott and Phoebe. 'Down the ladder and get to the van as quick as you can. I'll be back soon.'

Scott gave a thumbs-up sign, and Cushing made his way carefully down the poorly-lit corridor towards the room that he knew to be Sloane's study. He passed the impressive staircase and noted again the huge ancestral portraits that dominated the walls. 'Must have come as a job lot when Sloane bought the house,' thought Cushing, and was then horrified when he heard voices and footsteps coming up the stairs. Starting to panic, he hurriedly opened the nearest door and went into the dark room. He pulled the door closed behind him and heard a smattering of conversation. Two men, maybe three. One was Sloane, one the mysterious John whose voice Cushing had heard a month ago.

Sloane's voice came clearly through the door as they passed Cushing's hiding place. 'Leave us with the decanter, Murrall, and then I don't think we'll need you any more this evening.'

'Thank you, sir. Your Eminence.' This was a rougher voice, maybe the large butler who had removed Cushing from the house on the day of the ball. 'Good night, sir.'

'Good night, Murrall.' Footsteps passed and all was quiet.

"Your Eminence"? Cushing was shocked. This was the form of address for a cardinal, or a papal envoy. 'Is Sloane a Catholic? Are the Synarchists Catholic?' he mused to himself, fanning the fire of his long-held Church of England prejudices, and gently opened the door. The corridor was clear, and he tiptoed towards the door of Sloane's study, fearing a creaking floorboard with every step. He put his ear to the heavy wooden door, hoping that the men had remained in the study rather than having gone into Sloane's secret room, and was thrilled to be able to hear them speaking.

'They are beautiful, Charles, beautiful. The crown, and

285

the orb too. And is that really the Lapsit Exillis? After all these years? Well done. Very well done. A coup for Intelligence and Operations.'

Cushing longed to see into the room, and peered optimistically through the keyhole to catch a glimpse of the relics. The key was in the lock, and he could see nothing. He contemplated bursting in through the door, but realised that, unarmed as he was, this would be more than foolhardy.

'Thank you, John. Yes, they are beautiful. Do they really have the power we believe?'

'How can you doubt it? They represent everything our order believes in. Now we have the relics, we are ready to act. It will be the crowning moment, the flame of the new revolution...'

'And we will have plenty of time to position the jewels – the best part of a year.'

'Absolutely. Then we will all be kings ourselves. How have you arranged for the jewels to be fitted?'

'Gemp has control over a man at Garrard's who has the job of cleaning them every year, some German Jew called Bamberger. Gemp has traced the man's family in Europe, and he has no choice but to do what we demand.'

'Good. I hoped that you wouldn't have to break into the Tower of London.' Cushing heard the two men laughing. What on earth was all of this about? The Tower of London? Jewels? The Crown Jewels? Garrard's he knew to be the Crown jeweller, for he had passed their window in Mayfair many times. His heart racing, he continued to listen.

'I'm not happy about Gemp, though,' said John. 'His role in Amsterdam next week is going to be critical, both the planning and the execution.' There was a noise like a muffled laugh. 'It is a real dramatic statement. Can Gemp be trusted not to make a mess of it? This is a crucial step towards everything we have been working towards all these years.' John's voice grew intense.

'Forget Italy. This is so much bigger. Right and might are now on our side, and our action will be both the proof and the trigger...'

Sloane cut across John's outburst in a calming voice. 'Domvile has every faith in Gemp. He says that he is one of his best agents.'

'That's as maybe, but he has come up against this wretched bunch of interfering amateurs twice now, and still hasn't sorted it out. From what Domvile said earlier, he's even lost a couple of his men.'

'Shot one of them himself, I gather,' replied Sloane. 'The one who was captured.' Behind the door, Cushing shivered at the ruthlessness of Gemp's actions, and felt that Sloane sounded more than uncomfortable about it himself.

'Well, at least the man can't give away any secrets. Gemp now knows who they are, though they appear to have gone into hiding. One thing worries me, though, Charles, and I wanted to talk to you about this after the others had gone.'

'What's that?'

'Gemp has traced the owner of the car that these people were using in France.'

'Excellent.'

'Not really, Charles. It appears to be yours.'

'What?'

'The Rolls Royce. It belongs to you.'

'But – my stepdaughter. Phoebe. She was....'

'Quite. She has got herself mixed up with this lot somehow. I thought that you should deal with it yourself.'

'Well, yes, I will ask her...'

'And when you've finished asking her questions, Charles, I mean that I want you to deal with her.'

'But she's just a chit of a girl. She's my daughter. I can't...'

'She's only your stepdaughter. Just get rid of her. Permanently. This is too important and I don't want some silly little girl who knows too much causing any problems. If you don't, Domvile will have to manage it for you.'

Cushing listened for a few seconds to the protesting Sloane, and realised that he had to leave sharply, without fulfilling his aim of gaining access to the secret room. Sloane would be coming to see Phoebe, to question her at best, and would find her missing. Cushing shuddered. He found Phoebe irritating, but was becoming fond of her despite himself, and was bitterly angry at the thought of Sloane harming the poor girl. He crept back down the corridor and into Phoebe's room, and climbed in darkness down the ladder.

'What's happening, Padre?' whispered Scott, who had been waiting. 'Did you get into the study?'

'No,' responded Cushing. 'Let's get out of here, quickly.' The two men trotted across the lawns towards the wall. Cushing could hear shouting and, as he disappeared into the gloom, turned to see a figure silhouetted against Phoebe's window. He grinned, and slowed his pace.

As they neared the wall, however, they could hear more of a commotion behind them, together with the barking of dogs.

'Come on, Padre, quickly,' called Scott, who by now was yards ahead. Cushing began to run as fast as he could, and reached the short ladder conveniently left for them against the wall. Scott was already on top of the wall, calling for Lenny to start the van. Cushing climbed the ladder to join him as a dark shape hurled itself, slavering, at the wall just below his shoes.

'Forget the ladder,' he shouted, and they jumped, leaving the dog behind them. They bustled into the front of the van, squeezing in beside Phoebe, and Lenny drove them off into the darkness.

22

Friday 20th July 1928

Cushing and Scott brought Phoebe back to Badger's in the small hours of the morning. They thanked Lenny extensively and apologised for leaving the ladders behind. 'No problem,' he said, jauntily. Plenty more where they came from. I'll paint over the sign on the side before I go to bed. Night, all.'

Rachel Brock was up feeding the baby, and welcomed Phoebe, preparing her a glass of hot milk before taking her to her room. Cushing and Scott declined the milk, and Scott produced a voluminous hipflask. 'I'm for some shuteye,' he said, after taking a long gulp. 'Well done, Padre. I think it's time for a council of war in the morning.'

It was mid-morning by the time they sat round the table to work out their next steps. Before breakfast, Cushing had told Scott about John's order to Sloane to get rid of Phoebe, and a dour-faced Scott had been pacing round for half an hour. Cushing had not wanted to let Phoebe join the group, but Scott had convinced him. 'If they are planning to kill her, she's got as much right to sit round the table as the rest of us,' he said, grimly.

Cushing, who had already asked one of Badger's gang of helpers to post a letter to Stockington for him, started to explain his conclusions from what he had overheard at Longley Hall.

'First of all, the butler called this man John "Your Eminence", which means that he must be a Catholic cardinal. I'll get in touch with Gussie and see if there was a cardinal on the guest list at the ball. He would have stuck out like a sore thumb. Especially if he was dressed in red.' Badger stared out of the window and Scott drummed his fingers on the table.

'Is this really important?' he asked.

'Well yes, it is,' replied Cushing, earnestly. 'He's obviously senior to Sir Charles Sloane in this business, because he was giving him orders, and he sounds absolutely mad. He seems to believe in all this ritual stuff. You should have heard him froth. Now if we can identify him...'

'I know him,' said Phoebe. 'I've met him.'

'Excellent, Phoebe. Well done,' said Scott, enthusiastically. 'What's his name?'

'I don't remember,' she said, and the rest of the group leaned back in frustration. 'But he's French, I think, or Spanish, or something, though you would hardly know it to hear him speak. His name isn't John, either. It's Jean. The way the French spell it.'

'Thank you, Phoebe,' said Cushing. 'That's a good start. So we can start looking for a French or Spanish cardinal. There can't be that many, I suppose. Now I was wondering if this might be a Catholic conspiracy...'

'That's even more unlikely than it being a hundred per cent German,' interrupted Scott, petulantly. 'Come on. I want to hear more about the Amsterdam business.'

'What Amsterdam business?' asked Badger.

'Yes,' said Cushing. 'Gemp is off to Amsterdam to do something really important for the Synarchists. I don't know what, but they said that it was crucial. They've been working on this plot for years, and what they are planning now is some sort of culmination of it. We know that Horstmann was on his way there too, today, if you remember. We found that ticket for the boat train in his pocket.'

'But what are the wretched people up to?'

'I really don't know. He said that it would be a dramatic statement, the crowning moment of their plan, whatever it is. Or perhaps a step towards it, at least. And the relics are involved.'

'They have them, I suppose,' said Scott, gloomily.

'Oh yes. John, or Jean rather, said they were beautiful. They have all of them: the crown, the gems and the Lapsit Exillis. They were all just the other side of the door, with Sloane and Jean looking at them. It's such a shame.'

'More than a shame,' muttered Scott.

'But what is bizarre is that they want to do something specific with the gems. They mentioned a jeweller from Garrard's. They appear to be blackmailing him.'

'To do what?'

'Again, I don't know. But they joked about breaking into the Tower of London. Perhaps we should take a look?'

'Well yes, perhaps some tourism would be good while there's a major international conspiracy going on.'

'Don't be sarcastic, Geoffrey. They are planning to use the Templar relics somehow.'

'Fine. But in the meantime they are after us. And not just you and me, Padre.' He looked meaningfully at Phoebe. 'Shall I tell her?'

Cushing nodded, and Scott relayed the conversation between Sloane and Jean, his fists clenching. Phoebe blanched, and Badger, tight-lipped, said 'I'll have a word with Maurice. We can double the guard.'

'But how could he even think of it?' asked Rachel. 'I mean, asking the man to get rid of his own stepdaughter? It's barbaric.'

'He never liked me,' said Phoebe, and burst into tears. There was little point continuing with the meeting, so Cushing took the opportunity to telephone Gussie. He was pleased that she was safe in the country, but concerned that she might also have become a target. He knew that he would be far more comfortable if she were with the rest of them. She promised to call him back with any news about Cardinal Jean.

He then telephoned Grainger who he discovered had an appointment with Claude Schaeffer, the Ugarit archaeologist, that afternoon. Grainger agreed to meet Cushing at his Regent's Park house on Saturday lunchtime. Cushing exhorted him to say nothing of the additional tablets, at the risk of being assaulted again, and he hoped that Grainger had taken note this time.

He then approached the group, where Scott and Rachel had dried Phoebe's tears. 'Let's get some fresh air,' he said. 'How about a walk to the Tower of London?'

'You really have a bee in your bonnet about this, Uncle Kit,' mocked Scott. 'But you're right. I don't like being caged up.'

Cushing, Scott and Phoebe had not visited the Tower of London since they were at school, which for Cushing had been in the last century. They joined a little crocodile of tourists, mainly families enjoying the school holidays, walking from the underground station. Phoebe looked cool and fetching in a light silk dress, but the two men were uncomfortable in the heat in their jackets, waistcoats and hats.

After queuing with the crowds at the entrance to the Tower, they stopped to watch Tower Bridge opening to allow a ship to pass through, and then crossed the dry moat through the ancient gate. Several Yeoman Warders stood round in their colourful uniforms carrying pikes. While the famous Beefeaters might appear to be a charming anachronism, Cushing knew that they were tough and experienced old soldiers, backed up by a strong armed guard.

They passed the square White Tower, built by William the Conqueror, and went straight to the display of the Crown Jewels. Like the other tourists, they gawped at the priceless artefacts worn by the country's kings and queens, dominated by the glittering diamonds in Queen Victoria's state crown and the Imperial Crown of India. Phoebe cooed at the huge Kohinoor diamond, the Mountain of Light in Queen Mary's coronation crown, and Cushing indicated the enormous Star of Africa at the top of the great sceptre.

'Grainger pointed out that they used a crown, orb and sceptre in those ceremonies thousands of years ago,' he said. 'And he joked about how little the principles had changed. I hadn't realised how right he was. Here they all are.'

'But so what?' asked Scott, in a low voice. 'I mean I can understand why Phoebe's stepfather and his gang might want to steal them. I would, given half a chance. But what on earth do they need a jeweller for?'

They came out into the sunshine, and strolled round the Tower for another half hour, looking down from the walls at the river glinting in the light. 'At least we're safe in the Tower,' laughed Scott.

Eventually they returned to Whitechapel, to hear from Rachel that they had missed a call from Stockington. 'He's taking his son to a cricket match tomorrow afternoon,' she said, 'but he's going to come round to the vicarage at about five o'clock.'

'Oh well,' said Scott, 'I suppose a day won't make a lot of difference.'

'Well we're going to be deep in the throes of our party at that time,' said Rachel.

'Party?' asked Phoebe, excitedly.

'It's for the local children,' replied Rachel. 'There's a big football match tomorrow afternoon at the ironworks ground. It's the local Jewish lads playing the Christian boys. Philip has organised it. He's done so much for them all. The least we could do is have the children back here for tea. It's going to be a lovely day for it.'

'And I'm going to be helping.' A female voice came from behind him, and Cushing spun round.

'Gussie!' he exclaimed, delightedly, and threw his arms round her before recovering his composure and shuffling, embarrassed, from foot to foot. Scott grinned and Phoebe gave Gussie a huge hug herself.

'I thought I'd join you,' she said. 'I was getting a little bored down in West Meon. Though Rachel has been trying to persuade me not to go out shopping.'

'Well she's absolutely right,' said Cushing, a little pompously.

'Well we'll just have to see about that,' she said, wrinkling her nose. 'Anyway, it's too late to go out today, and Rachel has roped me in to help with the festivities tomorrow. But I've got some news. I think I've traced your Cardinal Jean.'

'Splendid. Tell us the details.'

'It's actually rather embarrassing. One of Sir Charles Sloane's personal guests was squeezed in at the last minute. Sir Charles was hosting the dinner, so he called the shots. I think we thought he was a woman, if you know what I mean, so I didn't think of a Jean when you asked for a John. No ecclesiastical title or anything, but the name was Jean de Mayol de Lupe.'

'Phoebe was right. It does sound Spanish. Do you know anything about him?'

'Sorry, Christopher, nothing else. I've checked in "Who's Who" but no mention. I thought that maybe he would be in Crockford's, but my friends in Hampshire didn't have a copy.'

Cushing snorted. 'Crockford's is C of E,' he said, 'but there is probably a Catholic equivalent. We can go to the Athenaeum library tomorrow.'

Cushing woke early. Looking at the bright sunshine streaming through the curtains, he wished, perhaps for the first time in his life, that he was in Manchester. As he and Scott had discussed the previous evening, rather annoying Gussie and Phoebe over the otherwise jolly dinner, today was the start of the second test match against the West Indians.

Leaving Gussie and Phoebe to help Rachel prepare for the children's party, Scott and Cushing took the underground to Regent's Park to visit Grainger. Over a long cool drink in the archaeologist's garden, he began to talk about his further work on the documents that they had given him a week ago. The visitors were more interested to hear about Schaeffer's investigations in Ugarit.

'I took your advice,' drawled the American, 'and didn't tell him anything else.' He was looking better after his ordeal, but was clearly still nervous. 'I'm sure he's on the level, but you can't be too sure. Those people who bashed me over the head, you know, the ones that you gentlemen have been so worried about, did so immediately after I last spoke to him.'

'What did you find out?'

'Well, what he told me was pretty interesting. He gave me chapter and verse about what they had uncovered. They had found a chamber containing a number of crusader artefacts, books, maps and so on. They had originally been concerned that their findings at the ancient site had been compromised in the twelfth century in some way, then realised that what they had found was itself significant.'

'And this was...'

'Among the various Ugaritic artefacts that he said the crusaders had uncovered were a number of parchments and references to other treasures. The problem is that some of these artefacts were stolen.'

'Sloane and Jean did talk about their men on site,' mused Cushing.

'Anyway, we now all agree that the first tablet you showed me had indeed been stolen from Ugarit. Then some of the crusader stuff also disappeared. He says he has his suspicions about who was responsible.'

'The map,' muttered Scott. 'Jean-Pierre said they had a map. Did they find a map of some sort?'

'Map? Yes, he left some photographs. There was one of a map.' He went to his desk and opened a large brown envelope. 'Here we are.'

Cushing and Scott flicked through a number of photographs and nodded familiarly at pictures of tablets and pieces of ancient writing from Ugarit, and then some of the crusader artefacts and documents. Cushing particularly pointed out Masonic links between some of the symbols on the documents – pyramids, compasses, stylised set-squares and the like – and those that he recognised from his own experience. The last photograph was of an old parchment. It was a map, similar in style and execution to that of Amalric de Montfort's map of the tunnels which they had found in Seborga. 'Look,' said Cushing. 'That must be the back way in. You know, the other entrance to the tomb...'

'That's as maybe,' interrupted Grainger, grumpily, 'but there's a difference between archaeology and treasure hunting. Or tomb robbing. If you really have found the tomb of Esclarmonde, let me be involved, please. You are amateurs; I am a professional, after all. This discovery belongs to the world.'

Cushing and Scott took the underground back to Piccadilly Circus with Grainger's words that echoed those of Stockington's still ringing in their ears, and, still uncomfortably hot, walked down to the Athenaeum.

Rafferty drew Cushing to one side as they entered. 'Those men who were looking for you last week, sir,' he said. 'One of them has been round again. Just thought you ought to know.'

Cushing thanked the porter effusively, and he and Scott walked into the wonderful panelled library. It took them some time to find the right volume, but eventually they were able to find some references to the mysterious Jean.

'He's not a cardinal in any normal sense that I can find,' said Cushing, reading. 'He was ordained in 1900 and then joined a French holy order, the Ecclesiastical Knights of Constantine and Saint George.'

'He's our patron saint, surely,' said Scott. 'What are the French doing with him?'

'He's not quite as English as Saint Edward the Confessor, of course,' said Cushing.

'Is this an order like the Templars and Hospitallers?'

'I'm not sure, I've never heard of them before. But this group is very public, and still active, whereas Sloane and Jean talked about their order as if it was a secret one.' He flicked through more references. 'Hmm, he's quite a hero. Served as a chaplain in the War, wounded and mentioned in dispatches. He got the Légion d'Honneur.'

'He sounds a bit like you, Uncle Kit.'

Cushing shuddered, as if something slimy had crawled over his leg. 'Except that I am not trying to kill the King of Italy and have that sweet girl Phoebe murdered,' he said. 'Yes, he appears to be a Monsignor, appointed in Rome, but there are references to other unnamed religious orders. Monsignor is sufficiently generic that he could be a bishop or its equivalent, or even higher. Presumably if he sets up a new order he can call himself whatever he wants. He sounded deranged enough to do that.'

'Where's he from?'

'Lupe is a tiny place not that far from Lyon,' replied Cushing.

'Pity,' said Scott. 'I thought he might have been from Montségur or somewhere like that. So we're not really a lot further forward.'

'Not really,' frowned Cushing. 'But there might be enough for Stockington to go on. We ought to get back to Whitechapel, though. It would be nice to help the girls, or even watch the football match.'

'Righto,' said Scott. 'But let's just pop back to my rooms. I need to pick up some more clothes. It looks as if we're going to be camping out for longer than I'd thought.'

They walked up Piccadilly towards Scott's apartment and were greeted by Clarence, who gave Scott his post and told him mournfully that a number of people had been calling and asking for him.

'Damn,' said Scott. 'Come on then, Padre. Let's make it quick.'

They climbed the stairs and entered the flat. Scott stared out of the window for a few seconds, then removed a picture from the wall and fiddled with a lock of a small concealed safe. He put some papers into his jacket pocket and then went into the bedroom, where he surreptitiously opened the wardrobe in which Cushing had hidden both golden reliquary chests. When he came out a few minutes later, Cushing noticed that his small suitcase looked to be surprisingly heavy, but thought little of it. 'I'm finished,' Scott said, and then peered out of the window again. The warnings from Clarence and the earlier discussion with Rafferty had made him nervous. 'This may not have been a good idea,' he observed, nonchalantly. 'I think we've got company.'

Cushing joined him cautiously at the edge of the glass and peered out. Scott pointed at two men, wearing hats and raincoats, standing under a street lamp. 'What makes you so sure? This is Piccadilly, after all. There are a lot of people around.'

'I think they followed us from the Athenaeum. Or maybe they've just been waiting here, I don't know. You probably shouldn't have been wearing your dog-collar. They've been standing there for the best part of half an hour. And no one else is wearing a raincoat in this weather. Come on. Out the back way. I wish I hadn't left my revolver at Badger's.'

They went down the stairs and found Clarence cleaning boots. The back door was locked. 'Clarence, old man, let us out the back way, would you, there's a good chap.'

'Well Mr. Scott, sir, I'm not sure if I have the key...'

'For heaven's sake, man, stop messing about.' He smacked a ten shilling note down on the porter's counter. 'We're in a hurry.'

Huffing and puffing, Clarence took a huge ring of keys from a hook and opened the back door, then led them through a small messy yard to a wooden gate, which he also unlocked. 'Have a nice day, sir,' he said, grinning.

Scott and Cushing bundled out of the gate and began a looping route up towards Regent Street. Cushing had immediately noticed two more men in raincoats keeping a regular march some thirty yards behind them.

'What shall we do?'

'Well we can't lead them back to Badger's,' said Scott. 'The girls are there. I wonder, though.... Do you have any pennies?' He stopped at a red telephone box and made a call. 'Right,' he said, as he came out of the box. 'Let them follow us. We're going to a pub and Badger is going to organise a little reception committee.'

They walked to the underground station, ostentatiously ignoring the men tailing them, and, as Badger had suggested to Scott, took a train back to Whitechapel. Scott, whistling tunelessly, turned several corners into Cable Street to find a grimy pub called the Britannia. Walking in, and looking over his shoulder to make sure that the men were still following, he greeted the man behind the bar jauntily and ordered two pints of beer.

'We're closed, sir,' said the publican, grumpily. 'Open at five.'

'Oh well, never mind,' said Scott, and at that point four men in raincoats entered the deserted pub behind them. They walked straight over to Cushing and Scott and one of them, a tall, cadaverous man with a thin moustache rather like Scott's, addressed them in well-spoken English.

'Now, gentlemen, we're the police. Perhaps you would come with us?' He showed them an obvious-shaped lump in his pocket.

'Police, eh?' blustered Cushing. 'Let me see your warrant.' At that word, the taciturn publican disappeared from view.

'Come on,' said one of the other men, in an Irish accent. 'We've been trailing round London all day. Let's have them.'

Cushing and Scott were searched for weapons and then ushered out of the pub, one of the men having relieved Scott of his suitcase. As they came out, blinking, into the sunlight, they saw a dozen men standing, menacingly, in a loose semicircle around the pub. They recognised some of them: the smiling figure of Lenny, carrying what looked like a pickaxe handle; Fred and Jim similarly armed. The enormous figures of Maurice and Chalky loomed over the others, Maurice carrying an old cricket bat.

'Now, gentlemen,' said Lenny. 'We have what I can only call a situation. How about if you just leave your weapons behind and we won't say any more about it? Mr. Scott, Father Christopher, just move away. Over there, that's right.'

Cushing and Scott did as they were told, with a leering Scott hurriedly snatching back his heavy suitcase. The tall man took the gun from his pocket and pointed it at Lenny. The man with the Irish accent drew a knife and tossed it from hand to hand, an evil sneer on his face. 'I don't think so,' said the tall man. 'I think this wins the argument, don't you?'

Lenny and his friends moved forward threateningly, raising their weapons. The four men stepped back towards the door of the pub as the group closed in, and the leader fired a warning shot into the air. As he did, the figure of the publican appeared behind him, smashing what appeared to be a life preserver onto the man's shoulder. The man's arm went limp and his gun flew off into the street.

'Get them, lads,' shouted Lenny, and his crew closed in on the four men. They disappeared under a flail of clubs and fists. There was one bloodcurdling yell, but in what seemed like only a few seconds it was all over. The four thugs lay battered and bleeding on the ground, and the sound of a police whistle could be heard in the distance.

Lenny was leaning over the form of Maurice, who was lying on the ground cursing volubly. Lenny was pressing a none-too-clean handkerchief against Maurice's side, and it was rapidly reddening with blood. 'Come on boys, we'd better get him to the doctor,' he said. 'Anyone else hurt? Jim, that bloke with the knife got you too, didn't he? Can you walk properly? Good. You'd better come to the doctor too.' He looked up at Cushing and Scott and grinned. 'Livens up the afternoon, eh? Haven't had so much fun since that bunch of fascists marched down the Commercial Road at Easter. You'd better make yourself scarce, sir. Go back to Father Badger's. Maurice will be all right.' He whistled and pointed at the groaning or unconscious bodies. 'Fred, Chalky, search these blokes and get out of here before the rozzers arrive.'

Cushing and Scott arrived back at the vicarage to find Gussie and Phoebe helping to set out tea for the children's party under Rachel's direction. Cushing absent-mindedly helped himself to a cake, and Gussie slapped his hand hard. 'Just you wait,' she snapped. 'I've had enough trouble keeping Phoebe and the children away from them.'

Half an hour later, Stockington appeared at the gate of the vicarage. 'There seems to be some sort of riot going on,' he said, mildly. 'Police cars, whistles. All very exciting. I wouldn't normally ask, but I assume that it's nothing to do with you gentlemen? Trouble does seem to follow you around.' Cushing and Scott blushed, and Gussie looked quizzically at them.

They ushered Stockington quickly into the vicarage, past a

bevy of women trying to squeeze more plates onto trestle tables already groaning with food. Cushing told him briefly that they had been followed from Piccadilly and threatened, before the locals lent a hand.

They made a pot of tea and told Stockington their conclusions about a "dramatic statement" in Amsterdam, and the identity of Jean. 'Jean de Mayol de Lupe. He's a French catholic priest, linked to some obscure religious order,' said Cushing, excitedly. 'We thought he was a cardinal, but he might just call himself that. Can't you get him arrested, or deported, or something?'

'Very interesting,' said Stockington, steepling his fingers. 'Yes, very interesting.' He stared into the distance, and then poured more tea. 'Now,' he continued languidly, 'just for interest, what have you done with the bodies you mentioned the other day? I don't want them turning up next year and causing a problem.'

Cushing promised to pass on the accurate location, and then remembered the business of the jeweller from Garrard's, continuing to bring Stockington up to date. 'Can you make some sort of official security visit on Monday?' he asked. 'And can we come?'

'Well I think it's appropriate that we keep in touch,' he said. 'Meet me outside Garrard's at noon on Monday.' He looked round as the door opened and the noise of excited children could be heard. 'Ah, we have company.'

Badger came into the room accompanied by the rabbi, a uniformed police officer and another man wearing a tweed jacket and baggy trousers. Introductions were made: Badger had invited Inspector Hodgson and his men who had come to quell the apparent riot to join the celebrations, and the other man was Patston, a middle-aged journalist, who had been covering the interdenominational football match and now scented a more important story.

'I dislike the fascists even more than I dislike the Bolsheviks,' said the journalist, earnestly. 'When they come along to a harmless game of soccer between the local Christians and Jews and start to cause trouble...'

'And that's what happened, Inspector?' asked Stockington, who had innocently introduced himself as FitzGerald.

'That's what it seems,' said the inspector. 'Though the four thugs in the back of the van are all pretty badly beaten up. They are under arrest, of course, or will be when they are wide awake enough to understand. One of my sergeants has taken them off to the station. It's a tough neighbourhood, this one.'

'Thank you, Inspector. Perhaps I could pop in and have a word with them at some time?' He flashed an identity card, and the policeman was visibly impressed.

'Yes, of course, sir,' he said.

'Look, Father Badger, Rabbi, I must be going,' said Patston. 'If I can file this copy tonight it might even make tomorrow's issue.'

'Thank you, Peter. Always a pleasure having you here covering the local colour and atmosphere.'

'Well, Father, after that scoop you gave me at Easter I'm always glad to help. God bless.' Patston shook hands and left.

'Well, gentlemen,' said Badger, 'shall we pop off and join the ladies outside? I think the party has already started.'

'I must be going too,' said Stockington. 'Father, Rabbi, gentlemen, it has been – well, a pleasure in every way.' He looked piercingly at Cushing. 'I'll see you on Monday.' Inspector Hodgson stood up to join him. 'No, no, Inspector. You and your men deserve a bit of relaxation.'

Cushing enjoyed the food and the singing that followed, but was particularly delighted when Lenny appeared. Avoiding the policemen, Lenny whispered in Badger's ear and then came over to join Cushing, Scott, Gussie and Phoebe. 'Thanks for the fun earlier,' he said. 'I just wanted to let you know that Maurice and

Jim are both fine. We had to take Maurice to hospital, and he's still there, but he'll be right as rain in a couple of days.'

'Thank you again,' said Cushing, and shook Lenny's hand warmly. 'We'll drop in and visit Maurice tomorrow, if you think that's appropriate.'

'I'm sure he'd be very pleased to see you, sir,' said Lenny. He grinned. 'Maurice likes grapes, I know, but a bottle or two of beer will go down even better.'

23

Sunday 22nd July 1928

Scott had monopolised the Sunday newspaper over breakfast. 'Tich Freeman took five,' he said, with satisfaction, having turned straight to the cricket scores. 'We bowled the West Indians out for two hundred and six. Good stuff.'

Cushing was torn between reading the report from Old Trafford and searching the news pages for anything about the incident the previous day. Sure enough, there was a short piece, blaming the affray on a group of fascist sympathisers who had hurled abuse at crowds watching an integrated junior football match. One of four men arrested was also charged with a firearms offence.

'There's a long quote from you, Badger,' called out Cushing to his fellow clergyman who was preparing for the Sunday service. 'Condemning the fascists and all.'

'Oh really?' replied Badger. 'I just let Patston make it up. He does it very well. He did a grand job for us when they had that march at Easter. He's a good bloke. Very much on our side.'

The party dutifully attended Badger's service, and again Cushing found it not to his taste. He saw Phoebe clapping in time with the tambourines and singing along enthusiastically, and found it most unbecoming. He also spotted Lenny, several pews behind him, with Fred, Jim, Chalky and a group of women and children. Lenny winked and the others also acknowledged him. 'I've just thought,' whispered Cushing to Gussie. 'Isn't Lenny Jewish?' 'It's a very broad church,' she shrugged.

After church, the group went to visit Maurice in the London Hospital. He was cheerily sitting up in bed, and was grateful for the beer that Cushing had smuggled in under the watchful eyes of the matron. Scott showed Maurice the newspaper article, then turned again to the sports pages. 'Hobbs and Sutcliffe have made a sound start,' he told Maurice, flipping the pages. 'Nice to see Hobbs back in the team. Mind you, he's almost as old as the Padre. And there's an interesting article here about Lord Burghley.'

'Oh really? Young David?' interrupted Cushing. 'He was at Magdalene with the son of a friend of mine. He's the athlete, isn't he?'

'Yes, the hurdler. Competed in Paris four years ago and tipped for gold at Amsterdam. A dead cert, they say. I should go to the bookies....'

He tailed off, and the two men looked at each other in silence.

'What's up, guv?' chirped Maurice.

'Amsterdam. The Olympics,' said Cushing, in horrified realisation. 'They start next week, don't they?'

Scott skimmed the rest of the article. 'Yes. The opening ceremony is next Saturday.'

'And it will be opened by the Queen of the Netherlands, presumably. Of course! Gemp is going to assassinate Queen Wilhelmina! Sloane and Jean talked about "execution" and a "crowning moment". "Forget Italy", he said.'

Scott snatched back the paper as Gussie and Phoebe thronged round, Maurice looking bemused from the bed.

Gussie, almost squeaking, stabbed her finger at a paragraph

near the end of the article. 'Look, look. It's not just Queen Wilhelmina. Look. "His Royal Highness King George V will attend the opening ceremony, with Queen Mary. They travel to Holland on Thursday. The Kings of Norway and Sweden, as well as other European heads of state, will also attend." Oh Christopher....'

'How can we have been so stupid?' snapped Cushing. 'Forget Italy. They're going to kill the King.'

'The King?'

'Yes, the King, our King. The King!' Cushing waved his hands in the air. 'The King Emperor. His Majesty King George the Fifth. Oh God. What are we going to do?'

'But what will killing the King achieve?' asked Gussie, hesitantly.

'They kill the King, and then they crown a new one! That's why they talked about a coronation. They can't crown a new king without murdering the existing one. They have to murder him, otherwise they would have to wait for him to die of natural causes.'

'But...'

'Remember when they spoke about the assassination attempt in Italy, they said that Prince Umberto wasn't a suitable candidate, and they had a better one?'

'Yes, but...'

'Well that's it. The Prince of Wales. They crown him, using the ancient jewels and relics. That's what they mean about crowning the true king. Then they control him in some way. Or maybe he's part of this ghastly conspiracy himself. Either way, they run the Empire.'

'We've got to stop them,' said Scott.

'But how?' asked Phoebe.

'We've got to tell Stockington,' said Gussie.

'You're right, but I'm sure that the authorities won't believe us,' concluded Cushing. 'I think we're on our own, and we've got to do it ourselves.'

'So Amsterdam here we come,' said Scott, cracking his fingers.

'We must. We've got to stop them. Come on, back to Badger's.' Cushing paused. 'Good luck Maurice. Sorry to leave you. Not a dickie bird about this!'

The whole party was seething in frustration. They had been unable to reach Stockington on Sunday, and, other than look at the times of the boat train, had done little but hypothesise about the conspirators' plans. With Sinclair still out of contact, they did not have access to the aeroplane, which would have helped them to cross the Channel more quickly.

Cushing and Scott arrived early at Bond Street to meet Stockington, impatient as they paced up and down outside the expensive shops. Unruffled, he appeared shortly before noon, and immediately Cushing began to blurt out their fears to him.

'They're going to kill the King, in Amsterdam, and use the gems we have been hunting for to crown a new one. We must have been idiots. It's so obvious!'

'Calm down, Reverend, please. I wondered how long it might take you to put two and two together. I'm already on the case. Now, let's do this security check.'

Completely lost for words, the two men followed Stockington into the jeweller's and watched as he summoned the manager, showed some identification and explained what they wanted to do. The manager sent an assistant to summon Bamberger and invited the three visitors through a secure door into a smart panelled room, glass cases showing off some fabulous exhibits.

'No chance of a free sample, I suppose,' said Scott, grinning.

Bamberger was a nervous, birdlike man in his late thirties, with lank, thinning hair and thick pebble glasses. The manager was gushing, describing Bamberger as one of his most talented jewel experts. 'The only man I would trust to clean the Crown Jewels,' he said.

'Thank you, Herr Simpson,' said Bamberger, in a heavy German accent.

'Yes, thank you, Mr. Simpson,' said Stockington. 'Perhaps we could discuss the process of cleaning the Crown Jewels with Mr. Bamberger alone? You have already done enough to explain the security measures for bringing the items to your vaults.'

The manager left, and Stockington began to ask some searching questions about the safety of the jewels while they were at Garrard's. 'So,' he concluded, 'when you are cleaning the jewels, there is no one supervising you. You could easily switch the jewels for others, couldn't you?'

'Svitch? Vot do you mean?'

'Exchange the jewels for others. Perhaps false ones, so that you could remove the real ones. Hypothetically, of course.'

Bamberger was starting to sweat. 'I vould not do such a thing...'

'Of course not, of course not. You are clearly not a criminal, are you? So you would have to have a good reason. Your family is in Germany, I believe...'

'No...'

'Now, Mr. Bamberger, we believe that some people may have threatened your family if you do not carry out a few, shall we say, little services for them.'

'But I have done nothing!'

'But am I right? Have they asked you to exchange certain gems, the next time the Crown Jewels are entrusted with you for cleaning?'

Bamberger started to whimper. 'Please...'

Stockington flexed his fingers. 'Tell me everything, and we will do everything in our power to protect your family and bring them to join you in England.'

An hour later they were out again in the bright sunshine, leaving Bamberger, wholly compliant, behind them. He had not been able to identify any of his blackmailers, but had confirmed the principles of the plan.

'Well, gentlemen,' said Stockington, 'this is curiouser and curiouser. It seems as if you are right.'

'At last,' said Cushing, somewhat surprised. 'You believe us.'

'Absolutely,' said Stockington. 'Which is why I'm going to Amsterdam myself on Wednesday.'

'Is everything under control now then?'

'Not exactly. I'm not able to go over in any official capacity, though I can still pull some strings.'

'You'll need some help, then,' said Cushing.

'Actually, I do. I don't like to admit it, but I think I'll need all the help I can get.'

'Excellent,' said Scott. 'We'll pack our bags.'

'Well, packing your bags might be a good idea' replied Stockington. 'You've clearly annoyed the opposition enough for them to raise the stakes.'

'What do you mean?' asked Cushing.

'Didn't I tell you?' said Stockington, casually. 'They've been pulling a few strings too. Domvile, I suspect. You're wanted.'

'What?'

'Wanted. At least the two of you are, and Mrs. Gordon and Miss Fairfax as well. For some reason they don't appear to have named your friend Badger. Rather sloppy of them, though I say so myself.'

'Wanted? What for?'

'Oh, murder, of course. Murder gets Scotland Yard so excited.'

'Who? Ross? Hitchcock? But we didn't...'

'I know you didn't. There might be questions asked about

the people who attacked you in Surrey last week, of course, but not if they haven't found the bodies. No, you're wanted for the murder of Ross.'

'But...'

'I know!' Stockington was becoming tetchy. 'Obviously they've trumped up this spurious charge against you. But that's not the point. The point is that in addition to a bunch of thugs pursuing you, you now have half the police force in the country with the same objective.'

'So what do we do?'

'Well, I suggest you leave the country. I hear that Holland can be a nice holiday destination at this time of year.' He smiled. 'I just wouldn't use your real names, that's all.'

'Can you get us some false passports?' asked Scott, conspiratorially.

'Sadly not,' replied Stockington, not looking sad at all. 'Too short notice, and I don't want to rock the boat officially, not yet at least. But I hear that the authorities are giving a special dispensation to let people use identity cards rather than passports for the Olympics. There are so many press and family and supporters going, as well as the competitors. I can't say that it appeals to me, but there we are. Shall I see you on the boat train on Wednesday?'

Back at Badger's vicarage, they affirmed that they would not risk any more public appearances. It was one thing to be pursued by Sloane's or Domvile's thugs, but another to be wanted for murder and chased by the real police. They could hardly resist arrest when the police were just doing their jobs.

'We're going to need identity cards,' said Badger. 'I know a man who can help.'

'But what are we going to do when we get to Amsterdam?'

asked Gussie.

'Now, Gussie...' said Cushing, protectively.

'Oh don't start that again, Christopher,' she snapped. 'I'm coming, and that's final. It's hardly safe for us in England, is it?'

'And I'm coming too,' said Phoebe, emphatically.

'So that's settled,' smiled Gussie. 'Now, we can't just go as spectators. Can we get press passes, or something?'

'Excellent idea,' said Scott. 'I say, Badger, your man Patston who was here on Saturday. Could he sort something out for us?'

'I'll give him a call,' said Badger, and disappeared to his study to use the telephone. When he came back ten minutes later he looked very pleased. 'Peter will be here at about six,' he said, 'and I've asked an old friend called Donald to come along as well. He should be able to help us with the identity cards. I suppose we'll all need them, though Stockington did say that I'm not wanted.'

'I don't even know what an identity card looks like,' said Phoebe.

'That's not a problem,' replied Badger. 'Donald will know exactly what to do.'

Donald certainly did know what to do. A quiet man with thick glasses and a fringe of hair around his bald pate, Donald managed never quite to catch the eyes of the party. He produced a sample identity card to confirm that this was what the party wanted, and said, dismissively, that he would be able to give them all new cards by lunchtime the following day.

'What names would you like?' he asked.

'I don't know,' said Cushing. 'John Smith?'

'Use a bit of imagination, Padre,' laughed Scott.

'Absolutely,' said Badger. 'Overdale, or Underhill. Something better than Smith, at least.'

'Why not Psmith with a P, like in those P G Wodehouse stories,' said Scott. 'Then I can be Mike Jackson, his cricketing chum.'

'Or you could go as Bertie Wooster,' contributed Badger. 'And I could be Jeeves. And Gussie could be his Aunt Agatha.'

'The dragon lady?' giggled Gussie. 'How dare you, sir!' She giggled again. 'You should go under the name of Sanders, Christopher. Like Winnie the Pooh.' Phoebe, sitting next to her, dissolved in laughter.

Donald coughed. 'Perhaps you would leave the names to me,' he said. 'Now, Badger, didn't you say something about a press pass as well?'

With perfect timing, there was a knock at the door and Patston arrived. He was puzzled when Badger asked if he could arrange five press passes for the party. 'By tomorrow? Not a chance, I'm afraid,' he said. 'What for?'

'We need to go to Amsterdam, for the Olympics,' said Badger, 'and we thought that you might be able to help. Never mind, Peter. Do you have your own pass we could have a look at?'

Patston obligingly passed over his card and Badger gave it to Donald, who shrugged. 'A five year old could do these,' he said. 'Can I borrow this for the night?'

'Yes, of course,' replied Patston, automatically, scenting a good story. 'What are you all up to? Amsterdam, eh? Can I come?'

The party were all tense the following morning, nervous about leaving the vicarage but desperate for some sort of action.

Scott was particularly irritated to read in the newspaper that his old enemy, Douglas Jardine, had made a big score at Old Trafford against the West Indies on the second day of the test match. 'Run out for eighty three,' he snarled. 'I'd have called him for a short one a lot earlier than that and left him stranded, I can tell you.'

Donald was as good as his word and arrived promptly at

the vicarage shortly after noon with the forged documents. Each member of the party had an identity card, and a suitably dog-eared press card accrediting them as representatives of various regional newspapers.

'Mrs Amelia Ffoulkes,' read Gussie. 'Two Fs. I suppose it could be worse. Who are you?'

'I'm Lucy Bathurst,' said Phoebe. 'Western Daily Press. Does that exist? Good heavens.' She peered at the other documents. 'You're Mr. Dewhurst,' she said to Badger, 'and you, Geoffrey, are Mr. Galveston.'

Scott leaned over. 'Let me see. Ah, Richard Galveston. That's good. At least it's not Piers. And you're Hastings, Padre,' he said. 'Donald has a sense of humour.'

The forger raised an eyebrow. 'I'm pleased you like my little joke.'

Cushing looked blank.

'Come on, Padre,' said Scott, jocularly. 'It's not like you to miss a literary reference. They are all in the League of the Scarlet Pimpernel. You know, saving the French aristocrats from the guillotine.'

Cushing, who had clearly not read the book, shrugged vaguely. 'Seems appropriate, I suppose, if we're flitting across the Channel on a similar mission,' he said, and turned to Donald to thank him profusely for his help.

'A pleasure, sir,' replied Donald, his eyes fixed strangely at a lampshade over Cushing's shoulder. 'Any friend of Badger's...'

'Is a friend of mine.' Scott completed the sentence for him and they all laughed.

'Right,' said Cushing, 'now we know what our noms de plume are, we had better book the tickets for the boat train tomorrow. Badger, as you're the only one of us not wanted for murder, could you pop to the station and do the honours?'

Badger nodded. 'Of course. Those gangsters will have stolen a march on us. They will already be in Amsterdam.'

24

Wednesday 25th July 1928

Cushing was feeling exhausted. He had set the alarm clock horribly early, then, fearfully looking over his shoulder all the time, travelled with the others from the vicarage to Liverpool Street station. They caught the train across the flat landscape of Essex to Harwich, from where they took the long, tedious and smelly Channel crossing to the Hook of Holland. The sea was millpond still, but Cushing and Badger both felt ill and cursed Gussie under their breath when she talked happily about the last time they had crossed the Channel in Sinclair's converted bomber. Even the newspaper report of England's win at the test match did not make them feel better.

They were, however, all delighted that their forged documents passed muster with both the English and the Dutch authorities, and gratefully joined the train to Amsterdam. The journey was routine, and Gussie pointed out of the window at the windmills dotting the flat and wet landscape of coastal Holland, criss-crossed with narrow canals. It was the middle of the evening when they finally pulled into Amsterdam's central station, a gothic building that Cushing thought reminded him of St. Pancras in London.

The urbane Stockington, who had previously told them

that he used a different name and passport when travelling "on business", gave the group of friends another warning. 'We are going to be met by one of my contacts. The city will be fairly busy, I think, but he will find you somewhere to stay.'

'Aren't you staying with us then?' asked Scott.

'Good heavens, no,' replied Stockington, dismissively. 'I thought of staying at the embassy, but as I'm here unofficially I felt I should just stay with a friend. But I'm warning you – keep a low profile, for pity's sake.'

They joined the milling throng on the station concourse, the men struggling to help the women with their bags, and a slovenly-looking man in a dirty jumper shuffled over towards them.

'Mynheer FitzGerald?' he said to Stockington. 'Welcome to Amsterdam, sir.' He eyed up the other members of the party. 'Dominee Cushing, Mynheer Scott, Dominee Brock, I presume? Good evening. Mevrouw Gordon, Jufrouw Fairfax. Welcome to Holland. My name is Willem.' Bright blue eyes twinkled under the man's battered hat as they shook hands, and Cushing noted that he sounded rather better-spoken than his outward appearance might have indicated. Cushing looked quizzically at Stockington, but he appeared to be completely relaxed, and Willem ushered them all towards the station exit.

'Most of the hotels are full because of the Olympics,' said Willem in fluent but accented English. 'Many of the teams are staying in boats at the harbour. The Americans certainly are. Some of the bigger European nations have taken over the best hotels, as you might expect. But my uncle has a small hotel with rooms for you all. It is clean, at least.' He laughed, and Cushing, who wanted nothing more than to have a quick meal and then a good sleep, was in no mood to argue.

They followed Willem for about half a mile along a maze of increasingly narrow cobbled pavements, lined by tall brick buildings. They crossed a number of canals and passed several well-lit smoky bars crammed with people.

'I could use a beer,' said Scott, but they agreed to leave their luggage in the hotel before they allowed themselves the pleasure of a drink.

Willem led them through the main entrance of a narrow building with a gabled roof and light shining from the windows. A burly, grey-haired man with a brocade waistcoat met them and embraced Willem expansively. 'Hoe gatt hat, Willem,' said the man, warmly, over the noise of conversation and the music of a piano. 'Friends, welcome.'

'Hoe gatt hat, Onkel,' replied Willem. 'This is my Uncle Piet,' he said, turning to the friends. 'Let's meet in half an hour or so. That will give you time to freshen up. I can take Mynheer FitzGerald to my house and be back to look after you by then.'

'Excellent,' said Stockington. 'I should be in time for dinner. I shall see you all tomorrow, perhaps.' He and Willem left, talking earnestly.

Piet threaded the party through the crowded smoky bar and took them up a winding staircase to three rooms in the attic. Gussie and Phoebe took the largest, and Cushing and Scott another. Badger, the shortest of the group, squeezed into the smallest room which had a steeply-sloping low roof.

After a quick wash, they made their way downstairs. Cushing was the first to return to the delft-tiled bar and ordered a well-earned beer from the pretty barmaid. Scott and Badger appeared at the far end of the bar, and he beckoned to them to join him, ordering another beer and a lemonade. By the time they had carved out a space, Gussie and Phoebe had also arrived, and Cushing went back to the bar to buy them each a gin and tonic.

He returned with the drinks. 'This is a lively place,' he said. 'I was chatting to a couple of girls on the stairs. They seemed very friendly, though I couldn't really understand the lingo. Piet's daughters, I think. Willem's cousins.'

Badger snorted into his lemonade and Scott grinned widely. 'I think you'll find they are working girls, Uncle Kit.'

'Well, of course they are. There must be a lot to do around the hotel....' He tailed off and blushed pinkly. 'Oh. I see.'

Gussie giggled and patted his hand. 'It's certainly not the Ritz, is it?' she said, and took a mouthful of gin and tonic. She coughed violently. 'What are you trying to do, Christopher?' she spluttered. 'Poison me?'

Scott leaned over and sipped at the drink. 'Dutch gin,' he said, laconically. 'Back to the bar, Padre. Ask for London gin. I'll have another beer too, please. And don't speak to any loose women on the way.'

'Don't call me Padre,' said Cushing, as he returned to the bar.

Piet brought over a huge wooden platter of bread, cheese and smoked sausage, and the group began to relax. Willem, looking much smarter without his disreputable hat and jumper, rejoined them, and they started to plan for the following morning. Convinced that the Synarchists would carry out whatever actions they had planned during the opening ceremony of the Olympic Games, the party determined to use their forged press passes to explore the stadium.

'What about you, Willem?' asked Scott. 'You don't have a press pass. Or do you?'

'I will be fine,' replied Willem, confidently.

'Do you work for Stockington, then?' asked Phoebe.

'Mr. FitzGerald, you mean?' replied Willem, smiling. 'No, not exactly. Though we are in the same line of business, you might say.' He looked round and called across the bar. 'Onkel Piet! More beer!'

In the morning, after a breakfast of bread, cheese and strong coffee, they dodged the bicycles which came at them from every direction and took a tram to the brand new Olympic stadium. The brick structure was a triumph of modern architecture, and flags bearing the three crosses that signified the coat of arms of Amsterdam were everywhere.

Building work had completed a while ago, with the stadium built on a promontory of reclaimed land between wide new canals, but armies of workmen were still there making finishing touches, erecting banks of chairs and so on. Flags bearing the five interlinked rings that were the sign of the Olympics were being run up poles around the stadium.

The confusion outside was exacerbated by the ranks of competitors and press who were all there to rehearse the opening ceremony, along with gymnasts, dancers and a marching band. Uniformed stewards optimistically tried to keep back hordes of spectators eager to catch a glimpse of their favourites. 'They look like bus conductors,' giggled Phoebe.

Flashing their press passes to a stressed gatekeeper, the party entered the stadium, followed by Willem who also showed a pass of some sort. They were immediately impressed at the size of the wide, sweeping arena. Cushing pointed out the brick built royal box on the opposite side to the main entrance. 'The King will be there on Saturday,' he said. 'Where is he now, I wonder?'

'As soon as he arrives, he will join Queen Wilhelmina and Prince Hendrik at a lodge in the royal forest,' said Willem, knowledgeably, and then flushed. 'So they say,' he muttered.

A fat man with a megaphone was trying to get the athletes into some sort of order and, jostled by the crowds of competitors, the party made their way across towards the box which they noticed was decorated with a stylised mural of half-naked athletes. Again showing their passes, they walked up the stairs into the box itself, and watched the teams of athletes forming themselves behind their flags as part of their practice. Scott admired the tower that stood over the entrance. 'It's as high as Nelson's Column,' he said. 'But that bowl at the top is pretty ugly.'

'They call it the ashtray,' said Willem.

'Why?' asked Phoebe.

'Because the KLM pilots fly over it as they go in and out of the airport. It is a Dutch joke, you see. They are so close they can flick their cigarettes into the top. Where they are going to light the Olympic flame.'

'What's that all about?' asked Scott.

'It is a new idea. As part of the opening ceremony, the Queen will light the flame that represents the Olympic spirit.'

Cushing looked at the throng milling around the stadium, forming and reforming on the grass in the middle of the race track. 'It's going to be a shambles,' he said, shaking his head. 'Come on, let's have a look round.'

They walked round the box and through the dining room and kitchens, dodging scurrying staff and feeling as aimless as the athletes struggling in the arena. They walked down some stairs to a door that seemed to be directly below the royal box, and opened it, finding a dusty store room full of old gymnastic equipment.

'Look at this wooden horse,' said Scott. 'You could hide anything in there. Even two of us. Well not you, Padre, obviously.'

They were interrupted by a uniformed steward. He spoke in Dutch and Scott brazenly presented his press pass. 'No, no. You must not be here. Please go away. Outside only. Thank you.' Not wishing to cause a scene, and feeling they had explored enough for the day, they rejoined the masses, hearing the chief steward berating one of his underlings for having let them in.

'This is hopeless,' sighed Gussie. 'There are so many people, and there is just no way we can guess what the Synarchists are doing.' Dispirited, they watched the rehearsal for another half an hour, then took a tram back to the old town. They spent the rest of the afternoon on borrowed bicycles scouring the many fully-occupied hotels in Amsterdam in search of Gemp. With only a vague description of him, however, and in the expectation that the villains would be using false names anyway, they realised that it was like trying to find a needle in a haystack. 'This is ludicrous,' said Gussie. 'There must be thousands of hotels. I want to go back and have a bath.'

When they returned to the hotel they found a note awaiting them from Stockington, asking them to meet him at the stadium by the hop, skip and jump pit at noon the following day. 'I'm heartily sick of the place already,' said Scott. 'Never mind. How about a beer?'

After two or three beers, Scott's enthusiasm had returned. 'Let's go back to the stadium,' he said. 'It's starting to get dark now. We may be able to break in and take a look around without anybody watching us.'

Gussie declined, but Cushing and Badger felt that they should support Scott. Phoebe was also keen. 'Is the Padre going to break into another bedroom?' she asked coquettishly. 'What a lark.'

Forty minutes later, the three men and Phoebe were standing outside the stadium, where Scott had pointed out a surprising number of people standing nonchalantly around smoking and reading newspapers. 'They can't be journalists,' he said. 'They'd all be in the pub by now. I bet they're security. It looks as if Stockington and his cronies are on the case.'

The party walked round the whole peninsula on which the stadium sat, and approached a darkened entrance at the rear. Badger started to peer at the lock, and as he did so Cushing saw two men walking purposefully towards them. 'No need to answer questions,' he said, and they bustled quickly back to the tram stop. Their pursuers slowed and stopped.

'Hang on,' said Badger, staring at the darkened stadium.

'Look at those two men over there, at the bottom of the tower. They're making a hasty exit too.'

Sure enough, two men were also walking quickly towards them, looking nervously over their shoulders. Before they reached the tram stop, they got into a waiting car. 'Come on,' urged Badger. 'They might lead us to Gemp.'

'You're clutching at straws here,' said Cushing.

'It's the best lead we've got,' replied Badger. 'We've been chasing shadows all afternoon. Let's follow them.' He flagged down a taxi. 'Follow that car!' he ordered, and laughed. 'I've always wanted to say that.'

The taxi followed the car through the evening traffic, and it became clear that they were heading towards the docks. The car stopped and the taxi drew up fifty yards behind. Badger paid the driver, and the party followed the men for five minutes through a melee of people. Cushing remembered that Willem had said how many visiting teams were staying in boats at the docks, and there were strolling groups of people talking in a myriad different languages all around them. He cursed as their path was blocked by a group of Frenchmen dancing in the street, and, when they had extricated themselves from the merry band, there was no sign of the men they were following.

'We've lost them,' said Cushing. 'This is hopeless.'

'I don't know,' said Phoebe. 'This looks like a great party.'

When the friends arrived at the stadium the following morning, a second rehearsal was already under way. Tempers were starting to fray as the organisers formed up the national teams in the car park. The press corps were laughing and joking, smoking heavily, as indeed were some of the athletes. Not wishing to expose themselves as fakes, the party queued to go inside the stadium again, talking to a group of Frenchmen standing behind them. The Frenchmen were talking animatedly to Phoebe, whose uninhibited dancing with their compatriots at the docks and then on board ship the night before had earned Cushing's disapproval.

The steward, coincidentally the one they had met at the royal box the previous day who had been vilified by his superior, spent a long time checking and rechecking their passes, until Willem pushed past and growled at the man in guttural Dutch. The steward crossly waved the party through, and then proceeded to shout rudely at the Frenchmen.

They crossed the track and the wide expanse of grass, and watched technicians grappling with complicated reels of cable and wire. Willem asked a few questions as two men staggered past them with enormous microphones, and was told that they were anticipating a long speech from the Queen and the master of ceremonies. Some of the other cables were part of the mechanism for lighting the Olympic flame. Press photographers were getting in everyone's way as they set up their equipment for the following day.

Cushing suddenly thought he saw a face he recognised. 'Look,' he cried. 'It's Gemp!'

'Where?'

'There, with the photographers. I think it was him. No, dash it all, I've lost him. But I'm sure it was.'

Silently, Willem passed Cushing a set of field glasses, and he scanned the crowd. 'No, maybe I was mistaken.'

'I can't see him either,' said Scott. 'Keep an eye open. In the meantime, it's five to twelve. Let's wait for Stockington.' He pointed towards the sand pit near the edge of the arena and the rest of the party followed him.

With a burst of sound, a brass band entered the arena followed by the flag of Greece and a small gaggle of competitors, marching in a haphazard manner. They watched for a while as groups of athletes from the various competing nations tramped in, and Cushing was prepared to admit that it was a more convincing effort than the previous day.

A troop of uniformed horse artillery passed close to them, wheeling to a halt and spraying Cushing with sand. The soldiers began to set up their guns and practised a salute. Stockington, punctual as always, joined them. 'Ah, ladies, gentlemen,' he said. 'What news?'

'The Padre thinks he spotted Gemp,' said Scott, 'but other than that, not a sausage.'

'Well I can report that His Majesty is in the country,' said Stockington. 'And that, bizarrely, Queen Wilhelmina will not be attending the opening ceremony.'

Willem looked surprised. 'Why not?' asked Cushing.

'She is taking a moral position against the fact that some of the events are being staged on the Sabbath,' he said. 'Prince Hendrik will open the games in her place. It will be all over the papers, I suppose. I don't think it's suspicious, but I just thought I'd mention it.'

'But the King is still going to attend?'

'Yes, so I believe.'

'And are you prepared? I mean, will you have security people in place, just in case...' Cushing tailed off.

'Cushing, please, give us some credit, we are the professionals, you know. That's why I'm here. Even unofficially I can help to sort out the security measures.' He frowned. 'And by the way, please don't try and break into the stadium again. It only causes embarrassment. I'm sure if you ask Willem he can get you a key.'

Back in the bar of the hotel that afternoon, the party were arguing again.

'We're not needed now,' said Gussie. Stockington has mobilised the security forces and has everything tied down. Can't we relax?'

'He can't have covered everything, not if he's here on his holidays,' said Scott.

'I agree,' said Cushing. 'I saw Gemp. And even if I didn't, we know that Gemp is here somewhere to kill the King. We need to be there.'

Willem, who had joined them, agreed. 'Every little helps,' he said. 'After all, no one else knows what this man Gemp looks like.'

'Thank you, Willem,' said Cushing, pleased that for once someone from authority was supporting him. 'I would never forgive myself if something happened and we hadn't done everything in our power to stop it.'

Willem had further news. 'The French have decided not to come to the ceremony tomorrow,' he said. 'There was some row with a gatekeeper who apparently insulted members of their team. There were fisticuffs, I believe.' His eyes twinkled. 'I think I know the man. Anyway, they are refusing to come to the ceremony and may boycott the games.'

'Then we can go to the opening ceremony as the French,' said Scott.

'Are you mad?' snapped Cushing.

'Not at all. I'll borrow a flag, they're all over the place. You said we needed to be at the ceremony, and we can get a lot closer to the royal box if we pretend to be competitors than we would be if we were just journalists.'

'But what if the real French team turn up after all?'

'Then we go in as journalists. Come on, Padre, where's your sense of adventure?'

'Christopher has a point,' said Gussie. 'I mean, we don't exactly look like athletes.'

'I don't know,' said Scott. 'I mean, look at the state of some of those Americans. They're as fat as the Padre here. In any case, not everyone is a marathon runner.'

'But we're too old,' retorted Cushing, crossly.

'Speak for yourself. Anyway, they might think you were part of the bowls team, or something.'

'Do they have bowls as an Olympic sport?' asked Gussie?

'And what about Gussie and Phoebe?' continued Cushing. 'Do they even have women competing?'

'For heaven's sake, Padre,' said Scott. 'What century are you living in?'

'They were banned in ancient Greece, you know,' said Cushing, huffily. 'Anyway, it's a crazy plan.'

'We don't have a better one,' laughed Scott, and again was surprised to get support from Willem. Cushing shook his head despairingly, but had to admit that there was merit in the plan if they could get closer to the royal box.

'We need uniforms,' said Gussie.

'I've got a white skirt,' said Phoebe. Gussie nodded. 'There we are then. White skirts for us. You men will need white trousers to match. And how about blue blazers and boaters? Come on Gussie, let's go to the shops before they close.'

25

Saturday 28th July 1928

After so many sunny days, it seemed as if the Ninth Olympiad would open under grey skies. The party dressed in their hastily-concocted uniforms and Scott proudly revealed a large French flag.

'Where did you get that from?' asked Cushing. Scott grinned, and Cushing looked away. 'No, don't tell me.'

They took the tram to the stadium where the crowds were already massing. The competitors were all there in matching outfits, the South Africans in bright red, the Belgians in pink, the Italians in military green and the Egyptians wearing fezzes. The massive contingent from the United States had just arrived en masse from the harbour, and the German delegation looked like ship's stewards, wearing Eton jackets and stiff shirts. 'First time the Germans have competed since the War,' said Scott. 'Hope we give them a good trouncing.'

As stewards tried to marshal the huge number of competitors, the spectators – Willem had said that the stadium had capacity for forty thousand – flowed past them. There was a flurry of excitement and the crowds parted as a series of horse-drawn carriages arrived, and the various royal parties stepped out and were escorted through the gates into the stadium. The party had to have the prince consort of the Netherlands and the Kings and Queens of Norway and Sweden pointed out to them, but King George V was unmistakeable, his bearded face visible under a huge plumed uniform hat. 'He's shorter than I thought,' said Scott.

The man holding the sign saying "Frankrijk" was surprised at the small size of the spurious French contingent, which was no larger than that of Monaco, but he happily summoned a steward with a flagpole to which Scott attached the stolen flag. 'I'll carry it,' said Badger. 'It's just like parading with the Boys' Brigade.'

'Good morning, gentlemen,' said a voice behind them, and they turned to see Willem, smartly turned out in a dark green military uniform with tight breeches and brightly polished boots, wearing the three pips of a captain on his shoulders. 'Ritmeester van der Merwe, Second Hussars, that's the Prince of Orange's Own you know, currently on special duties, at your service,' he said, clicking his heels and grinning at Phoebe who was now looking at him in a very different way. Scott, suddenly aware of his ill-fitting blazer, glared at him enviously, but Willem continued. 'I think your plan will work. The French have been, what is the word, mollified by a gift of champagne, and will compete in the games, but they will not be attending the opening event.'

A military band started to play and the march into the stadium began. Led by the Greeks, an innovation that seemed appropriately traditional, the procession filed slowly in, with the countries in alphabetical order thereafter. The Germans marched with military precision behind the sign marked "Duitsland" and their new flag, and a suffusion of pride filled the party as the large British contingent, preceded by the sign "Engeland" and the Union flag, began to move forward. The skirling of pipes announced their presence. Badger hoisted the red, white and blue flag of France at an angle, and the friends followed, waving shamelessly at the cheering crowd who were throwing their hats into the air as the competitors entered the stadium and made a circuit of the track.

Cushing scanned the crowd with the field glasses. How was he going to find one face among so many? He scrutinised the German contingent, and then dismissed the idea. Surely there was no way that Gemp would conceal himself as a German athlete. He focused on the royal box and watched the Italians marching past beneath it, giving a fascist salute. Prince Hendrik acknowledged the salute, while the King pointed at the Italians, frowned, and muttered something to his neighbour.

A huge roar announced the arrival of the Dutch contingent, bringing up the rear, and the party were called to stand in a line on the grass next to the British team, and behind the Finns. Cushing continued to sweep the crowds with his field glasses, and stopped excitedly, nudging Scott with his elbow. 'He's there. With the other photographers, behind that big camera, the one they make the news films with. Look, I know he's wearing a beard, but I'm sure it's Gemp.'

Scott snatched the field glasses and examined the man carefully. 'It could be. Yes, it probably is. What are we going to do?'

The Dutch team joined the other teams in the middle of the arena, and, as they did so, five biplanes flew low over the stadium in formation, red, white and blue smoke streaming from behind their wings. Cushing watched as the aeroplanes turned and crossed the stadium again from the other side, the lowest seemingly touching the "ashtray" on top of the tower.

As he did so, a sick realisation filled his stomach. 'Willem,' he said, urgently, 'what happens with the lighting of the Olympic flame? How is it done?'

'Prince Hendrik will make a speech and hit some sort of a button,' said the Dutch officer. 'It lights a fuse – pass over the field glasses and let me see.' Scott, who was still staring at the photographer, handed them over, and Willem focused on the royal box. 'Yes, there, in the middle of the flowers by that large microphone. He presses that button. That will light the flame in the ashtray.'

'But that's it,' said Cushing. 'They want a dramatic moment. And they talked about the flames of the new revolution. It's going to coincide with the lighting of the Olympic flame. There must be a bomb under the royal box. They will set it off with the same fuse.' He looked round hurriedly. 'Willem, am I right? Can the security people have covered every angle?'

'It's difficult to say, Dominee Cushing. We are keeping what you call a low profile. This is an unofficial operation, as you know.'

'All right. Let's assume that there may have been a security lapse. Willem, you try and catch Gemp. Over there, the photographer with the black beard. Badger, I'm sorry, you'll have to stay here with the flag, or everyone will realise that something is wrong. Phoebe, Gussie, you stay here too. Geoffrey, come with me.'

'What are we going to do?'

'Find the bomb, if there is one, and cut the fuse. And make sure that Prince Hendrik doesn't light the flame, or it will kill hundreds, let alone the King. Come on.'

Willem broke ranks and started to walk purposefully towards the raised wooden platform where the photographers were all standing, while Cushing and Scott marched resolutely across the track. As they did so, the flag holders started to be called forward one by one, and the band began to play the national anthems. 'Forty six countries,' said Cushing, breathlessly. 'We've got some time at least.'

They were surprised that no one stopped them entering the door to the building containing the royal box. 'They are all watching the parade,' said Scott. 'Come on, let's try downstairs first.'

Scott led the way, and Cushing suddenly heard a noise and turned to see Phoebe and Gussie behind him. 'What in God's name are you two doing?'

'Don't argue, Christopher. Many hands make light work.'

Scott turned round and grinned at Phoebe as the band started to play the opening bars of "God Save the King" for the fourth time. 'They're getting through those anthems quickly,' he said. 'That will be Australia, Canada, Great Britain and India. We haven't got much time. Stop bickering.' He paused at the door. 'It's locked,' he said. 'Oh well. No time for niceties.' The door survived the first kick from his boot, but flew open the second time.

As the band went remorselessly though the anthems, Cushing and Scott scoured the room. It was Gussie who pointed at a wire coming down into the top of a window and down the wall. Scott traced it to the large wooden horse in the middle of the store room. He lifted the top and let out a gasp. 'You were right, Padre. Gemp has got here. It's packed with explosives.'

'Get the girls out of here,' said Cushing. 'And make sure that no one presses that button. I'll try and defuse it.'

'But...' whimpered Gussie.

'For once, don't argue. Go!'

He heard the heels of Phoebe and Gussie go up the stairs, and breathed heavily. He looked up to see Scott still there. 'I told you to go.'

'You told the girls to go. I'm staying with you. They can warn the King as well as I can. Can you defuse a bomb?'

'I don't know,' said Cushing through gritted teeth. 'I've never tried. Have you?'

'Sorry, Uncle Kit. I haven't either. Good luck. Keep praying.'

As Cushing scanned the contents of the wooden horse, the words of the Twenty Third Psalm flowed unbidden through his mind. 'Yea, though I walk through the valley of the shadow of death,' he muttered, then interrupted himself. 'I've found where the wire is coupled to what looks like a detonator. I think I can disconnect it. If I can reach it, that is.'

'Be careful.'

'Will you be quiet!'

The band broke into "Stars and Stripes", but the sound could have been coming from a different planet.

Unable to breathe, Cushing gently fiddled with the wires for a couple of minutes, and eventually let out a deep sigh. 'Yes,' he said, slowly. 'I think I've done it.'

As he did so, there was a flurry of footsteps on the stairs, and a man burst into the room. Scott, intent on what Cushing had been doing, spun round, but was too late. It was Gemp. Holding a pistol, he swung it against Scott's head and the big Englishman collapsed like a felled ox.

Cushing roared and threw himself at Gemp, whose face was indeed concealed by a black beard. Gemp's pistol flew off into the corner of the room, and the two grappled on the floor, Cushing gouging and punching the younger man.

Gemp flailed out and caught Cushing on the side of the head, and Cushing retaliated by gripping Gemp wildly around the throat. Using force he did not realise he possessed he forced Gemp's head backwards, and then suddenly lost his grip. The false beard had slipped away from Gemp's face, and Cushing was clutching nothing but air.

Gemp kicked out blindly and then smacked his forehead into Cushing's face. Cushing stumbled backwards from the blow, and Gemp lashed into him several times. Gemp now had full advantage, and repeatedly smashed his fists into Cushing's body.

Cushing crumpled to the floor and Gemp stood over him, kicking him viciously twice in the ribs. 'Dreckiges englischer Schwein!' he screamed, and kicked him again.

Cushing, dazed, could only watch Gemp walk over to the wooden horse, lean over and pick up the detonator. The anthems outside had finished a while ago and Cushing was vaguely aware of the crowd roaring. He could have sworn he could hear Gussie's voice screaming in the distance, but it was drowned out by a series of explosions. He had failed.

Yet the explosives had not gone off. Cushing was still alive, and could still focus on the detonator in Gemp's hands. He saw Gemp reconnect one of the wires and curse as he began to fiddle with the second. With a last-ditch effort, Cushing groggily flung himself towards the triumphant German. He grabbed the man's legs and the two of them fell to the floor in a confused writhing heap. Again Gemp's fists smashed into Cushing's face, then there was a loud bang and Gemp's leering face disappeared in a red spray. He fell heavily onto Cushing who continued to struggle feebly before the room swam before his eyes and everything went dark.

'Dominee Cushing. Are you all right?' A weight was pulled from his body, and a dazed Cushing could see Willem leaning over him.

'The detonator,' mumbled Cushing weakly.

'It's fine,' said Willem. 'He was trying to connect it up, but I got him first.'

'You got him? Gemp...?'

'I shot him. I'm sorry I was so late. I made a mistake and went for the wrong photographer. Quite a few of them had beards, you see. By the time I realised I had collared the wrong man, I saw this one making his way towards the royal box. I got here just in time. Can you sit up?'

'Geoffrey...'

Willem propped Cushing up against the wooden horse and stepped over to Scott, who was groaning gently. 'He'll have a big bruise, but I think he's going to be fine too.'

Cushing stood up shakily. 'I'm sure I heard an explosion,' he said, blearily.

'Not the one that mattered,' said Willem. 'You heard the artillery doing a twenty one gun salute, I guess.' He laughed. 'Gemp might well have succeeded if they hadn't squeezed so much into the ceremony.' He dabbed blood from the wound on Scott's head and helped him to sit up as well.

'What's happening?' asked Scott. 'Did we win?'

Cushing clasped his hand. 'Yes, Geoffrey. We won.'

'If you can stand, Mynheer Scott, we should be going,' said Willem.

'I'm fine,' said Scott, blurrily. 'Bit of a headache, mind. Getting socked on the old noggin is getting to be a bit of a habit.'

Cushing helped Scott to his feet. 'Good God, Padre, you look a mess,' he said.

Willem checked Gemp's pockets. 'Hmm. A boarding pass for a boat at the harbour. I think we should go there as soon as possible.'

He helped the two Englishmen up the stairs, and was stopped by a small group of people at the top. Gussie, who was in front, screamed with joy and flung herself at Cushing. 'Christopher, Christopher! I'm so sorry, I couldn't stop them pressing the button, I tried.' She loosened her grip in sudden realisation. 'You're all covered in blood!'

'Am I?' he said, wincing painfully, disengaging his ribs from her grasp. 'I think it's Gemp's. And we disconnected the detonator. We did it.'

Phoebe hugged Scott and Badger joined them, clapping both men on the back.

Stockington, smiling, shook their hands. 'You were right,' he admitted. 'Despite the security we had been able to arrange, we would still have been too late. Well done.'

Willem saluted a grizzled man in uniform with colonel's

insignia on his epaulettes. 'Gentlemen, allow me to present Colonel Ypma,' said Stockington. 'You'll be pleased to know that his men have rounded up all the others.'

'Others?' said Scott, confused.

'Three bearded Bolsheviks,' said Stockington, casually. 'Innocent stooges. Well, not exactly innocent, as they were all carrying guns. But I think they were set up by the opposition to carry the can for the explosion.'

'Willem's found the boat that Gemp is on,' he said.

'It's the Dulcibella,' said Willem.

'Dulcibella?' asked Phoebe. 'That's my stepfather's yacht.'

'That's as maybe,' said Stockington. 'But I'll take it from here. You've all done enough now. I think it really is about time you left it to the professionals. Just for once...'

26

Friday 10th August 1928

Scott opened another bottle of champagne with a flourish and filled the glasses. 'I think we should have another toast,' he said. 'To freedom.'

'That's very profound,' said Cushing, as the others echoed the toast, Badger and Rachel raising their glasses of tonic water.

'Not at all,' grinned Scott. 'I mean our freedom. It's nice to know that our names have been cleared. We can go to the Oval tomorrow without some bobby arresting us for murder.'

'Phoebe and I have already been out to celebrate,' said Gussie. 'We spent yesterday shopping.'

Cushing laughed. 'I'm certainly glad to be able to look like a vicar again. Though I don't think Mrs. Sturdy will ever fully trust me. It's not every week she hears that her vicar is wanted for murder.'

'I'm sorry I couldn't sort it out sooner,' said Stockington. 'I've had rather a lot to do. Still, the five of you staying in Amsterdam for a week was probably for the best.'

'But it's so frustrating,' said Cushing. 'The Dutch police rushed us out of the stadium and kept us confined to our hotel for twenty four hours before you came and told us what had been going on.'

'I think he did have a lot to do, Christopher, to be fair,' said Gussie.

'I don't care about whether it was fair or not,' said Scott. 'After all, we saved the King's life, didn't we? And we were still treated like criminals.'

'There will be a formal apology and compensation for your efforts in due course,' said Stockington. 'I'm buying the champagne, for a start.'

'But you haven't told us what has happened to all the Synarchists,' said Cushing. 'I know that the Dutch police, or army, raided the yacht, and you got a lot more evidence. But what has happened to Sloane? And Domvile? And the Cardinal?'

'All the information you have given us has been very useful. Those carbons, for example. Excellent. We questioned your Jean de Mayol de Lupe for quite a long time, and then deported him. We wanted to send him to France, where he didn't want to go, or even Italy.'

'Italy?'

'Yes, it seems that he has been acting as tutor to the Italian royal family for years. But suddenly he's not welcome in Rome either, which may explain a thing or too about that assassination attempt. So he's declined both of those options and he's gone to Mexico.'

'Mexico?'

'Yes, funny that. Quite a few synarchist links to Central America. We'll keep tabs on him, don't worry. Oh, by the way, on the subject of assassinating kings, you'll be pleased to hear that we don't think the Prince of Wales was actively involved.'

'Well that's a relief,' said Gussie.

'Yes, indeed. They may have been grooming him, of course, but he doesn't appear to have much of a clue about anything sinister. Or about anything much at all, really.'

Cushing was about to chide Stockington for his rudeness to the heir to the throne, but thought better of it. 'And what about Domvile?' he asked.

'Domvile? Well, he's still working for SIS.'

'What?'

'He's a traitor, of course, but we're watching him. I'm running the department now. We can get more benefit from having him, and several others I could mention, under surveillance, rather than having them locked up or running around as loose cannons.'

'And I suppose it would be too much of an embarrassment if he were to go on public trial,' sneered Scott.

'Absolutely,' said Stockington, ignoring the jibe. 'And we picked up a few more names from the papers and from questioning the rest of the gang. One or two of the other conspirators have, how shall I put this? Disappeared from public life.'

'Too good for them,' muttered Scott.

'There can't be a trial, as I've said. None of this can become public.' He looked round. 'You have all signed the Official Secrets Act, by the way, haven't you?'

'And what about my stepfather?' asked Phoebe. 'Mummy is distraught. I saw her yesterday.'

'We can't find him, I'm afraid,' admitted Stockington.

'What?' shouted Cushing, almost dropping his champagne. 'I didn't know that.'

'I didn't know that either,' said Scott. 'And what about the jewels?'

'He's gone to ground,' said Stockington, shaking his head. 'He may even have left the country.'

Cushing banged his fist on the table. 'Have you searched his secret study properly?'

Stockington looked perplexed. 'What secret study? You never mentioned a secret study.'

Everyone looked accusingly at Cushing. 'Well, if you keep

us at arm's length, what do you expect?' he said. 'I found it when I broke in.' He glared at Scott and Phoebe. 'Stop looking at me like that. He's the secret service man, not me.'

'Well where is it? At Longley Hall, I presume?'

'Absolutely. Come on. Let's go. I'll take you there.'

'That's a very good idea,' said Stockington. 'May I use your telephone? I'll arrange for a couple of cars.'

The two large black cars swept up the drive of Longley Hall, driven by seemingly identical grim-faced, silent men. Badger and Rachel had returned to Whitechapel, but Scott, Gussie and Phoebe had accompanied Cushing and Stockington. Apart from a certain amount of continued mutual recrimination, the party had also spent much of the journey in silence.

Stockington, flanked by the burly drivers, knocked on the door which was answered by the pugilistic butler whom Cushing had met before.

'Mr. Murrall, isn't it?' said Stockington, brushing past him. The other members of the party followed. 'Lady Sloane is still in London, I believe?'

'Yes, sir…'

'Now I seem to recall you telling me when questioned that you had no idea of the whereabouts of Sir Charles Sloane. Is that correct?'

'That's right,' said the surly butler, unconvincingly.

'I'm going upstairs to the study,' said Stockington calmly, 'and if I find anything to contradict that statement, you'll be back in Pentonville.'

He strode up the stairs, Cushing trotting behind him. When he reached the top, he turned. 'Cushing, perhaps you could show me exactly where you mean. Gallagher, come with me. Summersgill, keep an eye on our friend Murrall here and make sure he doesn't try and leave. Mr. Scott, maybe you would stay here with the two ladies?'

Cushing led Stockington to Sloane's study, opened the door to the dressing room and showed Stockington the switch that opened the secret door. He fiddled until he heard a click and pushed the door open. 'Here's the study,' he said. 'This is the window from which he shot Hitchcock.' He looked at the grate and saw a pile of ash. 'Looks like someone has been destroying evidence. Could have been the butler, of course.' He pulled back the rug to reveal the trapdoor, which he opened. 'Here we go. Stairs, leading down. This isn't a priest hole, the house is too recent for that. I wonder who owned this place before Sloane bought it? He can't have built all this himself – can he? I don't know where the stairs go, though. Well, down, obviously.'

The light on the stairs was already on. Stockington and Gallagher started to make their way down, but Cushing stopped them. 'I've got a hunch,' he said. 'I'd lay odds that Sloane is down there. Let me go down alone first.'

Stockington shrugged. 'Fair enough, old man,' he said, and drew his pistol. 'But just in case, you might like to take this with you.'

Cushing thanked him, put the pistol in his pocket and walked cautiously down the narrow stone stairs. It was a long flight, turning back on itself more than once, and Cushing was sure that he well below the ground floor. He emerged into a vaulted cellar, his heart beating fast. In the light he could see books and papers scattered over the floor and dark-clothed tables together with the evidence of further burning in an ornate fireplace. He walked over to racks of robes and masks and fingered the rich fabrics, whistling softly. He had seen various Masonic rites, but nothing approaching this.

He pulled aside a heavy curtain and was confronted with a startling scene. Clearly extending for much of Longley Hall, this expansive room was no ordinary cellar. He gasped out loud, marvelling at the opulence. Dozens of candles flickered in cressets on the walls and in holders around the cellar. Many of the pillars were of magnificent marble, plush drapes and sumptuous tapestries covered the walls, and a circle of ritualistic symbols was clearly marked on the floor. In front of him was an altar with a pair of huge golden candlesticks, open books and an array of utensils that Cushing recognised as a parody of the Christian sacrament. Behind the altar, in front of a stylised golden sun that glinted in the candlelight, was a huge ornate seat, almost a throne, with black velvet cushions and with its back and arms formed of winged creatures that reminded Cushing of the statues in the British Museum. A dozen high-backed chairs were spaced evenly around the circle.

He began to cross the cellar towards the altar, but jumped back when he saw a figure standing by a pillar to his right, next to a case of leather-bound tomes. Thin and drawn, Sir Charles Sloane was a shadow of his former self.

'Good afternoon,' said Sloane, in a strained voice. 'Welcome, I should say. I wondered how long it would take. Do come over and join me.' Cushing reached for his pocket, but Sloane nonchalantly lifted his right hand and pointed a revolver at him. 'Hands where I can see them, if you please. Thank you. Just sit down, in that chair.' Cushing complied, and Sloane looked searchingly at him. 'Now you must be the meddlesome priest. Strange. You look familiar.'

'We did meet once,' admitted Cushing, struggling to remain calm. 'This display is a little over-dramatic, don't you think?'

'Ill-met by candlelight. It seemed appropriate, and I have been expecting you.'

'Very elaborate. Just as I might have imagined.'

'So you are the one who has interfered with our plans in France and in Amsterdam. Most irritating. And I assume that it was you and your friends who broke into my house and kidnapped my stepdaughter.'

'Hardly kidnapped,' said Cushing. 'You were going to kill her. And your men tried to kill the King.'

Sloane shrugged, and his mouth creased into an ugly grin. 'Whatever you have done to interfere, you have merely delayed the inevitable. You cannot halt our true purpose.'

'Is that so?' said Cushing, smugly. 'Your gang of conspirators has been rounded up while you've been skulking down here.'

'Really? One or two, perhaps. Ours is a worldwide movement, you know. You will barely have scratched the surface. Even I don't know all the members of the order. And you won't find anything in Longley Hall that will help. I've destroyed everything, you see – though I didn't have the heart to burn these beautiful books.' His demeanour changed and he lowered the revolver. 'But Reverend – perhaps I can call you Christopher? Surely you have sympathy with our aims? The Bolshevik menace must be defeated. We offer the best hope for the world. Why don't you join us, help us to build the future we want...'

Cushing laughed, nervously. 'A world ruled by you and your friends, backed up by Germany? A world where your thugs are free to murder...'

'You are a fool, Cushing,' sneered Sloane, lifting the revolver again. 'So be it.'

'Wait!' Cushing's voice was a little high-pitched. 'Wait. Tell me more. What's so important about the Baal ceremony? I mean, surely you and your friends can't take a three thousand year old ritual seriously? Can you?

'Despite your calling, Cushing, you understand so little of the true meaning. The physical and the symbolic, remember?' He laughed sardonically. 'The rituals you follow are – what, half as old as these?'

'So what have you done with the gems?' responded Cushing

rapidly. 'You know, the treasure of the Cathars. The gems from the crown. And the Lapsit Exillis, of course? Was it really the Lapsit Exillis?'

Sloane grinned. 'Ah, Reverend. I think you will allow me one or two little secrets.'

'It will all come out when you get tried for treason.'

'I don't think that's going to happen, do you? Really? After all, I am the one with the gun.' He raised the revolver and pointed it unshakingly at Cushing's chest.

'Shooting me will achieve nothing,' retorted Cushing, raising his voice. 'I'm not alone, you know.' The noise of footsteps could suddenly be heard on the stairs.

'No, I supposed you wouldn't be. Though it would give me the satisfaction of removing an irritant, of course.' Cushing swallowed, and Sloane sighed. 'Oh well. There it goes. I wouldn't have hurt the girl, you know.'

He turned his wrist and placed the muzzle of the revolver into his mouth.

'No!' shouted Cushing, and leaped from the chair, but Sloane's finger tightened on the trigger and the shot blew off the top of his head. His body fell back and crashed to the floor.

Stockington walked calmly across the inscribed circle and joined Cushing. 'Not a lot you could have done,' he said. 'Come on, let's go back upstairs. Gallagher, search this place thoroughly. Oh yes, and arrest that butler, Murrall, when you're finished, there's a good chap.'

Cushing and Stockington returned to join the others at the foot of the main staircase. Relief was visible on their faces as they surged forwards – they had clearly heard the shot. Scott drew his finger across his throat in a questioning gesture, and Cushing nodded. Phoebe began to cry as the group linked arms and walked out together into the sunshine.

Epilogue

Friday 31st August 1928

Cushing thought it odd to see Badger and Sinclair, who had returned from France the previous week, in morning suits. Badger looked particularly uncomfortable as he showed his invitation to the guards at the gate and passed through to join the throng of people at the garden party. Rachel Brock, however, was excited and bubbling like a schoolgirl.

Buckingham Palace was bathed in sunshine. Cushing spotted Gussie, who looked radiant in plum-coloured silk, deep in conversation with someone who looked vaguely familiar, perhaps an actor. He started to push his way through the crowd to speak to her.

All of the friends had received invitations a few days before. 'Stockington must have had a word or two in the right circles,' laughed Scott. 'But I'd still prefer hard cash.'

As if he knew that Cushing was thinking about him, Scott appeared at his elbow, accompanied by Phoebe, who seemed tired and frail.

'What ho, Padre,' said Scott.

'Hello, Geoffrey. How did...' Cushing tailed off. He knew that Sir Charles Sloane's funeral had been the day before and that

Scott had accompanied Phoebe. He had felt it inappropriate to attend himself.

'Pretty rough,' replied Scott, knowing what Cushing had meant. Phoebe was unusually quiet, and Cushing could see dark rings under her eyes. Gussie, who had left her actor friend, joined them and, ignoring the men, immediately gave Phoebe a huge hug.

She had done the same to comfort Phoebe the previous week at the funeral of Peter and Molly Clifford. The authorities had finally repatriated the bodies, and Cushing had been asked to officiate at the service. All of the friends were there, and it had been a grim affair. Cushing had wanted to tell the truth to the Cliffords' son, Harry, but Stockington had expressly forbidden him to mention the Cliffords' part in the business. The only good news from the day was when he heard that Grainger had made more breakthroughs in his studies of the archaeological treasures.

'I didn't know what to do,' he said, grumpily. 'They tipped me the wink that I'd get my FRS for the Ugarit research, but only on condition that I forgot everything I might have heard about Esclarmonde. I still haven't decided what to do about that tomb you told me about in Buckinghamshire or wherever. It's hardly something I can stumble on by accident, is it?'

The group had finished their tea and cucumber sandwiches and were walking round the gardens together. Scott had brought a flask of brandy, and was taking a surreptitious swig by the edge of the lake when a liveried servant walked up to them. 'Excuse me, ladies, gentlemen. Would you all please accompany me inside the Palace?'

A little nonplussed, they followed the servant inside, and he led the party down a long corridor past beautiful paintings and antique furniture. He opened a door and ushered them into a bright and airy drawing room where two figures rose to greet them. One was Stockington, wearing a morning suit; the other

Willem van der Merwe, wearing dress uniform. Scott was quick to notice that Willem's epaulettes bore the crown of a major. 'He's got something out of this affair, at least,' he whispered, before grinning and warmly shaking the Dutchman's hand.

The door opened again and a short bearded figure came into the room. All the men bowed deeply to the King and the girls curtsied.

'These are the men and women I told you about, Sir,' said Stockington.

The King coughed chestily, and Cushing thought how ill he looked.

'I gather from Mr. Stockington that we have a lot to thank you for,' he said. 'Under normal circumstances, you would all get medals from your grateful King and Country, but we have agreed that these are not normal circumstances. This act of treason should not be made public, so I am afraid that you must all keep the whole matter secret. But please, do be assured of our utmost gratitude.'

'Thank you, Your Majesty,' said Cushing, on behalf of them all.

'The Queen of the Netherlands has taken a different and rather personal view, however,' said the King, his eyes twinkling, 'and she has asked me to present you with these on her behalf. The Military William Order – it is the oldest and highest honour of the kingdom, I understand. Very smart, though I think a little flamboyant for my taste.'

One by one, the King shook the hands of Phoebe, Gussie, Badger and Scott, and placed the gold and blue ribbon with its white-enamelled gold cross over their necks. 'You are all now Knight Commanders of the Order,' he said. 'Congratulations.' Finally he came to Cushing. 'Her Majesty has seen fit to make you a Knight Grand Cross, Reverend Cushing,' he said, smiling warmly as he struggled with a complicated sash. 'You are in good company. The Duke of Wellington received one, I believe. Of course you still can't say what you did to deserve the honour.'

As Cushing stepped back and bowed again, Willem stood to attention and saluted the group of friends who now, technically at least, all outranked him in the Dutch army.

They talked with the King for ten minutes, but he was finding it increasingly difficult to speak and even to breathe, and Stockington led them all back out into the garden.

'I would like to add my own thanks,' he said. 'I trust that the country can call on you again if we need what Ross called "irregulars" at any time?'

They all nodded, and Stockington and Willem went back inside the Palace. 'I'll be in touch,' he said. 'Maybe sooner than you think.'

They went for a fine dinner to celebrate, and Scott spoke again bitterly about their lack of financial reward. 'Tea and medals are all very well,' he said, gloomily, then brightened up. 'At least I've got that gold and other stuff from France. And I can always pawn the medal. After all, Uncle Kit, it's pretty second rate compared to yours.'

When they left the restaurant, Cushing and Gussie made their farewells to the others and walked arm in arm down the Embankment, gazing at the lights on the Houses of Parliament. She disengaged from him and flagged down a taxi. 'I'll see you again, won't I?' he asked.

'Oh Christopher,' she said, affectionately. 'I've been down to Albury four times in the last fortnight. Your Mrs. Sturdy's curtains are twitching like nobody's business.' She put her hands on her hips and glared at him in a playful manner. 'Every time she sees me she looks down that nose of hers so much I think she's going to fall over backwards. Of course I'm going to see you again.' She kissed him goodnight and got into the taxi.

'I do hope so,' he said to himself, feeling a sense of emptiness despite Gussie's words as he waved at the taxi disappearing into the traffic.

Cushing was tired after all the excitement of the previous day and his late return to Albury, but had forced himself to get out of bed at the planned hour. He was marrying a couple at his church later in the morning, and he always liked to be there in good time when he was taking the service.

He finished his breakfast and peered out of the window. Mrs. Sturdy was already out in her garden, and he had hoped to avoid her on his way to the church. Gussie had laughed off her disapproving stares, but it was only a month or so ago that Cushing and his friends had been officially wanted for murder, and Mrs. Sturdy still regarded him with suspicion. Several of the villagers also continued to point at him in the street and mutter behind their hands, even though the newspapers had authoritatively cleared his name. 'Thank heavens for Stockington,' he thought.

He laughed hollowly to himself. A month ago he had been in Holland, saving the King's life; only three weeks ago he had faced down Sir Charles Sloane. And now his biggest problem was worrying about what the neighbours might think.

He had admitted to Gussie only recently, on one of her increasingly frequent visits, that he had begun to find the routine of "normal life" as a country vicar incredibly tedious. 'Thank heavens for Gussie too,' he thought, and stared out of the window at the flowers in his garden.

His reverie was interrupted by a knock at the door. He opened it to find the postman with a handful of letters and a parcel for him. Intrigued, he walked into his study and, taking a paper knife from his desk, attacked the brown paper of the parcel. He was astonished to find an envelope containing five brand new passports in the false names that he and the rest of the party had used on their trip to Amsterdam. The compliments slip from the Foreign Office looked genuine enough. He frowned to himself, but felt a frisson of excitement.

Puzzled, he flicked through the envelopes and saw an official-looking one with a Whitehall postmark. He reached again for the letter opener and scanned the short handwritten letter inside.

"Dear Reverend Cushing," he read. "It was delightful to see you and your chums earlier at the Palace. I trust that you are pleased with the honours that Her Majesty Queen Wilhelmina has bestowed upon you. And His Majesty's personal gratitude was heartfelt. Perhaps you would do me the honour of meeting me at our usual rendezvous on Monday at noon? Please bring your friends. With warmest regards. Yours sincerely, D. Stockington."

Fascinated, he started to read the letter again. As he did so, the telephone rang.

'St Peter and St Paul,' he said, picking up the receiver and hearing Scott's excited voice.

'Padre, is that you? It's Geoffrey. I've had a letter from Stockington.'

'Yes, so have I. He wants to meet on Monday.'

'Absolutely. I'm game. I was getting bored, I have to say.'

Cushing did not want to admit to his godson that he was feeling the same way, and grinned roguishly to himself.

'He's sent us a batch of passports, too. The game is afoot again, I think.'

'Top show. Now another thing, Padre. Have you seen The Times this morning?'

'No, I haven't even opened it yet. Why?'

'Look at page five. News from Albania. Zog has proclaimed himself king.'

'And why is that interesting?'

'He's being crowned today. Could it be them? The Synarchists?'

Cushing smiled affectionately as he listened to Scott's tinny voice continuing to rattle on at him down the line.

'Well, Geoffrey, I'm sure that Stockington will tell us everything we need to know on Monday.'

Scott's disembodied voice continued, but Cushing interrupted him. 'I'm sorry, Geoffrey, but it will all have to wait until then. I can't do anything just yet. I've got two young people I need to marry off first.'

He placed the receiver firmly down, cutting off Scott in mid-flow, and started to whistle a jaunty tune. Maybe life was not going to be so incredibly tedious after all.

Author's Notes

Many of the people, locations and incidents mentioned or encountered in Dark Designs are real – though in many cases a certain amount of literary licence has been taken and a liberal amount of fiction superimposed over the real history. We hope that this adds to the fun.

These are some of the real places and people who appear, largely as background, in the novel.

Albury

The mansion, set in an area of outstanding natural beauty near Guildford in Surrey, is mentioned in the Domesday Book – though it has now been converted into flats. The old Saxon church, closed in 1841 and left to decay after the new church was opened closer to the centre of the village, was reopened in 1921. The midsummer service still takes place.

Buckingham College, Cambridge

There is no Buckingham College at Cambridge – though Buckingham was, prior to 1542, the name of the college now called Magdalene.

Castrum Sepulchri

See Seborga.

The Cathars

Catharism was a Gnostic movement that originated in the tenth century, branded by the Roman Catholic church as heretical. Centred in the Languedoc in southern France, both the movement and the area were associated with intellectual and artistic advancement and with a high level of tolerance, including to the Moors and to the promotion of women. Church leaders, both men and women, were known as Parfaits.

The Albigensian Crusade against the Cathars (the Cathars were also known as the Albigenses, after the town of Albi) was first preached by Pope Innocent III in 1208 and prosecuted with vigour, particularly by the French kings Philip II and Louis IX who saw the opportunity to bring the Languedoc under control of the crown. The Crusade led to significant death and destruction – Carcassonne fell in 1209, Montségur not until 1244 – and also saw the beginning of the Inquisition. A leader of the crusaders was Simon de Montfort – no relation to the fictional de Montforts in the novel.

Craiglockhart

Requisitioned by the military in 1916, the building in Edinburgh was turned into a war hospital for the treatment of shell-shocked officers. Its most well-known patients included war poets Wilfred Owen, sent there in 1917 to recover from "neurasthenia" and Siegfried Sassoon, thus avoiding a court martial after his "Declaration against the War" was read in the House of Commons.

Aleister Crowley

Crowley was an infamous and influential English occultist,

born in 1875. He was associated with various esoteric groups including the Hermetic Order of the Golden Dawn and the Ordo Templi Orientis. His philosophy and leanings led him to be dubbed "the wickedest man in the world" in the contemporary press. He led an expedition to attempt to climb K2 in 1902 and was – subsequently – rumoured to have been a British spy.

Domvile

Admiral Sir Barry Edward Domvile had been a distinguished naval officer before becoming Director of the Department of Naval Intelligence in 1927, a post he held for three years. He held strong pro-German and anti-Semitic views and was eventually interned in 1940 for his Nazi sympathies.

Esclarmonde de Foix

Esclarmonde de Foix (1151-1215) was a prominent Cathar leader and Parfait. Esclarmonde (meaning "light of the world" in Occitan) was the daughter of the Count of Foix. It is believed by many that she fled the siege of Montségur – perhaps in the shape of a dove – taking the fabled Templar treasures with her. Her last resting place has never been found.

Flying Scotsman

The LNER Class A3 Pacific locomotive number 4472 "Flying Scotsman" was built in 1923. Its distinctive style and bright green livery made it a much loved fixture for many years between London and Edinburgh. The inaugural service was on 1st May 1928.

Gemp

The Gemp who appears in Dark Designs is a thug. Coincidentally, however, a Colonel Friedrich Gempp was head of the Abwehr-Abteilung (German intelligence) from 1921 to 1927, after an impressive period of military service. He retired in 1943 at the rank of Major General, and was declared dead in 1946, having been abducted by the Russians. Who knows if this more important Gempp was part of the conspiracy too?

Horchdienst

A German intelligence cipher operation, set up after the creation of the combined "Abwehr" intelligence service in 1928. The operation was known as B-Dienst by the navy, Horchdienst by the army and air force.

Hospitallers

The Knights Hospitaller were a religious and military order, originally founded in the 11th century to provide care for poor or sick pilgrims visiting the Holy Land. After the First Crusade, they were charged with the care and defence of the Holy Land. Along with the Knights Templar, they were a rich and powerful group, but they avoided the fate of the Templars. After the fall of Jerusalem, they operated from Rhodes and then from Malta.

Jean de Mayol de Lupe

Staunchly anti-Republican, he was ordained a priest and subsequently joined a number of pseudo-military ultra-orthodox catholic orders. Officially neither a cardinal nor a bishop, he was still addressed as "Monsignor". An army chaplain and decorated war hero during the Great War, he later supported the Vichy regime and served in the SS Legion Charlemagne in the German army, for which he was subsequently imprisoned.

Lapsit Exillis

First mentioned by Wolfram von Eschenbach (more famous for the Parsifal stories) in about 1200, the Lapsit Exillis was ostensibly the stone from Lucifer's crown when he fell from heaven. As such, it has been linked to Grail legend and the wider beliefs of many organisations, including the Masons.

Lombrives

An enormous cave system inhabited since 4000 BC and known for its archaeological treasures. After the fall of Montségur, the Cathar bishop Amiel Aicard and some 600 people were to die there. If Esclarmonde's tomb is indeed hidden in the caves, it has not yet been found.

London

Much of the action in the book is set in the streets and fine buildings of London and its suburbs. The Athenaeum and Travellers Clubs are still alive and well in Pall Mall; the Naval and Military Club has moved its premises to St. James's Square, but the pillars that give the "In and Out" Club its name remain in Piccadilly, along with the flats known as Albany. Many other hotels, stations, pubs, churches, vicarages and private houses referenced in the novel can still be found – and Aleister Crowley really did live by the cheese shop in Jermyn Street.

The famous pavilion at Lord's Cricket Ground is the home of cricket. The details of the matches referenced in the novel are accurate, though there is no evidence that Douglas Jardine, England captain during the notorious "Bodyline" tour to Australia, played at Oxford or Surrey with a Geoffrey Scott.

Montségur

A huge Cathar castle on a rocky outcrop, fought over during the Albigensian Crusade and eventually to fall in 1244 after a long siege. The survivors were given two weeks to renounce their faith; most refused and were burned alive in the fields below the castle.

1928 Olympics

The 1928 Summer Olympics (the IX Olympiad) were held in Amsterdam. Queen Wilhelmina did indeed boycott the opening ceremony, objecting to it being held on a Sunday, and the event was opened by Prince Henrik. The French team did indeed boycott the opening ceremony after a row. Many crowned heads of Europe were there, but not King George V – we made that bit up. The stadium is still open, including the iconic tower known as "the ashtray" (for reasons explained in the novel) and the royal box.

Parmoor

The house is situated in Buckinghamshire between Marlow and Henley on Thames, and was owned by the Templars in the 12th century. The cedar tree in the grounds was reputedly grown from a seed collected from Lebanon during the Crusades. There is absolutely no indication of a hidden tomb beneath the cedar. The first Lord Parmoor was a privy councillor, Lord President of the Council in Ramsay Macdonald's government, and subsequently Leader of the House of Lords. A high Anglican, he was prominent in the Church Assembly. His son was to become Chancellor of the Exchequer in Attlee's government.

Otto Rahn

A German medievalist, Rahn was fascinated by the Grail legends and the German epics popularised by Wagner. He was inspired by the Cathar movement and the massacre at Montségur, and one of the first to link Catharism with the Holy Grail, a subsequent theme of conspiracy fiction. His work drew the attention of Heinrich Himmler, and he was subsequently to join the SS before his apparent suicide in 1939.

Room 40

Founded at the outbreak of the Great War, Room 40 was the section in the Admiralty formed to intercept and decode German communications. It was staffed by a mixture of military and civilian personnel. Its greatest success was probably decrypting the Zimmermann telegram, which was to lead to the US entering the war. Room 40 merged with Military Intelligence in 1919 and subsequently relocated to Bletchley Park.

Seborga

The ancient castle, site of a religious order, was originally known as Castrum Sepulchri. After the unification of Italy, and now called Seborga, the small town near the French border still claims to be an independent principality with notional border posts and a variety of souvenir opportunities, some taking advantage of the local links to the early days of the Knights Templar.

Synarchists

The word "synarchism" is used to describe government (or power wielded by) a shadowy elite, such as a secret society or (even very recently in the Middle East) a well-financed international business with a private army. While synarchy is by definition the opposite of anarchy, it is frequently used to describe collections of revolutionary groups. In the 1930s in Mexico, the Synarchists were been an extreme right catholic party, and politicians of both extremes still use the name.

Templars

The Knights Templar, originally The Poor Fellow-Soldiers of Christ and of the Temple of Solomon, was probably the most famous religious and military order of the Middle Ages and the one which has sparked the most speculation about its money, motivation and power. As soldiers and bankers they amassed a phenomenal reputation and huge fortunes, building castles and properties across Europe and the Holy Land. Earning the enmity and jealousy of the King of France and the Pope, many were arrested on trumped up charges and tortured and killed in 1307 – Friday 13th October was the day that the Grand Master Jacques de Molay was arrested. The order was disbanded, but much of their treasure and alleged relics were never recovered.

Romolo Tranquilli

An acknowledged anarchist, he was arrested on suspicion of being part of the bungled bomb attack against Victor Emmanuel III, King of Italy, in 1928. He died in prison as a result of the beatings he suffered. His brother, Ignazio Silone, was probably a police informer.

Ugarit

An ancient city on the eastern Mediterranean coast, destroyed at the end of the Bronze Age, near what is now Ras Shamra in modern Syria. When excavated in the late 1920s, under the leadership of Claude Schaeffer of Strasbourg University, many archaeological treasures – including cuneiform tablets in the Ugaritic language that described the worship of the Canaanite Baal – were found.